The Legacy

A Journey of Conservation, ~~Cunin~~

Serena Knight

Copyright © 2024 by Serena Knight

All rights reserved. No part of this book may be used or reproduced in any form whatsoever without written permission except in the case of brief quotations in critical articles or reviews.

First Edition: October 2024

Table of Contents

Chapter 1 Final Preparations and Fundraising Efforts 1

Chapter 2: Assembling the Team 18

Chapter 3 Crossing into the Unknown 35

Chapter 4 Uneasy Beginnings 52

Chapter 5 Confronting Internal Conflicts 73

Chapter 6: First Signs of Danger 93

Chapter 7 Bonds Forged in Adversity 110

Chapter 8 Unexpected Allies 127

Chapter 9 Traps and Ambushes 143

Chapter 10 Strengthening Resilience 161

Chapter 11 Secrets of the Jungle 181

Chapter 12 Tensions Rise 198

Chapter 13 The First Encounter 214

Chapter 14 Strategies and Sacrifices 230

Chapter 15 Logistical and Environmental Challenges 247

Chapter 16 Ambush in the Wild 266

Chapter 17 Unraveling the Syndicate's Web 283

Chapter 18 Exploring Legacy and Identity 299

Chapter 19 Closing in on the Enemy 316

Chapter 20 Uncovering the Syndicate's Network 333

Chapter 21 The Poachers' Last Stand 351

Chapter 22 Choices and Consequences 371

Chapter 23 Resolution and Moving Forward 387

Chapter 24 New Paths and Partnerships 407

Chapter 25 A New Beginning 424

Epilogue A Legacy of Hope 443

Chapter 1
Final Preparations and Fundraising Efforts

The room buzzed with low murmurs as Mia Evans stepped into the conference hall of the Global Wildlife Conservation headquarters. The glass walls and modern decor exuded an air of sophistication, but the tension was palpable as she took her seat at the long, polished mahogany table. The air-conditioning hummed softly, a stark contrast to the relentless heat of the Congo she would soon be facing. Mia glanced around, taking in the expressions of the five representatives seated across from her—men and women whose decisions could determine the fate of her entire expedition.

"We've reviewed your proposal, Ms. Evans," began Dr. Andrew Keller, a graying man with sharp eyes that peered over the rim of his glasses. He set down the thick folder containing Mia's documents and folded his hands neatly. "It's... ambitious, to say the least. However, there are significant concerns regarding your experience and the feasibility of this project. You're proposing to enter one of the most hostile environments on the planet to combat a well-funded poaching syndicate. Why should we trust that you're up to the task?"

Mia squared her shoulders, forcing a calm she didn't quite feel. "My father spent most of his career in those environments, and I was with him for much of it. I know the land, the dangers, and the challenges. More importantly, I understand the urgency. Species like the Okapi and the Forest Elephant are facing extinction because of these poachers. I'm not just proposing this expedition—I'm committing to it, just as my father did."

A murmur ran through the group, some nodding thoughtfully, others exchanging skeptical glances. Mia caught the eye of Mr. Simon Grant, a senior board member known for his stringent approval standards. He leaned back in his chair, eyes narrowing slightly.

"And what makes you think you can succeed where others have failed? Your proposal mentions hiring an ex-special forces operative, Ryan McCallister. But from what I see, you've had no previous command experience. Leading an expedition is more than just research and passion—it's about handling people under extreme pressure. With respect, Ms. Evans, you're very young for such a venture. Isn't this more about honoring your father's legacy than actually being equipped to lead?"

Mia's heart hammered against her ribs. She'd anticipated this line of questioning but hearing it so bluntly still stung. She took a deep breath, letting the air fill her lungs, and then released it slowly. "It's true that I haven't led a full-scale expedition like this before," she began, meeting Mr. Grant's gaze evenly, "but I've spent years working in the field, right beside my father. I've seen what it takes to keep a team alive and on mission. More importantly, I'm not doing this alone. Ryan's experience will be invaluable in navigating dangerous situations, and I've consulted with local guides who are familiar with the terrain and the poachers' movements."

Dr. Keller cleared his throat, breaking the silence that followed. "Your passion is evident, and your credentials are solid. However, the cost of failure is high, not just in terms of finances but in potential loss of life. We need to ensure that this isn't driven purely by emotion."

"Emotion is part of it," Mia conceded, leaning forward. "My father dedicated his life to this cause. But this mission is not just about him. It's about stopping the decimation of entire ecosystems. The poachers are getting bolder, their traps more sophisticated. If we don't act now, we could lose species forever. I'm prepared to take that risk, and I have a team that is equally committed."

The representatives exchanged glances again, their expressions shifting from skepticism to consideration. Mrs. Eleanor Briggs, the head of the foundation's financial committee, finally spoke up. "Let's talk numbers. You're requesting a significant amount of funding. How will you ensure that every dollar is used effectively?"

Mia nodded, grateful for the shift in tone. "We have a detailed budget plan that prioritizes resources for tracking and surveillance equipment, field supplies, and local support. We'll also allocate funds for emergency extraction and medical aid, given the high-risk environment. Every expenditure will be documented and reported regularly. We're partnering with local conservationists to maximize the impact and minimize costs. It's all in the financial breakdown I've provided."

Mrs. Briggs glanced at the document, then back at Mia. "And if something goes wrong? What's your contingency plan?"

Mia hesitated, then spoke with quiet intensity. "There's always a risk of something going wrong. But that's why I have Ryan. He's trained for worst-case scenarios. We'll have communication set up with a base camp outside the conflict zone, and we've made arrangements for evacuation if necessary. We're not going in blind, and we're not taking unnecessary risks."

Silence fell over the room again. Mia's gaze shifted from one face to another, trying to gauge their reactions. Dr. Keller looked at her thoughtfully before leaning forward, hands clasped.

"I believe you, Ms. Evans. Your proposal is strong, and your commitment is clear. But passion alone won't keep you alive out there. We're willing to back this mission, but we want weekly reports and proof of progress. If at any point we feel the risk outweighs the reward, we'll pull the plug. Understood?"

Mia exhaled slowly, relief and anxiety mingling in her chest. "Understood. You won't regret this decision."

"See that we don't," Mr. Grant murmured, a slight smile breaking through his stern demeanor. "Good luck, Ms. Evans. And be careful. Your father was a good man. Let's make sure this mission does him justice."

Mia nodded, a surge of determination coursing through her. She rose to shake their hands, the finality of the decision sinking in. As she left the room, the weight of their approval—and the immense responsibility it carried—settled heavily on her shoulders.

The mission was officially greenlit. Now, she had to prove she was worthy of their trust.

Mia leaned against the edge of her kitchen counter, laptop open in front of her, a spreadsheet glowing on the screen. The small Brooklyn apartment was filled with half-packed gear and field equipment, each labeled with meticulous precision. As she scanned through the rows of items—satellite phones, medical kits, climbing gear—her phone buzzed on the countertop.

"Dr. Klein," she answered, recognizing the number instantly. She straightened, bracing herself for the conversation she knew was coming.

"Ms. Evans," Dr. Klein's voice came through, formal and steady. There was a hint of concern layered beneath the cordial tone. "I wanted to go over a few points regarding your team composition. You've made some... interesting choices."

Mia's brow furrowed as she adjusted the volume. "I assume you're referring to Ryan."

"Exactly," Dr. Klein confirmed. "I understand he's highly skilled, but his background is... unconventional for a conservation mission. Special forces operatives aren't known for subtlety or diplomacy. Are you sure he's the right fit for what you're trying to accomplish?"

Mia glanced at the framed photograph of her father on the mantle, his smiling face looking out at her. "Dr. Klein, I need someone who's used to handling unpredictable situations. Ryan's training makes him perfect for this. He knows how to operate in high-stress environments, and frankly, he's one of the best in the field."

"Yes, but you're leading a conservation expedition, not a military operation. There's a risk that his presence alone might attract the wrong kind of attention. You do realize how dangerous this could get, right?"

"I'm aware," Mia said firmly. She moved to her desk, fingers brushing over the neatly stacked files and expedition plans. "And that's exactly why I need someone like him. The Congo is unpredictable. It's not just about the animals; the poachers out there—they're heavily armed and dangerous. I can't afford to take any chances."

Dr. Klein sighed, the sound crackling softly through the speaker. "I understand your concern, Mia, but there's another issue. I've reviewed your team's background. You're pulling in people with very different skill sets. There's a possibility for conflict—different approaches, different philosophies. You need cohesion, not just competence."

"Which is why I've chosen carefully." Mia's voice tightened slightly. "Every person on this team has a role. Amina has the local knowledge, Ryan provides security, and Kato—well, Kato's our connection to the community. I know they come from different backgrounds, but that's the point. We need diverse perspectives to navigate this mission successfully."

"Does Ryan know his place in this structure?" Dr. Klein asked pointedly. "He's used to leading. You'll be the one in charge out there, but I'm concerned there might be friction if he tries to overstep. Have you had that conversation with him?"

Mia hesitated, her fingers tapping lightly against the desk. "He understands. We've discussed it. He knows I'm the expedition leader. His job is to provide support, not make decisions."

"And what happens if things get dangerous?" Dr. Klein pressed. "Will he stand back and let you call the shots, or will he take over? Because once you're out there, there won't be time for debates. You need to be certain, Mia."

"I am certain," she insisted, though the pause that followed betrayed her doubt. "Ryan respects me, and he understands the importance of this mission. He's not going to undermine me."

"I'm not questioning his respect for you. I'm questioning how clear the chain of command is in practice, not just in theory," Dr. Klein said, his tone softening slightly. "Mia, you're young, but you're capable. I've seen you in the field. But don't let personal connections cloud your judgment. You're trying to honor your father's legacy, and that's admirable. But it's also dangerous if it means you're making decisions based on sentiment rather than strategy."

Mia swallowed hard, staring at the list of equipment on her laptop. "Ryan was my father's friend. He trusted him, and I do too."

"Yes, your father trusted him in a different context," Dr. Klein pointed out gently. "A context where they were equals. This time, it's different. You're the leader, and Ryan's there to follow your lead. Can you be sure he'll remember that when it matters most?"

"I can," Mia said, though her voice lacked its usual certainty. She exhaled slowly, rubbing her forehead. "Dr. Klein, I know this isn't going to be easy. I know there's a lot at stake, but I've thought this through. I've gone over every scenario, every possible complication. I'm not going in blind."

"Alright," Dr. Klein relented, his tone turning more resigned. "Just... keep an open line of communication. If things start to go sideways, don't let pride stop you from making adjustments. This mission's too important."

"I will," she promised softly. "And thank you, Dr. Klein. Your advice means a lot."

"You're welcome, Mia. And for what it's worth, I believe in you. Just make sure your team believes in you too, all the way."

The call ended, leaving Mia staring at her phone screen. She looked back at the equipment list, then at the team roster pinned beside it. Ryan's name stood out like a bold declaration against the white paper.

"Just trust me, Ryan," she whispered to the empty room. "Trust me like my father did."

She shook her head, clearing her thoughts. With a deep breath, she returned to her laptop, her resolve hardening. There was no room for doubt now. The mission depended on it.

The door to Mia's apartment swung open, and Lina stepped inside, her expression a mix of anxiety and frustration. She paused just inside the threshold, taking in the chaotic scene before her: boxes stacked against the walls, duffel bags spilling over with gear, maps spread out across the coffee table. It was a familiar sight—one that reminded her too much of the nights before their father would leave on his expeditions.

"Wow, Mia, you've really outdone yourself this time," Lina muttered, voice tight. She shut the door with a soft click and folded her arms. "Looks like you're packing for war, not a research trip."

Mia glanced up from where she was kneeling on the floor, organizing a stack of notebooks and field guides. She brushed a stray lock of hair from her face, her expression guarded. "Lina, I didn't expect you to come by tonight. I thought you were still in D.C."

"Yeah, well," Lina shrugged, her gaze darting to the wall where a large map of the Congo basin was pinned, marked with red and yellow pins, "I figured I'd better see my sister before she disappears into the jungle again. We need to talk, Mia."

Mia sighed, pushing herself to her feet. "I don't have a lot of time right now. The team's arriving in two days, and I still have to finalize the equipment manifest, double-check the travel arrangements, and—"

"And what?" Lina cut in, stepping forward. "What then? Jump into a helicopter, fly out to the middle of nowhere, and hope for the best?" Her voice rose, eyes flashing with a mix of anger and concern. "This isn't a game, Mia. You're going after armed poachers. Real people with guns. This isn't like tagging butterflies in the Amazon. They could kill you."

Mia's jaw tightened. "I know that, Lina. I'm not naïve. I've been planning this for months. Everything is accounted for."

"Is it?" Lina challenged, taking another step closer. "Or are you just throwing yourself into this because you can't handle being here? Because you can't deal with the fact that Dad's gone?"

Mia flinched at the accusation, but she held her ground, meeting Lina's gaze evenly. "This isn't about Dad," she said quietly, but firmly. "This is about finishing what he started. The poachers have decimated populations of endangered species. If we don't act now, we could lose entire ecosystems. I'm not doing this just for him—I'm doing this because it's the right thing to do."

Lina shook her head, disbelief etched across her face. "You think I don't get that? I know what's at stake. But why does it have to be you? You've been chasing Dad's ghost ever since he died. But you're not him, Mia. You don't have to prove anything to anyone."

"I'm not trying to prove anything!" Mia snapped, her voice rising for the first time. She took a deep breath, struggling to keep her emotions in check. "Look, Lina, I'm not blind to the risks, okay? But I've trained for this. I have a team. Ryan's going to be there—"

"Ryan? Oh, great," Lina interrupted, sarcasm lacing her words. "So you're dragging Dad's old war buddy into this, too? I thought you wanted to lead this expedition, not have someone babysit you."

"That's not fair," Mia whispered, her voice barely audible. The words hit harder than she'd expected. "Ryan's there to support the mission, not babysit me. He's there because he believes in what we're doing. Because he cares, Lina."

"And what about me?" Lina shot back, her voice breaking. "Don't I care? Don't I get a say in this? You're my sister, and you're all I have left. I can't lose you, too, Mia. Not like we lost him."

The raw emotion in Lina's voice struck Mia like a punch to the gut. She looked away, blinking rapidly to clear the sudden sting of tears. "I'm sorry, Lina. I know you're worried, but I can't stay here and do nothing. I need to go. If I don't—if we don't—then everything Dad worked for, everything he gave his life for, will be for nothing."

Lina's shoulders slumped, the fight draining out of her. She looked at Mia, her expression a mixture of helplessness and love. "This isn't about him, Mia. This is about you. I just... I don't want you to get hurt. You've barely given yourself time to breathe since he died. You keep running, pushing yourself. And I'm afraid you'll burn out, or worse."

Mia stepped forward, placing her hands gently on Lina's shoulders. "I'm not running away, Lina. I'm running toward something. This is who I am. I've known it since I was a kid, since Dad took me on my first trip. And I promise, I'm not doing this recklessly. I have a plan. I'm ready."

Lina looked at her sister for a long moment, searching her face for any sign of uncertainty. Finally, she sighed, covering Mia's hands with her own. "Okay. But promise me you'll be careful. Promise me you'll call, check in whenever you can."

"I promise," Mia whispered, squeezing Lina's shoulders reassuringly. "I'll call every chance I get. And I'll be back before you know it."

"Yeah, well, you'd better," Lina muttered, blinking back tears. "Because if you get yourself killed, I'm gonna be really pissed."

Mia laughed softly, the sound strained but genuine. "Noted."

They stood there for a moment longer, the silence between them heavy with unspoken words. Finally, Lina stepped back, wiping her eyes with the back of her hand. "Just... take care of yourself, okay? And remember, you don't have to do this alone."

"I know," Mia murmured. "Thank you, Lina. For everything."

Lina nodded, offering a small, sad smile. "Just come back in one piece, sis. That's all I ask."

With a final glance around the cluttered apartment, Lina turned and walked to the door. Mia watched her go, the weight of her sister's words settling deep in her chest.

As the door closed behind her, Mia let out a long breath, turning back to the organized chaos that surrounded her. The determination in her eyes was undimmed, but Lina's voice echoed in her mind.

You don't have to prove anything to anyone.

Maybe not, she thought, but she did have something to prove to herself.

The apartment was quiet, save for the faint hum of the overhead light and the soft rustling of Mia's movements as she meticulously packed the last of her equipment. A rugged backpack lay open on the floor, filled with essentials—survival gear, first aid supplies, a GPS unit, and stacks of waterproof maps. She took a deep breath and picked up her father's old compass from the side table, the metal cool and familiar against her palm.

The compass had been with him on countless expeditions, the worn edges and tiny scratches on its surface a testament to the miles it had seen, the places it had mapped. Mia traced her thumb over the engraved initials on the back: **W.E.**—William Evans. She swallowed the sudden lump in her throat and slipped the compass into the front pocket of her bag. It was more than just a navigational tool—it was a piece of him, a tangible link to the man whose legacy she was trying to uphold.

She glanced at the framed photo propped up beside it. In it, she and her father stood side by side in front of a vast jungle canopy, their faces flushed with the thrill of discovery. She remembered that day vividly—the scent of the rainforest, the calls of birds echoing through the trees, the pride in her father's eyes as she had identified a rare plant species without his help. That photo had been taken just months before his last expedition, before everything changed.

"Mia, you can do this," she whispered to herself, the words echoing softly in the empty room. But even as she spoke, doubt crept in, gnawing at the edges of her resolve.

Her phone buzzed, shattering the silence. She fumbled for it, glancing at the screen—Ryan. She hesitated only a moment before answering.

"Hey, Ryan."

"Hey yourself," came the familiar, gravelly voice on the other end. "Just checking in. You all set for tomorrow?"

Mia nodded, even though he couldn't see her. "Yeah, just finishing up here. Going over the equipment one last time."

"Triple-checking everything, I bet," Ryan said, a hint of a smile in his tone. "That's good. Keeps us from being unprepared out there. I'm at the airport now, getting everything squared away with the gear transport. Thought I'd give you a heads-up."

"Thanks, I appreciate it." She glanced around at the scattered remnants of her life—clothes she wouldn't take, books left half-read on the shelves, pictures of family and friends that seemed to belong to another world entirely. "I'll be there first thing in the morning. You sure everything's good on your end?"

"Yeah, everything's fine," Ryan replied, but there was a slight hesitation, a barely perceptible shift in his tone. "Just... be ready. This is going to be intense, Mia. It's not like the trips you've done before. I need to know that you're one hundred percent in this. No looking back."

She bristled slightly, but forced herself to keep her voice steady. "I am in this. Completely. You know that."

"I do," he said quietly. "But I also know what happened the last time you were in the field. That injury wasn't your fault, but it was a wake-up call. I just want you to stay sharp. Trust your instincts, but don't let your emotions get in the way."

Her fingers tightened around the strap of her backpack. "You think I'm not ready?"

"That's not what I said," Ryan answered, a touch of frustration seeping into his words. "I know you're ready. I just don't want anything to happen that might—"

"Might what?" she cut in, her voice sharper than she intended. "Make me doubt myself? Make me question if I can do this without my father? Because I already do, Ryan. Every damn day."

Silence stretched between them, heavy and charged. When he spoke again, his voice was softer. "I'm not your father, Mia. But I promised him I'd have your back. Just let me do that, okay? Let me be the one to worry about everything else."

She closed her eyes, exhaling slowly. "I know. And I trust you, Ryan. But I have to lead this mission. Not because I want to, but because I need to. This is my chance to prove that I'm capable—not just to everyone else, but to myself."

"I understand," he said quietly. "And I'll be right there with you. First thing tomorrow."

"First thing tomorrow," she echoed softly.

They exchanged a few more logistical details, then ended the call. Mia stared at the phone for a long moment before setting it down. She turned back to the photo of her father, lifting it gently. The frame felt too light, almost fragile in her hands.

"Guess this is it, Dad," she murmured. "I'm really doing it."

She carefully wrapped the photo in a small cloth and tucked it into her bag, securing it between layers of clothing. As she zipped up the final compartment, she glanced around the room once more. There was so much she was leaving behind—not just physically, but emotionally. But there was one thing she couldn't leave unresolved.

Mia crossed to the kitchen counter, grabbed a pen and a notepad, and began to write:

Lina, I'm sorry about tonight. I know you're worried, and I know I haven't made this easy. But I hope someday you'll understand why I had to do this—why I had to see it through. You've always been there for me, and I'm so grateful for that. I promise I'll be careful, and I'll come back safe. Until then, please know that I love you. – Mia

She placed the note on the counter, folding it neatly. The apartment felt emptier now, each shadow and corner filled with the weight of unspoken goodbyes.

With one last look around, Mia hoisted her backpack onto her shoulder and reached for the door. Tomorrow, everything would change. She only hoped she was truly ready for what lay ahead.

"Goodbye, Lina," she whispered to the silent room. "Goodbye, Dad."

The door clicked shut behind her, leaving the apartment—and the life she'd known—behind.

Chapter 2:
Assembling the Team

The heat hit Mia like a wave as she stepped out of the air-conditioned terminal into the bustling Kinshasa airport. The sun was high in the sky, casting a golden glow over the chaotic scene. Travelers hurried past, taxis honked incessantly, and vendors shouted their wares in a mix of French and Lingala. Mia felt a surge of adrenaline. This was the starting point of her father's work, and now it was hers.

Ryan, always composed, walked beside her, scanning the area with the trained eye of a former special forces soldier. "Feels like a furnace out here," he commented, adjusting his duffel bag.

Mia smiled, her excitement barely contained. "It's part of the adventure, right? Plus, the real challenge begins once we hit the jungle."

They maneuvered through the crowd to the rendezvous point where Amina was waiting with her jeep. Amina waved as she spotted them, her smile broad and welcoming.

"Welcome to the Congo, Mia and Ryan!" Amina greeted them with enthusiasm. "I hope your flight was smooth?"

"As smooth as it could be," Mia replied, shaking Amina's hand. "Thank you for meeting us."

"It's my pleasure. Let's get your gear loaded and head to the base camp. We have a lot to discuss," Amina said, helping them with their bags.

The jeep ride through Kinshasa was a sensory overload. The streets were alive with activity, from street vendors selling vibrant fabrics and fresh produce to children playing soccer on dusty roads. Mia took it all in, her heart pounding with a mix of excitement and trepidation.

Ryan, ever the professional, kept his focus on their surroundings. "So, Amina, how's the situation on the ground? Have there been any recent sightings of the poachers?"

Amina's expression turned serious. "Yes, they've been more active lately. We've had reports of increased activity around the wildlife reserves. That's why your presence here is so crucial. We need to act fast."

Mia nodded, her determination solidifying. "We're ready. Whatever it takes to stop them."

The landscape gradually changed from the urban sprawl of Kinshasa to the lush greenery of the outskirts. Mia's mind wandered to the skills she had honed for this mission. Her father's training sessions, the survival courses, the countless hours studying the flora and fauna of the Congo—all of it had led to this moment.

They arrived at a modest but well-equipped base camp nestled at the edge of the jungle. A handful of conservationists and local guides were already there, busy with preparations. Amina introduced them to the team, and Mia felt a sense of camaraderie immediately.

"Everyone, this is Mia and Ryan. They'll be leading the mission to track down the poachers," Amina announced.

The team greeted them warmly, and Mia felt the weight of their expectations. She knew she had to prove herself, not just to them but to honor her father's legacy.

A young guide named Kato approached, his eyes wide with curiosity. "Is it true you're here to catch the poachers? Like in the movies?"

Mia laughed, ruffling his hair. "It's not quite like the movies, Kato. It's dangerous work, but we're here to protect the animals and stop the bad guys."

Kato's admiration was clear. "I want to help. I know the jungle well. My father taught me."

"Good to know, Kato. We'll need all the help we can get," Ryan said, patting the boy's shoulder.

As they settled into the camp, Mia and Ryan began unpacking their gear and organizing their supplies. Mia's meticulous nature shone through as she checked and double-checked everything.

"Looks like you've got everything covered," Ryan observed, watching her work.

"I've been preparing for this for a long time," Mia replied, her voice steady. "This mission means everything to me."

Ryan nodded, his respect for her growing. "I can see that. And don't worry, you're not alone in this. We've got each other's backs."

The day passed in a flurry of activity as they coordinated with Amina and the team, planning their next move. Mia felt a sense of satisfaction as they worked together seamlessly, each person contributing their expertise.

That evening, as they gathered around a campfire, the sounds of the jungle creating a symphony around them, Mia felt a deep sense of purpose. The journey ahead was fraught with danger, but she knew they were ready. She looked at Ryan, who gave her an encouraging nod.

"To new beginnings and successful missions," Mia said, raising a makeshift cup.

"To protecting what matters," Ryan added, clinking his cup against hers.

As the fire crackled and the stars began to appear in the sky, Mia knew this was just the beginning. The real adventure awaited them in the heart of the jungle, and together, they were prepared to face whatever challenges came their way.

The bustling local market was a whirlwind of colors, sounds, and smells. Vendors called out to passersby, displaying vibrant fabrics, exotic fruits, and intricate handicrafts. Mia and Ryan navigated through the crowded stalls, each step bringing them deeper into the heart of the Congo's culture.

Mia stopped at a fruit stand, examining a pile of mangos. The vendor, a middle-aged woman with a warm smile, greeted her in Lingala.

"Mbote! Moko nyoso ezali malamu?" the vendor asked.

Mia responded fluently, "Mbote! Ezali malamu, mersi. Nazali koluka biloko ya kolia mpo na mobembo."

The vendor's eyes lit up. "Oyebi malamu Lingala! Oyokaki yango wapi?"

Mia smiled. "Tata na ngai azalaki kolakisa ngai. Nazali na mikano ya kosunga Congo."

Ryan watched the exchange with admiration. "You speak the language really well, Mia."

"Thanks, Ryan. It's something my father insisted on. He always said you can't truly understand a place unless you speak its language," Mia explained, turning to him with a grin.

Ryan nodded. "He was a wise man. It definitely helps build trust with the locals."

Mia paid for the mangos and handed a couple to Ryan. They continued through the market, stopping occasionally to purchase other necessities. At one stall, Mia negotiated the price of some dried meat with a young vendor, her fluency and cultural understanding evident in every word.

As they walked away, Ryan couldn't help but comment, "You're a natural at this. It's impressive."

"I've had a lot of practice. It's all about respect and understanding. The more you show that, the more people are willing to help you," Mia replied.

They reached a stand selling traditional Congolese crafts, and Mia picked up a beautifully woven basket. As she admired the craftsmanship, an older man behind the stand began speaking to her in Lingala.

"Oyo ezali biloko ya maboko na ngai. Nalekisaki bangonga mingi mpo na kosala yango," he said proudly.

Mia nodded appreciatively. "Ezalaka na botali monene. Natangi mambi ya Congo mpe nalingi kosunga na lolenge nyonso."

The man smiled warmly. "Na kokamwa ndenge oyebi lisano na biso. Oyebi ete biloko oyo ekoki kosalisa mingi na boteki ya mboka."

Ryan, observing the interaction, felt a deeper appreciation for Mia's dedication. "You're really making a difference, Mia. These connections are invaluable."

"That's the goal. It's not just about the mission; it's about building relationships and understanding the community," Mia said, handing over money for the basket.

They moved on to the next stall, where a young boy was selling handcrafted bracelets. He looked up at them with wide, hopeful eyes.

"Bonjour! Voulez-vous acheter des bracelets?" the boy asked in French.

Mia knelt down to his level, switching to French. "Bonjour! Oui, je voudrais en acheter quelques-uns. C'est toi qui les a faits?"

The boy nodded enthusiastically. "Oui, madame. Je les ai faits avec ma mère."

"They're beautiful. I'll take three," Mia said, selecting a few and handing him the money.

Ryan watched the exchange, smiling. "You really connect with everyone, don't you?"

Mia stood up, smiling back. "It's important. Every interaction counts, especially when you're in a place like this."

They continued walking, their bags now filled with supplies. Ryan stopped at a stall selling hand-carved wooden animals, picking up a small elephant.

"These are incredible," he said, examining the intricate details.

The vendor, an elderly woman, spoke to him in Lingala, and Mia translated. "She says her husband carved them. They believe the spirit of the animal is captured in the wood."

Ryan nodded respectfully. "I'll take this one," he said, handing over the money.

As they left the market, Ryan turned to Mia. "I have to admit, I was skeptical at first, but seeing you in action, I understand why you're leading this mission. You have a way with people."

"Thanks, Ryan. That means a lot. I know this is just the beginning, but I'm confident we can make a difference," Mia replied, feeling a sense of accomplishment.

Ryan's expression softened. "You've already made a difference. Let's keep that momentum going."

They reached the jeep where Amina was waiting. She looked at their purchases and smiled. "Looks like you've had a productive morning."

"We have. Mia here is quite the negotiator," Ryan said, chuckling.

Amina nodded. "I knew she would be. Are you ready to head to the camp?"

"Absolutely," Mia said, climbing into the jeep.

As they drove away, Mia felt a renewed sense of purpose. The market visit had reinforced her belief in the mission and the importance of understanding and connecting with the local community. She glanced at Ryan, who gave her a reassuring smile.

"You're doing great, Mia. Let's keep this up," Ryan said.

"We will, Ryan. We definitely will," Mia replied, determination shining in her eyes as they journeyed deeper into the Congo.

The late afternoon sun filtered through the dense canopy as Mia, Ryan, and Amina arrived at the site for their first camp. The location was carefully chosen—a small clearing near a freshwater stream, with enough tree cover to provide shade and some concealment. The team of local guides had already started unloading the gear from the jeep.

"Alright, everyone," Mia called out, her voice clear and authoritative. "Let's get the camp set up before nightfall. Ryan, can you handle the tents?"

"On it," Ryan replied, already moving towards the pile of equipment.

Amina approached Mia with a smile. "You've chosen a good spot. The stream will be a reliable water source, and we're well-hidden from any potential poachers."

"Thanks, Amina. I've learned from the best," Mia said, returning the smile.

Ryan began assembling the first tent, his movements efficient and practiced. He glanced over at Mia, who was organizing the cooking supplies.

"Need any help over there?" Ryan asked, his tone friendly.

"I'm good, thanks. Just making sure everything's in order for dinner," Mia replied, pausing to look at him. "How's the tent coming along?"

"Almost done with the first one. These new models are pretty intuitive," Ryan said, securing the final pole.

One of the local guides, a young man named Kato, joined Ryan, eager to help. "Can I assist with the tents?"

"Absolutely, Kato. Grab that other end and help me with the next one," Ryan instructed.

As they worked together, Mia called out instructions to the rest of the team, ensuring that everyone was busy with a task. She moved around the campsite, checking on progress and offering assistance where needed. Her attention to detail and leadership were evident in every interaction.

Ryan and Kato finished setting up the second tent and moved on to the third. Ryan glanced at Kato, impressed by the young man's enthusiasm.

"You're pretty good at this, Kato. Have you done it before?" Ryan asked.

"Yes, with my father. We used to camp in the jungle often," Kato replied proudly.

"That's great. Your skills will be really useful on this mission," Ryan said, patting Kato on the back.

Mia approached them, a smile on her face. "Nice work, you two. The tents look solid."

"Thanks, Mia. Kato here is a natural," Ryan said, giving Kato a nod of approval.

Kato beamed with pride. "Thank you, Ms. Mia."

Mia turned to Ryan. "How's the rest of the setup going?"

"Smoothly. We should be done before dark," Ryan replied.

"Perfect. I'll start preparing dinner," Mia said, heading back to the cooking area.

As the sun began to set, the camp started to come together. The tents were up, a fire was crackling, and the aroma of cooking food filled the air. Mia stirred a pot of stew, her mind focused on the tasks at hand. Ryan joined her, carrying a stack of plates.

"Smells good," Ryan commented, setting the plates down.

"Thanks. It's a simple recipe, but it'll keep us going," Mia replied, her eyes on the pot.

Ryan watched her for a moment, then spoke. "You're a natural leader, Mia. The team respects you, and it's clear why."

Mia glanced at him, a hint of surprise in her eyes. "Thanks, Ryan. That means a lot coming from you."

"It's true. You've got a good head on your shoulders, and you're not afraid to get your hands dirty," Ryan said, his tone sincere.

Mia smiled. "I learned from the best. My father always said that a good leader leads by example."

"He was right. And you're doing a great job," Ryan said.

"Thanks, Ryan. I couldn't do it without everyone's support," Mia said, her gratitude evident.

As the team gathered around the fire for dinner, the camaraderie was palpable. They shared stories, laughed, and enjoyed the meal together. Mia felt a deep sense of satisfaction—everything was falling into place.

Amina raised her cup in a toast. "To our mission and to the success of our team. We've got a lot of work ahead, but I believe in each and every one of us."

"Hear, hear," Ryan added, lifting his cup.

Mia joined in the toast, feeling a surge of pride and determination. "To protecting what matters."

The evening continued with more conversation and planning. As the fire died down, Mia and Ryan walked the perimeter of the camp, ensuring everything was secure.

"Everything looks good. We're ready for whatever comes next," Ryan said, his voice steady.

"Agreed. We're off to a strong start," Mia replied, her confidence unwavering.

As they returned to the campfire, Mia looked around at her team, feeling a profound sense of purpose. The journey ahead was daunting, but she knew they were prepared. With Ryan's support and the dedication of her team, she was ready to face the challenges that awaited them in the heart of the Congo.

The sun was just beginning to rise, casting a warm golden glow over the village. The team gathered in the central square, their gear packed and ready for the journey ahead. The villagers had come to see them off, their faces a mixture of hope and concern.

Mia tightened the straps on her backpack and turned to Ryan. "Do you think we have everything we need?" she asked, her voice filled with determination.

Ryan nodded, checking his map one last time. "We've planned this route thoroughly. We should be fine, but we need to stay vigilant. The terrain can be unpredictable."

Amina joined them, her expression resolute. "We've trained for this. We'll be okay as long as we stick together and support one another."

Nia, standing nearby, gave them an encouraging smile. "You've got this. Remember, the village is counting on you. Stay safe out there."

Mia nodded, appreciating the support. "We will. Thank you, Nia."

Kato, the youngest member of the team, looked up at Mia with wide eyes. "Are you scared, Ms. Mia?"

Mia knelt down to his level, giving him a reassuring smile. "A little bit, Kato. But being brave doesn't mean you're not scared. It means you do what needs to be done, even if you are."

Kato nodded, his small face serious. "I'll be brave too."

Juma approached, his voice steady. "Remember, the first leg of your journey will be the toughest. The terrain is rough, and the weather can change quickly. Keep an eye on the sky and stay close to each other."

Ryan thanked Juma. "We appreciate the advice. We'll be careful."

As they prepared to leave, the village elder, Temba, stepped forward, holding a small, intricately carved wooden talisman. "This has been in our village for generations. It's a symbol of protection and unity. Take it with you as a reminder that you carry our hopes and prayers."

Mia accepted the talisman with reverence. "Thank you, Temba. We'll carry it with pride and remember why we're doing this."

The team turned to face the path ahead, their hearts filled with a mix of anticipation and determination. The villagers began to sing a traditional song, their voices rising in harmony, a melody of hope and strength.

As they started their journey, Amina glanced back at the village. "We'll make it back. We have to. There's too much at stake."

Ryan placed a reassuring hand on her shoulder. "We will. Together."

The team moved steadily forward, the village fading into the distance behind them. The path was rugged, with jagged rocks and steep inclines, but they pressed on, their spirits bolstered by the support of those they left behind.

As they reached the first hilltop, Mia paused to catch her breath, looking out over the vast landscape ahead. "It's beautiful, isn't it? Even with all the challenges, there's so much beauty in the world."

Amina nodded, her eyes scanning the horizon. "And it's worth fighting for. Every step we take brings us closer to making a difference."

Ryan checked his compass, ensuring they were on the right path. "Let's keep moving. We have a long way to go before we reach the next village."

Kato, who had been quietly observing everything, spoke up. "Ms. Mia, do you think the people in the next village will be like us?"

Mia smiled at his curiosity. "In many ways, yes. They'll have their own stories, their own struggles, but they'll also have hope and dreams, just like us. That's why we're here – to help them achieve those dreams."

The team continued their trek, the sun climbing higher in the sky. They moved in a rhythm, each step bringing them closer to their goal. As the day wore on, they encountered various challenges – a fallen tree blocking their path, a steep cliffside that required careful navigation – but they faced each obstacle with determination and teamwork.

As the sun began to set, casting a warm, golden hue over the landscape, Mia called for a break. They found a small clearing and set up camp for the night. The fire crackled softly as they gathered around it, discussing their progress and plans for the next day.

Amina looked at the map, tracing their route with her finger. "We've made good time today. If we keep this pace, we should reach the next village by tomorrow evening."

Ryan nodded in agreement. "We need to stay alert, though. The terrain is only going to get tougher."

Mia turned to Kato, who was watching the flames dance. "How are you holding up, Kato?"

Kato smiled, though his eyes were tired. "I'm okay. It's hard, but I'm trying my best."

Mia ruffled his hair affectionately. "You're doing great. Remember, it's okay to feel tired. We all do. What matters is that we keep going."

As the stars began to twinkle in the night sky, the team felt a deep sense of satisfaction and purpose. They were ready for whatever lay ahead, united by their mission and the bonds they had forged along the way. They knew the path ahead was long and filled with challenges, but they were prepared. Together, they were building a future, one step at a time.

Chapter 3
Crossing into the Unknown

The morning sun cast a golden hue over the dense foliage as Mia, Ryan, and the rest of the team set out from their new camp. The air was thick with humidity, and the sounds of the jungle—chirping insects, distant bird calls, and rustling leaves—created a symphony that surrounded them. Mia felt a sense of anticipation mixed with determination as they moved deeper into the heart of the Congo.

"Alright, everyone," Mia called out, pausing to consult her map. "We've got a long trek ahead. We need to reach the northern ridge by midday to set up our observation post."

Ryan, walking beside her, nodded. "We'll need to keep a steady pace. The terrain gets rougher as we go."

Kato, eager to contribute, piped up, "I know a good path. It's a bit longer, but it's safer and avoids the steep climbs."

Mia smiled at him. "Lead the way, Kato. We trust your judgment."

As they followed Kato's lead, the team settled into a rhythm. Mia walked near the front, Ryan beside her, while Amina and the other guides brought up the rear, keeping a watchful eye on their surroundings.

"Mia, how long do you think it'll take to get to the ridge?" Ryan asked, scanning the dense jungle ahead.

"About four hours if we keep a good pace," Mia replied. "We'll take short breaks every hour to stay hydrated and check our bearings."

Ryan nodded, satisfied. "Sounds like a plan. The humidity here is no joke. Everyone, make sure you're drinking plenty of water," he called back to the group.

As they trekked through the jungle, Mia and Ryan kept a close eye on the team, ensuring everyone was coping with the physical demands of the journey. The dense foliage and uneven ground made progress slow, but they pushed on, motivated by their mission.

"So, Mia," Ryan said during one of their breaks, "you mentioned your father trained you in survival skills. What was that like?"

Mia took a sip of water and smiled. "It was intense but rewarding. He believed that understanding the environment was key to surviving in it. We'd spend days camping in the wilderness, learning how to find food, water, and shelter."

Ryan nodded, impressed. "That training is definitely paying off. You handle yourself well out here."

"Thanks, Ryan. I just hope I can live up to his legacy," Mia said, her voice tinged with emotion.

"You're doing more than that. You're building your own legacy," Ryan replied, his tone sincere.

As they continued their journey, the jungle seemed to close in around them, the canopy thickening and the light dimming. The path Kato had chosen proved to be as safe as he'd promised, but the dense vegetation made for slow going.

A sudden rustling in the underbrush caused the team to halt. Mia held up a hand, signaling for silence. She and Ryan exchanged a cautious glance, their senses on high alert.

"What do you think it is?" Amina whispered, moving closer to Mia.

"Could be anything—wildlife, maybe. Let's stay quiet and see if it passes," Mia replied softly.

The rustling grew louder, and then a small group of monkeys burst from the foliage, chattering loudly as they swung through the trees. The team let out a collective sigh of relief.

"Monkeys," Ryan said with a chuckle. "False alarm."

Mia laughed, the tension easing. "They gave us quite a scare. Let's keep moving."

The hours passed as they made their way deeper into the jungle. The terrain grew steeper, and the humidity seemed to intensify. Despite the challenges, the team maintained a steady pace, their determination unwavering.

As they approached the ridge, Mia paused to consult her map again. "We're close. Just a bit further, and we'll have a clear view of the valley below."

Ryan looked around, taking in the dense foliage and the distant calls of wildlife. "This is prime territory. We'll be able to see any movement for miles."

Kato, who had been leading the way, stopped and pointed ahead. "There it is. The ridge."

The team climbed the last few feet to the top of the ridge, and the view that greeted them was breathtaking. The valley below stretched out, a sea of green with the river snaking through it. Mia felt a sense of accomplishment and purpose.

"This is perfect," she said, setting down her pack. "We'll set up our observation post here."

Ryan nodded in agreement. "Great work, everyone. Let's get to it."

As the team began to set up their equipment, Mia stood at the edge of the ridge, gazing out over the vast expanse of the jungle. This was the heart of their mission—to protect this beautiful, untamed land and the creatures that called it home. With renewed determination, she turned back to her team, ready for the challenges ahead.

The morning air was crisp and invigorating as the team broke camp and prepared for another day of travel. The sky was a brilliant blue, but the rugged terrain ahead promised a challenging journey. Mia looked at the map, tracing their path with a finger.

"The route today takes us through some rough country," she said, her tone serious. "We need to be extra cautious and watch out for each other."

Ryan adjusted his backpack, his expression determined. "We've trained for this. We just need to stay focused and move carefully."

Amina nodded, tightening the laces on her boots. "Let's make sure we have regular check-ins. If anyone spots something difficult or dangerous, call it out immediately."

Kato looked up at Mia, his eyes wide with a mix of excitement and apprehension. "Will it be really hard today, Ms. Mia?"

Mia smiled reassuringly. "It will be challenging, Kato, but we can handle it. Remember, we're a team. We help each other."

As they set off, the landscape quickly changed. The rolling hills gave way to rocky outcrops and steep, uneven ground. The team moved slowly, each step placed with care. The path was narrow, bordered by dense foliage and sharp rocks.

Ryan took the lead, his eyes scanning the ground for safe footing. "Watch your step here. The ground is loose."

Amina followed closely behind, using her walking stick to test the stability of the terrain. "Stay close and keep your balance. If you need help, just ask."

Kato, sandwiched between Mia and Amina, tried to mimic their careful movements. He stumbled slightly on a loose rock, but Mia's steady hand caught him before he could fall.

"Easy there, Kato," Mia said gently. "You're doing great. Just take your time."

They continued to navigate the difficult path, the sun climbing higher in the sky. The team's progress was slow but steady, each member working together to overcome the obstacles in their way.

After several hours, they reached a particularly challenging section of the trail. A steep incline loomed ahead, the ground littered with loose stones and debris. Ryan stopped and turned to face the group.

"This part is going to be tough," he said, his voice firm. "We need to take it one step at a time and help each other up. Amina, can you go up first and anchor a rope?"

Amina nodded, her expression focused. "I'll secure it to that tree up there. It looks sturdy enough to hold us."

Mia handed Amina a length of rope from her pack. "Be careful. We'll follow your lead."

Amina began her ascent, moving with practiced ease. She reached the top quickly, securing the rope to a large, sturdy tree. Once the rope was in place, she called down to the others.

"Rope's secure! Start coming up one by one. Use the rope for support."

Ryan went first, testing the rope's strength before climbing. He moved steadily, reaching the top without incident. Next was Kato, who looked up at Mia, his expression nervous.

"You can do this, Kato," Mia said encouragingly. "I'll be right behind you."

Kato gripped the rope tightly, his small hands shaking slightly. He began to climb, his movements careful and deliberate. Mia followed closely, ready to catch him if he slipped. With Ryan and Amina's encouragement from above and Mia's steady presence behind him, Kato made it to the top safely.

"Great job, Kato!" Ryan said, clapping him on the back. "You did it!"

Kato beamed with pride, his earlier nervousness forgotten. "Thanks, Mr. Ryan. That was really hard."

Mia climbed up next, her ascent quick and sure. Once at the top, she turned to help the next team member, ensuring everyone made it safely. When everyone had reached the top, they took a moment to rest, the difficult climb behind them.

As they continued their journey, the terrain gradually began to level out. The forest thickened, the path winding through dense trees and underbrush. The air was filled with the sounds of nature – birds singing, leaves rustling in the breeze, and the occasional rustle of small animals in the undergrowth.

Ryan led the way, his eyes constantly scanning for any signs of danger. "Stay alert. The forest can be deceptive. Keep an eye out for any sudden drops or unstable ground."

Amina nodded, her gaze sharp. "We're making good progress. Let's keep up this pace, but don't rush. Safety first."

Kato, despite the challenges, seemed to be enjoying the adventure. He walked with a newfound confidence, his earlier fears replaced by determination. "I like the forest, Ms. Mia. It's like an adventure book come to life."

Mia smiled at his enthusiasm. "It is, Kato. And just like in your books, we need to be smart and careful. Adventure is exciting, but safety is important."

As the sun began to set, casting long shadows through the trees, the team found a suitable place to camp for the night. They set up their tents and built a small fire, the warmth and light providing comfort after the day's exertions.

Sitting around the fire, Ryan looked at the team, pride evident in his eyes. "Today was tough, but we made it through because we worked together. Every challenge we overcome makes us stronger."

Amina nodded in agreement. "We faced some difficult terrain, but we supported each other. That's what will get us through this journey – our teamwork and determination."

Kato looked up at Mia, his eyes filled with curiosity. "What do we do tomorrow, Ms. Mia?"

Mia smiled, ruffling his hair. "Tomorrow, we keep moving forward. We'll face new challenges and see new sights. And we'll do it together, as a team."

As the fire crackled softly and the stars began to twinkle above, the team felt a deep sense of accomplishment. They had faced difficult terrain and come out stronger, their bonds forged even tighter by the day's challenges. They were ready for whatever lay ahead, united by their mission and their trust in each other.

As the sun rose, the team stirred, ready to face another challenging day in the jungle. The air was thick with humidity, and the sounds of the forest slowly woke up along with them. Mia was already up, making sure everything was in order.

Ryan stretched and walked over to where Mia was going over the map. "Morning. How did you sleep?"

Mia smiled faintly, not taking her eyes off the map. "About as well as you can in the jungle. We've got a tough day ahead. This area here," she pointed to a section on the map, "is known for its dense vegetation and steep inclines."

Ryan nodded. "We'll need to move carefully. Let's make sure everyone is ready and well-prepared."

Mia looked up and saw the rest of the team starting to gather. "Alright, everyone, gather around," she called out. "We've got a challenging route today. The terrain is rough, and we need to stay alert."

Kato stepped forward, his youthful enthusiasm evident. "Ms. Mia, I checked the area last night. There are signs of heavy animal traffic. We need to be cautious."

"Good work, Kato," Mia said appreciatively. "Everyone, keep an eye out for wildlife and any signs of poachers. Stay close and communicate constantly."

Amina joined them, adjusting her backpack. "I've packed extra water and snacks. It's going to be a long hike."

Ryan nodded in agreement. "Make sure you drink water regularly. Dehydration is a serious risk out here."

With the plan set, the team began their trek. The jungle seemed to close in around them as they moved deeper into the dense foliage. Mia led the way, her machete slicing through the undergrowth. Ryan followed closely, his senses on high alert.

The morning passed slowly as they navigated through the challenging terrain. The ground was uneven, and every step required careful attention. Mia and Ryan communicated constantly, ensuring the team stayed together and moved safely.

"Watch your step here," Mia advised, pointing to a particularly steep section. "It's slippery from last night's rain."

Ryan nodded, turning to the group. "One at a time, and use the ropes for support. Amina, you go first."

Amina secured the rope and began her descent, moving cautiously. She reached the bottom safely and signaled for the next person. One by one, the team followed, each movement deliberate and careful.

Halfway down, Kato slipped, and Mia quickly grabbed his arm, steadying him. "I've got you, Kato. Just take it slow."

"Thank you, Ms. Mia," Kato said, his voice shaky but grateful.

Once everyone was safely down, they continued their trek. The jungle was alive with sounds—birds calling, insects buzzing, and the occasional rustle of unseen animals. The humidity was oppressive, and the heat seemed to intensify with every step.

Ryan wiped sweat from his brow and glanced at Mia. "This heat is brutal. How are you holding up?"

Mia took a deep breath, feeling the weight of the journey. "It's tough, but we're making progress. We just need to stay focused."

The team took a short break to hydrate and rest. Mia handed out water bottles and checked in with each member. "Everyone doing okay?"

Amina nodded, taking a long drink of water. "It's hard, but we're managing. The terrain is tougher than I expected."

Kato looked around, his eyes wide with excitement. "This is amazing. I've never been this deep into the jungle before."

Ryan smiled at the boy's enthusiasm. "It's incredible, alright. Just remember to stay alert. The jungle is beautiful but dangerous."

After the break, they resumed their journey. The terrain grew steeper, and the vegetation thicker. Mia's machete worked tirelessly, clearing a path for the team. They moved slowly, every step a careful calculation.

Suddenly, Mia stopped, holding up her hand for silence. "Do you hear that?"

Ryan listened intently. "Sounds like running water. There must be a stream nearby."

"Let's head that way," Mia said, leading the team towards the sound.

As they approached the stream, the ground grew softer, and the air cooler. The sight of clear, running water was a welcome relief. Mia knelt by the stream, filling her water bottle.

"This will be a good place to rest and regroup," she said, looking up at Ryan.

He nodded in agreement. "We can refill our water and cool off. Good call, Mia."

The team settled by the stream, grateful for the break. As they rested, Mia and Ryan discussed the next part of their journey.

"The terrain ahead is even tougher," Mia noted. "We need to be prepared for anything."

Ryan agreed. "We've got a strong team. We'll make it through."

Mia looked around at her team, feeling a deep sense of responsibility. "Alright, everyone," she called out, "take a few minutes to rest and refill your water. We've got a tough climb ahead, but we can do this."

The team nodded, their determination evident. As they rested by the stream, the challenges of the jungle seemed a bit more manageable. They were a strong, united group, ready to face whatever came their way.

After resting by the stream and refilling their water bottles, the team prepared to continue their trek deeper into the jungle. The respite had been much needed, but the hardest part of their journey was still ahead.

Mia took a deep breath, her senses tuned to the sounds and sights of the jungle around them. "Alright, everyone, let's get moving," she called out, her voice steady and commanding. "We need to reach the observation point by nightfall."

Ryan checked his gear one last time and nodded. "Everyone ready? Stay close and watch your footing. The path ahead is steep."

The team set off, the sound of the running stream gradually fading behind them. The terrain grew increasingly challenging as they ascended a rugged incline. The dense vegetation made it difficult to see more than a few feet ahead, and every step required careful navigation.

The sun was high in the sky, casting dappled light through the canopy above. The humidity was oppressive, and sweat dripped from their faces as they climbed. Mia led the way, her machete slicing through the thick underbrush.

As they pushed forward, the jungle seemed to grow even more impenetrable. The path was narrow and treacherous, with loose rocks and hidden roots threatening to trip them up.

Kato, walking behind Mia, stumbled over a root and nearly fell. "Careful," Mia said, reaching back to steady him. "Watch your step."

"Thanks, Ms. Mia," Kato replied, his voice breathless but determined.

The team pressed on, their progress slow but steady. The sounds of the jungle surrounded them—bird calls, rustling leaves, and the distant roar of a waterfall. Mia found herself simultaneously exhilarated and exhausted. This was the kind of challenge she had trained for, but it was pushing her to her limits.

Ryan, walking beside Mia, glanced at her. "How are you holding up?"

Mia wiped sweat from her forehead and nodded. "I'm good. Just focused on getting us there safely."

"You're doing great. We're making good progress," Ryan reassured her, his voice steady and calm.

The path continued to climb, the incline growing steeper with each step. Mia paused to consult her map, then pointed to a ridge ahead. "We need to get to that ridge. From there, we should have a clear view of the valley."

Amina, catching her breath, joined them. "It's going to be tough, but we can do it."

With renewed determination, the team began the final ascent to the ridge. The climb was grueling, and the heat and humidity made it even more challenging. Mia's muscles ached, and her breath came in ragged gasps, but she pushed on, driven by her sense of purpose.

As they neared the top, the path narrowed even further, and they had to use ropes to help them climb the last few feet. Ryan went first, securing the rope and guiding the others up one by one.

When it was Mia's turn, she gripped the rope tightly and began her ascent. Halfway up, her foot slipped on a loose rock, and she felt herself start to slide. Ryan, seeing her struggle, reached down and grabbed her arm, pulling her up with a firm grip.

"Got you," Ryan said, his voice reassuring.

"Thanks," Mia replied, her heart pounding with adrenaline.

They finally reached the top of the ridge and stood, breathing heavily, looking out over the breathtaking view before them. The valley below was a sea of green, stretching out as far as the eye could see. The river wound its way through the landscape, glistening in the afternoon sun.

"We made it," Amina said, her voice filled with awe.

Mia nodded, feeling a sense of accomplishment wash over her. "This is it. We'll set up our observation post here."

The team quickly got to work, setting up their equipment and securing their campsite. Mia and Ryan surveyed the area, ensuring they had a clear view of the valley and could spot any movement below.

As the sun began to set, casting a golden glow over the jungle, Mia stood at the edge of the ridge, taking it all in. This was why they were here—to protect this pristine wilderness and the creatures that called it home. Despite the exhaustion and challenges, she felt a deep sense of purpose and determination.

Ryan joined her, looking out over the valley. "We did good today, Mia. This is a perfect spot."

Mia nodded, her eyes on the horizon. "It is. And it's just the beginning. We have a lot of work ahead, but we're ready."

Ryan placed a reassuring hand on her shoulder. "Together, we can do this."

As night fell, the team settled into their campsite, the sounds of the jungle creating a symphony around them. They had faced the challenges of the day and come through stronger and more united. The journey ahead was still uncertain, but they were prepared to face it together, driven by their shared mission and unwavering resolve.

Chapter 4
Uneasy Beginnings

The dirt road wound through the thick, lush jungle, the jeeps jostling and bouncing over roots and uneven ground. Mia held tightly to the door handle as they maneuvered through one final sharp turn and rolled to a stop. The roar of the engines faded, leaving only the hum of the rainforest—chirping insects, distant birdcalls, and the rustling of leaves in the gentle breeze. A sense of reverence and awe settled over Mia as she gazed out at the dense canopy that stretched in all directions.

"We're here," Ryan announced, shutting off the engine and pushing the door open. He stepped out, his boots sinking slightly into the damp soil, and took a deep breath. "Home sweet home… for the foreseeable future."

Mia climbed out of the vehicle, her gaze sweeping over their surroundings. The base camp area was a small clearing, surrounded on all sides by towering trees and thick underbrush. A narrow river wound its way along the camp's edge, its waters dark and still. The humid air clung to her skin, heavy with the scent of wet earth and blooming flowers. For a moment, she simply stood there, absorbing the jungle's vibrant energy.

"Not bad," she murmured, her eyes narrowing as she assessed the site. "Plenty of cover, close to a water source… It's perfect."

"Perfect?" Ryan echoed skeptically, stepping up beside her. His gaze was sharper, more critical, as he scanned the perimeter.

"I'd call it exposed. No clear lines of sight beyond the immediate clearing, and that river's a double-edged sword. It gives us water, but it also means we've got one more entry point to guard."

Mia stiffened, her jaw clenching slightly. She turned to face him, lifting her chin defiantly. "We chose this location because it's central to the areas where poacher activity has been reported. We need to be close if we're going to monitor their movements effectively. And the river's manageable. We'll set up additional sentry points if necessary."

Ryan crossed his arms, his expression hard. "You're thinking like a researcher, not a field operative. This camp is vulnerable—to poachers, to wildlife, to just about anything that decides to wander through. We're practically inviting trouble."

"Ryan, I get your concerns," Mia replied, keeping her voice calm despite the heat rising in her chest. "But this isn't just about safety. We need to be in the thick of it if we're going to do any good out here. We're not hiding—we're protecting."

Ryan's lips pressed into a thin line. "And if something happens—if we're overrun, or if the locals we're supposed to be helping get caught in the crossfire?"

Mia faltered, uncertainty flickering in her eyes for just a moment. But she straightened, pushing past it. "I've thought this through. This location gives us the best chance to make a difference. We'll be careful, and we'll be prepared."

"Guys, maybe we can just... breathe for a second," Amina interjected gently, stepping between them. Her voice was calm, soothing, like a cool breeze cutting through the tension. "We're all on the same team here. We need to trust each other's judgment. Ryan, I know you're worried about security, but Mia's right—we have to be close to the action. We can adjust our setup to minimize the risks."

Ryan exhaled slowly, some of the rigidity leaving his shoulders. He glanced at Amina, then back at Mia, his gaze softening marginally. "Fine. But I'm going to do a perimeter check. If I see anything that concerns me, we're going to have another conversation about this."

"Deal," Mia agreed, trying not to let the relief show too much on her face. "Check the area. Let me know if you find anything."

He nodded curtly and turned, heading off into the jungle with his rifle slung over his shoulder. Mia watched him go, tension knotting in her stomach. This was supposed to be a new beginning, a chance to prove herself, but already she felt the weight of expectations pressing down on her.

"Don't let it get to you," Amina murmured, placing a hand on Mia's arm. "He just wants to keep everyone safe."

"I know," Mia sighed. "But I can't have him second-guessing me every step of the way. I need him to trust my decisions."

"He'll come around," Amina said with a reassuring smile. "Give it time. You're doing great."

"Thanks," Mia replied softly, managing a small smile in return. "I appreciate it."

A rustling sound made them both turn. Kato emerged from the back of the second jeep, his face pale and eyes wide. He glanced around nervously, his gaze lingering on the thick foliage and shadowy undergrowth.

"Is… is this really safe?" he asked hesitantly, his voice barely above a whisper. "I mean… I knew we'd be in the jungle, but… it's so… wild."

"It's exactly what we expected, Kato," Amina said gently, stepping closer to him. "We're prepared for this. We've got protocols and security measures in place."

"But what if—" Kato began, his voice trembling slightly.

"Kato," Mia interrupted, keeping her tone firm but kind. "You've trained for this. We've all trained for this. You're part of the team, and we're going to look out for each other. I need you to trust yourself as much as I trust you."

Kato swallowed hard, then nodded slowly. "Okay… okay. I'll—I'll do my best."

"That's all I ask," Mia said, offering him a reassuring smile.

The rest of the team busied themselves setting up the tents and securing the equipment. The sound of hammers and drills filled the air, blending with the ambient noise of the jungle. As the camp slowly took shape, Mia moved between the groups, offering guidance and encouragement.

But as the shadows deepened and the campfire flickered to life in the center of the clearing, Mia couldn't shake the feeling of being watched. She glanced toward the edge of the clearing where Ryan had disappeared hours earlier, worry gnawing at the edges of her mind.

She squared her shoulders, pushing the unease aside. She had to be strong—for herself and for the team. This was her chance to prove she could lead, that she could make a difference.

"Everything's going to be fine," she whispered to herself, the words half reassurance, half prayer. "We're ready."

With a deep breath, she turned her focus back to the camp, her resolve hardening. No matter what happened, they would make this work. They had to.

This was just the beginning.

The midday sun hung high overhead, casting sharp shadows through the canopy as the team moved about the camp, each person focused on their respective tasks. The clearing buzzed with activity—tents were being erected, equipment unpacked, and the radio communications system tested and retested to ensure they could maintain contact with the outside world.

Mia crouched beside a stack of crates, cross-checking the inventory list in her notebook with the items already unpacked. Sweat trickled down the back of her neck, and the paper beneath her hand felt slightly damp from the humidity. Despite the heat and discomfort, she forced herself to focus, running a critical eye over the gear.

"Two crates of rations, one of medical supplies, field kits…" she murmured to herself, ticking each item off the list. "Camera traps, batteries, fuel canisters… What's missing?"

A frown creased her brow as she reached the end of the list. Her gaze darted over the stacked crates again, double-checking, but the nagging suspicion didn't go away.

"Something wrong?" Ryan's voice broke through her thoughts. She looked up to see him standing over her, his expression unreadable.

"I don't know yet," she admitted, chewing on her lower lip. "I'm missing one crate. It should have been with the initial supply drop, but it's not here."

Ryan crouched down beside her, his gaze sharp as he surveyed the supplies. "What's in the missing crate?"

"Tools and spare parts for the field kits," Mia replied, flipping through her notebook quickly. "Nothing critical, but it's still important to have, especially if we're going to be here for a while."

Ryan's frown deepened. "If it's not critical, then why does it bother you?"

"It's not the missing crate itself," Mia said slowly, closing her notebook and looking up at him. "It's what it represents. Everything was supposed to be accounted for, and if we're already missing supplies, what else might go wrong?"

Ryan's eyes narrowed slightly, his gaze shifting from the crates to the surrounding jungle. "We should do a full check of everything—make sure there's nothing else missing. And then I think we need to reconsider whether this is the best spot for camp. I don't like that something's gone wrong on the first day."

Mia straightened, her back stiffening at his words. "We've already started setting up, Ryan. We can't just pick up and move at the first sign of trouble."

"This isn't about trouble, it's about being smart," Ryan insisted, his tone firm. "We're in unfamiliar territory. We need to make sure we have a solid base of operations—one we can defend, one that's secure. If something as simple as a supply drop goes wrong, what's that going to mean when we start running into poachers or wildlife issues?"

Mia's jaw clenched, irritation flaring. "I get that you're concerned, but I don't want to lose precious time moving camp just because of a misplaced crate. We're here to protect these animals and document the poachers' activities, not to hide out in the safest place we can find."

Ryan shook his head, his gaze never leaving hers. "It's not about hiding, Mia. It's about being prepared. You know that better than anyone. If we're not set up right, we could jeopardize everything we're trying to do."

"And moving camp isn't going to solve that," Mia countered, her voice rising slightly. She took a breath, forcing herself to calm down. "We can't keep second-guessing every decision, or we'll never get anything done."

A tense silence fell between them, the unspoken challenge hanging in the air. Amina, who had been nearby checking the radio system, glanced over, sensing the rising tension. She stood and walked over, placing herself between them with an easy, practiced smile.

"Hey, hey—let's not get too heated here," Amina said lightly, her tone a deliberate attempt to defuse the situation. "We've all been working hard, and it's been a long day. Why don't we take a step back and reassess? We've got enough supplies to hold us over for now. How about we finish setting up, run a perimeter check, and then decide if we need to move?"

Ryan exhaled slowly, his shoulders relaxing just a fraction. "I just don't want us to get caught off guard. This place feels… exposed."

Mia felt a pang of frustration, but she swallowed it back. "We'll secure the perimeter, Ryan. And if we find anything that gives us cause for concern, I promise we'll revisit the idea of moving.

But for now, we need to focus on getting set up. We're losing daylight."

He studied her for a long moment, then finally nodded. "Fine. But I'm going to do another sweep of the perimeter after we finish here. Just to be sure."

"Good," Mia agreed, her tone softer. "And thank you."

Ryan didn't respond immediately. He just nodded again and turned away, heading toward the edge of the camp where Kato was setting up motion sensors. Mia watched him go, her shoulders sagging slightly with the release of tension.

"Don't worry about it too much," Amina murmured, nudging Mia gently with her elbow. "He's just looking out for us."

"I know," Mia sighed, rubbing the back of her neck. "It's just… this is our first day out here, and I already feel like I'm messing up."

"You're not messing up," Amina said firmly. "You're leading. And leadership isn't about always having the right answer. It's about being willing to listen, adjust, and make the best decision with what you've got. And that's exactly what you're doing."

"Thanks," Mia murmured, a small smile tugging at her lips. "I just hope the rest of the mission goes smoother than today."

"It will," Amina assured her. "Once we're fully set up and everyone's settled, things will feel less chaotic."

As if on cue, Kato approached, his face pale and his gaze flickering nervously between Mia and Amina. He cleared his throat awkwardly. "Um, I just wanted to say that… I think Ryan has a point. I mean, about checking everything again. We should probably double-check… just in case."

Mia's smile faded, replaced by a look of quiet determination. "We will, Kato. But we also need to trust in the work we've already done. I know you're worried, but we have to find a balance between caution and action."

"Right," Kato muttered, nodding rapidly. "I just—okay, yeah, I get it. Sorry."

"Don't apologize," Mia said gently. "I appreciate your input. We all need to be on the same page if we're going to make this work."

Kato offered a hesitant smile, then shuffled back to his equipment. Mia let out a slow breath, glancing at Amina.

"See?" Amina said with a grin. "You've got this."

Mia shook her head, but a small smile crept back onto her lips. "I hope so. Because right now, it feels like I'm just trying to keep my head above water."

Amina laughed softly. "Welcome to leadership. But you're not alone. We're all here, and we've got your back."

Mia looked around at the bustling camp, at the team members working hard to bring her vision to life. For better or worse, this was her responsibility. And she wasn't going to let a missing crate or a few disagreements derail their mission.

"Thanks, Amina," she said quietly. "Let's get this camp finished."

They turned back to the task at hand, the unease lingering in the back of Mia's mind. The jungle loomed around them, silent and watchful, as if waiting to see if they truly belonged.

But Mia refused to give in to the doubt. This was where they needed to be—where *she* needed to be. And she would make it work, no matter what.

The thick canopy above filtered the late afternoon sunlight into a soft, dappled glow, casting shifting patterns on the forest floor as the team moved quietly through the underbrush. The air buzzed with the sounds of life—the chittering of insects, the distant calls of birds, and the occasional rustle of leaves as unseen creatures scurried away from the intruders. Mia took the lead, her eyes scanning the dense foliage and thick roots of the towering trees, noting every detail as they walked.

"Remember, we're not here to engage or draw attention," she murmured softly over her shoulder. "This is just reconnaissance. We need to get a feel for the area and see if there's any sign of wildlife or human activity."

Ryan, a few paces behind her, nodded, his expression serious. "Understood. But stay alert. This close to the camp, we can't afford any surprises."

Kato, his movements tentative but careful, trailed slightly behind Ryan. He glanced around, his gaze darting nervously from shadow to shadow. "How do we know if it's safe? I mean... there could be traps anywhere, right?"

Mia paused, turning back to give Kato a reassuring look. "That's why we're taking it slow, step by step. Look for disturbed soil, bent grass, or any unnatural markings. Most traps are set to blend in, but they still leave traces if you know what to look for."

Kato nodded, swallowing hard. "Right. Okay. Got it."

They continued their exploration, moving in a loose formation that allowed them to cover as much ground as possible while still staying within sight of each other. Amina, who had been keeping an eye on the tree line, suddenly stopped, her gaze narrowing.

"Mia, over here," she called softly, motioning to a massive tree with roots as thick as a man's arm winding in all directions.

Mia moved quickly to Amina's side, crouching low as she inspected the ground. Nestled between two roots, half-hidden beneath a layer of leaves, was a crude snare. It looked old and rusted, but the noose of wire was still intact, lying in wait for any unsuspecting animal that might wander too close.

"An old snare," Mia murmured, her voice tight. "But still dangerous."

She reached out carefully, her fingers deftly working to dismantle the trap. The wire snapped with a soft metallic twang as she disarmed the mechanism, and she set the remnants of the snare aside, her expression dark.

"This is why we're here," Mia said, her voice low but filled with resolve. "To stop this kind of thing. One snare like this could kill or injure multiple animals, and it's just one of hundreds, maybe thousands, in this area."

Amina nodded, glancing around warily. "Do you think it's been here long? It looks like it's been abandoned."

"Maybe," Mia replied, standing up and dusting off her hands. "But we can't assume anything. This could just as easily be a marker—poachers sometimes leave old traps behind to gauge the presence of people or animals. If something or someone interferes, they know the area's being monitored."

"Great," Ryan muttered, his eyes scanning the surroundings, his posture tense. "So now we're not just watching for traps—we're potential bait."

Mia turned to face him, her expression firm. "We knew this wasn't going to be easy, Ryan. But that's why we're here. If we don't take these risks, who will? We have to be vigilant, but we also have to act."

Ryan sighed, running a hand through his hair. "I'm not saying we shouldn't act. I'm just saying we need to be smart about it. Finding a trap this close to camp means they're either careless or bold. Either way, it's a problem."

"I know," Mia said quietly, meeting his gaze. "And we'll handle it. But we can't let fear paralyze us. This is what we came for—to stop this kind of activity, to make a difference."

Kato stepped forward hesitantly, his brow furrowed. "How do we know if there are more traps? Is there a pattern to where they set them?"

Ryan's expression softened slightly as he turned to Kato. "Good question. Poachers usually set traps along animal trails, watering holes, or other high-traffic areas. They look for signs of animals—tracks, scat, broken branches. Once you know what to look for, it gets easier to spot potential traps."

Kato nodded, listening intently as Ryan continued to explain. The tension between them from earlier seemed to dissipate as Ryan shifted into mentor mode, his voice steady and patient.

"See the way these roots are disturbed?" Ryan gestured to the base of the tree. "That's from an animal—probably a small mammal or a rodent—scrambling over the roots. If poachers notice a spot like this being used frequently, they'll set up a snare or a pit trap nearby."

Kato crouched down, inspecting the area with new eyes. "So, if we find a spot like this, we should check for traps even if we don't see one right away?"

"Exactly," Ryan confirmed with a nod. "And don't just look at ground level—check higher up too. Some traps are set to snag animals at chest height or higher. Always think like a predator—where would you set something to catch your prey?"

Mia watched the exchange, a small smile tugging at her lips. Ryan's protective instincts might cause friction sometimes, but they were rooted in genuine concern and experience. And seeing him guide Kato with such patience reminded her why she valued his presence on the team.

"Thanks, Ryan," Mia said softly. "For sharing that. It's important we're all on the same page."

Ryan glanced at her, his gaze lingering for a moment before he nodded. "No problem. We need everyone sharp out here. We can't afford to miss anything."

"Agreed," Amina said, stepping back and surveying the surrounding jungle. "So, what's the plan? Keep moving or head back to camp?"

Mia straightened, her gaze sweeping over the shadowy expanse of trees. "We keep moving for now. We need a better sense of the area before night falls. Let's see if we can find more signs of traps or activity."

With a shared look of understanding, the team fell back into formation, their senses heightened. As they moved deeper into the jungle, Mia's heart thudded steadily in her chest. The discovery of the snare had been a stark reminder of what they were up against. This wasn't just a research expedition—it was a fight for the jungle itself.

But Mia was ready.

She had to be.

"Stay sharp," she whispered to herself, glancing over her shoulder to check on the team. "We're just getting started."

The jungle came alive as the sun dipped below the horizon, casting the dense foliage into a web of shadows and shifting darkness. The transition from day to night was almost seamless—one moment the last rays of sunlight were streaming through the trees, and the next, a thick blanket of darkness enveloped everything. But the darkness didn't bring silence. It was as if the jungle itself awoke with a newfound energy, the chorus of chirping insects and croaking frogs rising to a deafening crescendo.

Mia sat cross-legged on the ground, staring into the flickering flames of the small campfire that crackled softly in the middle of the clearing. The warm light cast long shadows, playing across the faces of her team as they gathered around, eating their simple meal of dried fruits, nuts, and a few preserved rations. The earlier tension from the day's events had eased somewhat, but a quiet unease still hung in the air, mingling with the unfamiliar sounds of the night.

She glanced around the circle, noting the pensive expressions on Amina's and Ryan's faces, the nervous energy still radiating from Kato as he picked at his food. Mia shifted, the weight of her father's old compass pressing against her chest. She reached up and pulled it out from where it hung around her neck, the cool metal grounding her as she turned it over in her hand.

"So," Amina began softly, breaking the silence. Her voice was low, thoughtful, as if she didn't want to disturb the night around them. "I've been thinking about how we're going to approach the local communities. If we want their cooperation, we need to make sure we're presenting ourselves as allies, not outsiders coming in to disrupt their way of life."

Mia looked up, nodding slowly. "You're right. If we go in with a 'we know best' attitude, we'll lose their trust before we even start. We need to listen more than we talk. Understand what they need, what they fear."

"Agreed," Amina said, poking the fire with a stick and watching the embers flare up. "And we should consider bringing in some of the village leaders early on, show them what we're doing and how it benefits them directly. Maybe even have them help with the patrols or the data collection."

"Are we sure they'll be willing to get involved?" Kato asked hesitantly. "I mean… they must know about the poachers. Why haven't they done something about it already?"

Ryan glanced at Kato, his gaze thoughtful. "It's not that simple. They're caught between protecting their land and surviving.

Poachers can be ruthless. Some of these villages might have already been threatened, or worse."

Mia nodded in agreement. "Ryan's right. It's not just about willingness. It's about fear, survival, and often, lack of resources. If we can show them that we're here to support and not to judge, we can build a real partnership. That's the key—empowerment, not control."

Amina leaned forward, her expression intense. "What if we set up workshops? Educational programs where they can learn about conservation, but also where we can learn from them. They've lived here for generations—they know this land better than we ever could."

Mia felt a swell of gratitude for Amina's insight. She shifted, her fingers absently tracing the edge of the compass. "That's exactly what I want this project to be about. Not just protecting the land and the animals, but building a legacy of trust and collaboration with the people who live here."

She glanced around the circle, seeing the light of understanding in Amina's eyes and the thoughtful consideration on Ryan's face. Even Kato seemed more engaged, his nervousness easing as the conversation flowed.

"If we can get the communities on our side," Mia continued, her voice gaining strength, "then we'll have more eyes and ears in the jungle. We'll know where the poachers are operating, where the animals are moving. We'll be stronger together. This project—it's not just about what we're bringing to them. It's about what we can build together."

Ryan's gaze met hers, and for the first time since they'd arrived, Mia saw a glimmer of respect in his eyes. He gave her a small, almost imperceptible nod—a silent acknowledgment that spoke louder than any words. It was a moment of unspoken understanding, a bridge being built between them after the tension and disagreements earlier in the day.

"You're right," Ryan said quietly. "We have to do this differently. We can't just come in, set up traps, and patrol. We need their trust, and we need to earn it."

"Exactly," Mia agreed softly, feeling a surge of hope. "This is just the beginning. If we can do this right, we can make a real impact."

Amina smiled, her eyes shining with determination. "I believe we can. We're here to make a difference, and I think we're already on the right path."

The fire crackled between them, sending up a thin wisp of smoke that curled into the night sky. For a moment, they all fell silent, the weight of their mission settling around them like a heavy blanket. But it was a comforting weight, a shared burden that bonded them together.

The jungle continued its symphony around them, the sounds both familiar and strange. Mia stared out into the darkness, the flames casting soft shadows across her face. She felt the enormity of what lay ahead—the dangers, the challenges, the sacrifices they might have to make. But she also felt a sense of clarity, a certainty that had been elusive until now.

"We're going to change things here," she murmured, almost to herself. "One step at a time."

As the conversation turned to more practical matters—logistics, schedules, and strategies—Mia found herself drifting into her own thoughts, the firelight flickering in her eyes. She glanced down at the compass in her hand, the metal cool and smooth against her skin.

This was why she was here. Not just for her father, not just for the animals or the land. But for the people—for the communities who needed a voice, for the generations that deserved a chance to thrive alongside the wilderness.

With a deep breath, she slipped the compass back beneath her shirt and looked up at the stars peeking through the canopy. "This is just the beginning," she whispered softly, her voice barely audible over the crackling fire and the jungle's nocturnal chorus.

Her gaze lingered on the darkness beyond the fire's glow, a small smile tugging at her lips.

"Just the beginning."

As the fire burned lower and the team began to settle in for the night, Mia remained by the dying embers, watching as the flames danced and flickered. The weight of the jungle, the mission, and her own aspirations pressed down on her shoulders, but this time, it felt right.

With one last glance at the camp, she stood and turned away, stepping into the shadows at the edge of the clearing. The world beyond was vast, untamed, and filled with uncertainty.

And Mia was ready to face it, one step at a time.

Chapter 5
Confronting Internal Conflicts

Mia's breaths came in shallow gasps as she dangled from the climbing rope, her fingers slipping against the rough, craggy surface of the rock face. Her hands burned, and sweat stung her eyes, but she kept her gaze fixed on the small outcropping above her. She could almost hear her father's voice cutting through the rushing wind, calm and steady despite the height and danger.

"Don't rush it, Mia. Slow down. You've got this."

She squeezed her eyes shut, focusing on the memory. Her father had been perched above her that day, his silhouette framed against the clear blue sky. The day had been bright and crisp, the kind of perfect weather that felt almost like a promise. She had been twelve—small, determined, and desperate to make him proud.

"Use your legs more," he'd called down to her. "You're pulling too much with your arms. Find a foothold and push yourself up."

"I'm trying!" she'd shouted back, her voice tinged with frustration. She had been so close—just a few feet from where he stood—but the muscles in her arms were trembling with exhaustion, her grip threatening to fail.

"Stop trying. Just breathe. Remember what I told you? It's not about brute strength. It's about focus and control. Your mind is stronger than your body. Now, what's the next move?"

Mia had paused, clinging to the rock face with all the strength her small frame could muster. She remembered the feeling—the way her heart had pounded, not from fear, but from the intense desire to prove herself. To show him that she was capable, that she belonged in the wild with him. Slowly, she had forced herself to look down, scanning for a foothold. Her eyes had found it, just a few inches below, a tiny ledge big enough for the toe of her boot.

"Good," her father had encouraged. "Now shift your weight and push. Don't think about falling. Don't think about anything but that next step."

And she had. Mia had shifted, reached up, and pulled herself higher, inch by inch, until she had finally grasped his outstretched hand. His grip had been firm and warm, pulling her up the last few feet until she stood beside him, panting and flushed with triumph.

"See?" he'd said, his smile wide and bright against his suntanned face. "I knew you could do it."

She'd beamed up at him, her heart soaring at the approval in his eyes. "Really? You're not just saying that?"

"Mia," he'd said softly, kneeling down to her level so that their gazes were locked, "I wouldn't say it if it wasn't true. You've got more strength in you than you know. But remember, strength isn't just about climbing rocks or running faster. It's about staying calm when everything else is falling apart. It's about making decisions with a clear mind."

She had nodded eagerly, drinking in his words, committing them to memory. In that moment, she'd felt invincible, like there was nothing she couldn't do with him by her side.

"Promise me something," he'd said, his expression turning serious. "Promise me that you'll always stay true to who you are, no matter what happens. Don't let fear—or anyone else's expectations—dictate your path."

"I promise, Dad," she'd whispered, her voice small but fierce. "I'll be strong, just like you."

The memory faded, dissolving into darkness, and when Mia opened her eyes, she was back in the present—lying in her tent, the canvas walls faintly illuminated by the early dawn light filtering through. The jungle outside was alive with the sounds of chirping insects and distant bird calls. For a moment, she remained still, the lingering warmth of her father's presence both comforting and painful.

Slowly, Mia sat up, running a hand through her hair. It had been years since that climb, since that promise. And yet, here she was, thousands of miles from home, still chasing that feeling, still trying to prove that she was strong enough. Strong enough to lead. Strong enough to live up to his legacy.

She pushed herself out of the sleeping bag, blinking away the last traces of sleep. The tent was cramped, filled with equipment and notes, but everything was in perfect order—just the way she liked it. She needed that sense of control now more than ever.

"Couldn't sleep?" a voice murmured from the tent's entrance.

Mia glanced up to see Ryan crouched just outside, his broad frame silhouetted against the soft morning light. He looked relaxed, but there was a keen awareness in his eyes—always alert, always assessing.

"Just... thinking," Mia replied, her voice still thick with the remnants of her dream. "Old memories."

"Your father?" Ryan guessed, his tone gentle.

Mia nodded, swallowing the sudden tightness in her throat. "Yeah. I—I dreamt about that time he took me climbing up Mount Hood. It's funny. I haven't thought about that day in years, but now... it's like he's everywhere. I keep hearing his voice, seeing his face."

Ryan nodded slowly, his gaze steady. "That's not surprising. He was a good man. And you're out here doing exactly what he'd be doing—trying to protect what's left. It's natural to think of him."

"Yeah, maybe," Mia murmured, glancing down at her hands. "But I don't know if I'm doing it for him or for me. Sometimes it's hard to tell the difference."

Ryan was silent for a moment, then he shifted, moving closer. "You don't have to decide that now. What matters is that you're here, making a difference. Your father would be proud of you, Mia. I'm sure of it."

Mia looked up, meeting his gaze. There was something in his eyes—a quiet, unspoken understanding that made her want to believe him. She nodded slowly, a small, tentative smile curving her lips.

"Thanks, Ryan. I—needed to hear that."

"Anytime," he said softly, giving her shoulder a light squeeze before standing. "Now come on. We've got a long day ahead. Let's show them what we're made of."

Mia took a deep breath, letting the cool, damp air fill her lungs. Then she stood, straightening her shoulders.

"Yeah," she said quietly. "Let's do this."

With one last glance at the fading tendrils of the dream, she stepped outside the tent, ready to face whatever the day—and the jungle—had in store.

The dense undergrowth parted reluctantly as Mia pushed forward, her eyes scanning the jungle floor for any signs of disturbance. The team moved in a loose formation, each step deliberate to minimize noise. The morning humidity wrapped around them like a heavy blanket, and the air was thick with the scent of wet earth and decaying foliage. Ahead, Ryan raised a hand, signaling them to stop. He crouched low, peering intently at something on the ground.

"What is it?" Mia whispered, stepping closer. She adjusted her grip on the machete at her side, feeling the familiar rush of adrenaline.

Ryan glanced over his shoulder at her, his expression tense. "Tripwire," he murmured, pointing to the barely visible thread stretched between two trees. "And not the amateur kind. This was set up by someone who knows what they're doing."

A chill ran down Mia's spine as she studied the trap. It was simple but effective—anyone who walked through without noticing would trigger a silent alarm, alerting the poachers to their presence. "How far do you think their camp is?" she asked quietly.

"Could be close, could be miles away," Ryan replied, his gaze sweeping the surrounding area. "But this isn't just a random setup. They've got a perimeter established. We're in their territory now."

Mia's jaw tightened. The thought of poachers operating so openly, so brazenly, made her blood boil. She took a step forward, scanning for more traps. "Then let's keep going. If we're close, we can find their camp and—"

"Wait, Mia," Amina interjected, her voice calm but firm. She moved beside them, her dark eyes narrowing as she examined the tripwire. "We need to think this through. We don't know how many there are or how well-armed they might be. Charging in could get us killed."

Mia turned to face her, frustration simmering just below the surface. "We can't just stand here and do nothing, Amina. These traps aren't meant for us—they're for the animals. Every second we waste, more wildlife is at risk."

"I know that," Amina said gently. "But we have to be smart about this. If we get caught, we can't help anyone. And if we get killed, what good will that do?"

Ryan nodded, his gaze locked on Mia's. "She's right. We document this, report back, and then plan our next move. We can't rush in blind, Mia."

Mia opened her mouth to argue, but the look on Ryan's face stopped her. There was no doubt in his eyes, no hesitation. Just the cold, hard logic of someone who had seen too many missions go wrong because of a single reckless decision. She knew he was right—knew it in the same way she knew that being out here was dangerous, that every step they took could be their last.

But the anger wouldn't go away. It roared through her like a wildfire, threatening to consume her rationality. *What would Dad have done?* The question echoed in her mind, taunting her. He would have found a way. He wouldn't have let fear hold him back.

"We've got a chance to catch them off guard," she insisted, lowering her voice. "If we can take down just a few of them, send a message—"

"No." Ryan's voice was quiet but unyielding. "We don't even know their numbers. We don't know their firepower. This isn't a simple recon mission, Mia. One wrong move, and they'll be on us before we can blink."

Mia stared at him, her hands clenching and unclenching at her sides. "So what, then? We just leave? Let them keep slaughtering animals while we play it safe?"

"Calm down," Ryan said, his tone softening. "We're not leaving. We're assessing the situation. That's different. We document every trap we find, get the coordinates, and then we send it to the local authorities. We don't have the manpower or firepower to engage right now."

"But—"

"Mia, look at me," Ryan interrupted, his gaze steady and intense. "You're not thinking straight. I get it—you want to take them down. So do I. But rushing in without a plan isn't going to help anyone. We've got a team to think about. Amina, Kato, the people counting on us back home. You want to help? Then we do this the right way. Got it?"

Mia's chest heaved as she struggled to rein in her emotions. She glanced at Amina, who gave her a small nod of encouragement, and then at Kato, who stood a few feet away, his face pale but determined.

"Fine," Mia muttered, turning away. "We document it."

Ryan exhaled softly, the tension easing from his shoulders. "Good. We'll cover more ground if we split up. Amina, you and Kato take the eastern perimeter. Mia and I will handle the west."

"Got it," Amina agreed, already pulling out her camera to begin photographing the tripwire and its setup.

Ryan stepped closer to Mia, lowering his voice. "Hey. I know this isn't easy. But you made the right call."

"Did I?" Mia shot back, her voice barely more than a whisper. "Because it doesn't feel like it."

"You did," he insisted. "And when the time comes, we'll hit them hard. But not until we're ready."

Mia nodded reluctantly, watching as Amina and Kato disappeared into the dense foliage. "Just... promise me we won't let them get away with this."

Ryan's jaw tightened. "I promise. Now let's move."

They worked in tense silence, documenting each trap they found, recording every makeshift campsite and abandoned snare. Mia's mind raced as she noted the patterns, the way the traps were placed with a precision that sent chills down her spine. These weren't amateurs. Whoever was behind this knew what they were doing.

When they regrouped an hour later, Amina's face was grim. "This is worse than I thought. They've set traps in every direction. And from the look of it, they're checking them regularly. We're dealing with professionals."

Mia looked down at her notes, frustration and anger coiling tight in her chest. "We need to stop them. Soon."

"And we will," Ryan assured her. "But we do it smart. One step at a time."

Mia nodded, but the fire in her eyes didn't dim. "One step at a time," she repeated quietly, her voice carrying a promise.

The team fell into silence, the weight of their discovery pressing down on them like the heavy jungle air. They had come face-to-face with the reality of the threat they were up against. And while caution would dictate their next steps, Mia knew one thing for certain: this was only the beginning.

And she wouldn't stop until the poachers were brought down.

The afternoon sun filtered through the dense canopy, casting dappled shadows across the forest floor. Kato crouched low behind a thick cluster of ferns, his face scrunched up in concentration as he tried to follow Ryan's instructions. Mia stood a few feet away, leaning against a tree trunk, arms folded across her chest. Her gaze was focused on the two of them, watching the way Ryan moved effortlessly through the underbrush, silent and fluid like a shadow.

"Okay, Kato, what did I say about movement?" Ryan's voice was low, almost a murmur, but it carried through the stillness of the jungle.

"Uh... less is more?" Kato guessed, wincing as he shifted his weight and a twig snapped under his boot.

"Right, but that means you need to be aware of every step. Don't just look at where you're placing your foot—feel it out first. The ground here is tricky. Listen before you step, feel before you shift. It's like you're trying to become part of the forest."

Kato nodded, his expression serious as he mimicked Ryan's stance, eyes fixed on the ground. He moved slowly, carefully testing each step before putting his full weight down. Mia raised an eyebrow, a faint smile tugging at the corner of her lips. She had to admit, the kid was a quick learner.

"Good," Ryan said approvingly, his voice soft. "Now, blend in. Think of yourself as... a chameleon. Your job is to make yourself as invisible as possible. What do you notice around you?"

"Um, the trees? And the vines. And the way the light falls in patches," Kato replied hesitantly, glancing up at Ryan for confirmation.

Ryan nodded. "Right. Those shadows, the broken lines of light—they help you disappear. Use them to your advantage. Don't stand out in the open. Move from cover to cover, but don't rush. The more you try to force it, the more noise you'll make."

Kato bit his lip, his gaze shifting back to the trees. He took a few tentative steps, weaving between the trunks, his body low and his movements deliberate. Ryan watched him closely, nodding in encouragement.

"Better," Ryan murmured. "Now, stop. Stay still."

Kato froze mid-step, his eyes darting nervously to Ryan. "What did I do?"

"Nothing. That's the point," Ryan said with a grin. "Sometimes, the best move is no move at all. Stillness is just as important as silence. Animals do it all the time when they sense danger—they freeze, blending into their surroundings. If you're not sure what to do, just... stop. Take a breath. Don't draw attention to yourself."

Kato stood still, his face scrunched in concentration. "Like this?"

"Exactly like that," Ryan replied, his voice a whisper now. "You're doing great, Kato. Just remember—always stay aware. The jungle's always talking to you. You just have to listen."

Mia's smile widened slightly as she watched the interaction. Ryan had a way of explaining things that made even the most complex skills seem manageable. He was patient, guiding Kato with gentle nudges rather than heavy-handed instructions. For a moment, she saw a different side of him—one that wasn't all about strategy and survival. One that was willing to teach, to nurture.

"Alright, now, let's talk about camouflage," Ryan said, glancing over at a nearby patch of mud and leaves. He picked up a handful of dirt and smeared it across his forearm. "See this? This is nature's paint. Mud, leaves, even moss—anything that breaks up your outline. Kato, give it a try."

Kato hesitated, then reached down and grabbed a clump of wet earth, mimicking Ryan's actions. He smeared it across his cheeks, a grin breaking out on his face as he looked up. "Like this?"

"Perfect. Now, if you were a predator—or a poacher—would you see yourself easily?"

Kato shook his head. "No, I guess not."

"Exactly." Ryan nodded approvingly. "Remember, visibility is your enemy out here. The less of you they see, the better."

Mia pushed off the tree and approached them, clapping softly. "Not bad, Kato. You're picking this up quicker than I did."

"Really?" Kato's eyes widened, surprise and pride warring on his face.

"Really," Mia confirmed, glancing at Ryan with a smile. "But that's only because I had a pretty strict teacher."

Ryan chuckled softly, shaking his head. "You weren't a bad student. Stubborn as hell, sure, but never bad. You just needed to learn to trust yourself more."

Mia's smile faltered, a flicker of something shadowing her gaze. She turned away, pretending to inspect a nearby bush. "Yeah, well... that's always been my problem, hasn't it?"

Ryan stepped closer, lowering his voice. "You know, your father used to say the same thing about himself. He didn't always have it figured out, either. But you—Mia, you've got more than what it takes. You just have to believe that."

She looked up at him, a hint of skepticism in her eyes. "Is that supposed to be some kind of pep talk, Ryan?"

"Take it however you want," he said lightly, but his gaze held hers, unflinching. "Look, I know what it's like to live under a shadow. My old man was a legend in the military, one of the best. And every day, I felt like I had to prove that I could measure up. That I wasn't just some kid riding on his coattails."

Mia frowned, tilting her head. "I didn't know that. You never talked much about your dad."

"There's not much to say," Ryan shrugged, but there was a tightness in his jaw, a hint of old pain. "He had a way of making me feel like I'd never be good enough. And that's why I left the military. I couldn't keep trying to live up to his expectations."

Mia's expression softened. "And now?"

"Now, I try to live up to my own expectations," Ryan said quietly. "It's not easy. But it's better than trying to be something I'm not. And Mia... you don't have to be your father to be successful. You just have to be you."

She stared at him, the weight of his words sinking in slowly. "I don't know who I am without him, Ryan. I've been chasing his shadow for so long... I don't know where he ends and I begin."

Ryan reached out, his hand gentle on her shoulder. "Then stop chasing. Start walking your own path. You'll find it."

Mia nodded slowly, her gaze dropping to the ground. "I'll try. But... thank you. For this. For everything."

"Anytime," he murmured, stepping back. "Now, let's see if Kato can out-camouflage us both."

Kato's eager grin returned, and the tension melted away as they fell back into the rhythm of the jungle. But Mia's thoughts lingered on Ryan's words, a quiet resolve forming deep within her.

Maybe it was time to stop living in the past and start creating her own future.

The jungle was quieter now, the oppressive weight of the midday heat dampening even the sounds of the wildlife. Mia and her team gathered around a makeshift table fashioned from a fallen log, maps and notepads spread out before them. The tension was palpable as they huddled in the small clearing, each of them acutely aware of the magnitude of what lay ahead.

Mia drew a deep breath, glancing at each of her team members in turn—Ryan's steady, expectant gaze, Amina's calm yet alert expression, and Kato's eager but wary eyes. This was the moment. It was up to her to pull them together, to make them trust not just her judgment, but each other's as well.

"Alright," Mia began, her voice low but firm. She gestured to the map of the region, where red pins marked the locations of the poachers' traps they'd discovered earlier. "We've documented a pattern here. Most of the traps are concentrated in this area—" she pointed to a cluster of red pins "—which means their main camp is likely somewhere nearby. But if we go in too fast, we risk alerting them and losing the chance to take them down properly."

"Which is why we need to approach this strategically," Amina interjected, her fingers lightly tracing the route on the map. "They know this terrain better than we do. They've had time to set up surveillance points. We need to find those, eliminate them, and then move in on the main camp."

Mia nodded thoughtfully. "Agreed. But I also don't want to waste too much time on recon. The longer we wait, the more animals they'll trap—or worse, kill. We need to strike a balance between gathering intel and taking action."

Ryan cleared his throat, drawing Mia's attention. "If we split up, we can cover more ground faster. Amina and Kato should scout the lower paths along the riverbanks. The poachers might be using them as supply routes. Meanwhile, you and I can take the higher ground. We'll get a better vantage point, see if there are any lookouts or patrols."

Kato's eyes widened slightly, glancing between Mia and Ryan. "Split up? Are you sure that's safe?"

"It's a risk," Mia admitted, meeting Kato's gaze steadily. "But it's a calculated one. We've been careful so far, and we'll stay that way. Besides, if we're going to make a real impact here, we can't afford to be timid. This is what we came here to do."

Ryan leaned forward, his eyes never leaving Mia's. "The key is communication. We stay in constant contact. If anyone sees something, you don't engage—you pull back and radio in. We regroup and hit them when we're ready. Understood?"

Kato nodded slowly, a determined look settling on his face. "Got it. I won't let you down."

Mia offered him a small smile, then turned back to Amina. "You okay with this plan?"

Amina raised an eyebrow, a hint of a smile playing on her lips. "You're actually asking for my opinion?"

Mia's smile widened slightly. "Yeah, well, I'm learning."

"Good," Amina murmured, her tone softening. "Because I think it's a solid plan. We'll move quietly along the riverbanks, see if we can pinpoint any movement. If we find a supply route, it could lead us straight to their main camp."

Mia nodded, relief and a sense of accomplishment washing over her. This felt right—like they were finally acting as a cohesive unit. "Okay, then it's settled. Amina, you and Kato head out in twenty minutes. Ryan and I will take the ridge and set up a vantage point. We'll stay in touch every fifteen minutes, and if anything goes wrong—"

"We retreat and regroup," Amina finished, her gaze serious. "Don't worry, Mia. We've got your back."

Ryan's gaze shifted from Amina to Mia, his voice low but clear. "You're doing good, Mia. This—" he gestured to the map and the team surrounding it "—this is what leadership looks like. You're trusting us, and we're trusting you."

Mia felt something loosen inside her, a knot of anxiety and self-doubt that had been tightening since the moment she'd stepped into this jungle. She nodded, meeting Ryan's eyes with a steadiness she hadn't felt in days. "Thank you, Ryan. That means a lot."

He nodded back, a faint smile softening his normally stern features. "We're all here for the same reason. We want to stop them. But it's more than that, isn't it? It's about proving something—to ourselves, to the world. And the only way we do that is by working together."

"Together," Mia echoed softly, her gaze drifting back to the map. "I guess it's taken me a while to realize that."

Ryan reached out, placing a hand on her shoulder. "You're realizing it now, and that's what matters. You've got what it takes to see this through, Mia. Just remember, you don't have to carry it all alone."

Mia swallowed hard, a rush of gratitude and something deeper welling up inside her. "I know. And I won't."

"Good." Ryan's voice was firm, but there was a warmth there too. He straightened, turning to Kato and Amina. "Alright, team, you know what to do. Let's get out there and show these poachers what happens when you mess with the wrong people."

Amina and Kato nodded, the resolve in their eyes mirroring the intensity in Mia's own gaze. They moved to gather their gear, their movements brisk and efficient. Mia lingered for a moment, watching them with a sense of pride and purpose.

As Amina and Kato disappeared into the thick foliage, Mia turned to Ryan, who was already adjusting his pack and checking his radio.

"You really think this will work?" she asked, her voice quieter now that it was just the two of them.

Ryan paused, glancing back at her. "I do. Because it's not just about the plan—it's about the people. And I believe in them. I believe in you."

Mia's heart tightened, a strange mix of hope and fear twisting inside her. She gave a short nod, her lips curving into a determined smile. "Then let's go show them what we're made of."

With a final glance at the map, she shouldered her pack and followed Ryan into the jungle, their footsteps merging into the rhythm of the wild. The sense of unity, of trust, buoyed her spirits, pushing back the shadows of doubt.

Whatever lay ahead, they would face it together. As a team

Chapter 6:
First Signs of Danger

The village was a small oasis of civilization amidst the dense jungle. Thatched-roof huts surrounded a central clearing where children played and elders gathered. Mia, Ryan, and the team approached with a sense of purpose, their packs heavy with supplies and equipment.

Mia led the way, her eyes scanning the village. She was looking for one person in particular—Kato's father, a respected local guide named Temba. As they walked, villagers paused their activities to watch the newcomers, curiosity and caution in their eyes.

Kato, walking beside Mia, pointed towards a group of men near the largest hut. "There he is, Ms. Mia. That's my father."

Temba stood out among the men, his tall frame and authoritative presence unmistakable. He spotted Kato and broke into a wide smile, striding forward to meet them.

"Kato! You've returned safely," Temba said, embracing his son warmly. "And you've brought friends."

"Father, this is Ms. Mia and Mr. Ryan. They're leading the mission to stop the poachers," Kato introduced proudly.

Temba extended his hand to Mia, his grip firm. "Welcome to our village. I've heard much about your work. We are grateful for your efforts."

"Thank you, Temba. We're honored to be here," Mia replied. "We've brought supplies and equipment to share with your community, and we're hoping to learn from each other."

Temba nodded. "Come, let's talk. There's much to discuss."

He led them to the central hut, where a small group of elders were seated. The atmosphere was respectful as Temba introduced Mia and Ryan, explaining their mission and the purpose of their visit.

Mia addressed the elders, her tone respectful. "We're here to protect the jungle and its wildlife from poachers. But we can't do it alone. We need your knowledge and support."

An elder named Nia, her eyes sharp with wisdom, spoke first. "Our people have lived in harmony with the jungle for generations. We know its ways and its secrets. What can we do to help?"

Ryan stepped forward, spreading out a map on the table. "We've identified areas with high poacher activity. With your help, we can monitor these areas and set up patrols."

Temba studied the map, nodding slowly. "We know these places. They are sacred to us. We will help you protect them."

The elders discussed the details, their voices a mix of concern and determination. It was clear that they shared Mia and Ryan's commitment to preserving the jungle. After a lengthy discussion, a plan was formed.

"We will set up patrols and use your equipment to monitor the poachers," Temba said. "But we must also educate our people about the dangers and how to protect themselves."

Mia agreed. "Education is key. We've brought materials and training guides that we can share with your community."

As the meeting concluded, Mia and Ryan distributed the supplies they had brought—medical kits, radios, and educational materials. The villagers accepted them gratefully, their faces lighting up with hope.

Outside the hut, Mia and Ryan walked with Temba and Kato, discussing the next steps. "We'll start training tomorrow," Mia said. "We need to ensure everyone knows how to use the equipment and what to do in case of an encounter with poachers."

Temba nodded. "Our people will be ready. We have a strong community, and we will stand together."

Kato looked up at his father, pride evident in his eyes. "I want to help too, Father."

"You already are, Kato," Temba replied, placing a hand on his son's shoulder. "You've shown courage and dedication. We're proud of you."

Ryan smiled at the exchange. "We're all in this together. And with your help, we can make a real difference."

The rest of the day was spent integrating with the community. Mia and Ryan, along with Amina and the other team members, shared meals with the villagers and participated in their daily activities. They learned about the local customs and traditions, deepening their understanding of the people they were working with.

As evening fell, a sense of camaraderie and unity settled over the village. The team gathered around a fire with the villagers, sharing stories and building bonds that would strengthen their efforts.

Mia looked around, feeling a deep sense of gratitude and determination. "We're not just here to protect the jungle," she said to Ryan. "We're here to support this community and work alongside them. Together, we can achieve so much more."

Ryan nodded, his eyes reflecting the firelight. "We're building something important here. And it's just the beginning."

As the fire crackled and the sounds of the jungle filled the night, Mia felt a renewed sense of purpose. They were not alone in their mission. With the support of the community, they were stronger and more determined than ever to protect the jungle and its inhabitants. The next phase of their journey was about to begin, and they were ready to face it together.

The next morning, the village was alive with activity. Mia, Ryan, and the team had a full day ahead of them. They were going to gather additional supplies from the nearby town, a half-day's hike from the village. Temba had arranged for a few of the villagers to accompany them as guides.

Mia was packing her backpack when Ryan approached her. "Ready for another trek?" he asked, adjusting his gear.

"Always," Mia replied with a smile. "We need to make sure we get everything on our list. We can't afford to miss anything."

Ryan nodded. "I've double-checked the list. We need medical supplies, food provisions, and some additional equipment for the patrols."

Kato, ever eager, bounded over. "Ms. Mia, can I come with you to town?"

Mia smiled at his enthusiasm but shook her head. "Not this time, Kato. We need you here to help with the training. Plus, it's a long hike, and we need to move quickly."

Kato's face fell, but he nodded in understanding. "Okay, Ms. Mia. I'll help with the training."

Temba approached, ready to lead the way. "The path to town is well-traveled but still challenging. Stay close, and we'll make good time."

Mia and Ryan, along with a few team members and villagers, set off down the narrow trail leading to the town. The jungle was dense, the path winding through thick foliage and over uneven terrain. The morning sun filtered through the canopy, casting dappled light on the forest floor.

As they walked, Temba shared stories about the region, pointing out various plants and animals. "This tree," he said, touching the bark of a massive trunk, "has been here for generations. It's a sacred tree to our people."

Mia listened intently, absorbing the knowledge. "It's incredible how much history is here. Every part of this jungle has a story."

Ryan, walking beside Temba, asked, "How often do you make this trip to town?"

Temba smiled. "Often enough. We trade with the townspeople regularly. They know us well."

After a few hours of steady hiking, the dense jungle began to thin, giving way to more open terrain. The sounds of the forest were gradually replaced by the distant murmur of human activity. Soon, they could see the outskirts of the town—a cluster of buildings surrounded by small farms and gardens.

The town was bustling with activity as they entered. Market stalls lined the main street, vendors calling out their wares. The scent of fresh produce, spices, and cooked food filled the air.

"We'll split up to cover more ground," Mia said, handing out portions of the supply list. "Temba, can you help us find the best places to get these items?"

Temba nodded. "Follow me. I know just where to go."

Mia and Ryan followed Temba to a large market stall selling medical supplies. They greeted the vendor, a middle-aged woman with a warm smile.

"Welcome," she said. "What can I help you with today?"

Mia handed her the list. "We need these medical supplies. Do you have everything?"

The vendor looked over the list and nodded. "Yes, I have most of these items. Give me a moment to gather them."

While the vendor collected the supplies, Mia and Ryan looked around the market. The variety of goods was impressive—everything from fresh fruits and vegetables to handmade crafts and tools.

Ryan turned to Mia. "This town has a lot to offer. We should be able to get everything we need."

"Agreed," Mia replied. "Once we have the medical supplies, let's get the food provisions next."

The vendor returned with a box filled with medical supplies. "Here you go. Is there anything else you need?"

"This is perfect," Mia said, paying the vendor. "Thank you."

With the medical supplies secured, they moved on to the food market. Temba led them to a stall brimming with fresh produce and grains. The vendor, an elderly man with a friendly demeanor, greeted them warmly.

"We need enough provisions to last our team and the villagers for the next few weeks," Ryan explained, handing over the list.

The vendor nodded. "I can provide everything you need. Let me start packing it up for you."

As the vendor packed their provisions, Mia looked around, taking in the vibrant energy of the market. It was clear that this town was a lifeline for the surrounding villages, providing essential goods and a place for the community to come together.

With their supplies gathered, they reconvened with the rest of the team. Everyone had successfully found what they needed. Mia felt a sense of accomplishment. "Great work, everyone. Let's get these supplies back to the village."

The journey back was slower, the added weight of the supplies making the trek more challenging. But the team was in high spirits, buoyed by their successful mission.

As they approached the village, they were greeted by the villagers, who helped carry the supplies the rest of the way. Kato ran up to Mia, his eyes shining with excitement. "Ms. Mia, did you get everything?"

"We did, Kato," Mia replied, ruffling his hair. "Now we can focus on the next part of our mission."

Temba clapped a hand on Mia's shoulder. "You've done well. These supplies will make a big difference."

Mia looked around at the villagers, feeling a deep sense of connection and purpose. "We're in this together. Let's get to work."

As the sun set, the village buzzed with activity, everyone pitching in to organize the supplies and prepare for the days ahead. Mia knew that with the support of this community, they were well-equipped to face whatever challenges lay ahead.

The next morning, the village was abuzz with anticipation. Mia, Ryan, and the team had organized a training session to teach the villagers how to use the equipment and supplies they had brought. The central clearing was transformed into a makeshift training ground, with tables set up for different stations.

Mia stood in the center, addressing the gathered villagers. "Thank you all for coming. Today, we're going to go over how to use the equipment and supplies we brought. This will help us work together to protect the jungle and keep everyone safe."

Ryan stepped forward, holding up a walkie-talkie. "Let's start with communication. These walkie-talkies will help us stay in touch over long distances. Temba, would you like to try?"

Temba nodded and stepped up, taking the walkie-talkie from Ryan. "How does it work?"

Ryan demonstrated, showing him how to turn it on and switch channels. "Just press this button to talk. Let's do a quick test."

Temba pressed the button and spoke into the device. "Testing, testing. Can you hear me?"

The walkie-talkie crackled, and Amina's voice came through from across the clearing. "Loud and clear, Temba."

Temba grinned, clearly pleased. "This will be very useful."

Mia moved to the next station, where Amina was showing a group of villagers how to use the medical kits. "These kits have everything you need for basic first aid. Bandages, antiseptics, pain relievers. Let's go over how to use them."

Amina picked up a bandage and demonstrated how to properly wrap a wound. One of the villagers, an elderly woman named Nia, watched closely. "This is very important. We often have injuries from working in the fields."

Mia nodded. "Exactly. Knowing how to treat wounds quickly can prevent infections and save lives."

Kato was at another station, learning how to use the cameras and motion sensors. Mia joined him, showing him the basics. "These cameras will help us monitor the jungle for poacher activity. Once set up, they'll capture any movement and send the images to our base."

Kato's eyes lit up with excitement. "I can help set them up! Show me how."

Mia handed him a camera and walked him through the setup process. "It's simple. Just place it at the right height, secure it to a tree, and make sure it's pointing in the right direction."

Ryan approached them, carrying a small generator. "We also have portable generators to power the equipment. Let's go over how to use them."

As the training continued, the villagers grew more confident, their enthusiasm palpable. Mia and Ryan moved from station to station, answering questions and providing guidance. The sense of collaboration and mutual respect was strong.

After a few hours, Mia gathered everyone together for a final review. "You've all done an amazing job today. Remember, this equipment is here to help us protect the jungle and keep our community safe. If you have any questions, don't hesitate to ask."

Temba stepped forward, addressing the group. "We are grateful for your help and guidance. Together, we will protect our home and our way of life."

Nia added, "This knowledge will make a big difference. Thank you, Mia and Ryan."

Mia smiled, feeling a deep sense of satisfaction. "We're all in this together. Let's keep working as a team."

As the villagers dispersed, Mia and Ryan stood back, watching the scene. "That went well," Ryan said, a note of pride in his voice.

"It did," Mia agreed. "They're eager to learn and ready to help. We're building something important here."

Ryan looked at her, his expression serious. "We couldn't do this without you, Mia. Your leadership is inspiring."

Mia felt a warmth spread through her. "Thank you, Ryan. But it's not just me. It's all of us, working together."

Later that afternoon, Mia and Ryan sat with Temba and a few other village leaders to discuss the next steps. "We need to set up patrols and start monitoring the key areas immediately," Mia said, pointing to the map.

Temba nodded. "We can organize groups to cover these areas. With the equipment you've provided, we'll be more effective."

Ryan added, "And we'll be here to support you. We'll join the patrols and help with the monitoring."

Nia spoke up, "Our people are ready. We understand the importance of this work. The jungle is our home, and we will protect it."

Mia looked around at the determined faces. "We're stronger together. Let's get started."

The next few days were a flurry of activity as the team and villagers set up patrols, installed cameras, and began monitoring the jungle. The sense of unity and purpose was tangible, everyone working towards the common goal of protecting their home.

One evening, as the sun set and the jungle settled into its nocturnal rhythm, Mia stood at the edge of the village, looking out over the darkening trees. Ryan joined her, silent for a moment before speaking. "We've done good work here, Mia."

"We have," she replied, feeling the weight of their accomplishments and the challenges still ahead. "And we'll keep going. For the jungle, and for the people who call it home."

Ryan nodded, his gaze steady. "Together."

As the stars began to twinkle above, Mia felt a deep sense of hope. They had made significant progress, and with the continued collaboration of the villagers, they would make even more. The journey was far from over, but with their united efforts, they were on the right path to protect the jungle and its inhabitants.

As dusk fell over the village, the team and the villagers gathered in the central hut for a crucial meeting. The day had been productive, with the successful training sessions bolstering everyone's confidence. Now, it was time to plan their next move.

Mia stood at the head of the room, a large map of the jungle spread out on the table before her. Ryan, Amina, Temba, and several village leaders flanked her, their faces reflecting the seriousness of the discussion.

"Thank you all for coming," Mia began, her voice clear and steady. "We've made great progress today, but our work is far from over. We need to strategize our next steps to effectively protect the jungle and our community."

Temba nodded, his expression thoughtful. "The training went well. Our people are ready to assist with patrols and monitoring. We've already identified key areas that need immediate attention."

Ryan pointed to several marked spots on the map. "These are the hotspots where we've seen the most poacher activity. We need to set up surveillance and increase patrols in these areas."

A village elder, Nia, leaned forward, her eyes sharp. "We also need to think about communication. How will we coordinate between the patrols and the village?"

Amina spoke up, holding a walkie-talkie. "We'll use these. We've distributed them among the patrol leaders and key members of the village. They're reliable and will keep us connected."

Kato, eager to contribute, raised his hand. "Ms. Mia, can I join the patrols too? I want to help protect our home."

Mia smiled at his enthusiasm. "You've done great work, Kato. We'll need everyone's help, including yours. Just remember to stay safe and always follow the instructions of the patrol leaders."

Ryan looked around the room, his gaze steady. "We also need to consider our resources. We have a limited supply of equipment and medical kits. We need to use them wisely and ensure we're prepared for any emergencies."

Temba added, "We've already started stockpiling food and water. If the poachers become more aggressive, we might need to defend our village."

Mia nodded. "That's a good point. We need to be prepared for any situation. Let's talk about setting up a response team in the village that can act quickly if needed."

The discussion continued, with ideas and strategies flowing freely. The atmosphere was one of determination and unity. Mia felt a deep sense of gratitude for the support and commitment of the villagers and her team.

As the meeting wrapped up, Mia addressed the group once more. "We have a solid plan, but we need to stay vigilant and flexible. Things can change quickly in the jungle. Let's stay connected and support each other."

Ryan nodded in agreement. "We're stronger together. If we stick to the plan and stay united, we can protect the jungle and our community."

Temba stood, his presence commanding attention. "We will do whatever it takes. This is our home, and we will defend it."

The meeting concluded, and the villagers and team members began to disperse, each with a renewed sense of purpose. Mia and Ryan remained behind, discussing a few final details.

Ryan looked at Mia, his expression serious. "You're doing an incredible job, Mia. The villagers trust you, and you've given them hope."

Mia felt a surge of emotion. "Thanks, Ryan. I couldn't do it without you and the rest of the team. We're in this together."

Ryan nodded. "Absolutely. We've got each other's backs."

As they stepped out into the cool night air, Mia took a moment to breathe deeply, the sounds of the jungle a comforting presence around her. She felt a hand on her shoulder and turned to see Temba standing beside her.

"You're a strong leader, Mia. My people trust you, and so do I," Temba said, his voice filled with respect.

"Thank you, Temba. That means a lot to me," Mia replied, her voice sincere.

Temba nodded, looking out at the village. "We have a long road ahead, but I believe we can make a difference. Together, we will protect our home."

Mia looked around at the village, the people she had come to care for deeply. "Yes, together we will."

As the night deepened, Mia, Ryan, and Temba stood in silence for a moment, each lost in their thoughts. The challenges ahead were daunting, but the unity and strength of their community gave them hope.

"We should get some rest," Ryan said finally. "Tomorrow is another big day."

Mia nodded, feeling a sense of peace and determination. "Goodnight, Temba. Goodnight, Ryan. Let's be ready for whatever comes next."

"Goodnight, Mia," Temba replied, his voice calm and steady. "We'll be ready."

As Mia walked back to her tent, she felt a renewed sense of purpose. The bonds they were forming and the plans they were making were crucial steps toward protecting the jungle and its inhabitants. The journey was far from over, but with the support and collaboration of her team and the villagers, Mia knew they were on the right path. Together, they would face the challenges ahead and work towards a safer, more secure future for their home.

Chapter 7
Bonds Forged in Adversity

The village was quiet as dawn broke, the sky painted with the soft hues of sunrise. Mia, Ryan, and Temba stood around the central table in the main hut, a detailed map of the jungle spread out before them. The mood was tense but focused. They had gathered all the intelligence they needed and were now planning their next move: infiltrating the poachers' camp.

Mia pointed to a spot on the map marked with red ink. "This is where we believe their main camp is located. It's heavily guarded and well-hidden. We need to be extremely careful."

Ryan nodded, his expression serious. "From our observations, their security measures include patrols, traps, and possibly surveillance cameras. We'll need to disable those if we want to get in and out undetected."

Temba studied the map, his brow furrowed. "We know the terrain well. There are a few hidden paths that could get us close without being seen. But once we're inside, we'll need to move quickly."

Amina, who had been listening intently, spoke up. "What's the primary objective? Are we gathering evidence, disrupting their operations, or both?"

Mia looked at her, her eyes steely with determination. "Both. We need solid evidence to take to the authorities, but if we can disrupt their activities and set them back, that's even better."

Ryan tapped a spot on the map. "We'll split into two teams. Team A, led by me, will handle the surveillance equipment and traps. Team B, led by Mia, will gather evidence and document everything we find."

Temba nodded. "I'll go with Team B. My knowledge of the area will help us navigate quickly and quietly."

Kato, standing at the edge of the group, piped up. "Ms. Mia, can I come too? I want to help."

Mia looked at Kato, her expression softening. "Kato, I appreciate your eagerness, but this mission is very dangerous. We need you here to help coordinate from the village."

Kato's face fell, but he nodded. "Okay, Ms. Mia. I'll do my best here."

Ryan placed a reassuring hand on Kato's shoulder. "You're an important part of this team, Kato. We're counting on you to keep things running smoothly here."

Mia turned back to the map, her mind racing with the details of their plan. "We move at dusk. That'll give us the cover of darkness. Everyone needs to be ready and alert."

The group dispersed, each member preparing for the mission ahead. Mia and Ryan went over the equipment one last time, ensuring they had everything they needed. The air was thick with anticipation.

As the sun began to set, casting long shadows across the village, Mia gathered the team for a final briefing. "Remember, our primary goal is to gather evidence and disrupt their operations. Stay focused, stay together, and stay safe."

Ryan added, "If anything goes wrong, we regroup here. Don't take unnecessary risks. We'll have other opportunities if this one doesn't work out."

Temba adjusted his gear, his face set with determination. "We're ready. Let's do this."

The team set out, moving silently through the jungle. The path was treacherous, but Temba's guidance was invaluable. As they approached the poachers' camp, they slowed their pace, every sound and movement scrutinized.

Ryan raised his hand, signaling for the team to stop. He pointed to a small clearing where a surveillance camera was partially hidden among the trees. "There. We need to disable that without raising any alarms."

Mia nodded, moving closer to Ryan. "How do we do it?"

Ryan pulled out a small device from his backpack. "This jammer should do the trick. It'll disable the camera without alerting anyone. Cover me while I set it up."

Mia and Temba took up positions, keeping a lookout while Ryan worked quickly and efficiently. Within moments, the camera was disabled, and they continued their approach.

They reached the edge of the camp, hidden by the dense foliage. Mia peered through the leaves, her heart pounding. The camp was bustling with activity—men armed with rifles patrolled the perimeter, while others worked on processing illegally obtained animal parts.

"We need to split up here," Mia whispered. "Ryan, take your team and handle the traps and other surveillance equipment. Temba and I will gather the evidence."

Ryan nodded. "Be careful. We'll meet back here in one hour."

Mia, Temba, and Amina moved stealthily into the camp, their movements synchronized and silent. Mia's eyes scanned the area, noting the locations of various pieces of evidence. She pulled out her camera, snapping photos of documents, illegal animal parts, and the poachers' equipment.

Temba whispered, "Over here, Mia. There's a ledger. It looks like it contains records of their activities."

Mia hurried over, taking detailed photos of the ledger's pages. "This is exactly what we need. Great find, Temba."

Just as they finished documenting the evidence, a noise behind them made Mia freeze. One of the poachers was approaching, his flashlight sweeping the area. Mia signaled for Temba and Amina to hide, and they ducked behind a stack of crates.

The poacher stopped just a few feet away, his flashlight lingering on the ground. Mia held her breath, her heart racing.

After what felt like an eternity, he moved on, disappearing into the darkness.

Mia exhaled slowly, signaling for Temba and Amina to follow her. They retraced their steps, moving quickly but cautiously back to the rendezvous point. Ryan and his team were already there, waiting.

"Did you get everything?" Ryan asked, his voice low but urgent.

Mia nodded. "We got it. Let's move."

The team retreated through the jungle, the adrenaline still coursing through their veins. As they approached the village, a sense of relief washed over them. They had successfully infiltrated the camp and gathered the evidence they needed.

Back at the village, they gathered in the central hut to review their findings. Mia spread out the photos and documents on the table, her voice filled with determination. "This is it. This is the evidence we need to take to the authorities. We're one step closer to shutting down the poachers for good."

Ryan looked around at the team, his expression one of pride. "We did it together. This is just the beginning. With this evidence, we can make a real difference."

Temba nodded, his eyes shining with hope. "Our fight is far from over, but tonight, we've taken a crucial step forward."

Mia felt a surge of pride and gratitude for her team and the villagers. They had faced incredible risks, but their courage and determination had paid off. Together, they would continue to protect the jungle and its inhabitants, no matter the challenges ahead.

Back in the safety of the village, the team gathered in the central hut to review the evidence they had collected from the poachers' camp. The room was filled with a sense of urgency and anticipation. Mia spread out the photos, documents, and other items on the large wooden table, each piece a crucial part of their mission.

Ryan stood beside her, organizing the evidence. "This is solid proof of their activities," he said, holding up a photo of the ledger they had found. "It details their operations, including the names of buyers and locations of their other camps."

Temba leaned in, studying the documents closely. "This information is invaluable. It's enough to take to the authorities and demand action."

Amina pointed to a map they had found, marked with various locations. "These are their supply routes. If we can intercept these, we can cut off their resources and cripple their operations."

Mia nodded, her mind racing with the possibilities. "We need to act quickly. The longer we wait, the more time they have to relocate and cover their tracks."

Ryan agreed. "We should contact the authorities immediately. This evidence is more than enough to get their attention."

Kato, who had been listening intently, spoke up. "Ms. Mia, can we use the radios to call for help?"

Mia smiled at his eagerness. "Yes, Kato. That's exactly what we're going to do. We'll use the radios to contact the nearest ranger station and send someone to deliver this evidence in person."

Temba added, "I can lead a group to the ranger station. It's a few hours' journey, but we can get there and back by nightfall."

Ryan looked around at the team, his expression determined. "Let's split up. Temba, you take a few villagers and the evidence to the rangers. Mia, Amina, and I will stay here and continue to monitor the situation."

Everyone nodded in agreement, the plan taking shape quickly. Temba gathered a small group of trusted villagers, and Mia handed him the evidence, carefully packed in a waterproof bag.

"Be careful," Mia said, her voice steady. "This evidence is crucial. We're counting on you."

Temba gave her a reassuring smile. "We'll get it there safely. Stay vigilant."

As Temba and his group set off, Mia, Ryan, and Amina turned their attention to the surveillance equipment. They needed to keep a close watch on the jungle for any signs of the poachers' movements.

Mia adjusted the settings on one of the motion-activated cameras. "We'll place these around the perimeter of the village and along the main paths. If they try to come this way, we'll know."

Ryan checked the batteries on the portable radios. "We'll need to maintain constant communication. If anything happens, we need to be ready to act."

Amina set up the remaining cameras, her movements quick and efficient. "We'll also need to set up a few traps and alarms. It's better to be overprepared."

As they worked, the tension in the air was palpable. They knew that the poachers could retaliate at any moment, but they also knew that they were ready. The villagers were alert and prepared, their training and determination evident in their actions.

By midday, the surveillance system was in place, and the team gathered in the central hut to review their setup. Mia looked around at the faces of her team and the villagers, feeling a surge of pride and solidarity.

"We've done everything we can to prepare," she said, her voice firm. "Now we wait for Temba and the others to return. In the meantime, stay alert and stay safe."

Ryan added, "Remember, we're in this together. We've faced challenges before, and we've come through stronger. This is no different."

The hours passed slowly as they waited for Temba's return. Mia and Ryan took turns monitoring the cameras and radios, their eyes constantly scanning the screens for any signs of movement. The jungle was eerily quiet, the usual sounds of wildlife replaced by a tense silence.

As evening approached, a crackle came over the radio. Mia grabbed the receiver, her heart pounding. "Temba, is that you?"

Temba's voice came through, clear but urgent. "We're on our way back. The rangers are mobilizing a team. They'll be here by nightfall."

Mia felt a wave of relief wash over her. "Good work, Temba. We'll be ready."

Ryan looked at her, his expression one of determination and resolve. "This is it, Mia. We've done our part. Now we wait and hope the authorities act quickly."

Mia nodded, her gaze fixed on the horizon. "We've come this far. We won't let the poachers win."

As night fell over the village, the team and the villagers prepared for whatever lay ahead. They had taken a crucial step in their mission, and now it was up to the authorities to act. With their unity and determination, they were ready to face whatever challenges came their way.

Night had fallen over the village, casting it in a shroud of darkness punctuated by the soft glow of lanterns. Mia, Ryan, and the villagers waited with a mixture of anticipation and tension. The evidence had been delivered, and now they awaited the arrival of the authorities.

Mia stood by the central hut, her eyes scanning the edge of the jungle. Ryan joined her, his presence a steadying force. "They should be here soon," he said, checking his watch.

Mia nodded, her thoughts racing. "I just hope they understand the urgency. We've done everything we can, but without their help, we can't stop the poachers."

As if on cue, the sound of engines broke through the silence. The villagers gathered, their faces illuminated by the approaching headlights. A convoy of vehicles emerged from the darkness, coming to a stop in the clearing. Armed rangers and officials stepped out, their expressions serious and determined.

Temba, leading the group, approached Mia and Ryan. "The rangers are here. They've reviewed the evidence and are ready to take action."

The lead ranger, a stern-faced man named Captain Mbani, stepped forward. "Ms. Mia, Mr. Ryan, we've received your evidence. It's compelling and thorough. We're here to help."

Mia felt a surge of relief. "Thank you, Captain Mbani. The poachers are a well-organized group. We need to move quickly to catch them off guard."

Captain Mbani nodded. "We've planned a coordinated raid on their main camp. Our teams will move in from different directions to encircle them. We'll need your help to guide us through the jungle."

Ryan stepped forward. "We've mapped out the area and can lead you to the key locations. Timing is crucial. If we move now, we can catch them by surprise."

Captain Mbani turned to his team, issuing orders with practiced efficiency. "Teams Alpha and Bravo, prepare to move out. Ms. Mia and Mr. Ryan will lead us to the targets. Everyone else, secure the perimeter and prepare for possible retaliation."

As the rangers mobilized, Mia and Ryan gathered their team. "This is it," Mia said, her voice steady. "Stay close, stay alert, and follow the plan. We're going to shut them down for good."

The convoy moved out, Mia and Ryan leading the way through the dense jungle. The path was narrow and treacherous, but their determination kept them focused. The rangers moved silently, their training evident in their careful steps and watchful eyes.

After an hour of steady trekking, they reached the edge of the poachers' camp. The rangers spread out, taking up strategic positions around the perimeter. Mia pointed to a cluster of tents and makeshift structures. "That's where they store the illegal goods. We need to secure that area first."

Captain Mbani nodded, signaling his team. "Alpha Team, move in on my command. Bravo Team, secure the perimeter and watch for any escape attempts."

Ryan, crouched beside Mia, whispered, "This is it. Are you ready?"

Mia's heart pounded in her chest, but her resolve was unshaken. "Yes. Let's do this."

Captain Mbani raised his hand, and the rangers moved in with precision. Shouts and gunfire erupted as the poachers, caught off guard, tried to defend their camp. Mia and Ryan stayed close, guiding the rangers and providing crucial information about the layout of the camp.

Mia spotted a group of poachers attempting to flee through a hidden path. "Over there!" she shouted, pointing them out.

Ryan relayed the information to Captain Mbani, who quickly dispatched a team to intercept them. Within minutes, the poachers were surrounded and forced to surrender.

The rangers moved swiftly, securing the camp and rounding up the remaining poachers. The air was thick with the smell of gunpowder and the sounds of chaos slowly subsiding. Mia and Ryan watched as the rangers confiscated the illegal goods and dismantled the poachers' operations.

Captain Mbani approached them, his expression one of satisfaction. "We've got them. Thanks to your help, we were able to take down their entire operation."

Mia felt a wave of relief and pride. "Thank you, Captain. We couldn't have done it without your support."

Ryan nodded in agreement. "This is a significant victory. We've made a real difference here."

As the rangers continued their work, Temba and the villagers arrived, their faces filled with gratitude and admiration. "You've done it," Temba said, his voice choked with emotion. "You've saved our home."

Mia looked around at the gathered villagers and rangers, feeling a deep sense of unity and accomplishment. "We did this together. This is just the beginning. We'll keep fighting to protect the jungle and its inhabitants."

Captain Mbani nodded. "You have our support. We'll continue to work together to ensure the safety and preservation of this area."

As the dawn began to break, casting a soft light over the jungle, Mia felt a renewed sense of hope. They had faced incredible challenges and come through victorious. With the continued collaboration of the rangers, the villagers, and her dedicated team, they were ready to protect and preserve the jungle for generations to come.

Ryan placed a hand on Mia's shoulder, his voice filled with pride. "We did it, Mia. We really did it."

Mia smiled, her eyes reflecting the dawn's light. "Yes, we did. And we'll keep doing it. Together."

The adrenaline from the raid on the poachers' camp was still coursing through Mia's veins as the rangers finished securing the area. The camp, which had once been a hub of illegal activity, now lay in disarray, with captured poachers being led away in handcuffs. The sun was beginning to rise, casting a golden hue over the jungle and symbolizing a new dawn for the protected land.

Mia, Ryan, and Captain Mbani stood together, surveying the aftermath. "We did it," Mia said, her voice filled with a mix of relief and triumph.

Captain Mbani nodded, his expression serious but satisfied. "This is a significant blow to their operations. We'll need to remain vigilant, but this is a major victory."

Ryan looked around, taking in the scene. "We've shut down their main camp and captured their leaders. It's a huge step forward."

Temba approached, his face beaming with pride. "The villagers will be relieved to hear this. You've given us hope."

Mia turned to him, her eyes reflecting the weight of their shared struggle. "We couldn't have done it without your help, Temba. Your knowledge and bravery were crucial."

Temba nodded, his gaze steady. "We all played our part. Now, we must ensure this victory is lasting."

As the rangers began cataloging the evidence and preparing the site for a thorough investigation, Mia gathered her team and the key villagers for a debrief. "Everyone, gather around," she called out, her voice carrying over the sounds of the camp.

The group assembled, their faces showing signs of exhaustion but also a palpable sense of achievement. Mia took a deep breath, feeling the weight of the moment. "We've accomplished something incredible today. The poachers' camp is shut down, and their leaders are in custody. This is a victory for all of us."

Ryan stepped forward, his voice clear and strong. "This was a team effort. Everyone played a crucial role, from gathering evidence to executing the raid. We've shown that when we work together, we can achieve great things."

Kato, standing beside Temba, raised his hand hesitantly. "Ms. Mia, what happens next? How do we make sure they don't come back?"

Mia smiled at the young boy's determination. "We'll continue to work closely with Captain Mbani and the rangers. We'll set up regular patrols and maintain our surveillance to ensure the area stays secure. And we'll keep educating and training everyone in the village to be vigilant."

Captain Mbani added, "We'll also push for stronger legal measures to protect this region. The evidence we've gathered will support our case for increased enforcement and harsher penalties for poaching."

Amina, who had been quietly listening, stepped forward. "We should also think about the future. How can we use this momentum to continue protecting the jungle and its inhabitants?"

Mia nodded, her mind already racing with ideas. "We need to focus on sustainable development and conservation efforts. We'll work on projects that benefit both the environment and the local community, ensuring that everyone has a stake in protecting this land."

The group continued discussing their plans, the conversation filled with optimism and resolve. As the sun climbed higher, casting its warm light over the clearing, Mia felt a deep sense of fulfillment. They had faced incredible challenges and emerged victorious, but the journey was far from over.

Later, as the rangers prepared to transport the captured poachers and the evidence, Captain Mbani approached Mia and Ryan. "Thank you both for your leadership and dedication. You've made a significant impact here."

Mia shook his hand firmly. "Thank you, Captain. We couldn't have done it without your support. This is just the beginning of our partnership."

Ryan nodded in agreement. "We'll stay in touch and coordinate closely. There's still much work to be done."

As the convoy of rangers and captured poachers departed, Mia and Ryan stood at the edge of the clearing, watching them go. The jungle, which had been a battleground just hours before, now seemed peaceful and full of promise.

Ryan turned to Mia, his expression thoughtful. "What's next for us?"

Mia smiled, feeling a renewed sense of purpose. "We continue our mission. There are more areas to protect, more communities to empower. This victory gives us the momentum we need to keep going."

Temba joined them, his presence a steady reminder of their shared commitment. "We'll stand with you. Together, we'll protect our home."

Mia looked around at the faces of her team and the villagers, feeling a profound sense of unity and strength. "Yes, together we'll make sure this land is safe for future generations. We've achieved something incredible, and we'll keep building on this success."

As the sun set on a day filled with both challenges and triumphs, Mia knew that their journey was far from over. But with the support of her team, the villagers, and the rangers, she was ready to face whatever came next. Together, they would continue to protect and preserve the jungle, ensuring that its beauty and biodiversity endured for generations to come.

Chapter 8
Unexpected Allies

The village was buzzing with activity in the days following the raid. With the threat of the poachers neutralized, the focus shifted to rebuilding and strengthening the community. Mia, Ryan, and their team worked tirelessly alongside the villagers, ensuring that everyone was prepared for the future.

Mia stood in the central clearing, a sense of satisfaction washing over her as she watched the collaborative efforts unfolding before her. Ryan approached, carrying a crate of supplies. "Morning, Mia. Ready for another day of hard work?"

Mia smiled, her determination unwavering. "Always. We have a lot to do, but the villagers are motivated. It's inspiring to see everyone coming together."

Ryan nodded, setting the crate down. "We've made great progress already. The new training programs are a hit, and the security measures are being well-received."

Just then, Temba arrived, his presence commanding as always. "Mia, Ryan, can we discuss the next steps for the village's security?"

Mia gestured for him to join them at a nearby table, which was covered with maps and plans. "Of course, Temba. Let's go over what we have so far."

Temba pointed to several key locations on the map. "We need to set up permanent watch posts here, here, and here. These are strategic points that will give us a clear view of any approaching threats."

Ryan nodded in agreement. "I've also been thinking about integrating more advanced surveillance technology. We can install motion-sensor cameras and alarms to cover the blind spots."

Kato, who had been listening from a distance, stepped forward hesitantly. "Ms. Mia, can I help with the watch posts? I've been practicing with the equipment."

Mia smiled warmly at the young boy's eagerness. "Absolutely, Kato. Your enthusiasm and dedication are exactly what we need. You'll be a great asset."

Kato beamed with pride. "Thank you, Ms. Mia. I won't let you down."

As the discussion continued, Amina joined them, carrying a notebook filled with ideas. "I've been thinking about how we can expand our conservation efforts. We should start a community garden to provide sustainable food sources and also focus on reforestation."

Temba nodded thoughtfully. "A community garden would be a great addition. It will provide food and teach valuable skills. And reforestation will help restore the balance in our ecosystem."

Mia looked around at her team, feeling a deep sense of pride. "We're not just protecting the jungle; we're building a future for this community. Let's make sure we have a solid plan for both security and sustainability."

Ryan tapped the map again. "I've already started gathering the materials we need for the watch posts. We'll need volunteers to help with the construction."

Temba smiled. "We have plenty of willing hands. The villagers are ready to do whatever it takes."

With the plan set, the team dispersed to their various tasks. Mia and Kato led a group of villagers to the first watch post location. As they worked, Kato asked, "Ms. Mia, do you think the poachers will come back?"

Mia paused, considering her answer carefully. "It's possible, Kato. But we're taking every precaution to ensure we're ready if they do. The important thing is that we're prepared and working together."

Kato nodded, his face serious. "I'm glad we're doing this. It makes me feel safe."

Mia smiled, placing a reassuring hand on his shoulder. "That's the goal, Kato. We want everyone to feel safe and secure in their home."

As the day progressed, the new watch posts began to take shape. The villagers worked tirelessly, their determination and teamwork evident in every nail hammered and beam secured. By evening, the first watch post was nearly complete.

Ryan joined Mia and Kato, wiping sweat from his brow. "This is looking great. Once we get the cameras and alarms installed, it will be fully operational."

Mia nodded, satisfaction evident in her expression. "We're making real progress. This is just the beginning of what we can achieve together."

As the sun set, casting a warm glow over the village, Mia gathered everyone for a brief meeting. "I want to thank each and every one of you for your hard work and dedication. We've faced incredible challenges, but we've come through stronger and more united. Together, we can protect our home and build a brighter future."

Temba stepped forward, his voice filled with pride. "We are a strong community, and with your help, we will continue to grow and thrive. Thank you, Mia, Ryan, and the entire team, for standing with us."

Ryan smiled, looking around at the faces of the villagers. "We're honored to be part of this community. Let's keep moving forward, together."

As the villagers dispersed, Mia stood with Ryan, Temba, and Kato, feeling a deep sense of fulfillment. They had made significant strides, but there was still much to be done. With the unwavering support of the community and the dedication of her team, Mia knew they were on the right path.

"We've accomplished a lot, but our work is far from over," Mia said, her voice resolute. "Let's continue to build, protect, and thrive, together."

Ryan nodded, his gaze steady. "Agreed. We're just getting started."

As the night settled over the village, Mia felt a renewed sense of hope. They had faced the darkness and emerged stronger. Now, it was time to build a future filled with promise and possibility. Together, they would protect and preserve the jungle, ensuring it remained a sanctuary for generations to come.

The days following the raid were filled with renewed energy and purpose. The villagers, inspired by their victory over the poachers, were eager to continue building a safer and more sustainable future. Mia, Ryan, and the team worked tirelessly alongside them, expanding their efforts to ensure the community's resilience.

One morning, Mia and Ryan gathered the village leaders and key team members in the central hut to discuss the next phase of their plans. The atmosphere was one of determination and hope.

Mia spread out a map on the table, pointing to several areas. "We've secured the main entry points to the village, but we need to think about long-term sustainability. We've discussed a community garden and reforestation. Let's finalize those plans and assign tasks."

Amina, holding her notebook, nodded enthusiastically. "I've been working on a layout for the community garden. We'll need to clear some land and start planting as soon as possible. The garden will provide fresh produce and medicinal herbs."

Temba added, "We also need to focus on reforestation. Planting native trees will help restore the balance and create a barrier against future encroachments."

Ryan leaned in, examining the map. "We should identify the best locations for the garden and reforestation efforts. The soil quality and water sources will be crucial factors."

Kato, who had been listening intently, raised his hand. "Can I help with the garden, Ms. Mia? I've been learning about different plants and how to take care of them."

Mia smiled warmly. "Of course, Kato. Your enthusiasm is exactly what we need. You'll be a big help."

Captain Mbani, who had stayed to assist with the ongoing efforts, spoke up. "We've also received additional supplies from the rangers. We have more tools, seeds, and saplings to get started. This will give us a great boost."

Mia looked around the room, feeling a deep sense of unity. "Let's get to work. We have a lot to do, but together, we can achieve anything."

The group dispersed, each member taking on their assigned tasks with determination. Mia and Kato led a team to the designated area for the community garden. The villagers worked tirelessly, clearing the land and preparing it for planting.

Kato, kneeling beside Mia, examined a handful of soil. "Ms. Mia, do you think this soil is good for the garden?"

Mia took the soil, feeling its texture. "It looks good, Kato. It's rich and dark, perfect for growing our plants. Let's start marking the rows."

As they worked, Ryan and Temba led another team to the reforestation area. They carried saplings and tools, ready to begin planting the first batch of trees. Ryan explained the process to the villagers.

"We need to dig holes deep enough for the saplings to take root. Make sure the soil is packed firmly around them. These trees will grow strong and provide a natural barrier."

Temba added, "These trees are native to the area. They'll support the local wildlife and help restore the ecosystem."

As the day progressed, the village was filled with the sounds of progress. The community garden began to take shape, rows of freshly planted seeds promising future harvests. In the reforestation area, saplings stood proudly, a testament to their commitment to preserving the jungle.

Mia and Kato took a break, sitting under the shade of a large tree. "You're doing great work, Kato. The garden is going to be amazing," Mia said, handing him a water bottle.

Kato grinned, wiping sweat from his forehead. "I'm really excited, Ms. Mia. It feels good to be doing something that will help everyone."

Ryan and Temba joined them, their faces reflecting the satisfaction of a hard day's work. "The saplings are all planted," Ryan reported. "It's a good start. We'll need to keep an eye on them and make sure they're well taken care of."

Temba nodded. "This is just the beginning. We're building something that will last for generations."

As evening approached, the villagers gathered in the central clearing to celebrate their progress. Mia stood before them, her heart swelling with pride. "Today, we've taken significant steps toward securing our future. The community garden and reforestation efforts are just the beginning. Together, we can create a sustainable and thriving home."

Captain Mbani stepped forward, his voice strong. "Your dedication and hard work are inspiring. The rangers will continue to support you in any way we can. This community is a shining example of what can be achieved when people come together."

The villagers cheered, their spirits high. Mia looked around, feeling a deep sense of fulfillment. They had faced incredible challenges, but their resilience and unity had carried them through.

Ryan stood beside her, his expression one of pride and determination. "We've accomplished so much, Mia. But there's still more to do."

Mia nodded, her eyes shining with resolve. "We'll keep going. We've built a strong foundation, and we'll continue to grow and protect our home."

As the sun set over the village, casting a warm glow over the newly planted garden and saplings, Mia felt a renewed sense of hope. They had not only protected their land but had also laid the groundwork for a brighter, more sustainable future. With the continued efforts of the community and the unwavering support of her team, Mia knew they were on the right path. Together, they would ensure that the jungle and its inhabitants thrived for generations to come.

In the days that followed, the village continued to thrive. The community garden was beginning to sprout green shoots, and the reforestation efforts were showing promise as the saplings took root. Mia, Ryan, and the team worked closely with the villagers to ensure that every need was met and that the village was on a path to sustainability.

One afternoon, Mia called a meeting in the central hut to address some pressing concerns. The villagers gathered, their faces reflecting both hope and the desire for continued progress. Mia stood at the front, ready to lead the discussion.

"Thank you all for coming," Mia began, her voice steady and clear. "We've made incredible progress, but there are still some needs we need to address to ensure our long-term success."

Amina, holding her notebook, spoke up first. "One of the main concerns is access to clean water. The stream nearby is our primary source, but it's not always reliable, especially during the dry season."

Ryan nodded. "We've been discussing the possibility of installing a well. It would provide a consistent and clean water source for the village."

Temba, always practical, added, "We also need to think about water storage. If we can collect rainwater and store it, we'll have a backup supply during dry periods."

Mia turned to Captain Mbani, who had been listening intently. "Captain, do you think the rangers could assist us with the well installation and water storage systems?"

Captain Mbani nodded thoughtfully. "Absolutely. We have engineers and resources that can help. It's a critical need, and we're committed to supporting your efforts."

Kato, who had been sitting quietly, raised his hand. "Ms. Mia, what about education? Can we set up a place for the children to learn more about the jungle and how to take care of it?"

Mia smiled warmly at his suggestion. "That's a wonderful idea, Kato. Education is vital for our future. We can start by setting up a small learning center where we can teach about conservation, agriculture, and other important skills."

One of the elders, Nia, spoke next. "We also need to ensure we have adequate medical supplies. The jungle can be dangerous, and we must be prepared for any emergencies."

Ryan agreed. "We've already received some supplies, but we need to establish a more comprehensive medical station. Training more villagers in first aid will also be beneficial."

The discussion continued, with everyone contributing ideas and suggestions. The sense of unity and collaboration was palpable, and it was clear that the village was committed to building a strong and sustainable future.

After the meeting, Mia and Ryan walked to the edge of the village, where the new garden was flourishing. The green shoots were a testament to their hard work and dedication.

"We've come a long way," Ryan said, looking out over the garden. "But there's still so much to do."

Mia nodded, her expression thoughtful. "We're building something lasting, Ryan. It's not just about the immediate needs but creating a foundation for future generations."

Ryan turned to her, his gaze steady. "You've been an incredible leader, Mia. The villagers look up to you, and you've given them hope."

Mia felt a warmth spread through her. "Thank you, Ryan. But it's been a team effort. We couldn't have done it without everyone's hard work and dedication."

As they stood there, watching the villagers work together to build a brighter future, Temba joined them. "We've laid the groundwork, but we must keep pushing forward. The challenges will continue, but we're ready."

Mia placed a hand on Temba's shoulder. "We'll face them together, Temba. This village is a family, and we'll support each other through everything."

Kato ran up to them, his face beaming with excitement. "Ms. Mia, we found some more seeds we can plant! Can we start a new section in the garden?"

Mia smiled, her heart swelling with pride. "Of course, Kato. Let's keep growing."

As the sun began to set, casting a golden glow over the village, Mia felt a renewed sense of purpose. They had made significant strides, but there was still much work to be done. With the continued efforts of the community and the unwavering support of her team, Mia knew they were on the right path. Together, they would build a sustainable future, ensuring that the jungle and its inhabitants thrived for generations to come.

The village was alive with energy and anticipation as preparations for a celebratory feast were underway. The community had accomplished so much, and tonight was a time to reflect on their achievements and look forward to the future. Tables were set up in the central clearing, adorned with colorful fabrics and fresh flowers from the jungle. The scent of cooking food filled the air, and children ran about, their laughter echoing through the trees.

Mia and Ryan stood by the new community garden, admiring the rows of sprouting plants. "It's amazing how far we've come," Mia said, her voice filled with pride.

Ryan nodded, his eyes scanning the vibrant garden. "It really is. The villagers have put in so much hard work. They deserve this celebration."

Temba approached, a warm smile on his face. "The feast is almost ready. The elders would like to say a few words before we start."

Mia smiled back. "That sounds perfect. Let's gather everyone."

As the sun began to set, casting a golden glow over the village, the community gathered in the clearing. Mia stood with Temba, Ryan, and the elders at the front, ready to address the villagers.

Nia, one of the respected elders, stepped forward first. "Tonight, we celebrate not just our survival, but our strength, unity, and progress. We have faced many challenges, but together, we have overcome them. Let us give thanks for the blessings of our land and the hard work of our people."

The villagers cheered, their faces reflecting their joy and pride. Mia stepped forward next, her heart swelling with emotion. "I want to thank each and every one of you for your incredible dedication and effort. We have built something truly special here. This garden, these trees, this community—they are a testament to our resilience and unity."

Ryan joined her, his voice strong and clear. "This is just the beginning. We have laid a strong foundation, but there is still much to do. Together, we will continue to grow and protect our home. Let's keep moving forward, supporting each other every step of the way."

The villagers applauded, their enthusiasm filling the air. Temba raised his hand for silence, then spoke with a voice full of conviction. "We have shown that by working together, we can achieve great things. Let us enjoy this feast and remember that our strength lies in our unity."

As the celebration began, Mia and Ryan moved through the crowd, talking and laughing with the villagers. The tables were filled with delicious food, a mix of traditional dishes and fresh produce from the new garden. Children played games, their laughter a joyful soundtrack to the evening.

Kato found Mia and Ryan, his face beaming with excitement. "Ms. Mia, Mr. Ryan, come see what we've done!"

He led them to a corner of the clearing where a group of children had created a small, makeshift stage. They were preparing to put on a play, reenacting the village's triumph over the poachers and the subsequent rebuilding efforts.

Mia and Ryan watched with pride as the children performed, their enthusiasm infectious. The play was a heartwarming reminder of how far they had come and the bright future ahead.

After the play, Captain Mbani approached, his expression one of admiration. "You've built something remarkable here, Mia. The rangers are proud to support such a resilient and inspiring community."

Mia nodded, her eyes shining. "Thank you, Captain. We couldn't have done it without your help. This is a collective victory."

As the night wore on, the celebration continued with music, dancing, and storytelling. The bond between the villagers and the team grew stronger with every shared laugh and heartfelt conversation.

Temba, standing beside Mia and Ryan, raised a toast. "To our community, to our future, and to the friends who have stood with us. May we continue to grow and thrive together."

The villagers raised their glasses, their voices united in a resounding cheer. "To our future!"

Mia looked around, feeling a profound sense of fulfillment. They had faced incredible challenges, but they had emerged stronger and more united. The journey was far from over, but with the unwavering support of her team and the villagers, Mia knew they were on the right path.

As the stars twinkled above and the sounds of celebration filled the air, Mia leaned towards Ryan. "We've accomplished so much, but this is just the beginning. There's so much more we can do."

Ryan smiled, his eyes reflecting the flickering light of the lanterns. "Together, there's nothing we can't achieve."

Mia felt a surge of hope and determination. "Let's keep building, protecting, and growing. Our future is bright, and we'll face it together."

As the night drew to a close, Mia stood with Ryan, Temba, and the villagers, feeling a deep connection to each of them. They had built not just a community, but a family. And together, they would continue to nurture and protect their home, ensuring it flourished for generations to come.

Chapter 9
Traps and Ambushes

The morning after the celebration dawned with a sense of calm and hope. Mia was sitting in the central hut, going over plans for the new projects when Ryan rushed in, his face pale with concern.

"Mia, we need to talk," Ryan said, his voice urgent.

Mia looked up, her heart skipping a beat at his tone. "What is it, Ryan? What's happened?"

Ryan took a deep breath, trying to steady himself. "We've received word from the rangers. There's been an incident at one of the nearby villages. Poachers have attacked, and they've taken several people hostage."

Mia felt a wave of shock and anger wash over her. "Hostages? How did this happen?"

Ryan shook his head. "We don't have all the details yet. Captain Mbani is on his way to brief us. He should be here any moment."

As if on cue, Captain Mbani entered the hut, his expression grim. "Mia, Ryan, I'm afraid we have a serious situation. The poachers have retaliated. They attacked a village last night, and several villagers were taken hostage."

Mia stood up, her resolve hardening. "We need to act quickly. What's the plan, Captain?"

Captain Mbani unfolded a map on the table, pointing to the location of the attacked village. "The poachers are holding the hostages here, in a heavily fortified camp. We've already mobilized a rescue team, but we need your help to navigate the terrain and ensure the safety of the hostages."

Ryan nodded, his jaw set. "We're with you, Captain. What do you need us to do?"

Captain Mbani looked at them both, his eyes filled with determination. "We'll split into two teams. One will create a diversion to draw the poachers' attention, while the other team moves in to rescue the hostages. Mia, I need you to lead the rescue team. Ryan, you'll handle the diversion."

Mia and Ryan exchanged a glance, their unspoken communication clear. "We're ready," Mia said firmly. "Let's save those people."

Temba entered the hut, having overheard the conversation. "I'll go with Mia. My knowledge of the area will be crucial."

Mia nodded gratefully. "Thank you, Temba. We need all the help we can get."

As they prepared for the mission, Mia addressed her team. "We've faced challenges before, and we've come through stronger. This is another test of our strength and unity. Remember, the safety of the hostages is our top priority. Stay focused, stay together, and we will succeed."

Ryan stepped forward, his voice steady. "Team, the diversion is critical. We need to create enough chaos to draw the poachers away from the hostages without endangering ourselves. Follow my lead, and we'll give Mia's team the best chance to succeed."

Kato, who had been listening quietly, spoke up, his voice filled with determination. "Ms. Mia, please be careful. We're all counting on you."

Mia smiled at him, feeling a surge of pride and responsibility. "We'll bring everyone back safely, Kato. I promise."

With their plans in place, the two teams set out. Mia's team moved silently through the jungle, using Temba's knowledge to navigate the dense foliage and avoid detection. The air was thick with tension, every sound amplified in the quiet of the early morning.

Mia turned to Temba, her voice a whisper. "How much further?"

Temba pointed ahead. "We're close. The camp is just beyond that ridge."

As they reached the ridge, Mia signaled for the team to stop and crouch down. She peered through the foliage, spotting the poachers' camp below. Armed guards patrolled the perimeter, and makeshift structures were scattered throughout the clearing.

Mia turned to her team, her voice low but firm. "We need to move quickly and quietly. Temba, you lead the way. I'll cover the rear."

Temba nodded and began to lead the team down the ridge, their movements silent and deliberate. As they neared the camp, they could hear the muffled cries of the hostages. Mia's heart ached, but she forced herself to stay focused.

Ryan's voice crackled over the radio, barely audible but clear. "We're in position. Ready to create the diversion on your signal."

Mia pressed the button on her radio, her voice steady. "Copy that, Ryan. On my mark."

She turned to her team, her eyes filled with determination. "This is it. Ryan's team will create the diversion, and we'll move in to rescue the hostages. Be ready."

As the signal was given, the sound of explosions and shouting erupted from the other side of the camp. The poachers, caught off guard, scrambled to respond to the diversion. Mia and her team took advantage of the chaos, slipping into the camp and heading straight for the hostages.

They found them huddled together in a makeshift cage, fear etched on their faces. Mia quickly picked the lock, her hands steady despite the adrenaline coursing through her veins.

"Everyone, stay calm. We're here to get you out," Mia said, her voice firm but reassuring.

The hostages began to move, their hope rekindled. Temba led them towards the jungle, while Mia and the rest of the team provided cover. The sound of gunfire and shouting continued in the background, but Mia kept her focus on getting everyone to safety.

As they reached the edge of the camp, Ryan's voice crackled over the radio again. "We're pulling back. How's the rescue going?"

Mia responded quickly. "We have the hostages. Moving to the extraction point now."

Ryan's relief was evident in his voice. "Good work. We'll meet you there."

The teams regrouped at the extraction point, their mission successful. The hostages were shaken but safe, their gratitude evident in their eyes.

Mia turned to Ryan, her expression one of relief and pride. "We did it."

Ryan nodded, a smile breaking through his serious demeanor. "Yes, we did. Together."

Captain Mbani approached, his face filled with gratitude. "Thank you, Mia, Ryan. Your bravery and quick thinking saved lives today."

Mia felt a deep sense of fulfillment. "It was a team effort, Captain. We couldn't have done it without everyone's courage and determination."

As the sun rose over the jungle, casting a new light on the village, Mia knew that their work was far from over. But with their unwavering unity and resolve, they were ready to face whatever challenges lay ahead. Together, they would continue to protect their home and ensure the safety of their community.

With the hostages safely returned and the immediate threat from the poachers neutralized, the village began to settle back into a routine. However, the recent attack had left a mark on everyone, a reminder of the constant vigilance required to protect their home.

Mia and Ryan called a meeting with the village leaders and their team to reassess their strategies and plan the next steps. They gathered in the central hut, the atmosphere somber but determined.

Mia spread out a map on the table, highlighting key areas of concern. "We need to reinforce our defenses and improve our communication with neighboring villages. This recent attack showed us that the poachers are still a significant threat."

Temba nodded, his expression serious. "We also need to rebuild the trust and confidence of our people. They need to know that we are taking every possible measure to ensure their safety."

Ryan added, "I've been thinking about setting up a more advanced surveillance system. We can use drones to monitor the surrounding area and detect any suspicious activity early."

Amina, holding her ever-present notebook, chimed in, "Education is key. We need to continue training the villagers in self-defense and emergency procedures. Everyone should know what to do if another attack occurs."

Mia agreed, her mind racing with ideas. "We'll also need to strengthen our alliances with the rangers and other organizations. Their support was crucial in the last operation, and it will be vital moving forward."

Captain Mbani, who had stayed to assist with the rebuilding efforts, stepped forward. "We're ready to offer any assistance you need. We can help set up the surveillance system and provide additional training for your villagers."

As the meeting continued, the group discussed various strategies and assigned tasks. The sense of unity and purpose was strong, and everyone was committed to making the village safer and more resilient.

After the meeting, Mia and Ryan took a walk around the village, discussing the next steps in more detail. "We've come a long way, but there's still so much to do," Mia said, her voice reflecting both determination and concern.

Ryan nodded. "The drones will be a big help. They can cover a lot of ground quickly and give us a real-time view of the area.

We'll need to set up a control center and train a few villagers to operate them."

Mia looked around at the villagers, who were already hard at work reinforcing structures and repairing damages from the attack. "We also need to keep morale high. The villagers need to feel confident and supported."

Ryan agreed. "A community meeting would help. We can update everyone on the new measures we're taking and address any concerns they might have."

Mia smiled, feeling a surge of hope. "Let's organize it for tomorrow. We'll make sure everyone knows they're an important part of this effort."

The next day, the entire village gathered in the central clearing for the meeting. Mia stood before them, her heart swelling with pride at their resilience and unity.

"Thank you all for coming," Mia began, her voice strong. "The recent attack was a harsh reminder of the challenges we face. But it also showed us the strength of our community. Together, we rescued the hostages and protected our home."

Ryan stepped forward, his presence a steadying force. "We're taking several new measures to ensure our safety. We'll be setting up a drone surveillance system, improving our defenses, and continuing with our training programs. Your participation and support are crucial."

Kato, standing at the front, raised his hand. "Ms. Mia, how can we help with the drones?"

Mia smiled at his eagerness. "We'll need volunteers to learn how to operate them. It's an important job, and I know you'll do great."

Nia, one of the elders, spoke up. "We trust you, Mia. We trust all of you. Thank you for your dedication and leadership."

Mia felt a wave of gratitude. "Thank you, Nia. We're all in this together. By working as a team, we'll ensure our village remains a safe and thriving home."

As the meeting concluded, the villagers dispersed with renewed determination. Mia and Ryan continued their walk around the village, checking on the progress of various projects and offering support where needed.

Mia turned to Ryan, her eyes reflecting both resolve and hope. "We've faced incredible challenges, but we're stronger for it. We'll keep moving forward, building a brighter future together."

Ryan nodded, his gaze steady. "Absolutely. Together, we can overcome anything."

With the village united and focused on their shared goals, Mia felt a renewed sense of purpose. They had come through a difficult time, but their bond was stronger than ever. With continued vigilance and teamwork, they would protect their home and ensure a safe, prosperous future for all.

The sun was high in the sky as the village buzzed with activity. The recent community meeting had invigorated everyone, and the villagers were hard at work implementing the new strategies discussed. Mia and Ryan were at the center of it all, overseeing the progress and ensuring everything ran smoothly.

Mia stood near the newly established control center, where a group of villagers was being trained to operate the drones. Ryan was explaining the details to the eager learners, his voice confident and encouraging.

"These drones will give us an aerial view of the surrounding area," Ryan said, pointing to the monitor displaying the drone's camera feed. "We can spot any unusual activity long before it reaches the village. Let's go over the controls again."

Kato, who had been paying close attention, raised his hand. "Mr. Ryan, how do we know when to take off and land?"

Ryan smiled, appreciating the boy's curiosity. "Good question, Kato. We'll set up a schedule for regular patrols, but you'll also need to be ready to launch the drones if we get any reports of suspicious activity. Let's practice with this drone."

Mia watched as Ryan guided Kato through the process, feeling a sense of pride at the progress they were making. She turned to Temba, who was standing beside her. "The villagers are really taking to this new technology. It's going to make a big difference."

Temba nodded, his expression thoughtful. "It's a powerful tool. But we must remain vigilant. The poachers won't give up easily."

Mia agreed. "That's why we're reinforcing our defenses and continuing the training programs. We need to be prepared for anything."

Just then, Amina approached, her notebook in hand. "Mia, we've finished setting up the first rainwater collection system. The villagers are really excited about it."

Mia smiled. "That's great news, Amina. Let's check it out."

They walked over to the newly constructed rainwater collection system, where a group of villagers was gathered. One of the villagers, an elderly man named Juma, greeted them warmly. "Ms. Mia, Mr. Ryan, thank you for this. It's going to make a big difference, especially during the dry season."

Ryan nodded. "We're glad to help, Juma. How's it working so far?"

Juma pointed to the large barrels connected to the gutters. "We've already collected a good amount of water from the last rain. It's easy to use and maintain."

Mia looked around at the smiling faces of the villagers. "This is exactly what we hoped for. Let's make sure everyone knows how to use and take care of the system."

As they continued their tour of the village, they stopped by the community garden, where new rows of plants were sprouting. The garden was thriving, thanks to the hard work of the villagers and the training they had received.

Mia knelt beside Kato, who was tending to a row of young plants. "You're doing a fantastic job, Kato. The garden looks amazing."

Kato beamed with pride. "Thank you, Ms. Mia. I've learned a lot from you and Mr. Ryan."

Ryan joined them, his face reflecting the same pride. "It's a team effort, Kato. Everyone's hard work is paying off."

As the day went on, Mia and Ryan gathered the key members of their team for a final review of their progress. They met in the central hut, the atmosphere filled with a sense of accomplishment and determination.

"Today has been a great success," Mia began, her voice filled with confidence. "We've made significant strides in our defense and sustainability efforts. But we can't become complacent. We need to keep pushing forward."

Ryan nodded in agreement. "The drone surveillance system is up and running, the rainwater collection system is operational, and the community garden is thriving. We're on the right track, but we need to stay focused."

Temba added, "We've also made progress in training the villagers in self-defense and emergency procedures. They're becoming more confident and prepared."

Amina spoke up, her voice thoughtful. "We should continue to expand our education programs. The more knowledge we share, the stronger our community will be."

Mia looked around the room, feeling a deep sense of unity and resolve. "Let's keep this momentum going. We've faced challenges before, and we've overcome them together. We'll continue to protect and build our home, one step at a time."

As the meeting concluded, the team dispersed to continue their work. Mia and Ryan stood together, watching the village bustling with activity and purpose.

"We've accomplished so much, Mia," Ryan said, his voice filled with pride. "But there's still more to do."

Mia nodded, her eyes reflecting determination and hope. "We'll keep going, Ryan. Together, we'll ensure the safety and prosperity of our village."

With the village united and focused on their shared goals, Mia felt a renewed sense of purpose. They had come through difficult times, but their bond was stronger than ever. With continued vigilance and teamwork, they would protect their home and build a brighter future for all.

As dusk began to fall, the village was winding down from a day of hard work. Mia and Ryan were finishing up their final checks when suddenly, a young boy came running towards them, his face pale with fear.

"Ms. Mia! Mr. Ryan! There's smoke coming from the north side of the forest!" he shouted, pointing urgently.

Mia's heart skipped a beat. "Smoke? How far from the village?"

The boy shook his head. "Not far. It looks like a fire!"

Ryan immediately grabbed the radio and called Captain Mbani. "Captain, we've got a possible fire on the north side of the forest. We're heading there now."

"Roger that, Ryan. We'll meet you at the location," Captain Mbani's voice crackled back.

Mia turned to the villagers who had gathered around. "We need to move quickly. Temba, gather a team to help with the fire. Amina, alert the rest of the village and start preparing the evacuation plans just in case."

Temba nodded. "On it, Mia. We'll grab the tools and meet you at the north side."

As they sprinted towards the source of the smoke, Ryan turned to Mia. "If this is a wildfire, it could spread quickly. We need to contain it fast."

"I know," Mia replied, her mind racing with possible scenarios. "Let's hope it's not too large yet."

When they reached the north side, the sight that met them was both alarming and heart-wrenching. Flames were licking at the underbrush, and the fire was spreading rapidly through the dry foliage. Captain Mbani and his rangers were already there, trying to control the blaze.

Captain Mbani saw them and shouted, "We need to create a firebreak to stop it from spreading to the village. Start clearing the vegetation!"

Mia and Ryan grabbed tools and joined the effort. Mia turned to the team of villagers Temba had brought. "Form a line and start clearing everything that can burn. We need to create a gap that the fire can't cross."

As they worked, the heat from the flames grew intense. Sweat poured down their faces, but they kept going, driven by the urgency of the situation.

Temba called out, "Mia, we've got a clear path here! We need to widen it!"

Ryan looked over, assessing the situation. "Good work, Temba. Keep at it! We're holding it off for now, but we need more water."

Just then, Amina arrived with more villagers carrying buckets of water and wet blankets. She ran to Mia, breathless. "We've brought everything we could find. How can we help?"

Mia pointed to the line of firebreak. "Soak the blankets and lay them on the ground here. We need to stop the fire from advancing."

The combined efforts of the villagers and rangers began to pay off. The firebreak was holding, and the flames were starting to die down. But the air was thick with smoke, and visibility was poor.

Kato, who had been helping to fetch water, came running up to Mia. "Ms. Mia, I saw something moving in the smoke. I think there are animals trapped!"

Mia's heart sank. "Ryan, we need to check for any trapped animals. Can you handle things here?"

Ryan nodded, his face grim but determined. "Go, Mia. Be careful."

Mia and Kato moved towards the smoke, their eyes scanning for any signs of movement. Through the haze, they spotted a group of small animals huddled together, terrified and unable to escape the encroaching flames.

"There!" Mia pointed. "We need to get them out."

Kato nodded, his young face set with determination. "I'll help guide them, Ms. Mia."

They worked quickly, carefully picking up the frightened animals and carrying them to safety. As they brought the last of them out, Mia heard a loud crackling sound behind her. She turned to see a large tree, weakened by the fire, beginning to fall.

"Kato, look out!" Mia shouted, grabbing the boy and pulling him to safety just as the tree crashed to the ground, sending a shower of sparks into the air.

Breathing heavily, Mia checked Kato for injuries. "Are you okay?"

Kato nodded, wide-eyed but unharmed. "I'm okay, Ms. Mia. Thank you."

They hurried back to the firebreak, where the combined efforts of the villagers and rangers had finally brought the fire under control. The flames were dying down, and the immediate danger seemed to have passed.

Captain Mbani approached, his face covered in soot but filled with relief. "We did it. The fire's contained. Excellent work, everyone."

Mia nodded, exhaustion and relief washing over her. "Thank you, Captain. And thank you, everyone. Your quick action saved our village."

Ryan joined them, his expression one of pride and gratitude. "We've faced another challenge and overcome it together. We couldn't have done it without each and every one of you."

The villagers cheered, their spirits lifted despite the exhaustion. Mia looked around at the faces of her community, feeling a deep sense of connection and pride.

"We're a strong community," she said, her voice filled with emotion. "We've proven that time and time again. Let's continue to support and protect each other, no matter what challenges come our way."

As the night settled in, the village began the process of cleaning up and assessing the damage. Mia, Ryan, and Temba stood together, their bond stronger than ever.

"We've got a lot of work ahead," Temba said, his voice steady. "But we've shown that we can handle anything."

Mia nodded, her resolve unwavering. "Yes, we have. And we'll keep moving forward, together."

Ryan placed a hand on Mia's shoulder, his voice filled with admiration. "You're an incredible leader, Mia. We're lucky to have you."

Mia smiled, feeling a deep sense of fulfillment. "Thank you, Ryan. But this is a team effort. We're all in this together."

As the stars twinkled above, the village settled into a quiet but determined calm. They had faced another crisis and come through stronger. With their unity and resilience, Mia knew they could overcome any challenge and build a brighter future for their home.

Chapter 10
Strengthening Resilience

The thick canopy overhead did little to dispel the oppressive heat of the jungle. Mia crouched beside the trunk of a massive baobab tree, the satellite phone gripped tightly in her hand. A soft breeze rustled the leaves, but it didn't reach the humid air where she sat. She glanced over her shoulder to where Ryan and Amina were sorting through equipment a few yards away. This was the best moment she'd have all day to make the call—before they moved deeper into uncharted territory, before the signal became too weak to reach anyone.

She took a deep breath and punched in the familiar number, her heart pounding a little harder with each ring. After what felt like an eternity, a familiar voice crackled through the static.

"Mia? Is that you?" Lina's voice sounded faint and strained, the distance between them palpable even through the distorted connection.

"Yeah, it's me," Mia said softly, leaning back against the rough bark of the tree. "Can you hear me okay?"

"Barely," Lina replied, and Mia could almost picture her sister frowning at the poor reception. "You're breaking up a little. Where are you? Are you safe?"

"We're fine, Lina. I'm calling from a clearing a few miles from the main river. We've been setting up some new camera traps to monitor movement, and we—" Mia hesitated, choosing her words carefully, "—we ran into some signs of poacher activity."

"Poachers?" Lina's voice rose, a sharp edge of fear and anger cutting through the static. "What kind of signs? Mia, please tell me you're not chasing after them. You promised you'd be careful."

Mia closed her eyes, leaning her head back and letting the coarse bark press into her scalp. "We're not chasing them, I swear. We're just documenting what we find, sending the intel to the authorities. We've been staying clear of any direct confrontations."

"That's not what I asked," Lina said, her voice tight. "You know what they're capable of, Mia. They're not just some small-time hunters—they're armed, and they're dangerous. I don't care how much equipment or backup you have, you're still risking your life out there."

Mia sighed, a mixture of frustration and guilt welling up inside her. She glanced at Ryan, who caught her eye and gave a small nod of encouragement. She turned away, lowering her voice. "I know you're worried, Lina. But we're being smart about this. We have a solid plan. We're taking every precaution."

"Precaution?" Lina's laugh was bitter, almost a sob. "Mia, you're halfway across the world, in the middle of a jungle full of people who wouldn't hesitate to shoot you if you got in their way. That's not being cautious—that's being reckless. How much longer do you think you can keep this up before something goes wrong?"

"I can handle it," Mia said quietly, but even to her own ears, the words sounded hollow. She tightened her grip on the phone, wishing she could reach through the connection and somehow make Lina understand. "I have to do this. You know why."

"Because of Dad, right?" Lina's voice softened, the anger ebbing away into something far more painful. "Because you feel like you owe it to him to finish what he started. But Dad's not here, Mia. He's gone. And I can't lose you too."

The raw plea in Lina's voice cut through Mia's defenses, leaving her feeling exposed and vulnerable. She glanced at the small photograph of their father she kept tucked in her pocket—the one she looked at every morning before they set out. He was smiling in the picture, his arm wrapped around a much younger version of herself, both of them grinning at some long-forgotten victory. How many times had she wondered if he'd be proud of her? How many times had she tried to measure up to the man who had always seemed larger than life?

"I know," Mia whispered, her voice barely audible. "I know I can't bring him back, Lina. But I can keep his legacy alive. I can make sure that everything he worked for doesn't disappear."

"And what about your legacy, Mia?" Lina asked softly. "What about your life? When are you going to stop living for him and start living for yourself?"

The words hung in the air between them, stark and undeniable. Mia blinked back the sudden sting of tears, swallowing hard. "I don't know. I don't have an answer for that yet."

There was a long silence on the other end, punctuated only by the crackling of the weak signal. Then Lina sighed, the sound filled with weary resignation. "Just promise me you'll be careful. And call me whenever you can. Even if it's just for a minute. I need to know you're okay."

"I promise," Mia said, her voice breaking slightly. "I'll call every chance I get. I love you, Lina."

"I love you too," Lina replied softly. "Just... don't make me regret letting you go."

The line went dead, the silence that followed almost deafening in its finality. Mia stared at the phone for a long moment, her heart heavy with the weight of Lina's words. She shoved the device back into her pocket, feeling more torn than ever.

She looked up to find Ryan and Amina watching her quietly. Ryan stepped forward, his gaze sympathetic. "Everything okay?"

Mia forced a smile, but it felt brittle. "Yeah. Just... family stuff."

Ryan nodded slowly, glancing at Amina before speaking. "You know, your dad had a saying whenever things got tough. He'd say, 'Sometimes the jungle gives you the answer you need, not the one you want.'"

Mia let out a shaky laugh, wiping her eyes. "That sounds like him."

"Maybe we need to take a moment," Amina suggested gently. "For him. For everything we're doing here. A moment of silence—to remember why we're fighting this fight."

Mia hesitated, then nodded, the knot of tension in her chest loosening just a fraction. She looked at Ryan and Amina, at Kato standing a little further back, and took a deep breath. "Okay. A moment of silence."

The team stood together in the clearing, their heads bowed. The jungle around them seemed to hush, the cacophony of sounds fading to a soft murmur. For the first time in a long while, Mia felt something close to peace.

When they finally lifted their heads, there was a sense of renewed purpose in the air. Mia glanced at Ryan, who offered her a small, supportive smile.

"Let's do this," she murmured, her voice steady. "Let's make him proud."

And with that, they turned back to the path ahead, their resolve stronger than before. The jungle, for all its dangers, seemed just a little less daunting now.

The team gathered around the small campfire, the flickering light casting shadows on their faces. Mia shifted uncomfortably, the notebook in her lap feeling heavier than it should. The jungle around them was alive with the hum of insects and the distant calls of nocturnal animals, but within the small circle of their camp, it felt oddly still. She took a deep breath, looking at the expectant faces of her team—Ryan, Amina, and Kato—all watching her with a mixture of curiosity and concern.

"I wanted to share something with you," Mia began, her voice wavering slightly before she steadied it. She glanced down at the worn leather cover of the notebook, her fingers brushing over the faded edges. "This... this was my father's. It's his research journal, filled with notes, sketches, maps... everything he dedicated his life to."

Amina leaned forward, her eyes softening. "You've never mentioned it before. What's in there, exactly?"

Mia hesitated, then opened the journal to a page covered in her father's neat, precise handwriting. "It's more than just research data. It's his thoughts, his hopes for the future of conservation. He believed that every species—no matter how small or insignificant—has a role to play in maintaining the balance of our world. He wrote about how even losing a single species can cause a ripple effect that throws entire ecosystems into chaos."

Ryan, sitting across from her, nodded thoughtfully. "That sounds like him. He was always talking about the 'butterfly effect' of conservation."

Mia's lips twitched into a small smile. "Yeah, exactly. He used to say that we're all part of the same web, and if one thread is cut, the whole thing can unravel. It's why he was so relentless—why he wouldn't give up, even when it seemed hopeless."

Kato tilted his head, his gaze fixed on the notebook. "Is that why you're doing this, Mia? To keep his work alive?"

Mia looked up, meeting Kato's gaze. There was something earnest and raw in his eyes that made it hard to hide behind her usual defenses. "I guess... yeah. I feel like if I can finish what he started, then maybe I can prove that everything he gave up—everything he sacrificed—wasn't in vain."

"But you're not him," Amina said softly. "You know that, right? You don't have to carry the weight of his legacy on your shoulders. Your work, your commitment—it's already enough."

Mia swallowed hard, the words hitting a vulnerable spot she hadn't realized was so exposed. "I know," she murmured. "But sometimes it's hard to separate what I want from what he wanted. It's like... his voice is always in the back of my mind, pushing me to do more, be more."

Ryan shifted, leaning forward slightly. "He was proud of you, Mia. He told me that every chance he got. He said you had more potential than he ever did. But potential doesn't mean carrying his burdens. You can honor him by doing things your own way."

Mia looked down at the journal again, flipping through a few more pages. Each entry, each diagram, was a testament to the countless hours her father had poured into his work. She paused at a hand-drawn map, filled with intricate details of the very area they were in now—the Congo basin. The notes scrawled beside it described migration patterns, plant species, and the delicate balance between predator and prey.

"He spent so much time mapping out this region," Mia said quietly. "He used to take me on these expeditions, and we'd spend weeks just following animal tracks, watching how they moved through the forest. He said that understanding the land—really understanding it—was the key to protecting it."

"And you've been doing just that," Amina said, her voice filled with quiet conviction. "Every day we're out here, you're proving that you've learned from him. But you're also adding your own knowledge, your own insights. That's what makes this mission special."

Mia's throat tightened. She looked around at their faces—Ryan's calm, unwavering support; Amina's quiet encouragement; Kato's youthful admiration—and something shifted inside her. A deep sense of gratitude, mixed with a profound realization that she wasn't alone in this.

"Thank you," she whispered, barely able to get the words out. "For believing in me. For being here. It means more than I can say."

Ryan reached over, placing a hand on her shoulder. "We're not just here for your father, Mia. We're here because we believe in *you*. And we believe in what you're trying to do."

Mia blinked rapidly, fighting back the sting of tears. "I just... I want to do right by him. But sometimes I'm not sure if I'm making the right decisions. There's so much at stake, and I don't want to let any of you down."

"You're not letting anyone down," Amina said firmly. "Every step we take, every trap we disable—it's a victory. And your leadership is what's making that possible."

Ryan nodded, glancing at the journal. "You're carrying on his legacy, but you're also creating your own. I think we should take a moment—to honor him. And to honor you, too. You've brought us together, and that's something he would've been proud of."

The suggestion hung in the air, the weight of it settling over the group like a gentle, comforting presence. Mia hesitated, then nodded, a soft smile tugging at her lips. "I'd like that."

They sat in silence for a moment, the quiet broken only by the crackling of the campfire and the distant calls of the jungle. Mia closed her eyes, letting the memories of her father wash over her. When she opened them again, she felt lighter, the burden on her shoulders easing just a bit.

"Thank you," she whispered again, her voice steadier now. "For everything."

Ryan smiled, his gaze warm and reassuring. "Anytime, Mia. We're a team. And we're going to get through this together."

Mia nodded, a sense of unity settling over them like a shield against the darkness that loomed just beyond the circle of firelight. Whatever challenges lay ahead, they would face them as one. And for the first time in a long while, she believed they could succeed—not just for her father's sake, but for their own.

The trail ahead narrowed sharply, the dense jungle giving way to a rugged, rocky incline that loomed ominously above them. Mia scanned the terrain, noting the jagged edges and loose stones scattered across the path. Every step would be a risk, one wrong move sending them tumbling down the steep slope. The midday sun hung heavy in the sky, casting a harsh glare that made the rocks shimmer like shards of glass.

"This is going to be tough," Mia said, turning to the others. Her gaze swept over each member of the team—Ryan, with his steady composure; Amina, whose calm eyes held no trace of fear; and Kato, whose determined expression wavered only slightly. "But we can do it. Just take it slow and keep an eye out for loose stones. Ryan, you cover the rear and make sure no one falls behind."

Ryan gave a curt nod, his gaze already assessing the path ahead. "Got it. Everyone, keep your weight balanced. Use your hands if you need to, and stay close to the wall whenever possible."

"Stay close to the wall," Kato muttered, glancing up at the sheer cliff face beside them. "Yeah, easier said than done."

Mia caught his unease and stepped closer, her voice gentle but firm. "You've got this, Kato. We've done worse than this before, remember? Just take it one step at a time. Don't think about the whole climb—just focus on the next foothold."

Kato nodded, swallowing hard. "Okay, yeah. One step at a time. I can do that."

With a final encouraging look, Mia turned and began the ascent, her boots finding purchase on the uneven surface. The sharp rocks bit into her gloves as she used her hands to pull herself up, inch by inch. Behind her, she could hear the sounds of the others following—Amina's steady breathing, Ryan's quiet reassurances to Kato. Each word of encouragement echoed in the stillness, pushing them all forward.

"Watch your left foot, Mia," Ryan called up from below. "There's a loose rock just under your boot."

Mia paused, shifting her weight carefully to avoid the unstable stone. "Thanks," she murmured, casting a quick glance over her shoulder. "Everyone doing okay?"

"We're good," Amina replied, her voice light but controlled. "Just keep moving. We're right behind you."

Kato's voice came next, strained but determined. "I'm okay. Just... trying not to look down."

Mia bit back a smile, her chest tightening with a mix of pride and concern. "Don't worry about what's behind you. Just focus on what's ahead. You're doing great, Kato."

They climbed in silence for the next few minutes, the only sounds the scrape of boots against rock and the occasional grunt of exertion. Mia's muscles burned with the effort, her breath coming in short, controlled bursts. The path grew steeper, the angle more treacherous, but she forced herself to keep going. Lina's voice echoed in her mind, a constant undercurrent of worry and doubt.

What about your legacy, Mia? What about your life?

She shook her head, gritting her teeth as she hauled herself up another jagged outcrop. This was her life. This mission, this struggle—she couldn't let herself falter now. Not when there was so much at stake.

"Hold up," Ryan's voice interrupted her thoughts. "Kato needs a break."

Mia glanced down, her gaze locking onto Kato's pale face. He was clinging to a narrow ledge, his chest heaving with each ragged breath. A sheen of sweat glistened on his forehead, his fingers trembling slightly.

"Kato," she called softly, her tone filled with gentle encouragement. "Take a deep breath. You're doing fine. Just a quick rest, okay?"

"I—I'm sorry," Kato gasped, his voice tight with frustration. "I'm slowing everyone down."

"You're not," Ryan said firmly, shifting closer to the younger man. He reached out, placing a steadying hand on Kato's arm. "You're doing great. This climb is brutal. No one's rushing you. Just breathe."

Kato nodded shakily, closing his eyes and leaning his forehead against the cool rock. Mia watched him for a moment, then looked at Ryan. Their eyes met, and she saw the unspoken question there: *Do we push on, or do we turn back?*

"We keep going," Mia murmured, answering the question neither of them had voiced. She glanced back at Kato, her voice softening. "But at your pace, Kato. We're not leaving you behind."

He took a few more deep breaths, then opened his eyes, nodding determinedly. "Okay. I'm ready. Let's keep moving."

"Atta boy," Ryan said with a small smile. He gave Kato's arm a reassuring squeeze before pulling back. "Alright, everyone, back to it. Slow and steady."

The next stretch was the hardest. The rocks became slick with moss, the air thinning as they ascended higher. Mia's muscles screamed in protest, her grip slipping more than once as she fought to keep her balance. But every time she glanced down, she saw Kato pushing himself, his face set in a mask of concentration and determination.

"Almost there," Mia called out, her voice tight with exertion. "Just a few more feet, and we'll reach a flatter spot."

Ryan's voice floated up to her, calm and steady. "We've got you, Mia. You're doing great."

With one final burst of effort, Mia pulled herself over the last ledge, her body trembling with exhaustion. She reached down, extending a hand to Kato, who was only a step behind.

"Here," she murmured, her voice breathless but firm. "Take my hand."

Kato hesitated, then grasped her hand tightly. Together, they hauled him over the edge, his legs nearly giving out as he collapsed onto the flat surface beside her. He lay there, chest heaving, his face flushed with equal parts exhaustion and triumph.

"I—I did it," Kato whispered, a small, incredulous smile spreading across his lips.

Mia dropped to her knees beside him, grinning despite the burning in her lungs. "Yeah, you did. We all did."

Ryan and Amina joined them moments later, and for a moment, they all sat in silence, staring out at the view below—the dense jungle sprawling out beneath them, the river snaking through the trees like a ribbon of silver.

"We made it," Amina murmured, a soft laugh escaping her lips. "That was intense."

"Worth it, though," Ryan added quietly, his gaze shifting to Mia. "You led us through that, Mia. You kept us going."

Mia looked at him, then at Kato, and finally at Amina. There was a sense of camaraderie here, a bond forged not just by shared hardship, but by trust and belief in one another. She felt a swell of pride, mixed with that ever-present pang of uncertainty.

"I couldn't have done it without all of you," she whispered, her voice filled with gratitude. "Thank you... for believing in me."

They stayed there for a few minutes longer, the weight of their accomplishment settling in. The climb had tested them all, but they'd come through it together. And as Mia looked out over the jungle, Lina's words still echoing faintly in her mind, she knew one thing for certain:

Whatever lay ahead, they were ready to face it—together.

The jungle's oppressive heat finally relented as dusk settled over their camp. The last slivers of sunlight filtered through the dense canopy, casting long shadows and bathing the clearing in a dim, golden glow. Mia sat alone at the edge of the camp, the gentle murmur of her team's voices drifting over from where Ryan and Amina were going over the next day's plans.

Kato was hunched over a small fire, stirring a pot of something that smelled vaguely like beans. It was a moment of quiet, rare and fragile, and Mia let herself lean back against a moss-covered boulder, her body sinking into the cool earth. She pulled out her satellite phone, staring at the screen for a long moment before pressing a button to check for messages.

One new voicemail.

She tapped to play it, her breath catching in her throat when she saw the number. Lina. A mix of anticipation and trepidation surged through her as she brought the phone to her ear. The first crackle of her sister's voice made her heart clench.

"Hey, Mia... It's me."

Lina's voice was soft, hesitant, and Mia immediately noticed the lack of anger that had colored their last conversation. She shifted, her fingers tightening around the phone as she listened.

"I just wanted to say... I'm sorry. For the way I acted earlier. I know I'm being unfair, and I—" There was a pause, the faint sound of a shaky breath on the other end. "I guess I'm just scared, Mia. Scared of losing you the way we lost Dad. But I know that's not a good enough reason to hold you back. I know you're doing what you believe in."

Mia closed her eyes, letting Lina's words wash over her. The guilt and frustration she'd been carrying seemed to unravel slightly, loosening its grip on her heart. She could almost picture Lina sitting alone in her apartment, staring out the window as she spoke, her expression tight with worry and love.

"I keep thinking about something Dad told me once," Lina continued, her voice barely more than a whisper. "It was a few months before his last expedition. You were away on some research trip—your first one without him, remember?"

Mia nodded, even though she knew Lina couldn't see her. She remembered that trip vividly. It had been a small project in Costa Rica, monitoring the nesting habits of sea turtles. She'd been so excited, so determined to prove she could handle it on her own. Her father had been proud, but she'd sensed a strange undercurrent of tension in his voice when he'd called to wish her luck.

"He told me that he was thinking of leaving fieldwork altogether," Lina said, the words sending a shock through Mia. "He said he'd been gone too much, missed too many birthdays, too many of your milestones. He thought about quitting and taking a more stable position—something that would let him be there for you, for both of us."

Mia's chest tightened painfully, and she sat up straighter, her breath hitching. She'd never known that. Never even suspected that he'd considered stepping away from the work he loved so much. Why hadn't he told her? Why had he kept that decision to himself?

"But then you came back from that trip," Lina went on, her voice gaining a bit of strength, "and you were just... glowing. You talked about the turtles and the ocean and the way the light hit the water at sunrise. And I remember him watching you—really watching you—and afterward, he looked at me and said, 'She's got it. That fire, that passion. I can't take this from her. I can't leave this life if it means she'll think it wasn't worth it.'"

Mia's throat felt tight, the familiar sting of tears building behind her eyes. She took a deep, shaky breath, staring blankly at the darkening sky above. Her father had stayed—continued risking his life in dangerous places, fighting for endangered species—not just for himself, but because he'd seen that same drive in her. He'd stayed for her, to show her that the work mattered.

"I think he wanted to be there more," Lina continued softly, her voice carrying a weight of understanding that pierced through Mia's confusion. "But he knew that if he quit, you'd think it was because it wasn't worth it. He didn't want to extinguish that flame in you. So he kept going, even when it hurt. And I guess... I guess I'm scared you're doing the same thing. Pushing yourself too hard because you think it's what he would have wanted."

Mia closed her eyes, tears slipping silently down her cheeks. *God, Dad... Why didn't you tell me?* She pressed her fingers to her lips, holding back a sob. The realization hit her like a punch—he'd stayed because he believed in her, because he'd wanted her to believe in herself.

"Mia, I just want you to know that it's okay to do this for yourself," Lina whispered. "It's okay to be here because *you* want to be. And it's okay to stop, too. He wouldn't want you to lose yourself out there. Not for him. Not for anyone."

There was another long pause, the faint sound of Lina exhaling slowly. "I love you, sis. Just... be careful, okay? Call me when you can."

The message ended with a soft beep, the silence that followed thick and heavy. Mia stared at the phone, her vision blurred by tears. She drew in a shuddering breath, wiping her eyes with the back of her hand. Her father's smiling face, the one in the photo she carried with her, flashed in her mind's eye. His voice—always so sure, so calm—seemed to whisper in her ear: *This is your journey, Mia. Make it your own.*

She stood slowly, the phone still clutched in her hand, and turned to where Ryan and Amina were now sitting quietly by the fire, their faces reflecting the flickering flames. They looked up as she approached, a question in their eyes.

"Mia?" Amina asked softly. "You okay?"

Mia took another deep breath, her resolve strengthening. "Yeah," she murmured, her voice firmer now. "I just... needed to hear something. I think I understand a little more now."

"About what?" Ryan asked gently.

Mia glanced down at the phone, then back up at them, a small, grateful smile tugging at her lips. "About why I'm really here. And what I'm fighting for."

They didn't press her for more, simply nodded and made space for her to sit down. And as she settled by the fire, the warmth seeping into her bones, Mia knew that she was no longer just chasing her father's dream. She was here because she believed in it too.

For herself.

For them all.

And that made all the difference.

Chapter 11
Secrets of the Jungle

The village was basking in the glow of its recent achievements, and a sense of optimism pervaded every corner. Mia and Ryan, however, knew that resting on their laurels was not an option. They gathered in the central hut with the village leaders and key team members to discuss the next phase of their journey: exploring new opportunities for growth and development.

Mia began the meeting, her voice filled with excitement. "We've made incredible progress in strengthening our village, but we must keep looking forward. There are opportunities out there that can help us grow even more."

Ryan nodded in agreement. "One area we should explore is partnerships with other communities and organizations. By sharing knowledge and resources, we can achieve even greater things."

Temba leaned forward, his eyes thoughtful. "What kind of partnerships are we thinking about, Ryan?"

Ryan smiled, appreciating Temba's curiosity. "For starters, we could partner with agricultural experts to enhance our farming techniques. We can also connect with conservation groups to protect our local wildlife and environment."

Amina, always brimming with ideas, added, "And what about education? We could collaborate with schools and universities to bring more learning opportunities to our village, especially for our children."

Mia nodded enthusiastically. "Exactly. Education is key to our long-term success. We need to equip our young people with the skills and knowledge they need to thrive."

Kato, who had been quietly listening, raised his hand. "Ms. Mia, could we also think about ways to use technology to help us? Like more advanced tools for farming or ways to connect with other villages?"

Mia smiled at his insight. "That's a great idea, Kato. Technology can play a big role in our development. We'll definitely explore that."

Captain Mbani, who had become a trusted advisor and ally, spoke up. "The rangers have connections with various organizations that could be beneficial. I can help facilitate introductions and collaborations."

Mia felt a surge of gratitude. "Thank you, Captain. Your support has been invaluable, and we'd appreciate any help you can provide."

As the meeting continued, the group brainstormed and discussed various ideas, the room buzzing with excitement and possibilities. They knew that these new opportunities could propel their village to new heights.

After the meeting, Mia and Ryan took a walk through the village, discussing their next steps. The air was filled with the sounds of villagers working and children playing, a testament to the vibrant community they had built.

Ryan turned to Mia, his voice filled with determination. "We need to start reaching out to potential partners right away. The sooner we establish these connections, the better."

Mia nodded in agreement. "I'll draft some letters and start making calls. We should also plan visits to nearby villages and organizations to discuss collaborations in person."

As they walked, they passed by the community garden, where Kato and a group of children were tending to the plants. Kato looked up and waved. "Ms. Mia, Mr. Ryan! Come see what we've done!"

Mia and Ryan approached, their hearts swelling with pride at the sight of the thriving garden. "You've all done a fantastic job, Kato," Mia said, kneeling down to inspect the plants. "The garden looks amazing."

Kato beamed. "Thanks, Ms. Mia. We're thinking of adding more types of vegetables and fruits. What do you think?"

Ryan nodded, his eyes twinkling with approval. "That's a great idea, Kato. Diversity in our crops will make our garden even more productive."

As they continued their walk, they stopped by the new tree planting area, where Temba was overseeing a group of villagers. The young trees were growing strong and healthy, a symbol of the village's resilience and growth.

Temba greeted them with a smile. "The trees are doing well, thanks to everyone's hard work. We're creating a sustainable future for our village."

Mia felt a deep sense of fulfillment. "You're right, Temba. And with the new opportunities we're exploring, we can make our village even stronger."

That evening, Mia and Ryan sat together, drafting letters to potential partners and planning their visits to nearby communities. The excitement of new possibilities filled the air, and they knew that their hard work was paving the way for a brighter future.

Ryan looked up from his writing, his expression serious but hopeful. "We're on the brink of something great, Mia. These partnerships could change everything for us."

Mia nodded, her eyes shining with determination. "I believe that, too. We've come so far, and we're just getting started. Together, we can create a future where our village thrives in every way."

As the stars began to twinkle above, Mia felt a renewed sense of purpose. They had faced incredible challenges and come through stronger than ever. With continued vigilance, teamwork, and the unwavering support of their community, they were ready to explore new horizons and build a future filled with promise and possibility.

The next day, Mia and Ryan set out to establish the partnerships they had discussed. Their first stop was a nearby village known for its agricultural innovation. As they arrived, they were greeted warmly by the village leader, a woman named Nia.

Nia smiled, extending her hand. "Welcome, Mia and Ryan. We've heard about the incredible work you've been doing in your village. How can we assist you?"

Mia shook Nia's hand firmly. "Thank you, Nia. We're looking to enhance our farming techniques and thought your village could share some of its expertise. We're also interested in collaborating on sustainable practices."

Nia nodded thoughtfully. "We'd be happy to share our knowledge. Let's start with a tour of our fields and then we can discuss specifics over lunch."

As they walked through the lush fields, Ryan couldn't help but admire the advanced irrigation systems and diverse crops. "Your systems are impressive, Nia. How did you implement such efficient irrigation?"

Nia gestured to a series of solar-powered pumps and drip lines. "We partnered with an environmental organization that provided us with the technology and training. It's made a huge difference in our productivity and sustainability."

Mia turned to Ryan, her eyes lighting up. "This is exactly what we need. Nia, do you think your partners would be interested in working with us as well?"

Nia smiled. "I don't see why not. I can set up a meeting with them. In the meantime, we can start by sharing our techniques and resources."

Over lunch, the three leaders discussed the specifics of their collaboration. "We can send a team to your village to help set up similar irrigation systems," Nia offered. "And perhaps you could share some of your conservation strategies with us."

Ryan nodded enthusiastically. "Absolutely. We've made great strides in reforestation and creating firebreaks. We'd be happy to exchange knowledge."

Mia felt a surge of hope and determination. "This partnership could be the start of something truly transformative for both our communities. Thank you, Nia."

Nia raised her glass in a toast. "To new beginnings and prosperous futures for our villages."

The next day, Mia and Ryan traveled to a nearby town to meet with representatives from an educational organization. They were greeted by Dr. Samuel, a passionate advocate for rural education.

"Thank you for meeting with us, Dr. Samuel," Mia began. "We're looking to expand educational opportunities in our village, particularly in areas like agriculture, technology, and conservation."

Dr. Samuel smiled warmly. "I'm impressed by your vision, Mia. We've been working to bring more resources to rural areas, and your village sounds like a perfect candidate for our programs. What specifically are you looking for?"

Ryan leaned forward, his excitement evident. "We'd love to set up workshops and training sessions for both adults and children. Practical skills, new farming techniques, and environmental education are our main focus areas."

Dr. Samuel nodded. "We can definitely help with that. We have a mobile education unit that can visit your village regularly. We can also provide materials and online resources for ongoing learning."

Mia's eyes sparkled with enthusiasm. "That sounds amazing. Our children are eager to learn, and this would provide them with so many opportunities."

Dr. Samuel smiled. "It's settled then. We'll start planning our first visit. I look forward to working with your community."

As they left the town, Mia and Ryan felt a renewed sense of purpose and excitement. They had laid the groundwork for two significant partnerships, and the future looked brighter than ever.

On their way back to the village, Ryan turned to Mia, his face beaming. "We've accomplished so much in just a few days. These partnerships are going to make a huge difference."

Mia nodded, her heart swelling with pride and determination. "Yes, they will. We're building a future filled with promise and opportunity for everyone in our village."

Upon returning to their village, Mia and Ryan called a meeting with the villagers to share the exciting news. The central hut was filled with eager faces as Mia began to speak.

"We have some wonderful news," Mia announced, her voice brimming with excitement. "We've established partnerships with a nearby village for advanced agricultural techniques and with an educational organization to bring more learning opportunities to our community."

The villagers erupted in applause, their faces glowing with anticipation. Kato raised his hand, his eyes wide with excitement. "Ms. Mia, what kind of new things will we be learning?"

Ryan answered, his voice full of enthusiasm. "We'll have workshops on new farming methods, technology, and conservation. There will be classes for both children and adults, so everyone can benefit."

Juma stood up, his expression filled with gratitude. "This is incredible news. Thank you, Mia and Ryan, for your hard work and dedication. Our village is truly blessed."

Nia, one of the elders, added, "These opportunities will change our lives. We're so proud to be part of this community."

Mia felt a deep sense of fulfillment. "This is just the beginning. With these new partnerships, we'll continue to grow and thrive. Together, we can achieve anything."

As the meeting concluded, the villagers dispersed with renewed energy and excitement. Mia and Ryan stood together, watching as their community came alive with hope and possibility.

"We've laid a strong foundation," Ryan said, his voice filled with pride. "Now it's time to build on it."

Mia nodded, her eyes shining with determination. "And we will. Together, we'll create a future where our village thrives in every way."

As the sun set over the village, casting a warm glow on the faces of the people they had come to love, Mia knew that their journey was far from over. But with their unwavering determination and the support of their new partners, they were ready to face whatever challenges lay ahead. Together, they would continue to build, protect, and grow, ensuring a brighter future for generations to come.

The following days were a whirlwind of activity as the village began to prepare for the arrival of their new partners. The anticipation was palpable, and everyone was eager to contribute to the next phase of their journey. Mia and Ryan were at the center of it all, coordinating efforts and ensuring that everything was in place for the upcoming collaborations.

Mia stood in the central hut, reviewing the plans with Ryan, Temba, and Amina. "We need to make sure we're ready to welcome our new partners and integrate their resources effectively," she said, her voice steady with determination.

Ryan nodded. "I've spoken with Nia from the agricultural village. Their team will arrive tomorrow to help us set up the new irrigation systems and share their farming techniques."

Amina added, "I've also been in touch with Dr. Samuel's team. They'll be here the day after tomorrow with their mobile education unit. We need to prepare a space for their workshops and classes."

Temba looked around the group, his expression serious. "We also need to ensure that the villagers understand the importance of these partnerships. They should be ready to participate and learn."

Mia agreed. "Let's call a village meeting to discuss the upcoming changes and get everyone on the same page."

The village gathered that evening, filling the central clearing with eager faces. Mia addressed them, her voice carrying a sense of excitement and purpose. "We've made incredible progress, but we're about to take a big step forward. Our new partners will be arriving soon to help us with agriculture and education. This is a tremendous opportunity for all of us."

Ryan stepped forward, his voice confident. "The team from Nia's village will help us improve our farming techniques and set up advanced irrigation systems. This will boost our productivity and sustainability."

Amina continued, "And Dr. Samuel's team will bring educational resources and training. There will be workshops and classes for everyone, from children to adults. This is a chance to learn and grow together."

Kato raised his hand, his eyes shining with enthusiasm. "Will there be new things for us to try in the garden, Ms. Mia?"

Mia smiled warmly. "Yes, Kato. We'll be learning new ways to care for our plants and grow even more types of fruits and vegetables."

Juma stood up, his voice filled with gratitude. "This is a wonderful opportunity. We're ready to learn and work hard. Thank you for bringing these partnerships to our village."

Nia, one of the elders, added, "We've always been a strong community. With these new resources, we'll become even stronger."

As the meeting concluded, the villagers dispersed with a renewed sense of purpose. Mia and Ryan continued their preparations late into the night, making sure everything was ready for the arrival of their partners.

The next morning, the team from Nia's village arrived, bringing with them a wealth of knowledge and resources. Mia greeted Nia warmly. "Thank you so much for coming. We're excited to get started."

Nia smiled, looking around at the eager faces of the villagers. "We're happy to be here. Let's begin with a tour of your fields and then we can start setting up the irrigation systems."

As they walked through the fields, Nia explained the advanced techniques they would be implementing. "These drip irrigation systems are highly efficient and will help you conserve water while maximizing crop yields."

Ryan, walking beside them, nodded. "We've been looking forward to this. The more we can learn, the better we'll be able to sustain our community."

The villagers worked alongside Nia's team, eagerly absorbing the new techniques and working hard to implement them. The atmosphere was one of collaboration and mutual respect.

The following day, Dr. Samuel's team arrived with their mobile education unit. Mia and Amina welcomed them warmly. "Thank you for coming, Dr. Samuel. The village is eager to start learning."

Dr. Samuel smiled. "We're excited to be here. We've brought a variety of resources and are ready to start the workshops."

The villagers gathered around the mobile unit, their faces filled with anticipation. Mia addressed them, her voice filled with encouragement. "This is a wonderful opportunity for all of us. Let's make the most of it and learn everything we can."

As the workshops began, the villagers eagerly participated, asking questions and engaging with the material. The atmosphere was electric with the energy of learning and growth.

Mia stood back, watching the scene with a deep sense of fulfillment. She turned to Ryan, her eyes reflecting her pride and hope. "We've built something truly special here, Ryan. These partnerships are just the beginning."

Ryan nodded, his voice filled with determination. "And with these new foundations, we'll continue to grow and thrive. Together, there's nothing we can't achieve."

As the sun set over the village, casting a warm glow on the bustling activity, Mia knew that their journey was far from over. But with the support of their new partners and the unwavering strength of their community, they were ready to face whatever challenges lay ahead. Together, they would build a future filled with promise and possibility.

The village was bustling with the energy of new beginnings as Mia and Ryan walked through the central clearing. The fields were alive with activity as the villagers and the team from Nia's village worked together to implement the new irrigation systems. Nearby, Dr. Samuel's team was setting up for the first educational workshop in the newly prepared space.

Mia turned to Ryan, her voice filled with satisfaction. "It's amazing to see everyone so engaged and eager to learn. These partnerships are already making a difference."

Ryan nodded. "Absolutely. The villagers are soaking up the new techniques and information. It's a testament to their resilience and willingness to adapt."

Just then, Nia approached, her face glowing with pride. "Mia, Ryan, I wanted to show you the progress we've made with the irrigation systems."

They followed Nia to a section of the fields where the new drip irrigation lines had been installed. Water trickled efficiently from the lines, nourishing the plants with precision.

"This is fantastic," Ryan said, examining the system closely. "These lines are going to save so much water and ensure the plants get exactly what they need."

Nia smiled. "It's a simple but effective system. Your team has picked it up quickly. We'll continue to monitor and make adjustments as needed."

Mia turned to the group of villagers working nearby. "How are you finding the new system?"

Juma, standing next to the lines, beamed with pride. "It's incredible, Ms. Mia. The plants are already looking healthier, and we're using much less water. Thank you for bringing this to us."

Ryan clapped Juma on the back. "You're doing great work, Juma. Keep it up, and we'll see the benefits in no time."

Leaving the fields, Mia and Ryan made their way to the educational workshop. Dr. Samuel was addressing a group of children and adults, explaining the basics of soil health and sustainable farming practices.

Mia watched as Kato eagerly raised his hand. "Dr. Samuel, how do we know if the soil is healthy?"

Dr. Samuel smiled, appreciating the question. "That's a great question, Kato. One way is to look at the soil's color and texture. Healthy soil is usually dark and crumbly. You can also do a simple test by putting some soil in a jar of water and seeing how it settles."

Kato's eyes widened with interest. "Can we try that with our soil?"

Dr. Samuel nodded. "Absolutely. After this session, I'll show you how to do it. It's a fun and easy way to learn about your soil."

Mia turned to Amina, who was standing nearby. "These workshops are going to be so beneficial. The villagers are really engaged."

Amina nodded. "Yes, and the children are especially eager to learn. This kind of hands-on education will make a lasting impact."

As the day progressed, Mia and Ryan continued to oversee the various activities, offering support and encouragement wherever needed. The sense of community and collaboration was stronger than ever, and it was clear that the new partnerships were already bearing fruit.

In the evening, the village gathered in the central clearing for a communal meal. The air was filled with laughter and the delicious aroma of food prepared with fresh produce from the garden. Mia stood to address the villagers, her heart full of pride and hope.

"Today has been a remarkable day," she began, her voice carrying over the crowd. "We've taken the first steps towards a brighter future. Our new irrigation systems are in place, and the educational workshops have been a tremendous success. None of this would be possible without the hard work and dedication of each and every one of you."

Ryan stepped forward, his voice filled with gratitude. "We also owe a huge thanks to our new partners. Nia and Dr. Samuel, your teams have brought invaluable knowledge and resources to our village. We're excited to continue working together."

Nia raised her glass, smiling warmly. "To new beginnings and strong partnerships. We're honored to be part of your journey."

Dr. Samuel echoed the sentiment. "And to the future. Together, we'll achieve great things."

The villagers raised their glasses, their voices united in a resounding cheer. "To the future!"

As the meal continued, Mia and Ryan moved through the crowd, talking and laughing with the villagers. The atmosphere was one of celebration and unity, and it was clear that the partnerships were already having a positive impact.

Later that evening, as the stars began to twinkle above, Mia and Ryan stood together at the edge of the clearing, looking out over the village. "We've achieved so much in such a short time," Mia said, her voice filled with awe. "And this is just the beginning."

Ryan nodded, his eyes reflecting the same determination. "We've laid the foundations. Now it's time to build on them and create something truly lasting."

As they stood there, watching the village come alive with hope and promise, Mia knew that their journey was far from over. But with the strength of their community and the support of their new partners, they were ready to face whatever challenges lay ahead. Together, they would continue to build, protect, and grow, ensuring a future filled with promise and possibility for generations to come.

Chapter 12
Tensions Rise

A month had passed since the new partnerships had been established, and the village was thriving. The advanced irrigation systems were working perfectly, the educational workshops were in full swing, and the community spirit had never been stronger. Mia and Ryan knew it was time to evaluate their progress and plan the next steps.

Mia called a meeting with the key leaders and representatives from the partner organizations in the central hut. The atmosphere was one of excitement and pride as everyone gathered to discuss their achievements.

"Thank you all for coming," Mia began, her voice warm and welcoming. "We've made incredible progress over the past month, and it's time to take a step back and evaluate what we've accomplished and where we can improve."

Ryan nodded in agreement. "Let's start with the irrigation systems. Nia, could you give us an update on how they're performing?"

Nia stood, her face beaming with pride. "The systems are working exceptionally well. We've seen a significant increase in crop yields, and the water usage has been reduced by nearly 40%. The villagers have adapted quickly to the new methods, and the fields have never looked better."

Juma, one of the villagers, added, "The new techniques have made such a difference. We're able to grow more food with less effort, and the quality of the produce has improved."

Mia smiled, feeling a surge of pride. "That's wonderful to hear. And how about the educational workshops? Dr. Samuel, what's your assessment?"

Dr. Samuel stood, his expression thoughtful. "The response has been overwhelmingly positive. The villagers are eager to learn, and the children are especially engaged. We've covered a wide range of topics, from soil health to sustainable farming practices. The next step is to introduce more advanced topics and hands-on projects."

Kato raised his hand, his face lit with enthusiasm. "Dr. Samuel showed us how to test the soil, and we've been doing it every week. It's fun and really helps us understand how to take care of our plants."

Amina added, "The educational sessions have brought a new energy to the village. People are not only learning but also sharing knowledge with each other. It's creating a culture of continuous improvement."

Temba nodded. "We've also seen a positive impact on our conservation efforts. The reforestation projects are thriving, and the early warning system for fires has already helped us detect and prevent a small brush fire."

Mia felt a deep sense of satisfaction. "It's clear that these partnerships have brought immense value to our village. But we must continue to look for ways to improve and sustain this progress."

Ryan agreed. "One area we can focus on is expanding our market reach. With increased production, we have the potential to sell surplus produce and generate additional income for the village. We can look into forming cooperatives or partnering with nearby towns."

Nia nodded. "We've had success with cooperatives in our village. I can share our model and help set up something similar here."

Dr. Samuel added, "We can also explore online platforms to sell products. It's a great way to reach a wider audience and increase sales."

Mia looked around the room, feeling a renewed sense of purpose. "These are excellent suggestions. Let's form a committee to explore these opportunities and come up with a plan. We've achieved so much already, and I'm confident we can continue to grow and thrive."

The meeting continued with more ideas and discussions, and by the end, there was a clear plan of action for the coming months. The sense of unity and determination was stronger than ever, and it was clear that the village was on a path to sustained success.

Later that day, as Mia and Ryan walked through the village, they reflected on the journey so far. "We've come a long way, Ryan,"

Mia said, her voice filled with pride. "And we've built something truly special here."

Ryan nodded, his eyes reflecting the same pride. "We have. And with the continued support of our partners and the hard work of our community, the future looks brighter than ever."

Mia smiled, feeling a deep sense of fulfillment. "Together, we've created a place where people can thrive and grow. It's a legacy we can all be proud of."

As they looked out over the bustling village, Mia knew that their journey was far from over. But with the strength of their community and the support of their new partners, they were ready to face whatever challenges lay ahead. Together, they would continue to build, protect, and grow, ensuring a future filled with promise and possibility for generations to come.

The village's progress over the past month had been remarkable, but new challenges were inevitable. As Mia, Ryan, and the villagers gathered for their regular community meeting, the atmosphere was one of cautious optimism. Everyone knew that sustaining their success required constant vigilance and adaptability.

Mia stood at the front of the group, ready to address the gathering. "Thank you all for coming. We've achieved so much together, but we know that our journey is far from over. Today, we need to discuss some new challenges and find solutions to keep moving forward."

Ryan nodded and stepped up beside her. "We've noticed a few areas that need our attention. One of the main issues is pest control. With our increased crop yields, we've also seen a rise in pests that threaten our plants."

Juma raised his hand, his brow furrowed with concern. "We've tried some traditional methods, but they aren't working as well as they used to. What can we do to protect our crops?"

Mia turned to Dr. Samuel, who had joined the meeting. "Dr. Samuel, do you have any advice on effective pest control methods?"

Dr. Samuel nodded, his expression thoughtful. "There are several sustainable pest control techniques we can implement. One effective method is using natural predators to control pest populations. For example, introducing beneficial insects like ladybugs can help keep aphids in check."

Amina chimed in, "We can also use companion planting. Certain plants can repel pests naturally. For instance, planting marigolds around crops can deter nematodes and other harmful insects."

Kato, always eager to learn, raised his hand. "Can we set up a demonstration to show everyone how to use these methods?"

Mia smiled warmly. "That's a great idea, Kato. Dr. Samuel, could you help us organize a workshop on sustainable pest control?"

Dr. Samuel agreed readily. "Of course. We'll set up a demonstration area and teach everyone how to implement these techniques."

Ryan looked around the group, ensuring everyone was following. "Another issue we've encountered is soil fertility. While our crops are thriving, we need to make sure the soil remains healthy and productive."

Temba nodded. "I've noticed that some areas of the fields are starting to show signs of nutrient depletion. We need to address this before it becomes a bigger problem."

Nia, who had experience with soil management, offered her expertise. "We can use crop rotation and organic composting to maintain soil fertility. Rotating different types of crops can prevent nutrient depletion, and composting adds vital nutrients back into the soil."

Mia turned to the villagers. "We can set up a composting station and start a crop rotation plan. This will help keep our soil healthy and ensure continued high yields."

Juma stood again, his face reflecting determination. "We'll need everyone's help to make these changes. But I know we can do it together."

Amina looked thoughtful. "We should also consider testing the soil regularly to monitor its health. This way, we can make adjustments as needed."

Dr. Samuel nodded in agreement. "Soil testing kits are readily available and easy to use. We can include this in our educational sessions to teach everyone how to conduct these tests."

Kato's eyes lit up with enthusiasm. "I'll help with the composting station! And we can make a schedule for soil testing."

Mia smiled, feeling the energy and commitment of the group. "Thank you, Kato. Your enthusiasm is inspiring."

Ryan addressed another concern. "We've also had some issues with water distribution. While the irrigation systems are working well, we need to ensure that all areas of the fields are getting adequate water."

Nia suggested, "We can adjust the placement of the irrigation lines and use moisture sensors to monitor water levels in different areas. This will help us make sure that every part of the field is properly irrigated."

Mia nodded. "Let's make those adjustments and set up a system for regular monitoring."

As the meeting continued, the group discussed various strategies and assigned tasks. The sense of unity and determination was palpable, and everyone was committed to overcoming the new challenges they faced.

Later that day, as Mia and Ryan walked through the village, they reflected on the meeting. "We've got a lot of work ahead, but the villagers are so dedicated," Mia said, her voice filled with pride.

Ryan nodded. "They believe in what we're doing, and that makes all the difference. With everyone working together, I know we can tackle these challenges."

Mia smiled, feeling a deep sense of fulfillment. "We've come a long way, and we'll keep moving forward. Together, we're building a future we can all be proud of."

As they looked out over the bustling village, Mia knew that their journey was far from over. But with the strength of their community and the support of their partners, they were ready to face whatever challenges lay ahead. Together, they would continue to build, protect, and grow, ensuring a future filled with promise and possibility for generations to come.

As the village continued to thrive, Mia and Ryan knew that maintaining strong community bonds was essential for their ongoing success. They decided to host a community day, filled with activities that would not only reinforce their unity but also provide an opportunity to share knowledge and celebrate their achievements.

The day began with a communal breakfast in the central clearing. The villagers gathered, bringing homemade dishes made from the fresh produce of their gardens. The air was filled with the delicious aroma of food and the sounds of laughter and conversation.

Mia stood up to address the crowd, her voice filled with warmth. "Thank you all for coming. Today is about celebrating our hard work and strengthening the bonds that make our village so special. We've achieved so much together, and I'm excited to share this day with all of you."

Ryan stepped forward, a smile on his face. "We have a full day of activities planned, from workshops to games. Let's make the most of it and enjoy the time together."

The first activity was a series of workshops. Dr. Samuel led a session on advanced farming techniques, showing the villagers how to use soil testing kits and implement crop rotation plans. Nia demonstrated the use of natural pest control methods, including the introduction of beneficial insects and companion planting.

Juma raised his hand during Dr. Samuel's workshop. "How often should we test the soil, Dr. Samuel?"

Dr. Samuel replied, "Ideally, you should test the soil at the beginning of each planting season and whenever you notice changes in crop health. Regular testing helps you understand the soil's needs and make necessary adjustments."

Kato, who was helping with the demonstration, added, "It's really easy to do, and the results can help us grow even better crops!"

Mia moved between the groups, feeling proud of how engaged everyone was. She stopped by Amina's workshop, where villagers were learning about composting and sustainable waste management.

Amina explained, "Composting is a great way to recycle organic waste and improve soil fertility. It reduces the need for chemical fertilizers and helps retain moisture in the soil."

One of the villagers, Lila, asked, "What can we compost, and what should we avoid?"

Amina smiled. "You can compost vegetable scraps, fruit peels, coffee grounds, eggshells, and yard waste like grass clippings and leaves. Avoid meat, dairy, and oily foods as they can attract pests and create unpleasant odors."

After the workshops, the villagers gathered for lunch, enjoying the fresh, home-cooked meals. The sense of camaraderie was strong, and it was clear that the day's activities were fostering a deeper connection among the community members.

In the afternoon, it was time for games and team-building activities. Mia and Ryan organized a series of challenges, from relay races to a tug-of-war competition. The villagers participated with enthusiasm, cheering each other on and celebrating every victory.

During a break, Temba approached Mia, a smile on his face. "This has been a great day, Mia. The villagers are not only learning but also having fun together. It's exactly what we needed to strengthen our community bonds."

Mia nodded, her heart swelling with pride. "I'm glad to hear that, Temba. It's important that we take time to celebrate and enjoy each other's company. It makes us stronger."

As the sun began to set, the villagers gathered around a large bonfire. The children roasted marshmallows while the adults shared stories and reflected on the day's events. The atmosphere was one of warmth and unity, and it was clear that the community day had been a resounding success.

Ryan stood up to address the group, his voice filled with gratitude. "Thank you all for making today so special. Our village is strong because of the bonds we share and the hard work we put in together. Let's continue to support each other and build a future we're all proud of."

Mia joined him, her eyes shining with emotion. "We've come a long way, and there's still so much more we can achieve. Together, we can overcome any challenge and create a thriving, sustainable community. Thank you for being part of this journey."

The villagers cheered, their faces glowing in the firelight. As the evening continued, Mia felt a deep sense of fulfillment. The strength of their community bonds was the foundation of their success, and she knew that with this unity, they could face any challenge that came their way.

As the stars twinkled above and the fire crackled warmly, Mia and Ryan stood together, watching the village they had helped to build. Their journey was far from over, but with the unwavering support of their community, they were ready for whatever the future held. Together, they would continue to build, protect, and grow, ensuring a bright future for generations to come.

The success of Community Day had brought the villagers closer together, but Mia and Ryan knew that they couldn't rest on their laurels. As the village continued to grow and develop, they had to think strategically about the future. They decided to hold a planning meeting to discuss long-term goals and ensure that the progress they had made would be sustained.

The meeting took place in the central hut, where the key leaders and representatives from their partner organizations gathered. The atmosphere was one of determination and collaboration.

Mia began the meeting, her voice steady and confident. "Thank you all for coming. We've accomplished so much, but we need to ensure that our success is sustainable. Today, we'll discuss our long-term goals and the steps we need to take to achieve them."

Ryan nodded. "One of our main priorities is expanding our market reach. We've increased our production significantly, and now we need to think about selling our surplus produce to generate additional income for the village."

Nia, who had experience in market expansion, offered her insight. "We can start by forming cooperatives and partnering with nearby towns. This will help us reach more customers and negotiate better prices for our products."

Juma raised his hand. "How do we start forming these cooperatives, Nia?"

Nia smiled. "It's a simple process. We need to organize groups of farmers and producers who can work together. We'll also need to create a management structure and set some guidelines for operation. I can help you with the initial setup."

Mia turned to Dr. Samuel. "What about educational initiatives? How can we continue to provide learning opportunities for our villagers?"

Dr. Samuel nodded thoughtfully. "We can establish a more permanent educational center in the village. This center can host regular workshops and training sessions on various topics, from advanced farming techniques to technology and entrepreneurship."

Amina added, "We can also use the center to provide online courses and resources. This way, our villagers can access a wide range of knowledge and skills."

Kato, always eager to learn, raised his hand. "Can we have a library with books and computers, too?"

Mia smiled warmly at his enthusiasm. "Absolutely, Kato. A library would be a wonderful addition to our educational center."

Ryan then addressed another important aspect. "We also need to focus on infrastructure. While our irrigation systems and housing improvements have made a big difference, we need to ensure that all our infrastructure is sustainable and resilient."

Temba agreed. "We should look into renewable energy sources, like solar panels, to power our village. This will reduce our reliance on external resources and make us more self-sufficient."

Mia nodded. "That's a great idea, Temba. Let's explore options for integrating renewable energy into our infrastructure."

As the discussion continued, the group brainstormed and developed a comprehensive plan for the future. The sense of unity and determination was strong, and everyone was committed to making their vision a reality.

Later that day, as Mia and Ryan walked through the village, they reflected on the meeting. "We've set some ambitious goals, but I know we can achieve them," Mia said, her voice filled with conviction.

Ryan nodded. "The villagers are dedicated and hardworking. With the right support and resources, there's nothing we can't accomplish."

As they approached the community garden, they saw Kato and a group of children tending to the plants. Kato looked up and waved. "Ms. Mia, Mr. Ryan! We've been talking about starting a composting project to make our garden even better."

Mia's eyes lit up with pride. "That's a fantastic idea, Kato. Composting will help improve our soil and reduce waste."

Ryan added, "Let's organize a workshop to teach everyone how to compost effectively. It's a great way to involve the whole community."

As they continued their walk, Mia felt a deep sense of fulfillment. They had laid the groundwork for a bright and sustainable future, and with the continued support of their community and partners, they were ready to achieve their long-term goals.

In the evening, the village gathered for a communal meal, celebrating their achievements and looking forward to the future. Mia stood up to address the crowd, her heart swelling with pride and hope.

"Thank you all for your hard work and dedication. We've accomplished so much together, and our future is bright. Let's continue to support each other and work towards our common goals."

Ryan joined her, his voice filled with determination. "We've shown what we can achieve when we work together. Let's keep this momentum going and build a future we can all be proud of."

The villagers cheered, their faces glowing with enthusiasm and pride. As the evening continued, Mia and Ryan felt a deep sense of connection to their community and a renewed determination to achieve their vision.

Under the starlit sky, Mia knew that their journey was far from over. But with the strength of their community and the support of their partners, they were ready to face whatever challenges lay ahead. Together, they would continue to build, protect, and grow, ensuring a future filled with promise and possibility for generations to come.

Chapter 13
The First Encounter

The momentum from the previous months had not waned. The village was thriving, and with their new long-term goals clearly defined, Mia, Ryan, and the villagers were ready to embark on the next phase of their journey. The excitement was palpable as they gathered in the central hut to kick off the new projects that would drive their future success.

Mia stood before the assembled group, her voice ringing with enthusiasm. "Thank you all for coming. Today, we're launching several new initiatives that will help us achieve our long-term goals. Each project is a crucial step towards a sustainable and prosperous future."

Ryan stepped up beside her, holding a list of the projects. "We'll be focusing on three main areas: expanding our market reach, enhancing our educational opportunities, and improving our infrastructure with renewable energy solutions."

Temba, who had been instrumental in planning the infrastructure improvements, spoke first. "For our renewable energy project, we'll be installing solar panels to power our village. This will reduce our reliance on external energy sources and help us become more self-sufficient."

Mia nodded, adding, "We've identified several key locations for the panels, and we'll need volunteers to help with the installation. This project will make a significant difference in our energy independence."

Nia, who had experience with market expansion, then took the floor. "We're also forming cooperatives to help us sell our surplus produce. By working together, we can reach more customers and negotiate better prices. This will generate additional income for our village."

Juma raised his hand. "How do we get started with the cooperatives, Nia?"

Nia smiled. "We'll begin by organizing groups of farmers and producers. We'll create a management structure and set some guidelines for operation. I'll help with the initial setup and provide ongoing support."

Ryan continued, "And for our educational initiatives, we're establishing a permanent educational center in the village. This center will host regular workshops, training sessions, and provide access to online courses and resources."

Dr. Samuel, who had been crucial in developing the educational programs, added, "We're also setting up a library with books and computers. This will provide a valuable resource for both children and adults to continue learning and growing."

Kato, who had been eagerly listening, asked, "When can we start using the library, Dr. Samuel?"

Dr. Samuel smiled warmly. "We're working on setting it up right now, Kato. It should be ready in a few weeks, and then you can start using it."

Amina, who had been coordinating the various projects, addressed the group. "We'll need everyone's help to make these projects successful. Whether it's volunteering for the solar panel installation, joining a cooperative, or helping set up the library, every contribution is important."

Mia looked around the room, feeling a deep sense of pride and unity. "These projects are a testament to what we can achieve when we work together. Let's make the most of these opportunities and build a future we can all be proud of."

The meeting concluded with a sense of determination and excitement. The villagers dispersed, ready to dive into their new roles and responsibilities.

As Mia and Ryan walked through the village, they could see the enthusiasm in everyone's faces. "It's incredible to see how far we've come," Mia said, her voice filled with pride. "And we're just getting started."

Ryan nodded. "The villagers are committed and hardworking. With the new projects, we're setting the foundation for long-term success."

They stopped by the site where the solar panels would be installed. Temba was already there, organizing a group of volunteers. "We'll start with the main building and then move on to the other key locations," he explained.

Mia smiled. "Thank you, Temba. This project is going to make a big difference in our energy independence."

Next, they visited the area designated for the educational center and library. Dr. Samuel and a group of villagers were busy setting up shelves and unpacking books. Kato was there too, helping organize the materials.

Mia approached Dr. Samuel. "How's the setup going?"

Dr. Samuel looked up, his eyes shining with enthusiasm. "It's going well. The villagers are eager to help, and we should have everything ready soon. This center will be a hub for learning and growth."

Ryan turned to Kato. "Are you excited about the library?"

Kato nodded vigorously. "Yes, Mr. Ryan! I can't wait to start reading and using the computers."

As the day went on, Mia and Ryan continued to check in on the various projects, offering support and encouragement. The sense of community and collaboration was stronger than ever, and it was clear that the village was on the right path.

That evening, as the sun set over the bustling village, Mia and Ryan reflected on the day's progress. "We've laid the groundwork for a bright future," Mia said, her voice filled with hope. "And with the continued dedication of our community, there's nothing we can't achieve."

Ryan smiled, his eyes reflecting the same determination. "Together, we'll build a future that's sustainable, prosperous, and filled with opportunity."

As the stars began to twinkle above, Mia knew that their journey was far from over. But with the strength of their community and the support of their partners, they were ready to face whatever challenges lay ahead. Together, they would continue to build, protect, and grow, ensuring a future filled with promise and possibility for generations to come.

As the new projects got underway, the village buzzed with activity and excitement. However, with progress came challenges, and the villagers quickly found themselves navigating unexpected obstacles. Mia and Ryan were determined to address these issues head-on to ensure the success of their initiatives.

One of the first challenges emerged with the installation of the solar panels. As Temba and his team worked on setting up the panels, they encountered difficulties with the wiring and positioning. Mia and Ryan arrived on the scene to assess the situation.

Temba greeted them with a determined look. "We're having trouble with the wiring, Mia. Some of the connections aren't holding, and we're not getting the expected output."

Ryan examined the setup closely. "It looks like we might need some additional equipment to secure the connections properly. Let's make a list of what we need and see if we can source it quickly."

Mia nodded. "We can't afford delays. Temba, can you coordinate with our partners to get the necessary equipment? In the meantime, let's keep working on the panels we can install without issues."

Temba agreed. "I'll handle it, Mia. We'll make sure the project stays on track."

As Temba and his team continued their work, Mia and Ryan moved to the site of the educational center. Here, they faced a different challenge: the logistics of setting up the library and ensuring that the materials were properly organized and accessible.

Dr. Samuel was overseeing the setup, a look of mild frustration on his face. "We've received a lot of books and equipment, but we're having trouble organizing everything efficiently. We need a better system."

Mia approached him, her expression thoughtful. "Let's break it down into smaller tasks. We can assign different groups to handle specific sections—one for books, one for computers, and another for educational materials."

Ryan suggested, "And maybe we can get some of the older children involved. It's a great learning opportunity for them and helps spread the workload."

Dr. Samuel nodded, a smile returning to his face. "That's a great idea. Let's get everyone organized and tackle this systematically."

As the villagers divided into groups and began working on their assigned tasks, the sense of collaboration and community grew even stronger. Kato, leading a group of children, was especially enthusiastic about organizing the computer area.

"We're setting up the computers in a way that makes them easy to use," Kato explained to Mia. "Each one will have a list of educational websites and programs."

Mia smiled. "That's excellent, Kato. Your efforts will make a big difference for everyone using the library."

While the solar panel and educational center projects faced their initial hurdles, the cooperative formation for market expansion also encountered some challenges. Nia was meeting with a group of farmers to discuss the cooperative structure and guidelines.

One of the farmers, Juma, voiced his concerns. "I understand the benefits of a cooperative, but how do we ensure fair distribution of profits and responsibilities?"

Nia addressed his concern with patience. "We'll establish clear guidelines and a management structure to ensure transparency and fairness. Each member will have a say in the decisions, and we'll rotate leadership roles to distribute responsibilities."

Mia added, "We're in this together, Juma. The success of the cooperative depends on mutual trust and cooperation. Let's take it step by step and make sure everyone feels heard and valued."

With these reassurances, the farmers began to see the potential benefits more clearly, and their initial hesitation started to fade.

As the day drew to a close, Mia and Ryan gathered with the village leaders to review the progress and address any remaining concerns. The atmosphere was one of determination and optimism, despite the challenges they had faced.

"We've made good progress today," Mia began, her voice strong and confident. "We encountered some obstacles, but we tackled them together and found solutions."

Ryan nodded. "The key is to stay adaptable and support each other. We'll continue to face challenges, but with our collective effort, we can overcome them."

Temba, speaking for the solar panel team, added, "We've made arrangements to get the additional equipment we need. The project is back on track."

Dr. Samuel reported on the educational center. "Thanks to everyone's help, we're well-organized now. The library should be fully operational soon."

Nia concluded, "The cooperative discussions are moving forward. We're addressing concerns and building a strong foundation for our market expansion."

Mia looked around at her team, feeling a deep sense of pride and unity. "We're on the right path. Let's keep pushing forward and supporting each other. Together, we'll achieve our goals and build a thriving, sustainable future."

As the stars began to twinkle in the evening sky, the villagers dispersed with renewed energy and determination. Mia knew that their journey was far from over, but with the strength of their community and the support of their partners, they were ready to face whatever challenges lay ahead. Together, they would continue to build, protect, and grow, ensuring a future filled with promise and possibility for generations to come.

The village had made significant strides in their new projects, but with progress came inevitable setbacks. As they tackled the challenges head-on, the community's resilience and determination shone through.

One morning, Mia and Ryan were informed of a problem with the newly installed solar panels. They quickly headed to the site, where Temba and his team were working.

Temba greeted them with a serious expression. "We've encountered an issue with the solar panels. Some of the connections are faulty, and it's affecting the overall output."

Mia looked at the array of panels, her mind racing with potential solutions. "What do we need to fix it?"

Temba replied, "We need replacement connectors and some additional tools. I've already contacted our partners, but it might take a few days to get everything."

Ryan nodded. "In the meantime, can we work on the panels that are functioning properly and ensure they're optimized?"

Temba agreed. "Yes, we can focus on maximizing the output from the panels that are working. We'll make sure everything else is ready for when the replacements arrive."

Mia addressed the team. "Let's keep pushing forward. We've come this far, and we'll overcome this setback too."

Later that day, Mia and Ryan visited the educational center to check on its progress. Dr. Samuel greeted them with a look of concern. "We've run into a problem with the internet connection for the computers. It's unstable, and we're struggling to set up the online courses."

Mia frowned, considering their options. "Have we reached out to the service provider? Maybe they can send a technician to help us stabilize the connection."

Dr. Samuel nodded. "I've contacted them, but it might take a while. In the meantime, we're trying to find temporary solutions."

Ryan suggested, "Can we download some of the course materials for offline use? That way, we can continue the workshops without relying on the internet."

Dr. Samuel smiled. "That's a great idea, Ryan. We'll start downloading the materials immediately."

As they left the educational center, Kato ran up to them, his face filled with excitement. "Ms. Mia, Mr. Ryan, we've finished setting up the composting station! Come see!"

Mia and Ryan followed Kato to the new composting area, where a group of children and villagers were busy turning the compost and adding organic waste.

Amina, overseeing the project, greeted them with a proud smile. "The composting project is off to a great start. Everyone is enthusiastic about it, and we're already seeing some good results."

Mia praised their efforts. "This is fantastic, Amina. Composting will make a big difference in our soil quality and waste management."

Ryan added, "Great job, everyone. Keep up the good work."

As the day continued, Mia and Ryan moved from one project to another, addressing concerns and providing support. Despite the setbacks, the village's determination remained unshaken.

In the evening, a village meeting was held to review the progress and discuss the challenges they faced. The central hut was filled with villagers eager to share their thoughts and find solutions together.

Mia began the meeting, her voice filled with encouragement. "We've made incredible progress, but we've also encountered some setbacks. It's important that we face these challenges together and find ways to overcome them."

Ryan spoke next. "With the solar panels, we've identified the faulty connections and are waiting for replacements. In the meantime, we're optimizing the panels that are working."

Temba added, "We're also making sure that everything is ready for when the new connectors arrive. We'll be back on track soon."

Dr. Samuel addressed the issue with the educational center. "We're working on stabilizing the internet connection, but in the meantime, we're downloading course materials for offline use. The workshops will continue without interruption."

Kato raised his hand, his face serious. "What about the library? Can we still use it even if the internet is down?"

Dr. Samuel smiled. "Yes, Kato. The library is still available, and we have plenty of books and offline resources you can use."

Juma spoke up, his voice steady. "We've faced challenges before and overcome them. We can do it again. Let's keep working together and supporting each other."

Mia felt a surge of pride. "Exactly, Juma. We're a strong community, and together, we can overcome any obstacle."

The villagers nodded in agreement, their faces reflecting determination and unity. The meeting concluded with a renewed sense of purpose and resolve.

As Mia and Ryan walked back to their quarters, they reflected on the day's events. "We've faced some tough challenges, but the villagers' spirit is unbreakable," Mia said, her voice filled with pride.

Ryan nodded. "They believe in what we're doing, and that makes all the difference. Together, we can overcome anything."

As the stars twinkled above, Mia knew that their journey was far from over. But with the strength of their community and the support of their partners, they were ready to face whatever challenges lay ahead. Together, they would continue to build, protect, and grow, ensuring a future filled with promise and possibility for generations to come.

The village had faced and overcome several setbacks with determination and resilience. As the projects began to stabilize and show promise, Mia and Ryan decided it was time to celebrate the small wins. They knew that recognizing these achievements would boost morale and reinforce the community's commitment to their long-term goals.

One evening, Mia called for a gathering in the central clearing. Lanterns were hung around, creating a warm and festive atmosphere. The villagers arrived, their faces filled with curiosity and anticipation.

Mia stood before them, her voice ringing with pride and enthusiasm. "Thank you all for coming. We've faced challenges and setbacks, but we've also achieved so much. Tonight, we're here to celebrate our small wins and the progress we've made together."

Ryan stepped forward, holding a list of achievements. "Let's start with the solar panels. Despite the initial issues, we've successfully optimized the panels that are working, and we've reduced our energy costs significantly. Temba and his team deserve a huge round of applause for their hard work."

The villagers clapped and cheered, and Temba stood, a humble smile on his face. "Thank you, everyone. We couldn't have done it without your support and determination."

Mia continued, "Next, our educational center and library. Dr. Samuel and his team have done an incredible job setting it up. The workshops have continued without interruption, thanks to the offline resources. Kato and the children have also been instrumental in organizing the materials."

Dr. Samuel stood, his expression proud. "The enthusiasm and eagerness to learn have been amazing. This is just the beginning of what we can achieve together."

Kato, standing beside him, beamed with pride. "We love the library! It's so much fun to learn new things."

Ryan added, "And our composting project, led by Amina, is off to a great start. The compost is already improving our soil quality, and the waste management has become more efficient."

Amina stood, her voice filled with gratitude. "This project has shown us the power of sustainability and community effort. Thank you all for your participation and support."

Mia smiled, feeling the unity and strength of their community. "We've accomplished all this because we believe in each other and our vision for the future. Let's keep this momentum going and continue to support each other."

As the celebration continued, the villagers enjoyed a communal meal, sharing stories and laughter. Mia and Ryan moved through the crowd, talking to everyone and soaking in the positive energy.

Temba approached them, holding a plate of food. "Mia, Ryan, this celebration is exactly what we needed. It's a great reminder of why we're doing all this."

Mia nodded, her eyes reflecting her pride. "Absolutely, Temba. Recognizing our achievements, no matter how small, keeps us motivated and united."

Ryan added, "We've got a long road ahead, but with this community, there's nothing we can't achieve."

As they continued to mingle, Dr. Samuel pulled Mia aside. "I wanted to discuss some ideas for expanding our educational programs. The villagers are eager to learn more, and I think we can introduce more advanced topics soon."

Mia's face lit up. "That sounds fantastic, Dr. Samuel. Let's schedule a meeting to plan the next phase of our educational initiatives."

Kato ran up to them, holding a book. "Ms. Mia, look at this! I found a book about plants that glow in the dark. Do you think we can grow some here?"

Mia laughed, her heart warmed by Kato's enthusiasm. "That sounds fascinating, Kato. We can definitely look into it."

As the evening went on, the atmosphere remained lively and joyful. The villagers danced and sang, celebrating their progress and looking forward to the future.

At the end of the night, Mia stood with Ryan, Temba, and Dr. Samuel, watching the villagers enjoy themselves. "This is what it's all about," she said softly. "Building a community that supports and uplifts each other."

Ryan nodded, his voice filled with determination. "And we'll keep doing that, every step of the way."

Dr. Samuel agreed. "We've created a foundation that will carry us through any challenge. I'm excited for what's to come."

Temba smiled, looking around at the happy faces. "We're a family, and together, we'll achieve great things."

As the stars twinkled above and the celebration continued, Mia felt a deep sense of fulfillment. They had come a long way, and there was still much to do, but with the strength of their community and the support of their partners, they were ready for whatever lay ahead. Together, they would continue to build, protect, and grow, ensuring a future filled with promise and possibility for generations to come.

Chapter 14
Strategies and Sacrifices

The festive energy from the celebration carried over into the next morning. The villagers were eager to continue their work, inspired by the progress they had made and the recognition they had received. Mia and Ryan knew it was the perfect time to set new, ambitious goals for the future.

Mia gathered the village leaders and key team members in the central hut. The atmosphere was one of excitement and determination. She began the meeting with a confident smile. "We've achieved so much together, but there's always room for growth. Today, we're going to set new goals that will push us to new heights and ensure our community continues to thrive."

Ryan stepped forward, holding a chart with various potential projects. "We've identified several areas where we can expand and improve. These include enhancing our agricultural practices, increasing our market reach, further developing our educational programs, and improving our infrastructure."

Amina, who had been instrumental in the composting project, spoke up. "For agriculture, I think we can explore more sustainable farming techniques. Crop rotation has been successful, but we can also look into agroforestry and integrating livestock to create a more balanced ecosystem."

Juma nodded in agreement. "I've heard about agroforestry and how it can improve soil health and increase biodiversity. It sounds like a great idea."

Temba added, "We should also consider expanding our irrigation systems to cover more areas. This will ensure all our crops get the water they need, especially during dry seasons."

Mia turned to Nia, who had been leading the cooperative efforts. "Nia, how can we enhance our market reach further?"

Nia replied, "We can start by building stronger relationships with neighboring villages and towns. Setting up regular market days will help us sell more produce. We can also look into online platforms to reach a wider audience."

Ryan nodded. "That sounds promising. Let's also consider diversifying our products. We can start producing value-added items like jams, dried fruits, and herbal teas. This will increase our income and attract more customers."

Dr. Samuel, who was always thinking about education, chimed in. "On the educational front, we can introduce vocational training programs. These programs can teach practical skills like carpentry, sewing, and mechanics, which will help villagers find additional sources of income."

Kato, sitting attentively, raised his hand. "Can we have more science workshops too? I want to learn more about how things work and maybe even do some experiments."

Mia smiled warmly at Kato. "Absolutely, Kato. Science workshops will be a great addition. We'll make sure they're fun and educational."

Ryan addressed the final area of focus. "For infrastructure, we've already made great strides with the solar panels and irrigation systems. Let's also consider building more community facilities, like a health center and a marketplace. These will improve our quality of life and support our economic activities."

The group discussed each idea in detail, assigning tasks and creating timelines. The sense of unity and purpose was stronger than ever, and it was clear that everyone was committed to achieving these new goals.

As the meeting concluded, Mia felt a surge of pride and determination. "We have ambitious goals, but I have no doubt that we can achieve them. Let's continue to work together, support each other, and build a brighter future for our village."

Later that day, Mia and Ryan walked through the village, discussing the plans in more detail. "These goals are ambitious, but they're exactly what we need to keep moving forward," Mia said, her voice filled with confidence.

Ryan agreed. "The villagers are ready for the challenge. We've built a strong foundation, and now it's time to reach even higher."

They stopped by the educational center, where Dr. Samuel was preparing for the next workshop. "Dr. Samuel, how soon can we start the vocational training programs?" Mia asked.

Dr. Samuel looked up, his eyes shining with enthusiasm. "We can start planning immediately. I'll reach out to some contacts who can help us develop the curriculum and find instructors."

Ryan added, "We can also involve some of the villagers who have skills in these areas. They can teach and share their knowledge."

As they continued their walk, they visited the fields where the irrigation systems were being expanded. Temba and his team were hard at work, ensuring that the new lines were properly installed.

"Temba, how's the expansion going?" Ryan asked.

Temba wiped his brow and smiled. "It's going well. We're making good progress, and the new areas will be ready for planting soon."

Mia felt a deep sense of satisfaction. "This is exactly what we need. Every step we take brings us closer to our goals."

As the sun began to set, casting a golden glow over the village, Mia and Ryan reflected on the day's progress. They knew that the road ahead would be challenging, but with the strength and unity of their community, they were ready to face whatever came their way.

"We've set ambitious goals," Mia said softly, her eyes reflecting determination. "But together, we can achieve anything."

Ryan nodded, his voice filled with confidence. "Together, we'll build a future that's sustainable, prosperous, and filled with opportunity for everyone."

As the stars twinkled above, Mia felt a renewed sense of purpose. Their journey was far from over, but with their unwavering commitment and the support of their community, they were ready to embrace new horizons and continue building a brighter future for generations to come.

The village's new goals infused everyone with energy and determination, but as they started implementing their plans, unexpected obstacles arose. Mia and Ryan knew that facing these challenges head-on would be crucial to their success.

One morning, Mia received troubling news from Temba. They met in the central hut to discuss the issue.

Temba's face was tense. "Mia, we've run into a problem with the irrigation expansion. Some of the new lines are leaking, and we're losing a lot of water."

Mia frowned. "Do we know why they're leaking? Could it be a problem with the installation?"

Temba nodded. "It looks like it. We didn't account for the pressure changes with the additional lines. We'll need to reconfigure the system and possibly get some new parts."

Ryan, who had been listening, spoke up. "Let's prioritize fixing the leaks. We can't afford to lose water, especially with the new crops coming in. Temba, can you make a list of the parts we need? I'll contact our suppliers and see if we can expedite the order."

Temba agreed. "I'll get on it right away. We'll also start working on reconfiguring the existing lines to reduce the pressure."

Mia added, "Make sure to keep the team informed. We need everyone on the same page to fix this quickly."

Later that day, Mia and Ryan visited the educational center to check on the progress of the new vocational training programs. Dr. Samuel greeted them with a concerned look.

"We've hit a snag with the vocational training," Dr. Samuel said. "Some of the instructors we planned to bring in are unavailable due to scheduling conflicts. We're short on teachers for several key courses."

Mia sighed, considering their options. "Can we find other qualified instructors? Maybe reach out to neighboring communities or even look online for remote teaching options?"

Dr. Samuel nodded. "I've already started reaching out, but it might take some time. We could also train some of our own villagers to become instructors, but that will require additional resources and time."

Ryan suggested, "What if we start with the courses we can cover and gradually introduce the others as we find instructors? This way, we won't delay the entire program."

Dr. Samuel smiled, relieved. "That's a good plan. I'll reorganize the schedule and focus on the courses we can start immediately."

As they left the educational center, Kato ran up to them, looking worried. "Ms. Mia, Mr. Ryan, some of the books in the library are missing pages. We didn't notice it at first, but now it's becoming a problem."

Mia knelt down to Kato's level. "Thank you for telling us, Kato. We'll look into it right away. It's important that we have complete and accurate materials."

Ryan looked thoughtful. "We should do a thorough inventory of the library. Let's gather a team to check all the books and make a list of the ones that need replacing."

Mia smiled at Kato. "Would you like to help us with that, Kato? You're always so good at organizing things."

Kato nodded enthusiastically. "Yes, I'd love to help!"

As they walked back to the village center, Mia and Ryan discussed the challenges they were facing. "We've hit quite a few obstacles," Mia said, her voice tinged with concern. "But I'm confident we can overcome them."

Ryan nodded. "We've faced tough situations before, and we've always found a way through. It's about staying focused and working together."

That evening, Mia called a village meeting to update everyone on the progress and challenges. The villagers gathered, their faces reflecting a mix of determination and concern.

Mia addressed the group. "We've made significant progress, but we're also facing some unexpected obstacles. Our irrigation system needs reconfiguring, we're short on instructors for the vocational training, and some of our library books need replacing."

Ryan added, "We're working on solutions for each of these issues. Temba is fixing the irrigation leaks, and Dr. Samuel is reorganizing the training schedule. We'll also do a full inventory of the library to address the missing pages."

Juma stood up, his voice steady. "We're with you, Mia and Ryan. Just tell us what we need to do to help."

Amina spoke up. "We can form teams to handle each problem. I'll help with the library inventory. We can get it done quickly if we all pitch in."

Temba nodded. "And I'll keep everyone updated on the irrigation repairs. We'll need all hands on deck to get it done efficiently."

Dr. Samuel added, "I'll focus on finding new instructors and setting up the initial courses. If anyone knows someone who can teach, please let me know."

Mia felt a surge of gratitude and pride. "Thank you all for your support. We'll get through this together, just as we always have. Let's stay focused and keep pushing forward."

The villagers nodded in agreement, their resolve clear. As the meeting concluded, Mia and Ryan felt reassured by the community's unwavering commitment.

Walking back to their quarters, Mia turned to Ryan. "We're facing some tough challenges, but the villagers' spirit is unbreakable."

Ryan smiled. "They believe in our vision, Mia. With their support, there's nothing we can't overcome."

As the stars began to twinkle above, Mia knew their journey was far from over. But with the strength of their community and the support of their partners, they were ready to face whatever challenges lay ahead. Together, they would continue to build, protect, and grow, ensuring a future filled with promise and possibility for generations to come.

The days that followed were filled with a flurry of activity as the villagers rallied to address the issues they were facing. The sense of unity and determination was palpable, and Mia and Ryan worked tirelessly alongside the villagers to ensure that their projects stayed on track.

Mia was in the field with Temba, inspecting the reconfigured irrigation lines. "How are the new adjustments holding up?" she asked, her voice filled with curiosity.

Temba wiped his brow and smiled. "Much better. The leaks have been significantly reduced, and we've managed to optimize the pressure across all the lines. It looks like we're back on track."

"That's great news," Mia said, relief evident in her voice. "Your hard work is paying off."

Meanwhile, Ryan was at the educational center with Dr. Samuel, helping to organize the first set of vocational training classes. "We've managed to secure a few more instructors," Dr. Samuel said. "They'll cover some of the courses we were missing."

Ryan nodded, looking at the schedule. "That's fantastic. Let's get these classes up and running. The sooner we start, the better."

As the village continued to address their challenges, they also made progress on the library inventory. Amina and Kato were busy checking each book for completeness.

"Kato, how many books have we checked so far?" Amina asked, glancing at the growing pile of inspected books.

Kato looked up, his face lit with enthusiasm. "We've checked almost half of them. We found a few more with missing pages, but most of them are in good condition."

"That's excellent work," Amina praised. "Let's keep going. We'll have this done in no time."

One evening, Mia and Ryan called a village-wide meeting to update everyone on their progress and celebrate the collective efforts. The villagers gathered in the central clearing, eager to hear the latest news.

Mia began the meeting with a smile. "I'm proud to say that we've made significant progress in addressing our challenges. Thanks to Temba and his team, the irrigation system is now functioning optimally."

The villagers applauded, and Temba nodded appreciatively.

Ryan continued, "We've also secured more instructors for the vocational training program. Classes will start next week, and we're excited to see everyone participate."

Dr. Samuel added, "The library inventory is nearly complete. Thank you to everyone who helped with this important task. We'll replace the missing pages soon."

Juma stood up, his voice filled with pride. "We've faced some tough challenges, but we've come through stronger. This community is amazing."

Amina spoke up, "It's inspiring to see everyone working together. We're proving that there's nothing we can't achieve when we unite."

Mia looked around at the faces of the villagers, feeling a deep sense of pride and connection. "We've accomplished so much, and we'll continue to push forward. Together, we'll build a future that's sustainable and prosperous for all."

The villagers cheered, their spirits high. The meeting concluded with a communal meal, celebrating their achievements and looking forward to the future.

Later that night, as Mia and Ryan walked through the village, they reflected on the day's events. "The villagers' resilience and determination are incredible," Mia said, her voice filled with admiration.

Ryan nodded. "They believe in our vision, and that makes all the difference. With their support, there's nothing we can't overcome."

As they approached their quarters, Mia turned to Ryan, her eyes reflecting hope and determination. "We've set ambitious goals, but we're on the right path. Together, we'll achieve them."

Ryan smiled, his voice filled with confidence. "Absolutely. The strength of this community is our greatest asset."

As the stars twinkled above, Mia knew their journey was far from over. But with the strength of their community and the unwavering support of their partners, they were ready to face whatever challenges lay ahead. Together, they would continue to build, protect, and grow, ensuring a future filled with promise and possibility for generations to come.

The village continued to thrive as they tackled their challenges head-on, and the progress they made was evident. However, Mia and Ryan knew that to sustain their growth, they needed to ensure that every villager felt included and valued. They decided to hold a community forum where everyone could voice their ideas and concerns.

The central clearing was filled with villagers of all ages, eager to participate. Mia stood at the front, her voice carrying the warmth of her determination. "Thank you all for coming. Today is about hearing from each of you. We want to make sure everyone has a voice in our future."

Ryan nodded. "We've come a long way, but we can always improve. Your input is crucial to our continued success."

Nia, who had been instrumental in the market expansion, was the first to speak. "I think we should look into diversifying our products even more. Maybe we can start making crafts or other handmade goods to sell alongside our produce."

Mia smiled. "That's a great idea, Nia. Expanding our product line can attract more customers and provide additional income."

Juma raised his hand. "We've been talking about setting up a cooperative store where we can sell all our products. This way, we can manage sales better and ensure fair prices."

Ryan agreed. "A cooperative store would be a fantastic addition. It would give us more control over our market and help build our brand."

Dr. Samuel stood up next. "On the educational front, I think we should introduce more advanced courses for the children. They're eager to learn, and we have the resources to challenge them further."

Kato, who was sitting attentively, raised his hand. "Can we have science experiments? I want to learn how to make things and understand how they work."

Mia laughed softly. "Of course, Kato. Science experiments will be a fun and educational addition. We'll make sure to include them."

Amina spoke up. "I've been thinking about our waste management. The composting project has been great, but we can do more. Maybe we can start recycling programs and reduce our waste even further."

Mia nodded. "That's a wonderful idea, Amina. Recycling can help us manage our resources more efficiently and keep our environment clean."

Temba added, "We should also think about improving our infrastructure even more. Better roads and pathways can make it easier to transport our goods and move around the village."

Ryan agreed. "Infrastructure improvements are definitely important. Let's prioritize the areas that need the most attention and start planning."

As the forum continued, more villagers shared their ideas and concerns. Each suggestion was met with thoughtful consideration, and it was clear that everyone was committed to the village's success.

Mia looked around the clearing, feeling a deep sense of pride and unity. "We've heard so many great ideas today. It's clear that our community is full of innovative and passionate people. Let's work together to make these ideas a reality."

Ryan added, "Your input is invaluable. We'll take all these suggestions into account as we plan our next steps. Together, we'll build a future that reflects the collective vision of our community."

After the forum, Mia and Ryan gathered with the village leaders to discuss the next steps. The atmosphere was filled with optimism and determination.

Mia began, "We've received a lot of great feedback today. Our next task is to prioritize these ideas and start implementing them. Let's divide into smaller teams to tackle each project."

Ryan nodded. "We'll need to set clear goals and timelines for each project. This way, we can monitor our progress and ensure that we're moving forward efficiently."

Nia spoke up. "I can lead the effort to diversify our products and set up the cooperative store. I'll work with the farmers and crafters to get everything organized."

Dr. Samuel added, "I'll focus on expanding our educational programs. We'll introduce more advanced courses and start planning for the science experiments."

Amina volunteered, "I'll take charge of the recycling initiative. We can start by educating everyone about what can be recycled and setting up collection points."

Temba said, "I'll oversee the infrastructure improvements. We'll start by assessing the current state of our roads and pathways and prioritize the areas that need the most work."

Mia smiled, feeling a surge of hope and determination. "Thank you all for stepping up. Together, we can achieve anything."

As they left the meeting, Mia and Ryan walked through the village, reflecting on the day's events. "We've set ambitious goals, but with everyone working together, I know we can achieve them," Mia said, her voice filled with conviction.

Ryan nodded. "The villagers are motivated and united. That's our greatest strength. We'll face any challenge and come out stronger."

As they approached their quarters, Mia turned to Ryan, her eyes reflecting hope and determination. "We're building something truly special here, Ryan. A future that's sustainable, prosperous, and filled with opportunity for everyone."

Ryan smiled, his voice filled with confidence. "And we'll continue to build it together, every step of the way."

As the stars began to twinkle above, Mia knew their journey was far from over. But with the strength of their community and the unwavering support of their partners, they were ready to face whatever challenges lay ahead. Together, they would continue to build, protect, and grow, ensuring a future filled with promise and possibility for generations to come.

Chapter 15
Logistical and Environmental Challenges

The oppressive humidity weighed down on the group as they gathered around their dwindling stash of food supplies. Mia crouched beside the opened crate, frowning as she took inventory of their rations. A few crumpled bags of dehydrated meals, a small stack of protein bars, and a handful of sealed water bottles—it wasn't nearly enough for the days they still had ahead of them.

"This can't be right," she murmured, shaking her head. "We had at least two weeks' worth when we set out. What happened?"

Amina knelt beside her, her expression grim. "It's the poachers. They raided the cache at our last campsite. Must have taken what they could and ruined the rest. I found some torn packaging in the underbrush. They knew exactly what they were doing."

"Great," Ryan muttered from where he leaned against a nearby tree, his arms crossed tightly over his chest. "Just what we needed. First they set traps, now they're starving us out. Classic guerrilla tactics."

Kato hovered at the edge of the clearing, glancing nervously between them. "So, what do we do? We can't just go back empty-handed. There's still so much to document, and we're getting close to finding their main camp."

Mia stood up, brushing the dirt from her knees. "I know, Kato, but we also can't push forward if we're running on empty. We're going to have to figure something out—fast."

Amina nodded thoughtfully. "We could try foraging. There's bound to be some edible plants around here. And I've seen signs of small game. We could set up some traps, catch a few rabbits or birds."

Mia hesitated, glancing at the map spread out on the ground. "But that would take time. Time we don't have. Every hour we spend hunting and foraging is an hour we're not getting closer to stopping those poachers."

"We don't have a choice," Ryan interjected, his tone firm. "Mia, look at what we've got." He gestured to the meager pile of food, a frown creasing his forehead. "That's not even enough for two days if we ration it strictly. We're already cutting back on water intake to make it last. If we don't replenish our supplies, we'll be too weak to continue."

"But—"

"Ryan's right," Amina said softly, placing a hand on Mia's shoulder. "I know you want to keep moving, but we won't make it if we're dehydrated and starving. We have to take care of ourselves if we want to have any chance of stopping them."

Mia's shoulders sagged, the weight of the decision pressing down on her like a physical force. She knew they were right, but every second they spent off-track felt like a concession to the poachers—like admitting defeat, even if only temporarily.

She rubbed her temples, trying to think clearly. "Okay. Fine. We'll split up for a few hours. Amina, you take Kato and search the area for edible plants and anything else we can use. Ryan and I will scout further down the riverbank and set up a few traps for small game."

Kato's eyes lit up with a mix of relief and determination. "I can help with foraging. My grandmother taught me a lot about identifying plants back home. I can show you some that we used to cook with, Amina."

"Good," Amina said, giving him a quick smile. "We'll stick close to the camp and see what we can find."

Ryan straightened, pushing off the tree and rolling his shoulders. "I'll get the snares ready. There's a small game trail a bit to the west of here. If we're lucky, we'll have something caught by morning."

Mia nodded, forcing herself to focus. "Be careful, both of you. Stay within radio range, and if you see or hear anything out of the ordinary, call it in immediately."

Amina and Kato gave her reassuring nods, then turned and headed into the jungle, their footsteps soon swallowed by the dense underbrush. Mia watched them disappear, worry gnawing at her. She turned to Ryan, who was already busy tying snares and setting up traps with practiced ease.

"I hate this," she murmured, frustration bleeding into her voice. "I hate that we're losing time because of something I should've been able to prevent. I should've hidden the supplies better or set up a watch rotation or—"

"Mia, stop." Ryan's voice was gentle but firm as he looked up at her, his gaze steady. "This isn't your fault. The poachers knew what they were doing. They've been in this jungle longer than we have. You can't blame yourself for every setback."

"But I do," Mia whispered, dropping her gaze. "I'm supposed to lead this team, and I keep making mistakes. If we don't find their camp soon, if something happens to any of you because of my decisions..."

Ryan stood, closing the distance between them in two strides. "Hey." He placed a hand on her shoulder, squeezing gently. "Survival isn't about never making mistakes. It's about adapting, overcoming challenges, and pushing forward. And that's exactly what we're doing."

She looked up at him, searching his face for any sign of doubt or frustration. But there was only calm, unwavering support. "You really think we'll make it through this?"

"I know we will," Ryan said softly, his eyes locking onto hers. "Because we've got you leading us. And because we're a team. We take care of each other, no matter what. We'll get through this, Mia. One way or another."

Mia felt a small, tentative smile tug at her lips. "Thank you, Ryan. For... well, for being you, I guess."

He chuckled, the sound low and warm. "Anytime. Now, come on. Let's get these traps set before night falls. We've got a mission to complete, and we're not going to let a few missing supplies stop us."

Mia nodded, feeling a flicker of hope reignite in her chest. They would find a way through this. They always did. With a final look at the dwindling supplies, she turned and followed Ryan into the dense foliage, the sounds of the jungle rising around them like a living, breathing promise.

They weren't done yet—not by a long shot.

The night air was thick with humidity, the sounds of the jungle a cacophony of chirping insects and distant animal calls. The fire crackled softly, casting flickering shadows on the faces of the team as they sat around it, exhaustion etched into their expressions. Amina and Kato were sorting through the small collection of edible plants they'd foraged earlier, their voices low as they discussed what they'd found.

"This one's called mbondo," Kato said, holding up a small leafy plant with a proud smile. "My grandmother used it to make tea when we were feeling sick. It helps with stomach aches."

Amina nodded thoughtfully, turning the plant over in her hands. "Good find. But remember, out here, even familiar plants can look similar to something poisonous. Always double-check before you eat anything."

"I did double-check," Kato replied, a touch of defensiveness in his voice. "I know what I'm doing, Amina."

Amina gave him a gentle smile. "I'm not doubting you, Kato. Just... we can't afford any mistakes right now."

"Yeah, yeah, I know." Kato rolled his eyes good-naturedly and reached for a small handful of bright red berries he'd set aside earlier. "I'm sure about these, too. They taste a little bitter, but they're safe."

Before Amina could respond, he popped a few of the berries into his mouth, chewing thoughtfully. Mia, who had been quietly observing from across the fire, glanced up sharply.

"Kato, what are those?" she asked, a hint of concern creeping into her tone.

"Some local berries," Kato replied with a shrug. "I've had them before. They're a little tart, but they're good for energy."

Mia's eyes narrowed. "Are you absolutely sure they're the same ones? The jungle has a lot of look-alikes, and some of them can be toxic."

Kato hesitated, then nodded, though his confidence wavered slightly. "Yeah, I'm sure. I mean, they look the same as the ones I used to eat back home."

Ryan, who had been silently cleaning his machete, looked up at Kato, his gaze sharp. "Back home isn't here, Kato. Let's hope you're right."

The unease settled over the group like a thick fog, but the conversation moved on. They ate a sparse meal of foraged greens and a small portion of their remaining rations, each bite a reminder of just how little they had left. The night grew quieter, the fire burned lower, and one by one, they settled into their tents.

Hours later, Mia woke to the sound of someone retching violently outside her tent. She shot up, her heart pounding as she scrambled out of her sleeping bag and unzipped the flap. The scene that greeted her was chaos.

"Kato!" she gasped, rushing to where Amina was kneeling beside him, holding his shoulders as he convulsed, dry heaving into the dirt.

"He's burning up," Amina said urgently, her hands shaking as she tried to keep Kato upright. "His skin is clammy. I think it's those berries."

Panic gripped Mia's chest as she knelt beside them, pressing the back of her hand to Kato's forehead. He was burning with fever, his face slick with sweat. "Damn it," she muttered, her voice shaking. "We don't have the right supplies to treat this. We need the medical crate—"

"That's not an option right now," Ryan's voice cut in firmly. He crouched beside her, his eyes intense but steady. "We have to work with what we have. What do we know about the berries? Symptoms, timeline?"

Amina shook her head, frustration and fear warring on her face. "They're a local variety, but they have a toxic look-alike that can cause severe stomach cramping, fever, and dehydration if ingested. He must have gotten them mixed up."

Kato groaned, his hands clutching his stomach as another wave of pain wracked his body. Mia felt a surge of helplessness, guilt clawing at her insides. *I should have checked. I should have insisted he wait until we verified everything.*

"We need to get him hydrated," Mia said, trying to keep her voice calm. "Ryan, grab the water bottles. Amina, can we use any of the herbs we have to counteract the toxins?"

"There's one—mbondo—but it's mild," Amina replied, her voice tight. "It might help with the stomach cramps, but it's not enough to stop the toxin itself."

Mia bit her lip, cursing under her breath. They didn't have time to look for an antidote, and without the medical crate, they were at a loss. "Kato, hang in there," she whispered, brushing his hair back from his damp forehead. "We're going to get you through this."

Ryan returned with a water bottle, carefully tipping it to Kato's lips. "Drink," he said gently. "Slow sips. We don't want you getting more nauseous."

Kato's eyes fluttered open, glazed with pain. "I—I'm sorry," he croaked, his voice barely a whisper. "I thought... I thought I knew..."

"Shh, don't talk," Mia murmured, her heart breaking at the sight of him struggling to breathe. "You're going to be okay. Just stay with us, alright?"

Ryan's gaze flicked to Mia's, his expression unyielding. "Mia, focus. This is the jungle—things like this happen. It's not your fault."

"But I should've—"

"No," Ryan interrupted, his voice firm. "Don't do that to yourself. Survival out here is about adapting to what's thrown at you, not about dwelling on what could have been done differently."

Mia swallowed hard, the guilt still a heavy knot in her chest, but she nodded. "Right. We keep moving forward. We adapt."

They worked through the night, taking turns monitoring Kato's condition, administering sips of water and small doses of the mbondo herb. Each minute stretched endlessly, but slowly, Kato's fever began to recede, the violent shivers lessening until he finally drifted into an uneasy sleep.

Mia leaned back, exhaustion weighing her down like a physical force. Amina sat beside her, their shoulders touching lightly.

"He's going to be okay," Amina murmured, more to herself than to Mia. "We caught it early enough."

Mia nodded, letting out a long, shaky breath. "Yeah. But we need to be more careful. One more mistake like that, and we might not be so lucky."

Ryan looked at both of them, his gaze calm but resolute. "We'll make it through this, Mia. All of us. This was a wake-up call, but we're stronger for it. We know what we're dealing with now."

Mia glanced down at Kato's sleeping form, her heart still aching with residual fear. "I just want to keep everyone safe," she whispered.

"And you will," Ryan said softly. "But it's not just on you. We're all in this together."

The night air felt cooler now, the worst of the crisis behind them. But the shadow of what could have happened lingered, a stark reminder of how unforgiving the jungle could be. As they settled back into their uneasy rest, Mia knew one thing for sure:

Every decision from now on had to be flawless. There was no more room for error.

The first raindrop hit Mia's cheek like a warning, cold and sudden against the oppressive humidity of the jungle. She glanced up at the sky, the thick canopy above barely providing cover as more drops began to splatter against the leaves. A deep rumble of thunder reverberated through the air, and within moments, the rain turned from a light sprinkle to a torrential downpour.

"Great," Mia muttered under her breath, pulling her jacket tighter around her shoulders. She turned to call out to the others, her voice barely audible over the roar of water hitting the ground. "We need to keep moving! We're too exposed out here!"

Ryan, who was a few paces ahead, paused to look back at her, his expression grim. "Moving where? We're not going to make much progress in this. The path's already turning into a river."

Mia glanced down. The once-solid trail was rapidly transforming into a slick, muddy mess, water pooling in every dip and crevice. The mud sucked at their boots, making each step a battle to keep upright. Kato and Amina struggled behind them, their movements slow and cautious as they tried to avoid slipping.

"We can't stop now!" Mia insisted, wiping the rain from her eyes. "If we set up camp, we'll lose even more time. We're already behind schedule."

Ryan's jaw tightened, his voice raised to be heard over the pounding rain. "Mia, this isn't about the schedule anymore. This is about safety. If one of us gets hurt out here, it's over. The ground's turning to sludge. We're going to get stuck if we're not careful."

Mia's frustration flared. She glanced around, her gaze darting over the dense foliage, now shrouded in a curtain of rain. The jungle, already a maze of tangled roots and undergrowth, had become a treacherous, slippery nightmare. Visibility was down to a few feet, and the sound of the rain made it nearly impossible to hear anything else.

"If we stop now, we're giving the poachers more time to regroup," Mia argued, her voice tight. "They're counting on the weather slowing us down. If we keep going, we can—"

"We can what?" Ryan interrupted, his tone sharp. "We can barely see two feet in front of us. We're not going to make any real progress in this. Setting up a temporary camp isn't giving up—it's being smart."

Mia opened her mouth to argue, but Amina's voice cut through the tension, her tone strained. "He's right, Mia. I hate losing time too, but look at Kato. He's struggling just to stay upright."

Mia turned, her heart sinking at the sight of Kato slipping and catching himself on a tree branch, his face pale with exertion. He gave her a weak smile, trying to appear unbothered, but the exhaustion in his eyes was unmistakable.

"Sorry, Mia," Kato panted, wiping the rain from his face. "It's just... this rain is... it's brutal."

Mia felt the fight drain out of her. She looked back at Ryan, who was watching her with that infuriating mix of patience and exasperation.

"Fine," she relented, throwing up her hands in frustration. "We'll set up camp. But just until the rain lets up a little."

Ryan nodded, his shoulders relaxing slightly. "Good call. Let's find higher ground so we don't get flooded out."

They trudged through the deluge, searching for a spot that wasn't already ankle-deep in mud. After what felt like an eternity, they found a small rise, slightly drier than the surrounding area. Ryan and Mia set to work securing the tarps and reinforcing the tents, while Amina and Kato gathered what dry wood they could find to start a small fire.

The rain continued to pour, unrelenting and unforgiving. The sound of it was deafening, a constant roar that drowned out any attempts at conversation. They worked in near silence, each of them absorbed in their own thoughts, the frustration and disappointment thick in the air.

Finally, with the tents up and a small fire sputtering bravely under the cover of a tarp, they huddled together, their clothes soaked through and their spirits dampened.

"Half a day's worth of progress, washed away," Mia muttered, staring at the small, feeble flames. "And for what?"

"For not getting hurt," Ryan said, his voice calm but firm. "For not risking ourselves just to gain a few extra miles. You know I hate this as much as you do, Mia, but we have to be smart out here."

"Smart?" Mia shook her head, bitterness edging into her tone. "We're supposed to be making a difference, and instead, we're stuck here like sitting ducks. If the poachers find us—"

"They won't," Ryan interrupted quietly, his gaze steady on hers. "They're dealing with the same storm we are. And if they are out there, moving in this, they're risking as much as we would be. No one's getting an advantage tonight."

Amina nodded in agreement, her eyes soft with empathy. "We did the right thing. We have to pick our battles, Mia. It's frustrating, but it's better than pushing ourselves to the point of collapse."

Mia looked around at her team, seeing the resolve in their eyes, the trust they placed in her. The anger and frustration simmered down, replaced by a grudging acceptance. She exhaled slowly, rubbing her temples.

"Okay," she murmured. "Okay, you're right. I just... I feel like we're losing ground every time we stop. I want to keep moving forward, no matter what."

"And we will," Ryan assured her, his voice gentle. "But sometimes, surviving is winning. And we're doing that, one day at a time."

Mia managed a small smile, though it was tinged with lingering worry. "Thanks. I just need to remember that."

"We're all here to remind you," Ryan said softly, his gaze never wavering. "We'll get through this, Mia. Together."

The rain continued to beat down, but inside the small circle of their camp, a fragile sense of calm settled. Mia nodded, feeling the tension ease slightly from her shoulders.

"Together," she echoed quietly.

And as the storm raged on outside, they huddled closer, their shared warmth and determination a small but steady light against the dark, unpredictable forces of the jungle.

The rain had finally slowed to a soft drizzle, the relentless downpour easing enough for Mia to hear her own thoughts. The team huddled under the makeshift tarp, the fire flickering weakly in the center, its flames a feeble defiance against the damp and cold. The tension in the air was almost palpable, the weight of the past few days pressing down on all of them like a heavy stone.

Amina was the first to break the silence, her voice edged with frustration. "I just don't see how we're supposed to do this, Mia. We've been out here for weeks, and what do we have to show for it? A few traps dismantled, some data on animal movements—meanwhile, the poachers are two steps ahead of us. Every. Single. Time."

Mia looked up sharply, her gaze locking onto Amina's. "We've made progress. We've mapped their activity zones, documented their tactics—"

"And they're still out there, hunting, raiding our supplies, setting traps," Amina interrupted, her tone heated. "What's going to happen if we run into them again, huh? We barely made it through the last time, and that was with a full stock of supplies. Now we're down to scraps and scavenging."

Ryan shifted beside Mia, his expression calm but alert. "Amina, I get it. You're frustrated. We all are. But this isn't just about what we've lost—it's about what we're learning. We're adapting, finding new ways to deal with them."

"Adapting?" Amina's eyes flashed as she turned to face him. "Is that what you call it? Kato almost died because we didn't have the right medical supplies. We're out here with barely enough food to last another week, and you think we're 'adapting'?"

"Amina," Mia said quietly, struggling to keep her voice steady, "I know you're scared. We all are. But giving up isn't an option. We have to keep going. We knew this wouldn't be easy."

"Easy?" Amina let out a bitter laugh. "No one expected it to be easy, Mia. But I don't think we expected it to be this hopeless, either. We're hanging on by a thread here, and if you can't see that—"

"That's enough," Ryan interjected, his voice firm but not harsh. He glanced at Mia, then back at Amina. "This isn't about whose fault it is or what we should have done differently. Right now, we need to focus on what we *can* do. We still have the element of surprise. They think they've crippled us, but that's our advantage. We can hit back, take down their traps, and make it harder for them to operate."

Mia nodded, her gaze never leaving Amina's. "We can do this, Amina. But only if we stick together. I get it—things are tough right now. We're dealing with more than we bargained for. But if we turn back now, everything we've done, everything we've sacrificed, will be for nothing."

Amina's shoulders slumped, the fight draining out of her as she looked between Ryan and Mia. "I just... I don't want to see anyone else get hurt. We came here to make a difference, but sometimes it feels like we're just surviving."

"And sometimes, surviving is making a difference," Ryan said gently. "Surviving means we're still in the game. We still have a chance to turn things around."

Kato, who had been silent up until now, shifted uncomfortably. "Amina... I know it's been hard. I know I made things worse by getting sick, and I'm sorry for that. But I'm not ready to give up. Not when we're this close. We can still do this."

Amina sighed, closing her eyes for a moment. When she opened them again, her gaze softened, and she nodded slowly. "I'm not saying I want to give up. I just... I needed to say it. Get it out there."

Mia reached out, placing a hand on Amina's arm. "And I'm glad you did. We have to talk about this stuff, or it's going to tear us apart. But I promise you—we're going to get through this. Together."

Amina managed a faint smile, though worry still clouded her eyes. "Okay. So what's the plan?"

Mia glanced at Ryan, then back at Amina and Kato. "We adjust. We conserve what food we have left, keep foraging, and stay close to the main path. We need to find more of their traps, see if we can figure out where they're setting up their base of operations. Once we have a better idea of their movements, we can make a real impact."

"And what about supplies?" Kato asked, glancing at the meager pile of rations. "If we keep burning through them like this, we won't have anything left in a few days."

"We'll ration even more strictly," Mia replied. "But I'm also going to reach out to the local authorities again. Maybe we can arrange for a drop-off, get the medical supplies we need."

Ryan nodded. "That's a good start. And we stay alert. The weather's unpredictable, and the jungle's not going to cut us any slack. But we adapt. Like we always do."

Silence settled over them for a moment, the only sound the soft patter of rain against the leaves above. Slowly, the tension began to dissipate, replaced by a cautious sense of resolve.

"We're still in this," Mia murmured, more to herself than to the others. "And we're not going to let them win."

Amina nodded, a small spark of determination reigniting in her eyes. "Alright. Let's see this through."

Ryan's gaze lingered on Mia, his expression unreadable. Then he smiled, just a little. "We're with you, Mia. Every step of the way."

Kato grinned, his usual optimism shining through despite the exhaustion etched into his features. "Yeah, what they said. I'm not going anywhere."

Mia took a deep breath, the weight of their shared commitment settling over her like a protective mantle. She looked around at her team—her friends—and felt a renewed sense of purpose.

"Thank you," she whispered. "All of you. Now, let's get some rest. Tomorrow, we move forward. No more doubts, no more second-guessing."

They nodded, and one by one, they turned back to the fire, the tension easing as conversation resumed, quieter now but filled with a sense of camaraderie that hadn't been there before.

Outside their small camp, the rain continued to fall, but inside, a fragile sense of hope began to bloom. They weren't beaten yet. Not by the jungle, not by the poachers, and not by their own fears.

Tomorrow, they would keep fighting—together. And that was what mattered most.

Chapter 16
Ambush in the Wild

The morning sun painted the sky in hues of pink and orange as the village stirred to life. The crisp air was filled with the sounds of birdsong and the soft rustle of leaves. Ryan, Mia, Amina, and Captain Morales stood in the central clearing, their eyes scanning the busy scene. Today was crucial; they needed to ensure that the village was ready to stand on its own.

Ryan addressed the group, his voice clear and commanding. "We need to focus on two main areas today: reinforcing the last of the barriers and conducting a full-scale communication drill. It's essential that we're thorough."

Kira, the village leader, nodded. "We're ready. We've come a long way, and we won't let our progress slip."

Mia adjusted her camera, capturing the determination on Kira's face. "You've all worked so hard. It's inspiring to see the transformation."

Amina smiled, setting up her medical kit under a large tree. "We'll do another round of health checks and focus on advanced first aid training. It's crucial that everyone knows how to handle emergencies."

The villagers dispersed into their assigned teams. Ryan and Captain Morales led a group to the perimeter to inspect the barriers. "Make sure the supports are deep and secure," Ryan instructed, watching as the villagers worked. "We can't afford any weak spots."

Yuki, one of the younger villagers, wiped sweat from his brow. "Like this, Ryan?"

Ryan nodded approvingly. "Exactly. You're doing great. Keep it up."

Nearby, Amina was showing a group of villagers how to treat severe injuries. "In case of a deep cut, apply pressure to stop the bleeding, then clean the wound thoroughly."

Mei practiced on a dummy, her hands steady. "How does this look, Amina?"

Amina adjusted Mei's grip slightly. "Perfect. Just remember to stay calm and act quickly. It can make all the difference."

Captain Morales was overseeing the setup of the communication system, instructing a group of villagers on its use. "These radios are your lifeline. Regular check-ins are crucial, especially if there's any unusual activity."

Hiroshi, one of the more experienced villagers, asked, "How often should we check in?"

Morales replied, "Twice a day, minimum. And if there's anything suspicious, report it immediately. Clear and concise communication can save lives."

Mia moved through the village, capturing the collaborative efforts and the growing confidence on everyone's faces. She paused by Kira, who was overseeing the construction of a new barrier. "Kira, how do you feel about the progress we've made so far?"

Kira smiled, her eyes reflecting pride and determination. "It's been incredible. We're stronger and more united. Your team has given us the tools to protect ourselves and thrive."

As the day progressed, the villagers' confidence grew. They worked tirelessly, reinforcing the barriers and mastering the use of the communication system. By late afternoon, the sense of accomplishment was palpable.

Ryan gathered everyone for a final debriefing. "You've all done an exceptional job. The barriers are solid, and the communication system is operational. You're ready for anything."

Amina added, "Health and hygiene are improving too. Keep practicing what you've learned and support each other."

Captain Morales nodded. "The drills have gone well. Remember, clear communication is key to staying safe."

Mia, filming the update, felt a deep sense of fulfillment. She turned to Yuki, who had been working diligently. "Yuki, what's been the most challenging part of this work?"

Yuki wiped sweat from his brow, his face set with determination. "It's hard work, but it's worth it. We're doing this for our future, for our families. Knowing that makes it easier."

As the evening approached, the team and villagers gathered around the central fire. The atmosphere was one of celebration and reflection. Ryan addressed the group, his voice filled with hope and determination.

"We've built more than just physical defenses. We've built a community that supports and protects each other. Keep working together, and you can achieve anything."

Kira stood beside him, her eyes reflecting the firelight. "We will. This is our home, and we'll protect it with everything we have."

Amina beamed. "Remember, we're linked together. Use the communication network to stay connected and help each other out."

Mia captured the scene, her heart swelling with pride. "We're building something lasting here. This village is becoming a beacon of hope and resilience."

As the night grew darker, the team gathered by the fire, discussing their next moves and reflecting on their journey. They had faced many challenges, but with each village they aided, they were crafting a legacy of strength, resilience, and unity. The bonds they had formed with the villagers were strong, and their shared vision for a brighter future was becoming a reality.

The work was hard, but it was meaningful, and it was making a difference. Together, they knew they could face whatever came their way, one village at a time. The path ahead was long, but they were ready. They were building a future, one step at a time.

The village awoke to the soft light of dawn filtering through the trees. The air was cool and filled with the sounds of morning activities. The team and the villagers were already gathering in the central clearing, ready for another day of work and preparation. The sense of unity and determination was palpable, as everyone knew the importance of the tasks ahead.

Ryan stood in the center, addressing the group. "Today, we're going to focus on two main areas: reinforcing the remaining barriers and conducting a full-scale communication drill. We need to ensure everything is functioning perfectly."

Hana, the village leader, nodded. "We're ready. We'll split into teams to cover more ground."

Mia, her camera at the ready, moved around capturing the moment. She caught sight of Amina preparing her medical kit. "Amina, what's on your agenda today?"

Amina smiled. "I'm going to do another round of health checks and then focus on teaching some advanced first aid techniques. We need to make sure everyone is prepared for any emergency."

The villagers dispersed into their assigned teams. Ryan led a group to the western edge of the village where the barriers needed reinforcement. He demonstrated how to secure the logs and branches. "It's crucial that these barriers are solid. They're our first line of defense."

Taro, eager to learn, asked, "What if we run out of materials?"

Ryan replied, "Use what you can find. Rocks, mud, anything that can add to the stability. Adaptability is key."

Meanwhile, Captain Morales gathered a group for the communication drill. "Today, we're going to simulate a real emergency. I need everyone to follow the protocols we've discussed. Clear, concise messages. No panic."

Kala raised her hand. "What's the scenario?"

Morales explained, "We'll simulate an incursion. Remember, it's just a drill, but treat it seriously. We need to identify any weaknesses in our system."

As the drill began, Mia captured the intensity and focus on everyone's faces. The villagers moved quickly, sending messages and coordinating their responses. The communication system crackled with voices, each one delivering precise information.

At the same time, Amina was in the makeshift clinic, teaching a group of villagers how to handle severe injuries. "If someone has a broken limb, you need to immobilize it immediately. Use anything rigid, like a branch, as a splint."

Mei, practicing on a dummy, asked, "What about bleeding?"

Amina showed her how to apply a tourniquet. "Only use this as a last resort, if the bleeding is severe and won't stop with pressure. Remember, every action you take can save a life."

The day progressed with a steady rhythm, the villagers working tirelessly under the guidance of the team. The barriers took shape, the communication drill highlighted areas for improvement, and the medical training instilled confidence and skills in everyone.

In the afternoon, the team reconvened with the villagers for a debriefing. Ryan started, his voice filled with pride. "The barriers are looking solid. Great job, everyone. We're creating a strong defense."

Captain Morales added, "The drill went well, but we did identify some areas that need work. We'll address those immediately. Overall, I'm impressed with how everyone handled the situation."

Amina spoke next. "The medical training sessions are going smoothly. You're all quick learners. Keep practicing these skills—they're crucial."

Mia, capturing the debriefing on camera, felt a surge of pride. She turned to Hana, who stood by her side. "Hana, how do you feel about the progress we've made?"

Hana smiled, her eyes reflecting gratitude and determination. "It's incredible. We're stronger, more united. We've learned so much from all of you."

As the evening approached, the team and villagers gathered around the central fire. The atmosphere was one of quiet satisfaction and growing confidence. Ryan addressed the group, his voice carrying over the crackling flames.

"We've built more than just physical defenses. We've built trust and a sense of community. Keep working together, and we can achieve anything."

Hana nodded, her eyes reflecting the firelight. "We will. This is our home, and we'll protect it with everything we have."

Captain Morales added, "And remember, we're all connected now. Use the communication system to stay in touch and support each other."

Mia captured the scene, feeling a deep sense of fulfillment. "We're building something lasting here. This village is becoming a beacon of hope and resilience."

As the night deepened, the team sat together by the fire, reflecting on the day's achievements and planning for the future. The challenges were many, but with each step, they were building a legacy of strength and unity. The bonds they had forged with the villagers were strong, and their shared vision for a better future was becoming a reality. The work was hard, but it was meaningful, and it was making a difference. Together, they knew they could face whatever came their way, one village at a time.

The next morning dawned bright and clear, the village bathed in the soft light of a new day. The air was filled with the sounds of preparation as the team and villagers gathered to tackle their final tasks. There was a sense of urgency, tempered by the confidence that had grown over the past days.

Ryan stood in the central clearing, addressing the group. "Today, we'll complete the reinforcement of the barriers and conduct another full-scale communication drill. This will be our final test before we move on to the next village."

Hana, standing beside Ryan, nodded. "We're ready. We've learned so much from you. Let's make sure everything is perfect."

Mia moved through the crowd, her camera capturing the anticipation on the villagers' faces. She paused by Amina, who was checking her medical supplies. "Amina, what's your focus for today?"

Amina smiled. "I'll be doing a final round of health checks and then leading a refresher course on emergency medical procedures. We need to ensure everyone feels confident in their skills."

Captain Morales was organizing the communication drill, her voice calm and authoritative. "We'll run through a simulated incursion again, but this time we'll include a few unexpected elements to test our adaptability."

Kala, one of the more experienced villagers, raised her hand. "What kind of unexpected elements?"

Morales responded with a smile. "You'll see. The goal is to prepare for the unexpected. Stay alert and communicate clearly."

The teams dispersed to their tasks, each group focused and determined. Ryan led his team to the barriers, inspecting the progress and providing guidance. "Make sure the supports are deep and secure. We need these barriers to withstand anything."

Taro, working diligently, looked up. "We're using extra rocks and mud for reinforcement. These should hold strong."

Ryan nodded in approval. "Good thinking, Taro. Keep it up."

Meanwhile, Amina was conducting her health checks under the shade of a large tree. She examined an elderly woman, her voice gentle and reassuring. "You're in good health, but make sure to stay hydrated and avoid overexertion in the heat."

Mei, assisting Amina, practiced applying a bandage on a dummy. "How does this look, Amina?"

Amina smiled. "Perfect, Mei. Remember, practice makes perfect. You're doing great."

Captain Morales initiated the communication drill, her voice clear over the radio. "This is a drill. We have a simulated incursion from the west. Report your positions and any sightings immediately."

The villagers responded quickly, their voices steady and precise. "West perimeter clear. No movement detected." "South watchtower reporting, all clear."

As the drill continued, Mia captured the intense focus and coordination. She turned to Hana, who was monitoring the drill. "Hana, how do you think they're doing?"

Hana's face reflected a mix of pride and concentration. "They're doing well. The training has paid off. We're becoming a well-oiled machine."

The drill progressed smoothly, with the unexpected elements introduced by Morales testing the villagers' adaptability. There were moments of confusion quickly resolved by clear communication and decisive action. By the end of the drill, the village had demonstrated its readiness and resilience.

Ryan gathered everyone for a final debriefing, his voice filled with pride. "You've all done an incredible job. The barriers are solid, and the communication system is functioning perfectly. You're ready for anything."

Captain Morales added, "Today's drill showed that you can handle the unexpected. Keep practicing and stay vigilant."

Amina spoke next, her tone encouraging. "Your health and safety are paramount. Keep up with the regular checks and continue practicing your medical skills. You're well-prepared."

Mia, filming the debriefing, felt a deep sense of accomplishment. She turned to capture the expressions of the villagers, their faces alight with confidence and determination.

As the sun began to set, casting a warm glow over the village, the team and villagers gathered around the central fire. The atmosphere was one of celebration and reflection. Ryan addressed the group, his voice carrying a note of finality.

"We've built something strong and lasting here. You've shown incredible dedication and resilience. Remember, you're not alone. Stay connected, support each other, and keep building on what we've started."

Hana stood beside him, her eyes reflecting the firelight. "We will. This is our home, and we'll protect it with everything we have. Thank you for your guidance and support."

Captain Morales added, "And remember, the network we're building is only as strong as its weakest link. Stay in touch and keep improving."

Mia captured the moment, feeling a profound sense of fulfillment. The village, once vulnerable and isolated, had transformed into a beacon of hope and resilience. The bonds they had forged were strong, and their shared vision for a better future was becoming a reality.

As the night deepened, the team sat together by the fire, discussing their next steps and reflecting on their journey. The challenges were many, but with each step, they were building a legacy of strength, unity, and hope. Together, they knew they could face whatever came their way, one village at a time.

The village buzzed with activity as the team prepared to say their goodbyes. The morning air was crisp, carrying the promise of a new day. The villagers moved with purpose, their newfound confidence evident in every step. Ryan, Mia, Amina, and Captain Morales gathered in the central clearing, ready to address the community one last time.

Ryan stood at the center, his voice carrying over the crowd. "We've achieved a lot together. Your dedication and hard work have transformed this village. Remember, this is just the beginning. Stay vigilant and keep building on what we've started."

Hana, the village leader, stepped forward, her eyes reflecting gratitude and resolve. "We will. You've given us the tools and knowledge we need. We'll continue to work hard and stay connected with the network."

Mia, her camera capturing every moment, moved around to document the final preparations. She paused to interview Mei, who had become a key figure in the village's health initiatives. "Mei, how do you feel about the changes we've made?"

Mei smiled, her eyes bright with determination. "It's been incredible. We've learned so much and become stronger as a community. We're ready for whatever comes next."

Amina was conducting a final health check-up, her voice gentle but firm. "Remember to keep up with the regular check-ups and hygiene practices. These small steps will keep everyone healthy."

One of the villagers, a young man named Kenji, asked, "What should we do if we run out of medical supplies?"

Amina replied, "Use natural remedies where possible and communicate with the network. We'll ensure you get what you need. Stay resourceful and proactive."

Captain Morales was overseeing the last communication drill, her tone authoritative yet encouraging. "This is the final drill. Make sure your messages are clear and concise. Report any unusual activity immediately."

Kala, practicing with the radio, responded confidently. "West perimeter all clear. No movement detected."

Morales nodded in approval. "Good. Keep up the regular check-ins. This system is your lifeline."

Ryan joined Morales, addressing the group. "We're proud of how far you've come. The communication system is crucial. Use it to stay connected and support each other."

As the drill concluded, the villagers gathered for a final debriefing. Ryan spoke first, his voice filled with pride. "The barriers are solid, and the communication system is functioning perfectly. You're ready for anything."

Amina added, "Your health practices have improved significantly. Keep up the good work and continue to learn and share knowledge."

Mia, filming the debriefing, felt a deep sense of fulfillment. She turned to Hana, who stood beside her. "Hana, any final thoughts?"

Hana's face lit up with a mix of pride and gratitude. "We're stronger, more united. We'll carry forward what we've learned. Thank you for everything."

The team and villagers moved to the central fire for a final gathering. The atmosphere was one of celebration and reflection. Ryan addressed the group, his voice resonating with hope and determination.

"We've built more than just physical defenses. We've built trust and a sense of community. Keep working together, and we can achieve great things."

Hana nodded, her eyes reflecting the firelight. "We will. This is our home, and we'll protect it with everything we have."

Captain Morales added, "And remember, the network we're building is only as strong as its weakest link. Stay in touch and keep improving."

Mia captured the scene, feeling a profound sense of accomplishment. "We're building something lasting here. This village is becoming a beacon of hope and resilience."

As the night deepened, the team sat together by the fire, discussing their journey and the road ahead. Ryan turned to Mia, his voice thoughtful. "We've made a real difference here. But there's still so much to do."

Mia nodded, her eyes shining with determination. "Every village we help strengthens the whole network. We're building a future, one step at a time."

Amina added, "And it's not just about defense. It's about creating a community that cares for each other, that's resilient and self-sufficient."

Captain Morales smiled. "We've laid a strong foundation here. Now it's up to them to keep it going."

The conversation turned to their next mission, the next village that needed their help. Ryan looked around at his team, his expression determined. "We'll keep moving forward, one village at a time. We're building a network of hope and resilience."

Mia captured the moment, feeling a sense of purpose and unity. "And we'll document every step of the way, showing the world what's possible."

As the fire crackled softly, the team felt a deep sense of fulfillment and anticipation for the challenges ahead. The bonds they had forged with the villagers were strong, and their shared vision for a better future was becoming a reality. Together, they knew they could face whatever came their way, one village at a time.

Chapter 17
Unraveling the Syndicate's Web

The journey to the next village was grueling, the path winding through dense jungle and rocky terrain. The air was thick with humidity, and the sounds of the jungle provided a constant, vibrant backdrop. Mia, Ryan, Amina, and Captain Morales moved with purpose, their determination unshaken by the challenges ahead.

Ryan led the way, his eyes scanning the path ahead. "We're almost there. This village is more isolated than the others, but that means they need our help even more."

Mia, her camera capturing the rugged beauty of their surroundings, nodded. "It's important to show the world the reality of these remote villages. Their stories need to be told."

Amina adjusted her medical kit, her expression thoughtful. "I'm worried about their health situation. Isolation often means a lack of basic medical supplies and knowledge. We need to assess and address that quickly."

Captain Morales added, "And we need to ensure their communication systems are up and running. If they're this isolated, they'll need to alert us immediately if there's any trouble."

As they approached the village, the sounds of daily life reached their ears—children laughing, the clatter of tools, the hum of conversation. The village was nestled in a small clearing, surrounded by dense foliage. The villagers, noticing the newcomers, paused their activities and gathered to meet them.

An older man, clearly the village leader, stepped forward. His face was lined with age and wisdom, his eyes sharp and inquisitive. "Who are you, and why have you come here?"

Ryan stepped forward, his voice steady and respectful. "We're here to help. We've been working with other villages to build defenses, establish communication systems, and improve health and education. We want to do the same here."

The leader, whose name was Takashi, scrutinized them for a moment before speaking. "We've heard of you. Some say you bring hope, others say you bring trouble. Why should we trust you?"

Amina stepped up, her voice calm and reassuring. "We bring knowledge and support. We work with you to strengthen your community. Everything we do is to empower you, not control you."

Takashi nodded slowly, his expression thoughtful. "Very well. Show us what you can do."

The team immediately set to work, dividing the tasks among themselves. Ryan and Captain Morales began assessing the village's defenses, noting the natural barriers and identifying areas that needed reinforcement. Amina set up a temporary clinic, starting with a health assessment to understand the villagers' needs.

Mia moved through the village, capturing their efforts on camera. She interviewed Takashi, who spoke candidly about the village's struggles and hopes. "We've managed to survive in this harsh terrain, but it's been difficult. If you can truly help us, we will welcome your support."

As the day progressed, the team and the villagers worked side by side, building trust and laying the foundation for a stronger, more resilient community. Mia documented every step, knowing these images and stories would inspire others.

In the afternoon, Ryan gathered the villagers in the central clearing. "We need to fortify your defenses, especially near the edges of the clearing. Use the natural landscape to your advantage."

One of the younger villagers, Yuki, asked, "What if we don't have enough materials?"

Ryan replied, "Use what you can find. Rocks, mud, anything that can add to the stability. Adaptability is key."

Taro, who had accompanied the team to share his experience, added, "We did something similar in our village. It makes a huge difference. You can do this."

Takashi, observing the interaction, nodded approvingly. "We'll follow your lead."

Amina, addressing the health needs, spoke to a group of villagers about basic hygiene and first aid. "Clean water and proper wound care are essential. These small steps can prevent serious illnesses."

Mei, practicing on a dummy, asked, "What about more serious injuries?"

Amina showed her how to apply a tourniquet. "Only use this as a last resort, if the bleeding is severe and won't stop with pressure. Remember, every action you take can save a life."

As the evening approached, the team and villagers gathered around a central fire. The sense of unity and purpose was growing stronger. Ryan addressed the group, his voice filled with hope. "Today, we've taken the first steps toward securing your village. Together, we can build something strong and lasting."

Takashi stood beside him, his eyes reflecting the firelight. "We are ready to work with you. Let us move forward together, as one."

Mia captured the moment, feeling a deep sense of fulfillment. The journey ahead was long, but with each village they helped, they were building a network of hope and resilience. The night deepened, and the team and villagers sat together, sharing stories and laughter, united by a common goal and a shared vision for a better future.

The following morning dawned clear and bright, the village slowly coming to life with the sounds of daily routines. The team had already convened near the central clearing, their agenda for the day set. Ryan, Mia, Amina, and Captain Morales moved with purpose, their determination evident in every step.

Ryan gathered the villagers, his voice carrying a sense of urgency. "Today, we'll focus on reinforcing the barriers and setting up a basic communication system. We need to ensure you're well-protected and connected."

Takashi, the village leader, nodded. "We understand. We'll split into teams to cover more ground."

The villagers dispersed into their assigned groups, each taking on a specific task. Ryan led a team to the village's perimeter, assessing the existing defenses and identifying areas that needed reinforcement. "Use the strongest materials you can find," he instructed. "We need these barriers to be solid and reliable."

Yuki, one of the younger villagers, asked, "What if we can't find enough strong materials?"

Ryan replied, "Improvise with what you have. Use rocks, mud, and branches to reinforce the weaker spots. The key is to make it as difficult as possible for anyone to breach."

Meanwhile, Amina set up a makeshift clinic under the shade of a large tree, conducting health assessments and providing basic medical training. She demonstrated how to treat common injuries, her voice calm and clear. "In case of a deep cut, clean the wound thoroughly and apply pressure to stop the bleeding."

Mei, assisting Amina, practiced on a dummy. "How does this look, Amina?"

Amina smiled, adjusting Mei's technique slightly. "Perfect. Remember, cleanliness is crucial. It prevents infections and speeds up healing."

Captain Morales was busy overseeing the setup of the communication system. She gathered a group of villagers and explained the importance of regular check-ins. "Communication is vital for your safety. We need to ensure you can alert us or neighboring villages in case of an emergency."

One of the villagers, Hiroshi, asked, "How often should we check in?"

Morales replied, "At least twice a day. More if there's any unusual activity. The more connected we are, the safer you'll be."

Mia moved through the village, her camera capturing the collaborative efforts and the determination on everyone's faces. She paused by Takashi, who was overseeing the construction of a new barrier. "Takashi, how do you feel about the progress we've made so far?"

Takashi's eyes reflected both hope and determination. "It's been a challenging journey, but we're making great strides. Your support has been invaluable."

As the day progressed, the villagers worked tirelessly under the guidance of the team. The barriers took shape, the communication system began to hum with activity, and the villagers gained confidence in their new skills.

In the afternoon, the team gathered the villagers for a progress update. Ryan spoke first, his voice filled with pride. "The barriers are looking solid, and the communication system is almost fully operational. We're making great progress."

Amina added, "Health and hygiene are improving too. Keep practicing what you've learned and support each other."

Captain Morales nodded. "The drills are going well. Remember, clear communication is key to staying safe."

Mia, filming the update, felt a deep sense of fulfillment. She turned to Yuki, who had been working diligently on the barriers. "Yuki, what's been the most challenging part of this work?"

Yuki wiped sweat from his brow, his face set with determination. "It's hard work, but it's worth it. We're doing this for our future, for our families. Knowing that makes it easier."

As the sun began to set, casting a golden glow over the village, the team and villagers gathered around the central fire. The atmosphere was one of quiet satisfaction and growing confidence. Ryan addressed the group, his voice carrying over the crackling flames.

"We've built more than just physical defenses. We've built a stronger, more united community. Keep working together, and we can achieve anything."

Takashi stood beside him, his eyes reflecting the firelight. "We will. This is our home, and we'll protect it with everything we have."

Amina added, "And remember, we're all connected now. Use the communication system to stay in touch and support each other."

Mia captured the scene, feeling a profound sense of fulfillment. "We're building something lasting here. This village is becoming a beacon of hope and resilience."

As the night deepened, the team sat together by the fire, discussing their next steps and reflecting on the day's achievements. The challenges were many, but with each step, they were building a legacy of strength, resilience, and unity. The bonds they had forged with the villagers were strong, and their shared vision for a better future was becoming a reality. The work was hard, but it was meaningful, and it was making a difference. Together, they knew they could face whatever came their way, one village at a time.

The next morning, the village buzzed with a palpable energy. The team and the villagers gathered early, ready to tackle the final tasks needed to fortify their community. The sense of purpose and unity was stronger than ever as they worked together, each person contributing to the shared goal of making their village safe and resilient.

Ryan stood in the central clearing, addressing the group. "Today, we'll complete the reinforcement of the barriers and conduct a full-scale communication drill. This will be our final test before we move on to the next village."

Takashi, the village leader, nodded firmly. "We're ready. We've learned a lot from you, and we'll make sure everything is perfect."

Ryan and Captain Morales led a group to the perimeter, inspecting the barriers. Ryan pointed to a section that needed more support. "Make sure the supports are deep and secure. We need these barriers to withstand anything."

Yuki, working diligently with the group, asked, "What if we run out of strong materials?"

Ryan replied, "Use what you can find. Rocks, mud, branches. Adapt and reinforce where necessary. The key is to make it as difficult as possible for anyone to breach."

Meanwhile, Amina conducted a final round of health checks under the shade of a large tree. She examined an elderly woman, her voice gentle and reassuring. "You're in good health, but make sure to stay hydrated and avoid overexertion in the heat."

Mei, assisting Amina, practiced applying a bandage on a dummy. "How does this look, Amina?"

Amina smiled, adjusting Mei's technique slightly. "Perfect, Mei. Remember, cleanliness is crucial to prevent infections and ensure quick healing."

Captain Morales gathered a group for the communication drill, her tone firm but encouraging. "This is the final drill. We'll simulate an emergency. Everyone needs to follow the protocols we've discussed. Clear, concise messages. No panic."

Hiroshi, practicing with the radio, asked, "What's the scenario?"

Morales explained, "We'll simulate an incursion. Treat it seriously and stay focused. The goal is to test our response and adaptability."

As the drill began, Mia captured the intensity and focus on everyone's faces. The villagers moved quickly, sending messages and coordinating their responses. The communication system crackled with voices, each one delivering precise information.

"West perimeter clear. No movement detected," reported Kala.

"South watchtower reporting, all clear," added Hiroshi.

Ryan monitored the drill, his face showing satisfaction as the villagers demonstrated their readiness. "You're doing great. Keep it up. Remember, clarity and calm are your best tools."

The drill progressed smoothly, with Captain Morales introducing unexpected elements to test the villagers' adaptability. There were moments of confusion, but they were quickly resolved by clear communication and decisive action. By the end of the drill, the village had shown it was ready to handle emergencies.

As the day wore on, the team and villagers worked tirelessly. The barriers were completed, and the communication system was functioning perfectly. The sense of accomplishment was palpable as they gathered for a final debriefing.

Ryan spoke first, his voice filled with pride. "You've all done an incredible job. The barriers are solid, and the communication system is operational. You're ready for anything."

Amina added, "Health and hygiene are improving too. Keep practicing what you've learned and support each other."

Captain Morales nodded. "Today's drill showed that you can handle the unexpected. Keep up the regular check-ins and stay vigilant."

Mia, filming the debriefing, felt a deep sense of fulfillment. She turned to Takashi, who stood beside her. "Takashi, how do you feel about the progress we've made?"

Takashi's face lit up with a mix of pride and gratitude. "It's been an incredible journey. We've become stronger and more united. Thank you for everything."

As the sun began to set, casting a golden glow over the village, the team and villagers gathered around the central fire. The atmosphere was one of celebration and reflection. Ryan addressed the group, his voice carrying a note of hope and determination.

"We've built more than just physical defenses. We've built trust and a sense of community. Keep working together, and we can achieve great things."

Takashi nodded, his eyes reflecting the firelight. "We will. This is our home, and we'll protect it with everything we have."

Amina added, "And remember, we're all connected now. Use the communication system to stay in touch and support each other."

Mia captured the scene, feeling a profound sense of fulfillment. "We're building something lasting here. This village is becoming a beacon of hope and resilience."

As the night deepened, the team sat together by the fire, discussing their next steps and reflecting on the day's achievements. The challenges were many, but with each step, they were building a legacy of strength, resilience, and unity. The bonds they had forged with the villagers were strong, and their shared vision for a better future was becoming a reality. The work was hard, but it was meaningful, and it was making a difference. Together, they knew they could face whatever came their way, one village at a time.

The village buzzed with energy as the final preparations were underway. The team and villagers worked in harmony, each task flowing seamlessly into the next. The sun hung low in the sky, casting a golden hue over the scene. Ryan, Mia, Amina, and Captain Morales moved through the bustling village, ensuring everything was set for the final drill.

Ryan addressed the group, his voice steady and commanding. "We're about to start our final communication and defense drill. This is the last test to make sure everything is in place."

Kira, standing at the front, nodded. "We're ready. Let's show them what we've learned."

The villagers dispersed into their teams. Ryan and Captain Morales headed to the perimeter, where the barriers stood strong and imposing. "Remember, the key is to stay calm and follow the protocols we've established," Ryan reminded them.

Yuki, one of the younger villagers, grinned. "We've got this, Ryan. We're ready for anything."

Meanwhile, Amina gathered her group under the large tree for the final medical training session. "Today, we're going to review emergency procedures," she explained. "It's important to stay calm and act quickly."

Mei practiced on a dummy, her hands steady. "Like this, Amina?"

Amina smiled, adjusting Mei's grip slightly. "Perfect. Just remember to keep the wound clean and apply pressure to stop the bleeding."

In the communication center, Captain Morales conducted the last drill. "This is the final test. Treat it like a real emergency. Clear, concise communication is key."

Hiroshi, operating the radio, responded confidently. "Understood, Captain. We're ready."

The drill began, and the village moved with precision. Messages crackled over the radios, each one clear and concise. "South perimeter clear," reported Kala. "No unusual activity," added Hiroshi from the north watchtower.

Ryan and Captain Morales monitored the drill, their faces showing satisfaction as the villagers demonstrated their readiness. "Excellent work," Ryan praised. "You've shown that you can handle any situation."

As the sun began to set, casting long shadows over the village, the team gathered for a final debriefing around the central fire. Ryan addressed the group, his voice filled with pride. "You've all done an incredible job. The barriers are solid, the communication system is operational, and you're well-prepared for any emergencies."

Amina added, "Your health practices have improved significantly. Keep up the good work and continue to support each other."

Captain Morales nodded. "Today's drill was flawless. Remember to keep up with the regular check-ins and stay vigilant."

Mia, filming the debriefing, felt a deep sense of fulfillment. She turned to Yuki, who had been instrumental in the barrier construction. "Yuki, what's been the most rewarding part of this experience for you?"

Yuki wiped sweat from his brow, his face glowing with pride. "Seeing our village come together and knowing we can protect ourselves. It's been hard work, but it's worth it."

As the night deepened, the atmosphere around the central fire was one of celebration and reflection. Ryan addressed the group, his voice filled with hope and determination. "We've built more than just physical defenses. We've built a stronger, more united community. Keep working together, and we can achieve great things."

Kira stood beside him, her eyes reflecting the firelight. "We will. This is our home, and we'll protect it with everything we have."

Amina grinned. "Keep in mind, we're all connected. Use the communication system to stay in touch and back each other up."

Mia captured the scene, her heart swelling with pride. "We're building something lasting here. This village is becoming a beacon of hope and resilience."

As the fire crackled softly, the team sat together, discussing their next steps and reflecting on their journey. The challenges had been many, but with each village they helped, they were building a legacy of strength, resilience, and unity. The bonds they had forged with the villagers were strong, and their shared vision for a better future was becoming a reality.

Captain Morales turned to Ryan, her voice thoughtful. "We've made a real difference here. But there's still so much to do."

Ryan nodded, his expression serious but hopeful. "Every village we help strengthens the whole network. We're building a future, one step at a time."

Amina smiled, her eyes reflecting the firelight. "And it's not just about defense. It's about creating a community that cares for each other, that's resilient and self-sufficient."

Mia, her camera capturing the moment, added, "We're documenting every step, showing the world what's possible when people come together."

The night air was cool and filled with the sounds of the jungle, a reminder of the wild beauty surrounding them. They were not just building defenses; they were building a future, one village at a time. Together, they knew they could face whatever came their way, united by a common goal and a shared vision for a better world.

Chapter 18
Exploring Legacy and Identity

Mia knelt beside the edge of the pond, her fingers brushing lightly against the surface of the still water. The pond was exactly as her father had described it in his journal—serene, secluded, and surrounded by the vibrant hues of rare orchids. The soft, earthy scent of wet moss and blooming flowers filled the air, mingling with the distant calls of birds and the gentle hum of the jungle.

"Mia, you okay?" Ryan's voice broke through her reverie, and she glanced up to see him standing a few feet away, his brow furrowed in concern.

"Yeah, I'm fine," Mia replied, though her voice was distant. She looked back at the pond, a memory tugging at the edges of her mind. "I just... I think I've been here before. With my dad."

Ryan took a step closer, his gaze following hers. "Here? Are you sure?"

Mia nodded slowly, her eyes drifting to the clusters of white and pink orchids that dotted the edge of the water. "He used to bring me to places like this all the time. He called them his 'sanctuaries.' He said they were places where nature's resilience was on full display—where life thrived against all odds."

She could almost hear her father's voice, deep and gentle, explaining the intricate balance of the ecosystem around them, how each plant and creature played a vital role. The memory was so vivid that for a moment, she felt like she was twelve years old again, staring up at him with wide eyes, hanging on to every word.

"He said these orchids were special," Mia murmured, reaching out to touch one of the delicate flowers. "They only bloom for a few weeks each year. When I was a kid, I couldn't understand why something so beautiful would only last for such a short time."

"What did he say?" Ryan asked quietly, his voice soft with curiosity.

Mia smiled faintly, the corners of her lips lifting with the bittersweet memory. "He said that's what made them special. Because they're fleeting. He told me that the most beautiful things in nature—the rarest, most vibrant things—are often the most fragile. But that's why they need protecting."

Ryan was silent for a moment, watching her with an intensity that made her want to look away. But she held his gaze, feeling a strange mix of emotions churning inside her—pride, longing, and a deep, aching sadness.

"He really loved this place," Ryan said softly. "And I think... he would've been proud of you for finding it again."

Mia swallowed hard, her throat tight. "I don't know about that. There's still so much I don't understand, so much of his work that feels... unfinished. It's like I'm chasing a shadow, trying to live up to something I can never quite grasp."

"You're not chasing a shadow, Mia," Ryan said firmly. "You're building on his legacy, yes, but you're also creating your own. You don't have to follow his exact path to make a difference."

"But what if I'm not doing it right?" Mia's voice broke, the frustration and uncertainty she'd been holding back spilling over. "What if I can't protect the things he cared about? What if I end up failing?"

Ryan knelt beside her, his expression gentle but unyielding. "Listen to me. You're not going to fail. You've been fighting every step of the way, making tough decisions, keeping us all together out here. Your dad's work is a part of who you are, but it doesn't define you. You define you."

Mia looked down, her fingers trembling slightly as she traced the delicate petals of the orchid. "But how do I do that? How do I separate what he wanted from what I want?"

"That's something only you can figure out," Ryan murmured. "But I know this—you're not alone. You've got us, and we believe in you. Whatever path you choose, we're with you."

Mia nodded slowly, letting his words sink in. But the weight in her chest remained, heavy and unyielding. She glanced around the pond again, the memory of her father's laughter and the warmth of his hand on her shoulder almost palpable.

"There's so much of him here," she whispered, her voice barely audible. "In this place, in these flowers... it's like he's still here. And it hurts, Ryan. It hurts to see all of this and know that he's gone. That I'll never hear him talk about these orchids again, never see him smile when I get something right."

Ryan reached out, placing his hand over hers. "I know it hurts. But that pain? It's a reminder that he's still a part of you. And as long as you're out here, fighting for the things he loved, he's not really gone. You're carrying him with you."

Mia's eyes stung, and she blinked rapidly, trying to keep the tears at bay. She took a deep breath, nodding shakily. "I just... I need a minute. I need to clear my head."

"Take all the time you need," Ryan said softly, giving her hand a gentle squeeze before letting go. "We'll be right here."

Mia offered him a grateful smile, then rose slowly to her feet. She glanced back at the tranquil pond one last time, the orchids swaying gently in the breeze. The memory of her father's voice seemed to linger in the air, a soft whisper that she couldn't quite catch.

With a heavy heart, she turned and stepped away from the group, needing space to process everything. As she walked through the underbrush, the sounds of the jungle faded into a distant hum. She closed her eyes, letting the quiet settle around her like a shroud.

I'll figure this out, she promised herself, her hands clenched into fists at her sides. *I'll find my own way. For him. And for me.*

And with that, she disappeared into the dense foliage, leaving the pond—and the memories—behind, if only for a little while.

Mia sat at the edge of the pond, her gaze fixed on the ripples spreading across the water's surface. The memory of her father's voice, his excitement when he'd spoken about places like this, still lingered in her mind. She sighed, the weight of the past few weeks pressing heavily on her shoulders. The jungle, once vibrant and alive, felt suffocating now—like it was closing in around her.

The soft crunch of footsteps drew her attention. Mia glanced up to see Amina approaching, her expression a mixture of concern and understanding. Without a word, Amina settled beside her on the mossy rock, their shoulders almost touching. For a moment, neither of them spoke, the silence between them broken only by the gentle rustling of leaves in the breeze.

"Beautiful, isn't it?" Amina murmured, nodding toward the pond. "It's like a hidden paradise out here."

Mia nodded absently. "Yeah. He used to say it was like finding a little piece of heaven in the middle of the chaos."

Amina tilted her head, studying Mia's profile. "Your dad?"

"Yeah," Mia replied softly, a wistful smile tugging at her lips. "He loved these spots—these places where nature seemed to stand still, untouched by everything else. He believed they were proof that no matter how much damage we did, there was still hope for recovery."

"Sounds like a wise man," Amina said gently. "I can see where you get it from."

Mia let out a quiet laugh, shaking her head. "I don't know about that. He always seemed so sure of himself, like he knew exactly what he was doing. And me? I'm just stumbling along, hoping I'm making the right choices."

Amina's gaze softened. "Mia, no one knows exactly what they're doing, especially when they're trying to live up to someone else's legacy. It's... overwhelming. You feel like you have to be perfect, like every decision you make has to match up to what they would have done."

Mia looked at her, surprise flickering in her eyes. "How did you—?"

"I know because I've been there," Amina interrupted gently. "My mentor, Dr. Kassem—he was like a second father to me. He taught me everything I know about fieldwork, about conservation. When he passed, I felt this crushing pressure to keep his work going, to make sure I didn't let him down. But somewhere along the way, I realized I was losing myself. I wasn't making decisions based on what I thought was right—I was trying to guess what *he* would have wanted."

Mia stared at Amina, caught off guard by the vulnerability in her voice. "What did you do?"

Amina sighed, glancing down at her hands. "I had to step back. I had to take a good, hard look at why I was doing what I was doing. I asked myself if I was truly honoring him, or if I was just afraid of disappointing him, even when he wasn't there to judge me. And you know what I realized?"

"What?" Mia whispered.

"That honoring someone's legacy doesn't mean you have to become a copy of them," Amina said softly. "It means taking what they taught you, what they inspired in you, and making it your own. It means finding your own path, even if it's different from theirs. Because if they truly believed in you, then they'd want you to be yourself—not a shadow of who they were."

Mia looked away, blinking back the sudden sting of tears. "I want to believe that. But I keep thinking... what if I'm not doing enough? What if I fail, and everything he worked for is lost?"

"You won't fail," Amina said firmly. "You're too strong, too determined for that. But even if things don't go the way you planned, that doesn't mean you've failed him. Your dad's legacy isn't just about the successes. It's about the passion he had for the work, the love he had for these places, for these creatures. And you carry that with you in everything you do."

Mia's shoulders slumped, a tear slipping down her cheek. "It's just... so hard. I miss him. I wish he were here to tell me what to do."

Amina's expression softened, and she reached out, placing a gentle hand on Mia's arm. "I know, Mia. But he's still here—in you. In every choice you make, every step you take. You're not alone in this, even if it feels like it sometimes."

They sat in silence for a moment, the stillness of the pond reflected in the quiet understanding between them. Mia took a deep breath, letting Amina's words sink in, letting them soothe the raw edges of her grief and self-doubt.

"I guess... I just need to figure out what my path is," Mia murmured. "What I want to achieve, beyond just continuing his work."

"And you will," Amina assured her, her voice filled with quiet confidence. "It takes time, and it's not always easy. But you'll find your way. Just don't be afraid to listen to your own instincts, your own heart. Your dad taught you to be strong, to fight for what you believe in. But you get to decide what that means for you."

Mia nodded slowly, wiping her eyes with the back of her hand. "Thank you, Amina. I needed to hear that."

Amina smiled, a warm, genuine smile that reached her eyes. "That's what I'm here for. We're in this together, remember?"

"Yeah," Mia said softly, a tentative smile forming on her lips. "Together."

Amina gave her arm a gentle squeeze, then stood, glancing back at the rest of the team setting up camp in the distance. "Come on. Let's get back before Ryan and Kato start worrying."

Mia hesitated, glancing one last time at the pond and the orchids swaying gently in the breeze. She took a deep breath, then nodded.

"Yeah, let's go."

As they walked back to camp, Mia felt a small but significant shift within her—a flicker of light breaking through the shadows of doubt. She wasn't just her father's daughter, living in the shadow of his accomplishments. She was Mia Evans, with her own dreams, her own goals.

And maybe, just maybe, she could honor his memory and forge her own path at the same time.

With Amina's words still echoing in her mind, Mia straightened her shoulders and quickened her pace, feeling just a little bit lighter, a little bit stronger. There was still so much ahead of them, so much to overcome. But for the first time in a long while, she felt like she was exactly where she was meant to be.

The late afternoon sun filtered through the dense canopy, casting dappled shadows on the forest floor. Mia followed a few steps behind Kato, her mind still lingering on her conversation with Amina. They moved quietly, each step careful and deliberate as they navigated through the thick underbrush. Ryan and Amina flanked them, the entire team on high alert.

"Over here!" Kato's voice was hushed but urgent as he motioned for the others to join him. He crouched beside a large tree, his fingers brushing against what appeared to be a carefully concealed line of twine.

"What is it?" Mia asked, kneeling beside him.

Kato glanced up, his expression serious. "It's a snare. Well-hidden, too. Looks like it's designed to trap anything that crosses this path—small mammals, even ground-dwelling birds. But look closer." He pointed to a set of nearly invisible loops running parallel to the ground.

Mia's breath caught as she realized what she was seeing. "Multiple snares, all linked together... It's not just for one animal. It's meant to catch as many as possible in a single sweep."

"Exactly," Kato said, his voice tight. "And there's more. I found another set about twenty feet back, and a couple more just beyond that ridge. This isn't just a random setup, Mia. It's an entire network."

Ryan moved beside them, his eyes scanning the area. "They've been busy. This must be how they're operating so effectively without leaving much of a trace. By the time we spot one or two traps, they've already moved to another location."

Amina nodded, her gaze somber. "They're targeting everything in this area, and if we don't dismantle it soon, we could lose a significant portion of the local wildlife population. Some of these animals are species your father documented as being on the brink of extinction."

Mia's heart twisted painfully at the mention of her father. She looked around, noting the placement of each trap, the meticulous way they'd been set up. The jungle seemed to close in around her, suffocating in its silence. But amidst the anger and sorrow building within her, something else stirred—something she hadn't felt in a long time.

Determination.

"I know these patterns," Mia murmured, her voice gaining strength as she spoke. "My father studied poaching tactics like this in his research. He always said the key to dismantling these networks is to understand how they think, how they set their traps to maximize their haul with minimum effort."

Ryan glanced at her, his gaze sharp with interest. "So, what's the next move?"

Mia stood, dusting the dirt from her knees. "We take it down. Every single one of these traps. But not just that—" She turned to face them, her eyes alight with renewed resolve. "We use his research. His journals have detailed maps of where these species move, where they feed, where they nest. We can predict where the poachers will set up next."

Amina's eyes widened. "You want to use your father's research to get ahead of them? To turn their own tactics against them?"

"Exactly," Mia said, her voice steady, confident. "If we can anticipate their moves, we can start dismantling these networks before they even get a chance to catch anything. We can make it so costly for them to operate here that they'll have no choice but to leave."

Kato's face lit up with excitement. "Mia, that's brilliant! They've been playing this game with us, always staying one step ahead. But if we use your father's work..."

"We can finally turn the tables," Mia finished, nodding. "And more than that, we can protect these species the way he would have wanted."

Ryan studied her for a moment, then nodded slowly, a small smile tugging at the corners of his lips. "I like it. It's bold. But we're going to need to be careful. If they realize what we're doing, they could become more aggressive."

"Then we'll just have to be smarter," Mia said, her voice firm. She glanced down at the notebook tucked into her pocket—the same one her father had filled with notes, sketches, and ideas. For the first time since she'd started this expedition, she didn't feel like she was simply following in his footsteps. She was forging her own path, using his wisdom as a guide but making her own decisions.

Amina's smile was soft but full of pride. "Mia, I think your father would be proud. Not just because you're carrying on his work, but because you're making it your own."

Mia swallowed hard, emotions swirling within her. She looked at each of them—Amina, Kato, Ryan—and felt a surge of gratitude for their support, their belief in her.

"This isn't just about me or my father," she said quietly. "This is about all of us. We came here to make a difference, and that's exactly what we're going to do. One trap at a time, one step at a time. We'll take back this jungle, and we'll make it safe again."

Ryan reached out, placing a hand on her shoulder. "We're with you, Mia. Every step of the way."

Kato nodded eagerly. "Let's do this."

Mia took a deep breath, feeling the strength of their resolve, their shared purpose, solidify around her like a protective shield. "Alright. Let's get to work."

They moved quickly, dismantling the traps with practiced ease, their movements fluid and efficient. Mia directed them using her father's notes, guiding them to likely hotspots for more snares. With each trap they removed, she felt a little lighter, a little more in control.

As the last snare fell away, Mia straightened, brushing the dirt from her hands. She looked around at the small clearing, now free of the cruel devices meant to capture and kill. The sun was setting, casting a warm, golden glow over the jungle.

"We did it," Amina murmured, a note of awe in her voice. "We actually did it."

Mia nodded, a quiet smile on her lips. "This is just the beginning. We're not just reacting anymore—we're acting. We're making our own moves."

She turned to face them, her gaze steady, her heart filled with a renewed sense of purpose. "We'll finish what we started. And we'll do it on our terms."

With a final look at the clearing, Mia led the way back to their camp, a sense of clarity and resolve guiding her every step.

She was no longer just following her father's legacy.

She was building her own.

The camp was quiet, the only sound the gentle crackling of the fire as it flickered and danced in the center of their small circle. The others had retired to their tents, the day's exertions finally catching up to them. But Mia remained outside, staring into the flames, the warmth brushing against her face like a comforting hand. The notebook lay open on her lap, its familiar pages filled with hastily scribbled notes and sketches. But this time, she wasn't focused on strategies or research. She was writing something entirely different.

Dear Dad,

She hesitated, the pen hovering over the paper. She'd written to him a hundred times since his death, filling pages with her thoughts and feelings. But those letters were always left unfinished, abandoned whenever the weight of her grief grew too heavy. Tonight, though, it felt different. Tonight, she needed to get the words out, to confront them.

Dear Dad,

I've been trying to keep it all together out here. Trying to make you proud, to do things the way you would have. But the truth is, I'm scared. I'm scared that I'm not strong enough, not brave enough, not good enough. Every time I make a decision, I wonder what you would've done. And every time I fail, I feel like I'm failing you too.

She paused, swallowing hard as the words blurred on the page. The flames flickered, casting shadows that seemed to move and twist with her emotions. She could almost hear his voice—deep, steady, always so sure.

What would you say if you were here? You'd probably tell me to take a breath, to think things through. You'd tell me that I'm doing fine, even if I don't feel like it. And I want to believe that. I really do. But it's so hard, Dad. It's so hard without you.

Mia blinked rapidly, wiping away the tears that had gathered in her eyes. She took a deep breath, forcing herself to keep going.

I thought that if I finished your work, if I followed in your footsteps, I'd feel closer to you. That I'd be able to carry on your legacy. But now, I'm starting to realize something. I can't just live in your shadow. I can't keep chasing this dream as if it's only yours.

She shifted, glancing around the empty camp. The jungle seemed to press in on all sides, vast and unyielding. But she didn't feel as lost as she had before. Something had changed. Amina's words, their discovery today—it had sparked something in her, something she hadn't known she'd been missing.

This mission... it's become more than just honoring your memory. It's become my mission, too. My fight. I want to do this for me, Dad. I want to make a difference because it's what I believe in, because I want to see these places thrive. I want to find my own way, even if it's not exactly how you would've done it.

She exhaled slowly, the tension in her chest loosening with each stroke of the pen. The words flowed more easily now, each sentence a release, a way to make peace with everything she'd been holding onto for so long.

I hope you'd understand that. I hope you'd be proud of the choices I make, even if they're different from yours. I'll always carry you with me, but I'm ready to step out of your shadow and into the light. I'm ready to be Mia Evans—not just William Evans' daughter.

She paused, reading over what she'd written. The fear, the uncertainty, the lingering grief—it was all there, laid bare on the page. But there was something else, too. A sense of hope, of determination. Of strength.

Mia's hand trembled as she reached for the edge of the page. Slowly, deliberately, she tore it out, the sound of ripping paper startlingly loud in the stillness of the night. She stared at the torn sheet for a long moment, her heart pounding. Then, with a deep breath, she tossed it into the fire.

The flames eagerly licked at the edges of the paper, curling it into ash as it burned. Mia watched, a strange sense of calm settling over her as the letter crumbled and disintegrated. It felt like a release—like she was letting go of the fear of disappointing him, of not living up to his legacy.

"I'm doing this for both of us," she whispered softly to the fire, her voice barely more than a breath. "But I'm doing it my way."

She closed her journal, the familiar weight of it comforting in her hands. For the first time since arriving in the Congo, she felt... lighter. Like a burden she hadn't realized she was carrying had been lifted.

As the last of the letter disappeared into the flames, Mia leaned back, staring up at the stars peeking through the canopy. Her father's memory would always be with her, but she wasn't chasing him anymore. She was choosing her own path, making her own mark.

She smiled faintly, the lingering warmth of the fire brushing against her cheeks. Tomorrow would bring more challenges, more struggles, but she felt ready. Ready to face whatever lay ahead.

"Goodnight, Dad," she murmured softly, closing her eyes. "I'll make you proud—by being proud of myself, too."

With a final glance at the dying flames, Mia stood and walked back to her tent, feeling at peace in a way she hadn't felt in a long time.

Chapter 19
Closing in on the Enemy

The sun had barely risen when the team began their preparations to leave the village. The air was crisp and cool, the promise of a new day heavy with the unknown. Ryan, Mia, Amina, and Captain Morales packed their gear with practiced efficiency, their minds already on the next challenge.

Ryan glanced at the map, tracing their path to the next village. "This next leg of our journey will be tougher. We'll be navigating through dense jungle and crossing a wide river. We need to stay alert."

Mia, adjusting her camera strap, nodded. "The more remote they are, the more critical it is to connect them. Their stories need to be told."

Amina checked her medical supplies, her face set with determination. "I'm ready for whatever comes our way. Isolation often means a lack of basic medical care. We need to be prepared for anything."

Captain Morales double-checked the communication equipment, her expression serious. "And we need to ensure our radios stay functional. If we run into trouble, communication will be our lifeline."

The villagers gathered to see them off, their expressions a mix of gratitude and concern. Kira, the village leader, stepped forward, her eyes filled with determination. "You've taught us so much. We'll continue to build on what we've learned."

Ryan clasped Kira's hand, his voice steady. "You've made incredible progress. Keep up the good work and stay connected. We'll be in touch."

As the team set off, the villagers' well-wishes echoed behind them. The path quickly became more challenging, the jungle closing in around them. The air was thick with humidity, and the sounds of wildlife were a constant reminder of the untamed environment.

They moved in single file, each person focused on the path ahead. Ryan led the way, his machete slicing through the dense foliage. "Stay close and keep an eye out for any signs of danger," he instructed.

The journey was grueling, the terrain unforgiving. They navigated steep inclines, crossed narrow ravines, and waded through streams. Each step was a test of their endurance and determination.

By midday, they reached the edge of a wide river. The water was fast-moving and deep, a formidable barrier between them and their destination. Ryan surveyed the scene, assessing their options. "We'll need to find a safe way across. This current is too strong to swim."

Captain Morales scanned the riverbank, her eyes sharp. "There might be a shallower spot upstream. We should check it out."

They followed the riverbank, the sound of rushing water filling the air. After some time, they found a spot where the river narrowed slightly, the current appearing less fierce. Ryan tested the depth with a long stick. "This looks manageable. We'll go across one at a time, using the rope for safety."

Amina secured one end of the rope around a sturdy tree, while Ryan tied the other end around his waist. He stepped into the river, the cold water swirling around his legs. "Take it slow and steady. Hold onto the rope for balance."

Mia followed, her camera securely packed in a waterproof bag. She gripped the rope tightly, feeling the force of the current tugging at her. "This is intense," she muttered, concentrating on each step.

One by one, they made their way across, the rope providing a lifeline in the treacherous waters. Finally, they all reached the other side, breathing a collective sigh of relief.

Ryan checked his map, orienting himself. "We're making good progress. The village should be another few hours' trek from here."

As they resumed their journey, the jungle seemed to grow denser, the path less defined. The team moved with caution, every sense alert for potential dangers. The sun was beginning to dip lower in the sky, casting long shadows through the trees.

Ryan called for a brief rest, allowing everyone to catch their breath and rehydrate. "We're close. Let's keep pushing forward. The village is just over that ridge."

With renewed determination, they pressed on. The final climb was steep and challenging, but their perseverance paid off. As they reached the top of the ridge, the sight of the village nestled in a small valley greeted them. Smoke curled lazily from chimneys, and the sounds of daily life floated up to meet them.

The team exchanged relieved smiles. They had made it through the toughest part of their journey. Now, it was time to bring their support and expertise to this new village, helping them build a stronger, more resilient community. The path ahead was still filled with challenges, but with each step, they were forging a future of hope and unity.

The team stood at the edge of the village, their arrival not yet noticed by the villagers busy with their daily routines. Ryan took a deep breath, surveying the scene. "We need to approach this carefully. Let's introduce ourselves and explain our mission."

Mia nodded, her camera poised to capture the first moments. "Ready when you are, Ryan."

They walked down the ridge, drawing the attention of the villagers. An elderly man, tall and with a commanding presence, stepped forward, his eyes sharp with curiosity. "Who are you, and why have you come here?"

Ryan raised his hands in a gesture of peace. "We're here to help. We've been working with other villages to build defenses, set up communication systems, and improve health and education. We want to do the same here."

The man scrutinized them for a moment before nodding. "I am Masaki, the village leader. We've heard of you. Some say you bring hope, others say you bring trouble. What makes you different?"

Amina stepped up, her voice calm and reassuring. "We bring knowledge and support. Everything we do is to empower you, not control you. We work with you to strengthen your community."

Masaki's gaze softened slightly. "Very well. Show us what you can do."

Ryan smiled, relieved. "Thank you, Masaki. Let's start by assessing your needs. We'll split into teams to cover more ground."

As they divided into groups, Ryan and Captain Morales focused on the village's defenses. "We'll begin by inspecting the perimeter. It's crucial to understand your current setup," Ryan said, leading the way.

Masaki accompanied them, pointing out various parts of the village. "We've done what we can with the resources available, but it's far from adequate."

Ryan examined the makeshift barriers, noting their weaknesses. "We can reinforce these with stronger materials. It'll provide better protection against any threats."

Meanwhile, Amina set up a temporary clinic under a large tree. She addressed a group of villagers, explaining the importance of hygiene and basic first aid. "Clean water and proper wound care are essential. These small steps can prevent serious illnesses."

A young woman named Hana raised her hand. "What should we do if someone is injured and we don't have the right supplies?"

Amina demonstrated how to improvise with available materials. "Use clean cloths for bandages and boiled water for cleaning wounds. It's not perfect, but it's effective."

Mia moved through the village, capturing these interactions on camera. She paused to interview a group of children who had gathered around her, curious about the newcomers. "What do you think of all the changes happening?"

A boy named Kaito spoke up, his eyes wide with excitement. "It's amazing! We're learning so much, and it feels like we can do anything."

Mia smiled, her heart swelling with pride. "You're part of something important. Every effort counts."

As the day progressed, the team reconvened in the central clearing to share their findings. Ryan addressed the group, his voice steady. "We've identified several areas where we can make immediate improvements. Let's focus on strengthening the barriers and setting up the communication system."

Captain Morales added, "We'll conduct a drill tomorrow to ensure everyone knows what to do in an emergency. Clear communication is key."

Masaki nodded, his expression thoughtful. "Your help is invaluable. We've struggled for so long, but now it feels like we have a chance."

Ryan looked around at the villagers, seeing a mix of hope and determination on their faces. "We're in this together. Let's get to work."

As they began their tasks, the atmosphere in the village shifted. There was a sense of purpose and unity, each person contributing to the common goal. Ryan and Captain Morales oversaw the construction of stronger barriers, guiding the villagers through the process.

"Make sure these supports are deep and secure," Ryan instructed, watching as the villagers worked diligently.

Yuki, a young man from the village, looked up from his task. "Is this right, Ryan?"

Ryan inspected the work and nodded. "Perfect. Keep it up."

Meanwhile, Amina continued her medical training, demonstrating how to handle severe injuries. "If someone is unconscious and not breathing, start CPR immediately. Remember, 30 compressions to 2 breaths."

Hana practiced on a dummy, her face tense with concentration. "Like this, Amina?"

Amina smiled, adjusting Hana's hands slightly. "Exactly. You're doing great. Just keep practicing."

Mia captured every moment, knowing these stories would inspire others. She turned to interview Masaki, who was watching the progress with a mix of pride and hope. "Masaki, how do you feel about the changes happening here?"

Masaki's eyes reflected his deep emotions. "It's overwhelming, in a good way. We've been struggling for so long, and now it feels like we have a real chance to thrive. Your team has brought us hope."

As the sun began to set, casting a warm glow over the village, the team and villagers gathered around the central fire. The air was filled with the sounds of laughter and conversation, a stark contrast to the tension of their arrival.

Ryan addressed the group, his voice filled with optimism. "We've made incredible progress today. Remember, this is just the beginning. Keep working together, and we can achieve great things."

Masaki stood beside him, his eyes reflecting the firelight. "We will. This is our home, and we'll protect it with everything we have."

Amina added, "And remember, we're all connected now. Use the communication system to stay in touch and support each other."

Mia captured the scene, her heart swelling with pride. "We're building something lasting here. This village is becoming a beacon of hope and resilience."

The night deepened, and the bonds between the team and villagers grew stronger. They shared stories and laughter, united by a common goal and a shared vision for a better future. The challenges ahead were many, but with each step, they were forging a path of strength, unity, and hope.

The next morning, the village awoke to the sound of hammers and saws as the team and villagers continued their work. The air was filled with a sense of urgency, tempered by the excitement of progress. Ryan, Mia, Amina, and Captain Morales moved through the village, each focused on their tasks.

Ryan gathered a group near the perimeter, his voice steady and instructive. "Today, we'll finish reinforcing the barriers and conduct a communication drill. It's crucial that everyone knows their role."

Masaki, the village leader, nodded. "We're ready. We've made great progress, thanks to your guidance."

Ryan smiled. "You've all worked hard. Let's keep up the momentum."

The villagers dispersed into their teams, and Ryan led his group to the perimeter to inspect the barriers. "Remember to check the supports. They need to be deep and secure," he said, watching as Yuki and the others worked.

Yuki, focused on his task, asked, "Is this deep enough, Ryan?"

Ryan inspected the trench and nodded. "Perfect. Let's get these supports in place."

Meanwhile, Amina was conducting another round of health checks and training. She gathered a group under a large tree, her voice clear and calm. "Today, we're going to review emergency procedures again. It's essential to stay calm and act quickly."

Hana, practicing CPR on a dummy, looked up. "Like this, Amina?"

Amina adjusted Hana's hands slightly. "Yes, exactly. Keep your compressions steady and firm."

Nearby, Captain Morales was preparing the villagers for the communication drill. She handed out radios, her tone firm but encouraging. "This is a simulation, but treat it seriously. Clear, concise communication is key."

Hiroshi, one of the more experienced villagers, tested his radio. "Ready when you are, Captain."

Mia moved through the village, her camera capturing the activity. She paused to interview Kaito, a young boy who had been watching the preparations with wide eyes. "Kaito, what do you think about all the changes happening here?"

Kaito's face lit up with excitement. "It's amazing! We're learning so much, and I feel like we can do anything now."

Mia smiled, her heart swelling with pride. "You're part of something important, Kaito. Every effort counts."

The day progressed with a steady rhythm, each team focused on their tasks. By mid-afternoon, the barriers were nearly complete, and the communication system was ready for testing.

Ryan gathered everyone in the central clearing for the drill. "This is a final test to ensure everything is in place. Treat it like a real emergency. Stay calm and follow the protocols."

Captain Morales took charge of the drill, her voice clear over the radios. "All teams, report in."

"North perimeter clear," Hiroshi's voice crackled. "No unusual activity."

"West perimeter clear," added Kala. "Everything is calm."

The drill proceeded seamlessly, with each team responding promptly and effectively. Ryan observed with satisfaction as the villagers showcased their preparedness. "Great job, everyone. You've proven that you can manage any situation."

As the drill concluded, Amina gathered her group for a final debriefing. "You all did great. Remember, the key is to stay calm and support each other. Your health practices have improved significantly."

Mia, filming the debriefing, turned to interview Masaki. "Masaki, how do you feel about the progress we've made?"

Masaki's eyes reflected his deep emotions. "It's been incredible. We've struggled for so long, but now it feels like we have a real chance to thrive. Your team has brought us hope."

As the sun set, casting a soft glow over the village, the team and villagers gathered around the central fire. The mood was one of quiet fulfillment and rising confidence. Ryan spoke to the assembly, his voice strong with hope and determination.

"We've developed more than just barriers. We've built a community that supports and defends each other. Continue collaborating, and you can achieve remarkable things."

Kira stood beside him, her eyes reflecting the firelight. "We will. This is our home, and we'll protect it with everything we have."

Amina gave a warm smile. "Remember, we're all linked. Use the communication system to stay connected and provide support."

Mia captured the scene, her heart swelling with pride. "We're building something lasting here. This village is becoming a beacon of hope and resilience."

As the night deepened, the team sat by the fire, mapping out their next steps and reflecting on their journey. The trials had been many, but with each village they assisted, they were building a legacy of strength, resilience, and unity. The relationships they had developed with the villagers were strong, and their collective vision for a brighter future was coming to life. The work was hard, but it was meaningful, and it was making a difference. Together, they knew they could face whatever came their way, one village at a time. The path ahead was long, but they were ready. They were building a future, one step at a time.

As dawn broke, the village was already abuzz with activity. The team and villagers moved with purpose, knowing this was their final day together. The air was filled with a sense of urgency and determination, but also a quiet confidence that had grown over their time together. Ryan, Mia, Amina, and Captain Morales gathered for a final briefing.

Ryan addressed the group, his voice calm and steady. "Today, we'll finalize everything. We need to ensure the barriers are perfect and the communication system is flawless. Let's give it our all."

Kira, standing at the forefront, nodded resolutely. "We're ready. Let's make today count."

The villagers dispersed into their assigned teams. Ryan and Captain Morales headed to the perimeter, inspecting the barriers one last time. "Make sure every support is deep and secure," Ryan instructed. "We can't afford any weaknesses."

Yuki, working diligently, asked, "Is this deep enough, Ryan?"

Ryan inspected the work and nodded. "That's perfect. Let's keep moving."

Meanwhile, Amina gathered a group under the large tree for a final health training session. "Today, we're going to review everything we've learned. It's crucial that you all feel confident in handling emergencies."

Hana, practicing CPR on a dummy, looked up. "Like this, Amina?"

Amina adjusted Hana's technique slightly. "Yes, exactly. You're doing great. Keep your compressions steady and firm."

Captain Morales prepared the villagers for a comprehensive communication drill. She handed out radios, her tone firm but encouraging. "This is our final drill. Treat it like a real emergency. Clear, concise communication is key."

Hiroshi, testing his radio, responded confidently. "We're ready, Captain."

The drill began, and the village moved with precision. Messages crackled over the radios, each one clear and concise. "North perimeter clear," Hiroshi reported. "No unusual activity."

"West perimeter clear," added Kala. "Everything is calm."

Ryan and Captain Morales monitored the drill, their faces showing satisfaction as the villagers demonstrated their readiness. "Excellent work," Ryan praised. "You've shown that you can handle any situation."

Amina gathered her group for a final debriefing. "You all did great. Remember, the key is to stay calm and support each other. Your health practices have improved significantly."

Mia, capturing the debriefing on camera, turned to interview Masaki. "Masaki, how do you feel about the progress we've made?"

Masaki's eyes reflected deep emotion. "It's been incredible. We've struggled for so long, but now it feels like we have a real chance to thrive. Your team has brought us hope."

As the day progressed, the final touches were added to the barriers and the communication system. The sense of accomplishment was palpable, each task bringing the village closer to readiness. By late afternoon, the work was complete.

Ryan gathered everyone in the central clearing for a final address. "You've all done an exceptional job. The barriers are solid, the communication system is operational, and you're well-prepared for any emergencies. You're ready."

Captain Morales nodded. "Today's drill was flawless. Keep up with the regular check-ins and stay vigilant."

Amina added, "Your health practices have improved significantly. Keep up the good work and continue to support each other."

Mia, filming the address, felt a deep sense of fulfillment. She turned to Yuki. "Yuki, how do you feel after all this hard work?"

Yuki wiped sweat from his brow, his face glowing with pride. "It's been tough, but it's worth it. We know we can protect our village."

As the sun began to set, casting a warm glow over the village, the team and villagers gathered around the central fire. The atmosphere was one of celebration and reflection. Ryan addressed the group, his voice filled with hope and determination.

"We've established more than physical fortifications. We've nurtured a community of mutual support and protection. Keep cooperating, and you'll achieve great things."

Kira stood beside him, her eyes reflecting the firelight. "We will. This is our home, and we'll protect it with everything we have."

Amina smiled broadly. "Don't forget, we're all connected. Use the communication system to maintain contact and support each other."

Mia captured the scene, her heart swelling with pride. "We're building something lasting here. This village is becoming a beacon of hope and resilience."

As the fire crackled softly, the team sat together, discussing their next steps and reflecting on their journey. The challenges had been many, but with each village they helped, they were building a legacy of strength, resilience, and unity. The bonds they had forged with the villagers were strong, and their shared vision for a better future was becoming a reality.

Captain Morales turned to Ryan, her voice thoughtful. "We've made a real difference here. But there's still so much to do."

Ryan nodded, his expression serious but hopeful. "Every village we help strengthens the whole network. We're building a future, one step at a time."

Amina smiled, her eyes reflecting the firelight. "And it's not just about defense. It's about creating a community that cares for each other, that's resilient and self-sufficient."

Mia, her camera capturing the moment, added, "We're documenting every step, showing the world what's possible when people come together."

The night air was cool and filled with the sounds of the jungle, a reminder of the wild beauty surrounding them. They were not just building defenses; they were building a future, one village at a time. Together, they knew they could face whatever came their way, united by a common goal and a shared vision for a better world.

Chapter 20
Uncovering the Syndicate's Network

The first light of dawn cast a soft glow over the village as the team prepared to depart. The morning air was crisp, filled with the promise of a new journey. Ryan, Mia, Amina, and Captain Morales stood together, surveying the village that had transformed before their eyes. The villagers gathered to see them off, their expressions a mix of gratitude and resolve.

Ryan turned to Kira, the village leader, his voice filled with admiration. "You've done an incredible job here. The village is stronger and more united than ever. Keep building on this foundation."

Kira nodded, her eyes shining with determination. "We will. Thank you for everything. You've given us the tools to protect ourselves and thrive."

Amina stepped forward, embracing Kira. "Remember to keep up with the health practices we've taught you. Regular check-ups and hygiene are key."

Kira smiled. "We'll take your advice to heart. You've shown us the importance of health and community."

Captain Morales addressed the group, her tone firm but encouraging. "Stay vigilant and keep your communication system active. Regular check-ins will ensure you stay connected and informed."

Hiroshi, one of the villagers responsible for the communication system, responded confidently. "We'll make sure to follow the protocols. Thank you for everything, Captain."

Mia moved through the crowd, capturing these final moments on camera. She paused to interview Yuki, who had been instrumental in reinforcing the village's defenses. "Yuki, how do you feel about the work you've done here?"

Yuki's face lit up with pride. "It's been hard work, but it's worth it. We know we can protect our village now. We're ready for anything."

As the team prepared to leave, Ryan addressed the villagers one last time. "This isn't goodbye. We're all part of a larger network now. Stay connected and support each other. Together, we're stronger."

Kira raised her hand in a gesture of solidarity. "We will. This is just the beginning for us."

The team set off down the familiar path, the villagers' well-wishes echoing behind them. The journey ahead was filled with uncertainty, but also hope. They walked in silence for a while, each lost in their thoughts about the road ahead.

Ryan broke the silence, his voice thoughtful. "Every village we help strengthens the whole network. We're building a future, one step at a time."

Mia nodded, her camera hanging at her side. "It's incredible to see the impact we're having. These stories will inspire others to take action."

Amina adjusted her medical pack, her expression determined. "And it's not just about defense. It's about creating a community that cares for each other, that's resilient and self-sufficient."

Captain Morales scanned the surroundings, ever vigilant. "We've laid a strong foundation here. Now it's up to them to keep it going. But we'll always be there to support them."

The path led them through dense jungle, the sounds of nature a constant companion. They moved with purpose, their steps sure and steady. The journey was grueling, but their resolve was unwavering. They knew the importance of their mission and the lives it impacted.

By midday, they reached a clearing and paused for a break. Ryan unfolded the map, tracing their route to the next village. "We've got another day's trek ahead of us. Let's stay focused."

Mia took a sip of water, her gaze thoughtful. "The more remote the village, the more crucial it is to connect them. Their stories need to be told."

Amina nodded in agreement. "Isolation often means a lack of basic necessities. We need to be prepared for anything."

Captain Morales checked their supplies, her expression serious. "And we need to ensure our radios stay functional. Communication is our lifeline."

As they continued their journey, the terrain grew more challenging. The jungle thickened, the path becoming less defined. They moved with caution, every sense alert for potential dangers. The sun dipped lower in the sky, casting long shadows through the trees.

Ryan led the way, his machete slicing through the dense foliage. "Stay close and keep an eye out for any signs of trouble," he instructed.

The team pressed on, their determination unwavering. They knew that each step brought them closer to another village in need, another opportunity to make a difference. The challenges were many, but so were the rewards. They were building a future, one village at a time, united by a common goal and a shared vision for a better world.

As dusk approached, they reached a ridge overlooking their next destination. The sight of the village nestled in the valley below filled them with renewed energy. They exchanged determined smiles, ready to bring their support and expertise to this new community. The path ahead was still long, but they were ready. Together, they knew they could face whatever came their way, one village at a time.

The morning sun pierced through the canopy, casting speckles of light on the ground as the team descended into the valley. The village below was still waking up, the soft sounds of daily life floating up to meet them. Ryan, Mia, Amina, and Captain Morales moved with purpose, their minds focused on the task ahead.

Ryan addressed the group as they approached the village edge. "Let's approach with respect and caution. We need to earn their trust."

Mia adjusted her camera, ready to document their first encounter. "I'll capture everything. It's important to show the world what we're doing."

Amina checked her medical supplies, her face set with determination. "I'm prepared for anything. We need to assess their health needs immediately."

Captain Morales ensured their communication devices were operational, her expression serious. "And we need to set up a communication system as soon as possible. It's crucial for their safety."

As they entered the village, the inhabitants paused their activities, watching the newcomers with curiosity and caution. An elderly woman, her posture straight and commanding, stepped forward. "Who are you, and why have you come here?"

Ryan raised his hands in a gesture of peace. "We're here to help. We've been working with other villages to build defenses, set up communication systems, and improve health and education. We want to do the same here."

The woman scrutinized them for a moment before speaking. "I am Emiko, the village leader. We've heard of you. Some say you bring hope, others say you bring trouble. Why should we trust you?"

Amina stepped forward, her voice calm and reassuring. "We bring knowledge and support. Everything we do is to empower you, not control you. We work with you to strengthen your community."

Emiko's gaze softened slightly. "Very well. Show us what you can do."

The team immediately set to work. Ryan and Captain Morales began assessing the village's defenses, noting the natural barriers and identifying areas that needed reinforcement. "We'll start by strengthening these weak points," Ryan explained. "It'll provide better protection against any threats."

A young man named Kenta, eager to learn, asked, "What materials should we use?"

Ryan replied, "Use what you can find—rocks, mud, anything that can add to the stability. Adaptability is key."

Meanwhile, Amina set up a temporary clinic under a large tree, starting with a health assessment to understand the villagers' needs. She spoke to a group of women about basic hygiene and first aid. "Clean water and proper wound care are essential. These small steps can prevent serious illnesses."

A woman named Yumi raised her hand. "What should we do if someone is injured and we don't have the right supplies?"

Amina demonstrated how to improvise with available materials. "Use clean cloths for bandages and boiled water for cleaning wounds. It's not perfect, but it's effective."

Mia moved through the village, capturing their efforts on camera. She paused to interview Emiko, who spoke candidly about the village's struggles and hopes. "We've managed to survive in this harsh environment, but it's been difficult. If you can truly help us, we will welcome your support."

Emiko's words were filled with a mix of skepticism and hope. "We've seen many promises come and go. What makes you different?"

Mia lowered her camera slightly, meeting Emiko's eyes. "We're not here to make promises. We're here to work with you, side by side, to create lasting change."

As the day progressed, the team and villagers worked side by side, building trust and laying the foundation for a stronger, more resilient community. Ryan and Captain Morales led groups to gather materials and reinforce barriers, while Amina continued her medical training sessions, ensuring everyone felt confident in their new skills.

By mid-afternoon, the sense of accomplishment was palpable. The barriers took shape, the villagers' confidence grew, and the communication system began to hum with activity. The village was transforming before their eyes.

Ryan gathered everyone for a progress update. "We've made incredible strides today. The barriers are taking shape, and the communication system is almost operational. We're on the right track."

Amina added, "Your health practices are improving too. Keep practicing what you've learned and support each other."

Captain Morales nodded. "We'll run a drill tomorrow to ensure everyone knows what to do in an emergency. Clear communication is key."

As the sun began to set, casting a golden glow over the village, the team and villagers gathered around the central fire. The atmosphere was one of quiet satisfaction and growing confidence. Ryan addressed the group, his voice filled with hope and determination.

"We've built more than just physical defenses. We've built trust and a sense of community. Keep working together, and we can achieve great things."

Emiko stood beside him, her eyes reflecting the firelight. "We will. This is our home, and we'll protect it with everything we have."

Amina's smile was radiant. "Keep in mind, we're all connected now. Use the communication system to stay in touch and help one another."

Mia captured the scene, her heart swelling with pride. "We're building something lasting here. This village is becoming a beacon of hope and resilience."

As the night settled in, the team huddled by the fire, contemplating their next actions and reflecting on their journey. The obstacles had been numerous, but with each village they supported, they were shaping a legacy of strength, resilience, and unity. The connections with the villagers were unbreakable, and their collective vision for a better future was becoming a reality. The work was demanding but significant, and it was making a difference. United, they believed they could face any challenge, one village at a time. The road ahead was long, but they were prepared. They were forging a future, one step at a time.

The morning sun cast a golden hue over the village as the team prepared for their second day of work. The air was filled with a sense of purpose, the villagers moving with a newfound confidence. Ryan, Mia, Amina, and Captain Morales gathered near the central clearing, reviewing their plan for the day.

Ryan addressed the group, his voice carrying a note of urgency. "Today, we'll focus on finalizing the barriers and conducting a full-scale communication drill. It's crucial that everyone knows their role and feels confident."

Emiko, the village leader, stood beside Ryan, her expression resolute. "We're ready. We've come a long way in a short time, thanks to your guidance."

Ryan nodded. "Let's keep up the momentum. We'll split into teams to cover more ground."

The villagers dispersed into their assigned groups. Ryan and Captain Morales led a team to the perimeter, inspecting the progress on the barriers. "Make sure the supports are deep and secure," Ryan instructed. "We need these barriers to be solid and reliable."

Kenta, working diligently, asked, "Is this deep enough, Ryan?"

Ryan examined the trench and nodded. "Perfect. Keep up the good work."

Nearby, Amina gathered her group for another health training session under the large tree. She demonstrated how to handle severe injuries, her voice calm and reassuring. "If someone is unconscious and not breathing, start CPR immediately. Remember, 30 compressions to 2 breaths."

Yumi, practicing on a dummy, looked up. "Like this, Amina?"

Amina adjusted Yumi's technique slightly. "Yes, exactly. You're doing great. Just keep practicing."

Captain Morales prepared the villagers for the communication drill, handing out radios and explaining their use. "This is our final drill. Treat it like a real emergency. Clear, concise communication is key."

Hiroshi, testing his radio, responded confidently. "We're ready, Captain."

Mia moved through the village, her camera capturing the activity and interactions. She paused to interview Emiko, who watched the preparations with a mix of pride and hope. "Emiko, how do you feel about the changes happening here?"

Emiko's eyes reflected her deep emotions. "It's overwhelming, in a good way. We've been struggling for so long, but now it feels like we have a real chance to thrive. Your team has brought us hope."

As the day progressed, the team and villagers worked tirelessly. The barriers took shape, the communication system was tested, and the villagers gained confidence in their new skills. By mid-afternoon, the sense of accomplishment was palpable.

Ryan gathered everyone in the central clearing for the drill. "This is the final test to ensure everything is in place. Treat it like a real emergency. Stay calm and follow the protocols."

Captain Morales took charge, her voice clear over the radios. "All teams, report in."

"North perimeter clear," Hiroshi's voice crackled. "No unusual activity."

"West perimeter clear," added Kala. "Everything is calm."

The drill ran smoothly, with each team reacting swiftly and efficiently. Ryan watched with pride as the villagers displayed their readiness. "Well done, everyone. You've demonstrated that you can handle any scenario."

Amina gathered her group for a final debriefing. "You all did great. Remember, the key is to stay calm and support each other. Your health practices have improved significantly."

Mia, filming the debriefing, turned to interview Kenta. "Kenta, what's been the most rewarding part of this experience for you?"

Kenta wiped sweat from his brow, his face glowing with pride. "It's been hard work, but it's worth it. We know we can protect our village."

As the sun began to set, casting a warm hue across the village, the team and villagers assembled around the central fire. The air was filled with a sense of quiet satisfaction and growing assurance. Ryan addressed the group, his voice resonating with hope and determination.

"We've built more than just physical protections. We've fostered a community that cares for and safeguards each other. Stay united, and you'll accomplish extraordinary things."

Emiko stood beside him, her eyes reflecting the firelight. "We will. This is our home, and we'll protect it with everything we have."

Amina's face lit up with a smile. "Remember, we're all interconnected. Use the communication system to stay in touch and support each other."

Mia captured the scene, her heart swelling with pride. "We're building something lasting here. This village is becoming a beacon of hope and resilience."

As darkness enveloped the night, the team gathered around the fire, discussing their upcoming plans and reflecting on their journey. They had encountered many challenges, but with each village they helped, they were building a legacy of strength, resilience, and unity. The bonds they had forged with the villagers were robust, and their shared vision for a better future was becoming a reality.

Captain Morales turned to Ryan, her voice thoughtful. "We've made a real difference here. But there's still so much to do."

Ryan nodded, his expression serious but hopeful. "Every village we help strengthens the whole network. We're building a future, one step at a time."

Amina smiled, her eyes reflecting the firelight. "And it's not just about defense. It's about creating a community that cares for each other, that's resilient and self-sufficient."

Mia, her camera capturing the moment, added, "We're documenting every step, showing the world what's possible when people come together."

The night air was cool and filled with the sounds of the jungle, a reminder of the wild beauty surrounding them. They were not just building defenses; they were building a future, one village at a time. Together, they knew they could face whatever came their way, united by a common goal and a shared vision for a better world.

The dawn brought with it a renewed sense of purpose as the village stirred to life. The team and villagers moved with a quiet determination, knowing that today marked the culmination of their efforts. Ryan, Mia, Amina, and Captain Morales gathered near the central clearing, ready to tackle the final tasks.

Ryan addressed the group, his voice calm and steady. "Today, we'll focus on refining the barriers and running a comprehensive drill to ensure everyone is prepared. Let's give it our best."

Emiko, the village leader, stood beside Ryan, her expression resolute. "We're ready. Let's make today count."

The villagers dispersed into their teams. Ryan and Captain Morales led a group to the perimeter to inspect and reinforce the barriers. "Check the supports one last time," Ryan instructed. "We need to make sure everything is solid."

Kenta, working diligently, asked, "Is this deep enough, Ryan?"

Ryan examined the trench and nodded. "Perfect. Let's get these supports in place."

Nearby, Amina gathered her group under the large tree for a final health training session. She demonstrated how to handle severe injuries, her voice calm and reassuring. "If someone is unconscious and not breathing, start CPR immediately. Remember, 30 compressions to 2 breaths."

Yumi, practicing on a dummy, looked up. "Like this, Amina?"

Amina adjusted Yumi's technique slightly. "Yes, exactly. You're doing great. Just keep practicing."

Captain Morales prepared the villagers for the comprehensive communication drill. She handed out radios, her tone firm but encouraging. "This is our final drill. Treat it like a real emergency. Clear, concise communication is key."

Hiroshi, testing his radio, responded confidently. "We're ready, Captain."

Mia moved through the village, capturing the activity and interactions on camera. She paused to interview Emiko, who watched the preparations with a mix of pride and hope. "Emiko, how do you feel about the changes happening here?"

Emiko's eyes reflected her deep emotions. "It's overwhelming, in a good way. We've been struggling for so long, but now it feels like we have a real chance to thrive. Your team has brought us hope."

As the day progressed, the team and villagers worked tirelessly. The barriers took shape, the communication system was tested, and the villagers gained confidence in their new skills. By mid-afternoon, the sense of accomplishment was palpable.

Ryan gathered everyone in the central clearing for the drill. "This is the final test to ensure everything is in place. Treat it like a real emergency. Stay calm and follow the protocols."

Captain Morales took charge, her voice clear over the radios. "All teams, report in."

"North perimeter clear," Hiroshi's voice crackled. "No unusual activity."

"West perimeter clear," added Kala. "Everything is calm."

The drill continued smoothly, each team responding quickly and efficiently. Ryan watched with satisfaction as the villagers demonstrated their readiness. "Excellent work, everyone. You've shown that you can handle any situation."

Amina gathered her group for a final debriefing. "You all did great. Remember, the key is to stay calm and support each other. Your health practices have improved significantly."

Mia, filming the debriefing, turned to interview Kenta. "Kenta, what's been the most rewarding part of this experience for you?"

Kenta wiped sweat from his brow, his face glowing with pride. "It's been hard work, but it's worth it. We know we can protect our village."

As the sun began to set, casting a warm glow over the village, the team and villagers gathered around the central fire. The atmosphere was one of quiet satisfaction and growing confidence. Ryan addressed the group, his voice filled with hope and determination.

"We've created more than just physical barriers. We've fostered a community that supports and protects one another. Keep collaborating, and you can accomplish great things."

Emiko stood beside him, her eyes reflecting the firelight. "We will. This is our home, and we'll protect it with everything we have."

Amina offered a kind smile. "We're all linked now. Use the communication system to stay connected and back each other up."

Mia captured the scene, her heart swelling with pride. "We're building something lasting here. This village is becoming a beacon of hope and resilience."

As the night progressed, the team sat together by the fire, strategizing their next steps and reflecting on their journey. The difficulties had been numerous, but with each village they aided, they were establishing a legacy of strength, resilience, and unity. The connections they had made with the villagers were strong, and their united vision for a better future was becoming a reality.

Captain Morales turned to Ryan, her voice thoughtful. "We've made a real difference here. But there's still so much to do."

Ryan nodded, his expression serious but hopeful. "Every village we help strengthens the whole network. We're building a future, one step at a time."

Amina smiled, her eyes reflecting the firelight. "And it's not just about defense. It's about creating a community that cares for each other, that's resilient and self-sufficient."

Mia, her camera capturing the moment, added, "We're documenting every step, showing the world what's possible when people come together."

The night air was cool and filled with the sounds of the jungle, a reminder of the wild beauty surrounding them. They were not just building defenses; they were building a future, one village at a time. Together, they knew they could face whatever came their way, united by a common goal and a shared vision for a better world.

Chapter 21
The Poachers' Last Stand

The jungle was still, as if holding its breath in anticipation. Mia crouched low behind a dense thicket, her eyes locked on the makeshift camp the team had set up as bait. The decoy camp looked hastily assembled, the tents and equipment scattered in a way that suggested vulnerability—an easy target for anyone looking to strike.

"Ryan, you in position?" Mia murmured into her radio, keeping her voice low and steady.

"Roger that," Ryan's voice crackled softly in response. "We've got eyes on the east perimeter. No movement yet, but we're ready."

Mia nodded, glancing over her shoulder at Amina and Kato, who were positioned a few yards behind her, hidden among the thick underbrush. Kato held the binoculars steady, scanning the area while Amina adjusted the remote trigger for the snares they'd placed around the camp.

"How are we looking?" Mia whispered to them, her gaze flicking between the two.

"Everything's set," Amina confirmed, her voice a mix of anticipation and resolve. "The moment they step into that clearing, we'll have them."

"And if they take the bait," Kato added, his tone cautious. "What if they figure out it's a trap?"

"They won't," Mia said firmly, though a small part of her shared his concern. "We've studied their patterns, and they're desperate. They'll think we're exposed, caught off guard. They'll come."

Kato nodded, but his brow remained furrowed with worry. "Just... be careful, okay?"

Mia offered him a reassuring smile, though the tension thrumming through her veins made it hard to keep it steady. "I will. Stay sharp."

She turned her attention back to the decoy camp, where everything appeared calm and undisturbed. The fire they'd set up flickered weakly, casting shadows that danced across the clearing. A false sense of tranquility that would lure the poachers into a false sense of security.

"Mia," Ryan's voice crackled through the radio again, this time tighter, more urgent. "We've got movement. Northwest quadrant. At least four of them. Approaching the camp slowly."

Mia's pulse quickened. "Copy that. Keep eyes on them, but don't engage until I give the signal. Amina, Kato—get ready. This is it."

Amina's hand hovered over the remote trigger, her gaze sharp and focused. "Ready when you are."

Minutes ticked by like hours as they waited, the tension in the air thick enough to choke on. Mia watched, her breath held, as shadows shifted at the edge of the clearing. Slowly, figures emerged from the undergrowth—cautious, scanning the area, their rifles glinting faintly in the firelight.

"Four confirmed," Ryan whispered through the radio. "Looks like their leader is hanging back. Probably waiting to see if it's safe."

Mia's eyes narrowed. This was exactly what they'd anticipated. The poachers were ruthless but careful, never exposing themselves unless they were certain the odds were in their favor. But today, the odds were anything but.

"They're moving in," Ryan continued. "Get ready."

Mia raised a hand, signaling to Amina and Kato to hold. The poachers stepped further into the clearing, their eyes darting around as they assessed the seemingly abandoned camp.

"Looks like they took the bait," Kato whispered, his voice strained with barely contained excitement.

"Not yet," Mia muttered, watching as the leader—the tall, broad-shouldered man they'd identified from previous encounters—finally stepped out from the shadows. He moved with the confidence of someone who believed he had the upper hand.

He gestured to his men, and they began spreading out, circling the camp. One of them approached the fire, kicking at the embers with a booted foot.

Mia waited until they were all fully inside the clearing. "Now!" she hissed into the radio.

Amina hit the trigger.

There was a sudden, sharp snap as the snares activated, ropes tightening around the poachers' ankles and pulling them off balance. Shouts of surprise and anger filled the air as two of the men were yanked off their feet, their weapons clattering to the ground.

"Go, go, go!" Ryan's voice barked through the radio.

Mia sprang forward, adrenaline surging through her veins as she burst into the clearing, Ryan appearing on the opposite side. Together, they moved quickly, efficiently, subduing the struggling poachers and securing their hands behind their backs.

"Don't move!" Ryan growled, pressing the muzzle of his rifle against the shoulder of the man struggling the hardest. "It's over."

The leader, still free, stood at the edge of the clearing, his eyes blazing with fury. "You think this changes anything?" he spat, his voice low and venomous. "You can't stop us. We'll be back. And when we come, you won't be so lucky."

Mia straightened, her breath coming hard and fast as she met his gaze head-on. "We're not the ones who need luck," she said coldly. "You're done here. The authorities are on their way, and they'll have a nice, long chat with you about illegal poaching and trespassing."

The leader sneered, but Mia saw the flicker of fear in his eyes, the realization that they'd been outsmarted. "You think you're some kind of hero, don't you?" he snarled. "But you're just a bunch of amateurs playing in the jungle. This isn't your world."

"It is now," Mia shot back, her voice steady. "And we're not going anywhere."

The leader glanced at his captured men, then back at Mia. With a final look of contempt, he turned and fled into the jungle, disappearing into the shadows.

"Should we go after him?" Kato asked breathlessly, stepping up beside Mia.

She shook her head, watching the darkness where the man had vanished. "No. We've got what we need. Let him go. We'll deal with him another time."

Ryan stepped closer, his gaze searching her face. "You okay?"

Mia nodded slowly, a rush of satisfaction flooding through her. "Yeah. We did it."

She looked around at her team, at the poachers they'd captured, and felt a sense of accomplishment settle over her—a feeling she hadn't experienced in a long time. This was just one victory, but it was theirs.

And it was just the beginning.

"Let's get these guys tied up," she said, her voice firm and confident. "We've got a lot more work to do."

With renewed resolve, the team set to work, their movements precise and coordinated. As they secured the captured poachers, Mia couldn't help but feel that, for the first time, they were finally one step ahead.

The jungle around them seemed to hum with life, the silence that followed the brief struggle a testament to their success. And as they worked, Mia knew, deep in her heart, that they were on the right path—one that was entirely their own.

The air crackled with tension as Mia and her team stood facing the captured poachers, the clearing still echoing with the sounds of their brief struggle. A few yards away, two of the poachers lay on the ground, wrists bound, glaring defiantly up at their captors. Their leader, however, was still standing, his arms held loosely at his sides, a dangerous smirk playing on his lips despite the rifle Ryan held pointed at him.

Mia stepped forward, her gaze locked on the leader. She could feel the weight of the moment pressing down on her—this was it. This was the culmination of weeks of planning, of sacrifice, of every choice they'd made since they set foot in the Congo. She took a deep breath, steadying herself.

"Does it feel good, huh?" the leader sneered, his voice dripping with contempt. "Catching a few foot soldiers? You think this is going to stop anything?"

Mia narrowed her eyes, refusing to be intimidated. "We know you're not working alone. This isn't just some small operation, is it? You're connected to something much bigger—a network that stretches beyond this region, maybe even across the continent."

The leader's smirk faltered, just for a fraction of a second, but it was enough for Mia to see. She pressed on, her voice calm but unyielding.

"You've been poaching endangered species, setting up traps in areas specifically protected by conservation laws. That takes coordination, resources—things a small band of thugs like you shouldn't have access to. So who's supplying you? Who's backing this?"

A flicker of surprise crossed his face, quickly replaced by anger. "You don't know what you're talking about," he spat. "You're just some clueless little girl playing in the jungle."

Ryan took a step closer, the muzzle of his rifle lifting slightly. "You'd better start talking, or we're going to make sure you don't get another chance to do this. Ever."

"Easy, Ryan," Mia murmured, though her gaze never left the poacher's face. She tilted her head, studying him. "You're scared. I can see it. You know we're getting closer to the truth, don't you? That's why you've been trying so hard to shut us down."

The leader bared his teeth in a snarl. "You have no idea what you're dealing with. You think you're going to waltz in here, break up a few camps, and go home heroes? This isn't your world. We own these forests. We own *you*."

"Not anymore," Amina said firmly, stepping up beside Mia. She gestured to the other captured poachers, who were watching the confrontation with wary eyes. "Your little reign of terror ends today. You're going to tell us everything you know about this network, or you're going to rot out here while your buddies move on without you."

The leader laughed, a harsh, humorless sound. "You think I'm afraid of a few conservationists? You think I'll just spill everything because you've got me tied up? Go to hell."

Mia took another step forward, lowering her voice. "You're right—I don't expect you to talk. But what do you think happens when we hand you over to the local authorities? When your employers find out you've been caught? Do you think they'll come to your rescue? Or will they tie up loose ends to make sure you don't say anything?"

The leader's bravado wavered, a flicker of doubt flashing in his eyes. Mia pressed on, her voice steady.

"We've got time. We can wait. And when you're ready to talk, we'll be here."

The leader glared at her, his jaw clenched so tight that a muscle in his cheek twitched. For a long, tense moment, no one spoke. Then, with a sharp jerk of his head, he looked away, refusing to meet her gaze.

"Take him down," Mia said quietly. "Secure the perimeter."

Ryan and Amina moved quickly, forcing the leader to his knees and binding his hands behind his back. Kato stepped in, his eyes wide with a mix of fear and awe as he helped tie up the remaining poachers.

Mia turned away, her chest tight with a strange mixture of satisfaction and lingering unease. They'd captured several of the poachers, but she knew this wasn't over—not by a long shot. The leader's words echoed in her mind. *You have no idea what you're dealing with.*

"Mia." Ryan's voice was soft but insistent, drawing her attention back to the present. He nodded toward the leader, who was watching her with a cold, calculating gaze. "What now?"

Mia took a deep breath, forcing herself to focus. "Now, we get as much information as we can out of them. They're going to talk, one way or another."

"And then?" Amina asked quietly.

Mia's gaze hardened. "Then we go after the rest of them. We track down every last person in this network, and we shut them down. For good."

Ryan nodded, a faint smile tugging at his lips. "That's what I like to hear."

Mia glanced back at the leader, who had turned his gaze to the ground, his shoulders tense with barely contained rage. "He knows something. We need to break him."

Amina frowned. "We need to be careful. If we push too hard—"

"I know," Mia interrupted, her voice softer now. "But this is our chance. We need to get ahead of them, figure out who's pulling the strings. Otherwise, we're just playing catch-up."

Ryan stepped closer, his voice low. "We'll get him to talk. But you need to keep your head, Mia. This guy's dangerous."

"I know," she murmured, her gaze never leaving the leader's slumped form. "But we're not backing down. Not now."

She turned away, motioning for the others to follow as they began securing the perimeter. The poachers' threats still hung in the air, but Mia felt a surge of determination rise within her. This wasn't just about her father's legacy anymore. This was about protecting everything they'd fought for, about proving that they could stand up against something bigger than themselves.

And they would win.

The jungle seemed to settle around them, the silence heavy but charged with purpose. As Mia looked out over the captured poachers, she knew they were ready for whatever came next. This was just the beginning, and they weren't going to stop until every last piece of the network was brought down.

"Let's get to work," she said softly, a fierce light in her eyes. "We've got a lot more ground to cover."

The jungle was still, the only sound the faint rustling of leaves as the wind whispered through the trees. Mia stood a few feet away from the captured poachers, her gaze sharp and unyielding. The leader of the group, now bound and seated on a rough patch of dirt, glared up at her with a mixture of defiance and fear. His hands twitched behind his back, as if he still thought he might somehow break free and turn the tables.

Ryan and Amina flanked Mia, their expressions equally determined. Kato hovered nearby, his eyes darting between the poachers and Mia, a nervous energy radiating from him. The clearing felt charged, like a storm on the brink of breaking.

"Start talking," Mia said quietly, her voice low but carrying an edge that demanded attention. "Who's running this operation? Who's supplying you?"

The leader spat at the ground, his lips curling into a sneer. "You think I'm just going to spill everything because you ask nicely? You really are naive, girl."

Ryan took a step forward, his jaw clenched. "You might want to rethink your attitude. We're not the only ones who want answers. Once the authorities get their hands on you, you're going to wish you'd talked to us first."

The poacher shifted uncomfortably, his gaze flicking between Mia and Ryan. A small bead of sweat trickled down his temple. For all his bravado, he was clearly starting to crack.

"You don't get it, do you?" the poacher growled, leaning forward as much as his restraints would allow. "You're not dealing with some backwater gang. This is a network—big, organized. We've got people everywhere, in places you can't even imagine. You think you're safe just because you caught a few of us? There are others, hundreds more, just waiting to take our place."

Mia's heart pounded, but she forced herself to stay calm. "Who are they? Names, locations—give me something I can use."

The poacher's lips twisted into a cruel smile. "It's bigger than you know. And you're already in too deep, just like your father."

Mia stiffened, a chill running down her spine. "What do you mean?"

"He was digging where he shouldn't have been," the poacher sneered. "Poking around, asking questions. It didn't matter how careful he was—we knew. We were watching. He became a problem for the wrong people, and now you're doing the same thing."

Amina sucked in a breath, her eyes widening. "You're saying Mia's father was targeted? Deliberately?"

The poacher shrugged, a slow, deliberate motion. "He was getting too close. Too much of a threat. So we had to shut him down. And now you're making the same mistake."

Mia's blood ran cold. Her father's death had always been a mystery—an accident, they'd said. But now, hearing this, everything seemed to shift, the pieces falling into a darker, more sinister picture. "Are you saying you had something to do with his death?"

The leader's grin widened. "Not me, personally. But people I work for? Let's just say they have ways of taking care of obstacles."

Mia's vision blurred for a moment, rage and grief surging through her. She forced herself to breathe, to focus. Losing her cool now would only give him more power.

"So that's why you're targeting us," she said slowly, her voice deadly calm. "Because we're carrying on his work."

"Exactly," the leader hissed. "You and your team, running around like you're going to make a difference—it's pathetic. You're just painting targets on your backs. They'll come for you, too, just like they came for him. And when they do, you won't see it coming."

Ryan moved forward, his eyes blazing. "You talk a big game, but we've already taken down your little operation here. You think we're just going to back off now?"

The leader's gaze shifted to Ryan, a flicker of uncertainty passing over his face. "This isn't over," he spat. "There's a whole syndicate out there. Multiple countries, dozens of groups just like mine. You're just poking at the edges. You don't even know what you're up against."

Mia's hands trembled, but she tightened them into fists, steeling herself. "We'll find out. And we'll take every one of you down, no matter how long it takes."

The leader's smile turned bitter, mocking. "You're welcome to try. But by the time you figure it all out, it'll be too late. They'll crush you just like they crushed him."

Mia took a deep breath, the words stinging but not breaking her. "We're not backing down. You can either help us, or you can rot in a cell while we tear your syndicate apart."

The poacher's jaw tightened, his gaze darkening. He looked like he wanted to say more, but then his shoulders slumped, and he glanced away, refusing to speak.

"Get him out of here," Mia said softly to Ryan, her voice steady despite the turmoil churning inside her. "Secure the perimeter, and keep an eye on the others."

Ryan nodded, giving the poacher a hard shove. "You heard her. Move."

As Ryan and Amina led the prisoners away, Kato stepped up beside Mia, his face pale. "Mia, are you okay? What he said about your dad…"

Mia swallowed hard, shaking her head slightly. "I don't know if it's true, Kato. But if it is…" She trailed off, staring into the distance, her thoughts racing. "If it is, then we're in more danger than I thought."

"What do we do now?" Kato asked quietly.

Mia glanced back at the remnants of the poachers' camp, her resolve hardening. "We keep going. We follow the trail, no matter where it leads. If they killed my father because he was close to something big, then we finish what he started. We're not just stopping a few poachers, Kato. We're going to expose the whole network."

Kato nodded, his expression determined. "I'm with you, Mia. All the way."

Mia managed a small, tight smile. "I know you are. And we're going to need that strength, because this just got a lot more complicated."

The jungle seemed to close in around them, but Mia felt a sense of clarity settle over her. Her father's work, her mission—it was all connected. The stakes were higher now, but so was her resolve.

"We're not turning back," she murmured, more to herself than to Kato. "Not until we've taken down every last one of them."

And with that, she turned away, ready to face whatever came next.

The jungle seemed to pulse with a tense energy as Mia and her team slipped through the underbrush, moving with practiced precision. The capture of the poachers had been a victory, but the revelations that followed weighed heavily on them. They couldn't afford to stay at the camp, not when the threat of retaliation hung over them like a dark cloud.

"Here," Ryan whispered, pointing to a small clearing surrounded by dense foliage. "This should be safe for now. We've got good cover and a clear view of any approach."

Mia nodded, glancing around the area. "Good. Set up a perimeter and keep watch. We don't know how many more might be out there."

Ryan and Amina moved quickly, their movements fluid and efficient as they secured the clearing. Kato remained by Mia's side, his face tense with lingering worry.

"Are you sure we should be stopping here?" he asked quietly, his voice barely more than a whisper. "What if they track us?"

Mia turned to him, placing a reassuring hand on his shoulder. "We need a moment to regroup and plan our next move. If we keep running without a strategy, we'll be right where they want us—scattered and vulnerable. This is temporary, just until we can decide on our next step."

Kato nodded, though the anxiety in his eyes didn't fully disappear. "Okay. I just... I don't want to see anyone else get hurt."

"None of us do," Mia said softly, her gaze shifting to where Amina and Ryan were setting up the last of the motion sensors. "But we're not alone, Kato. We've got each other, and we're going to see this through. No matter what."

Satisfied that the area was as secure as it could be, Mia gestured for the team to gather. They formed a small circle in the center of the clearing, the flickering light from their portable lantern casting long shadows on their faces.

Ryan crossed his arms, his expression serious. "We have a few hours, at most, before they start looking for their missing people. We need to decide our next move."

Amina nodded, glancing at Mia. "We've disrupted their local operation, but they know we're here. If we stay, we'll be facing reinforcements—and not just a few more poachers. We're talking a full-scale response."

"Which means we need to go on the offensive," Mia said, her voice calm but firm. "We have the upper hand right now. They think we're just a small team in over our heads. We need to hit them hard, fast, before they can regroup."

"And how do we do that?" Kato asked, a hint of uncertainty in his voice. "We don't even know how many more there are, or where they're based."

"We'll start by interrogating the ones we captured," Mia replied. "Get as much information as we can—locations, numbers, their communication methods. They're not going to give it up easily, but we'll find a way to make them talk."

Ryan raised an eyebrow, his expression thoughtful. "What about the rest of the network? We know this isn't just a local problem. If we go after the big players, we'll be putting ourselves in even more danger."

"I know," Mia said quietly. She looked around at her team, seeing the resolve etched into their faces. "But this isn't just about us anymore. My father... he knew there was something bigger going on. He died trying to stop it, and I'm not going to let that be in vain. We need to take down this whole network, not just the small fry."

The silence that followed was heavy, charged with the weight of her words. Kato looked down, his hands clenching and unclenching. Amina's gaze was steady, unwavering. Ryan's jaw tightened, but then he nodded slowly.

"You've come a long way, Mia," Ryan murmured. "You're not just following in his footsteps anymore. You're leading us, making decisions he would have never dreamed of."

Mia felt a strange mix of emotions rise within her—pride, determination, and something bittersweet. "I'm not trying to replace him," she said softly. "But I know now that honoring his memory doesn't mean doing everything the way he would have. It means standing up for what we believe in, even if it's dangerous. Even if it means pushing ourselves to our limits."

"You're right," Amina agreed, her voice firm. "We came here to protect this place, to fight for these species. And now we know it's bigger than that. We're not just protecting the wildlife—we're fighting against a system that's exploiting everything we're trying to save."

Kato glanced between them, his eyes wide but filled with resolve. "So what's the plan? What do we do next?"

Mia looked at each of them in turn, feeling a surge of gratitude and fierce determination. This team—her team—had stood by her through everything, and they were still here, ready to follow her into the unknown.

"We move out at first light," she said firmly. "We'll split up. Amina and I will take the prisoners to a secure location and get what we need out of them. Ryan, you and Kato stay here and monitor their communications. We'll need to be ready to strike as soon as we have actionable intel."

Ryan nodded, his gaze steady. "And after that?"

Mia's eyes hardened. "After that, we take the fight to them. We expose their network, piece by piece, until there's nothing left."

The silence that followed was filled with unspoken promises. Each member of the team exchanged glances, a sense of unity settling over them.

"We're with you, Mia," Amina said softly. "All the way."

Kato nodded, his shoulders squaring. "Whatever it takes."

Ryan's lips twitched into a faint smile. "Let's make some noise, then."

Mia smiled, a fierce, determined expression that mirrored the fire in her eyes. "Then let's get ready."

They dispersed to make final preparations, each of them moving with purpose. As Mia watched them, a deep sense of satisfaction filled her. She wasn't just leading them—she was part of something bigger, something that mattered.

She glanced up at the dark sky, the stars peeking through the canopy. Her father's memory was still with her, but it wasn't a shadow hanging over her anymore. It was a guiding light, a reminder of the strength and courage she'd found within herself.

"Dad, I'm ready," she whispered, the words carried away by the breeze. "This time, I'm ready to see it through."

And with that, Mia turned back to the camp, her resolve unshakable. The final confrontation was coming, and she was prepared to face it head-on—no matter what it took.

Chapter 22
Choices and Consequences

The team set off early the next morning, leaving behind the village that had transformed before their eyes. The air was cool and crisp, the jungle around them alive with the sounds of birds and rustling leaves. Ryan, Mia, Amina, and Captain Morales moved with purpose, their minds already focused on the next challenge ahead.

Ryan led the way, his machete slicing through the dense foliage. "We've got a long trek ahead of us. Stay close and keep an eye out for any signs of trouble."

Mia followed closely, her camera ready to capture the journey. "Each village we visit feels like a new chapter. I can't wait to see what's next."

Amina adjusted her medical kit, her expression thoughtful. "Every village has its unique needs. We need to be prepared for anything."

Captain Morales brought up the rear, her eyes scanning the surroundings. "And we need to ensure our communication system stays operational. It's our lifeline."

As they walked, the terrain grew more challenging. The path became steeper, the jungle thicker. They moved with caution, every sense alert for potential dangers.

After several hours of trekking, they reached a clearing and paused for a break. Ryan unfolded the map, tracing their route.

"We're making good progress. The next village should be just over that ridge."

Mia took a sip of water, her gaze thoughtful. "The more remote the village, the more crucial it is to connect them. Their stories need to be told."

Amina nodded in agreement. "Isolation often means a lack of basic necessities. We need to be prepared for anything."

Captain Morales checked their supplies, her expression serious. "And we need to ensure our radios stay functional. Communication is our lifeline."

As they continued their journey, the sun climbed higher in the sky, casting long shadows through the trees. The path led them through a dense thicket, the undergrowth thick and tangled.

Ryan stopped suddenly, holding up a hand. "Wait. Do you hear that?"

The team paused, listening intently. In the distance, they could hear the sound of rushing water.

Mia's eyes lit up. "A river. That could be a good sign. It might lead us to the village."

Ryan nodded. "Let's follow it. But stay alert. The terrain could be tricky."

They moved carefully, following the sound of the water. The jungle thinned out, revealing a wide river cutting through the landscape. The water was fast-moving and clear, a welcome sight in the dense jungle.

Ryan scanned the riverbank, looking for a way across. "We need to find a safe place to cross. The current is too strong here."

Captain Morales pointed upstream. "There might be a shallower spot up there. Let's check it out."

They followed the riverbank, the sound of rushing water growing louder. After some time, they found a spot where the river narrowed slightly, the current appearing less fierce.

Ryan tested the depth with a long stick. "This looks manageable. We'll go across one at a time, using the rope for safety."

Amina secured one end of the rope around a sturdy tree, while Ryan tied the other end around his waist. He stepped into the river, the cold water swirling around his legs. "Take it slow and steady. Hold onto the rope for balance."

One by one, they made their way across, the rope providing a lifeline in the treacherous waters. Finally, they all reached the other side, breathing a collective sigh of relief.

Ryan checked his map, orienting himself. "We're making good progress. The village should be just over that ridge."

As they climbed the final incline, the sounds of the jungle gave way to the distant hum of activity. Cresting the ridge, they saw the village spread out below them, a cluster of huts surrounded by cultivated fields and grazing livestock.

Ryan turned to the group, his voice filled with determination. "This is it. Let's make a difference."

Mia adjusted her camera, capturing the scene. "Another chapter in our journey. Let's see what this village has in store."

Amina smiled, her eyes reflecting the morning light. "Every village we help brings us closer to our goal. Let's get to work."

Captain Morales nodded, her expression serious but hopeful. "Stay vigilant and stay connected. We've got a lot to do."

As they descended into the valley, the villagers looked up from their tasks, curiosity and caution evident in their eyes. The team approached with a sense of purpose and determination, ready to bring their support and expertise to this new community. The path ahead was still long, but they were ready. Together, they knew they could face whatever came their way, one village at a time.

The team walked into the village, their presence attracting the attention of the villagers who paused their activities to observe the newcomers. An elderly man, his posture dignified despite his years, approached them. He wore a simple robe, and his eyes held a mixture of curiosity and caution.

"Who are you, and what brings you to our village?" the man asked, his voice steady and authoritative.

Ryan stepped forward, offering a respectful nod. "We're here to help. We've been working with other villages to build defenses, set up communication systems, and improve health and education. We want to do the same here."

The man studied them for a moment before nodding. "I am Kaito, the village elder. We've heard of your work. Some say you bring hope, others say you bring change. What makes you different?"

Amina stepped forward, her voice warm and reassuring. "We bring knowledge and support. Everything we do is to empower you, not control you. We work with you to strengthen your community."

Kaito's gaze softened slightly. "Very well. Show us what you can do."

The team split up to begin their assessments. Ryan and Captain Morales focused on the village's defenses, inspecting the perimeter. "Your barriers are minimal," Ryan observed. "We need to fortify them to ensure safety."

A young man named Kenji, eager to help, asked, "What materials should we use?"

Ryan replied, "Use what you can find—rocks, mud, anything that can add to the stability. Adaptability is key."

Meanwhile, Amina set up a temporary clinic under a large tree. She began with a health assessment, addressing a group of villagers about basic hygiene and first aid. "Clean water and proper wound care are essential. These small steps can prevent serious illnesses."

A woman named Hana raised her hand. "What should we do if someone is injured and we don't have the right supplies?"

Amina demonstrated how to improvise with available materials. "Use clean cloths for bandages and boiled water for cleaning wounds. It's not perfect, but it's effective."

Captain Morales gathered a group of villagers to set up the communication system. "These radios will keep you connected with us and the other villages. Regular check-ins are crucial."

A boy named Toshi, holding a radio, asked, "How often should we check in?"

Morales replied, "Twice a day, minimum. And if there's any unusual activity, report immediately. Clear and concise communication can save lives."

Mia moved through the village, capturing the collaboration on camera. She paused to interview an elderly woman weaving a basket. "How has life been here, isolated from the other villages?"

The woman, named Suki, looked up, her eyes thoughtful. "It's been hard. We survive, but we lack many things. Medicine, education, safety. If you can help us with these, we will be grateful."

As the day progressed, the team and villagers worked tirelessly. The barriers took shape, the villagers' confidence grew, and the communication system was almost operational. By late afternoon, the sense of accomplishment was palpable.

Ryan gathered everyone in the central clearing for a progress update. "We've made incredible strides today. The barriers are taking shape, and the communication system is nearly operational. We're on the right track."

Amina added, "Your health practices are improving too. Keep practicing what you've learned and support each other."

Captain Morales nodded. "Tomorrow, we'll conduct a full-scale drill to ensure everyone knows what to do in an emergency. Clear communication is key."

Kaito listened intently, then spoke. "We are grateful for your help. We've struggled for so long, and now it feels like we have a real chance."

Ryan placed a reassuring hand on Kaito's shoulder. "We're in this together. Let's get to work."

As the sun began to descend, casting a soft glow over the village, the team and villagers came together around the central fire. The atmosphere was one of serene satisfaction and increasing confidence. Ryan spoke to the crowd, his voice infused with hope and determination.

"We've built more than just physical defenses. We've built trust and a sense of community. Keep working together, and we can achieve great things."

Kaito stood beside him, his eyes reflecting the firelight. "We will. This is our home, and we'll protect it with everything we have."

Amina's smile was encouraging. "Don't forget, we're all connected now. Use the communication system to stay in touch and assist each other."

Mia captured the scene, her heart swelling with pride. "We're building something lasting here. This village is becoming a beacon of hope and resilience."

As night fell, the team sat around the fire, planning their next moves and reflecting on their progress. The challenges had been numerous, but with each village they helped, they were establishing a legacy of strength, resilience, and unity. The relationships with the villagers were solid, and their common vision for a better future was coming to fruition. The work was tough but significant, and it was making an impact. United, they knew they could tackle any obstacles, one village at a time. The path ahead was long, but they were prepared. They were shaping a future, one step at a time.

The sun rose over the village, casting a soft, golden light on the bustling activity below. The team and villagers were already hard at work, the sense of urgency palpable. Today was the final day to ensure everything was in place before the team moved on to the next village.

Ryan and Captain Morales were at the perimeter, inspecting the barriers. The sturdy structures stood tall, a testament to the villagers' hard work and dedication. "These barriers are solid," Ryan said, running his hand along the wooden stakes. "You've all done an incredible job."

Kenji, one of the young villagers, beamed with pride. "Thanks, Ryan. We couldn't have done it without your guidance."

"Remember to check the supports regularly and make repairs as needed," Ryan continued. "These barriers will only protect you if they're maintained."

Meanwhile, Amina was conducting a final health training session under the large tree. She demonstrated how to handle severe injuries, her voice calm and reassuring. "If someone is unconscious and not breathing, start CPR immediately. Remember, 30 compressions to 2 breaths."

Hana, practicing on a dummy, looked up. "Like this, Amina?"

Amina adjusted Hana's hands slightly. "Yes, exactly. You're doing great. Keep your compressions steady and firm."

Captain Morales was overseeing the communication system, ensuring everything was operational. She gathered a group of villagers, explaining the importance of regular check-ins. "These radios are your lifeline. Make sure to check in twice a day and report any unusual activity immediately."

Toshi, holding a radio, asked, "What if we encounter interference?"

Morales replied, "Move to a higher ground or an open area to get a better signal. And always keep the batteries charged."

Mia moved through the village, capturing the collaboration on camera. She paused to interview Suki, the elderly woman she had spoken to earlier. "Suki, how do you feel about the changes happening here?"

Suki smiled warmly, her eyes reflecting the morning light. "It's wonderful. We've lived in isolation for so long, but now we feel connected and protected."

As the day progressed, the sense of unity and purpose grew stronger. The team and villagers worked tirelessly, each task bringing them closer to their goal. By mid-afternoon, the barriers were complete, and the communication system was fully operational.

Ryan gathered everyone in the central clearing for a final debriefing. "We've made incredible strides these past few days. The barriers are solid, and the communication system is operational. You're ready."

Amina added, "Your health practices have improved significantly. Keep practicing what you've learned and support each other."

Captain Morales nodded. "Tomorrow, we'll conduct a full-scale drill to ensure everyone knows what to do in an emergency. Clear communication is key."

As the sun set, spreading a warm glow across the village, the team and villagers gathered around the central fire. The ambiance was one of quiet contentment and rising confidence. Ryan addressed the gathering, his voice full of hope and determination.

"We've established more than just walls and defenses. We've nurtured a community that looks out for and protects one another. Keep working together, and you can accomplish wonders."

Kaito stood beside him, his eyes reflecting the firelight. "We will. This is our home, and we'll protect it with everything we have."

Amina's smile was reassuring. "Remember, we're all connected. Use the communication system to stay in touch and support each other."

Mia captured the scene, her heart swelling with pride. "We're building something lasting here. This village is becoming a beacon of hope and resilience."

As the night wore on, the team gathered by the fire, discussing their upcoming plans and reflecting on their journey. The obstacles had been many, but with each village they aided, they were constructing a legacy of strength, resilience, and unity. The bonds with the villagers were strong, and their shared vision for a better future was becoming a reality. The work was demanding but meaningful, and it was making a difference. Together, they knew they could face any challenge, one village at a time. The journey ahead was lengthy, but they were ready. They were building a future, one step at a time.

The first light of dawn broke over the village, casting a serene glow on the now fortified community. The team and villagers moved with a renewed sense of purpose, knowing this was their final day together. The air buzzed with a mix of excitement and determination as they prepared for the final drill and wrap-up.

Ryan, Mia, Amina, and Captain Morales stood in the central clearing, going over their plans for the day. Ryan addressed the group, his voice steady. "Today, we conduct the final drill. This is the last test to ensure everything is in place."

Kaito, the village elder, nodded firmly. "We're ready. We've come a long way, and we're eager to show what we've learned."

The villagers dispersed into their teams. Ryan and Captain Morales headed to the perimeter, making final checks on the barriers. "These barriers are looking solid," Ryan commented. "Your hard work is paying off."

Kenji, adjusting one of the supports, smiled. "Thanks, Ryan. It feels good to see everything come together."

Nearby, Amina gathered her group under the large tree for a final health training session. She demonstrated how to handle severe injuries once more, her voice calm and reassuring. "In case of a deep cut, apply pressure to stop the bleeding, then clean the wound thoroughly."

Hana, practicing on a dummy, asked, "And if we don't have clean cloths?"

Amina nodded, showing a sterilization technique. "Boil water and sterilize the cloths. It's essential to keep everything as clean as possible."

Captain Morales prepared the villagers for the comprehensive communication drill. She handed out radios, her tone firm but encouraging. "This is our final drill. Treat it like a real emergency. Clear, concise communication is key."

Toshi, testing his radio, asked, "What should we do if we lose signal during an emergency?"

Morales replied, "Move to a higher ground or an open area. And always keep spare batteries handy."

Mia moved through the village, capturing the collaborative efforts on camera. She paused to interview an elderly man named Yuto, who had been instrumental in organizing the villagers. "Yuto, how do you feel about the changes happening here?"

Yuto's eyes twinkled with pride. "It's been hard work, but it's worth it. We've become a stronger, more united community."

As the day progressed, the team and villagers worked seamlessly together, finalizing preparations for the drill. By mid-afternoon, everything was in place. Ryan gathered everyone in the central clearing for a final briefing.

"This is it, everyone. Our final drill to ensure we're ready for any situation. Stay calm, follow the protocols, and communicate clearly," Ryan instructed.

Captain Morales took charge, her voice clear over the radios. "All teams, report in."

"North perimeter clear," Hiroshi's voice crackled. "No unusual activity."

"West perimeter clear," added Kala. "Everything is calm."

The drill continued smoothly, each team responding quickly and efficiently. Ryan and Captain Morales monitored the drill, their faces showing satisfaction as the villagers demonstrated their readiness. "Excellent work, everyone," Ryan praised. "You've shown that you can handle any situation."

Amina gathered her group for a final debriefing. "You all did great. Remember, the key is to stay calm and support each other. Your health practices have improved significantly."

Mia, filming the debriefing, turned to interview Kenta. "Kenta, what's been the most rewarding part of this experience for you?"

Kenta wiped sweat from his brow, his face glowing with pride. "It's been tough, but it's worth it. We know we can protect our village."

As the sun lowered in the sky, casting a gentle light over the village, the team and villagers assembled around the central fire. The mood was one of calm satisfaction and building confidence. Ryan spoke to the group, his voice filled with hope and determination.

"We've created more than physical defenses. We've built a community of mutual support and protection. Keep cooperating, and you'll achieve extraordinary things."

Kaito stood beside him, his eyes reflecting the firelight. "We will. This is our home, and we'll protect it with everything we have."

Amina smiled gently. "We're all in this together. Use the communication system to keep in touch and support one another."

Mia captured the scene, her heart swelling with pride. "We're building something lasting here. This village is becoming a beacon of hope and resilience."

As the fire crackled softly, the team sat together, discussing their next steps and reflecting on their journey. The challenges had been many, but with each village they helped, they were building a legacy of strength, resilience, and unity. The bonds they had forged with the villagers were strong, and their shared vision for a better future was becoming a reality. The work was hard, but it was meaningful, and it was making a difference. Together, they knew they could face whatever came their way, one village at a time. The path ahead was long, but they were ready. They were building a future, one step at a time.

Chapter 23
Resolution and Moving Forward

The air was thick with tension as Mia and her team crept through the dense jungle, each step silent and deliberate. The coordinates they'd extracted from the captured poachers had led them to a remote compound hidden deep within the rainforest, far off the beaten path. This was it—the heart of the syndicate's operations, the place where everything they'd been fighting for would either come to a triumphant conclusion or a devastating end.

Mia glanced at her team, their faces set with determination. Ryan moved beside her, his gaze sharp and alert, while Amina and Kato flanked them, keeping low and quiet as they approached the clearing where the syndicate's leader was waiting.

"Everyone ready?" Mia whispered, her voice barely audible over the rustling leaves. She felt her pulse quicken, the familiar rush of adrenaline surging through her veins.

"Ready," Ryan murmured back, his rifle held steady. "We go in fast, disarm the guards, and secure the perimeter. You handle the leader. We'll cover you."

Mia nodded, a sense of clarity settling over her. She'd been preparing for this moment ever since she'd set foot in the Congo. The realization that her father's death had been orchestrated by these people had ignited a fire within her—a fire that burned with a need for justice, not revenge.

"Let's go," she whispered, signaling them forward.

They moved as one, slipping into the clearing. The compound was a crude structure of metal and wood, guarded by a handful of armed men. The guards barely had time to react before Amina and Ryan swept in, subduing them with swift, precise movements. Kato followed, securing their weapons and binding their wrists.

Mia's gaze locked on the man standing in the center of the compound. Tall and broad-shouldered, the syndicate leader watched them with a calm, calculating gaze, his hands clasped loosely behind his back. He didn't seem surprised—if anything, there was a hint of amusement in his eyes as he looked at Mia.

"So, you finally made it," he drawled, his voice low and smooth. "I must say, I'm impressed. You're just as relentless as your father was."

Mia's breath caught in her throat, but she forced herself to remain steady. "You knew my father."

The leader's smile widened, a cruel glint in his eyes. "Oh, I knew him very well. He was always so... determined. So convinced he could make a difference. Just like you."

Mia took a step forward, her jaw clenched. "What did you do to him?"

The leader tilted his head, as if considering her question. "What did I *do* to him? Well, I didn't pull the trigger, if that's what you're asking. But I made sure he understood the price of meddling in affairs that were beyond him."

Mia's fists tightened, but she kept her voice even. "You killed him because he was getting too close to the truth. Because he threatened your precious operation."

The leader shrugged, his gaze never wavering from hers. "He was a threat. And threats need to be eliminated. It's as simple as that. I thought you would have learned from his mistake. But I suppose the apple doesn't fall far from the tree, does it?"

"Maybe not," Mia said softly, taking another step closer. "But I'm not my father. I'm not here to make the same mistakes."

"Then why are you here?" he taunted, raising an eyebrow. "To finish what he started? To prove yourself? Or are you just seeking vengeance for a man you could never live up to?"

Mia felt a surge of anger, but she forced herself to push it down. She looked at the man who had orchestrated so much pain, who had shattered lives for profit, and she felt a strange sense of calm settle over her.

"I'm here to stop you," she said quietly. "To make sure you never hurt anyone else again."

The leader laughed, a harsh, mocking sound that echoed through the clearing. "You think capturing me is going to change anything? There are hundreds more like me. Take me down, and another will take my place. You're fighting a war you can't win, little girl."

"Maybe," Mia said, her gaze unwavering. "But it starts here. With you."

She moved then, faster than he expected. Before he could react, Mia closed the distance between them, knocking his legs out from under him and slamming him to the ground. He grunted in surprise, but Mia didn't let up. She pressed a knee into his back, pinning him down as she pulled out a pair of zip ties and secured his wrists.

"You're done," she said softly, leaning close enough that he could feel the intensity of her words. "It's over."

The leader struggled, but Mia held firm. She felt the rage bubbling just below the surface, the urge to do more—to make him pay for what he'd done. But then she remembered her father's voice, his belief in justice, not vengeance.

She took a deep breath and stepped back, releasing the man to Ryan and Amina, who dragged him to his feet and forced him to kneel.

"You think this changes anything?" the leader spat, his eyes blazing with fury. "They'll come for you, for all of you. They'll tear you apart."

"Let them try," Mia said calmly. "We're not afraid of you or your syndicate. And we're not stopping until every last one of you is brought to justice."

The leader glared at her, but Mia turned away, signaling to Kato, who had been standing off to the side, watching with wide eyes.

"Are you okay?" Kato asked hesitantly, stepping closer.

Mia looked at him, a small smile tugging at her lips. "Yeah, I'm okay. This was the right thing to do. My father... he wouldn't have wanted me to become like them."

Kato nodded slowly, then straightened his shoulders, a determined expression on his face. "Mia, I've been thinking... after all this is over, I want to continue. To keep working with you, fighting for the things your father believed in. I want to be a conservationist, like you."

Mia's heart swelled with pride and something deeper—hope. She placed a hand on his shoulder, squeezing gently. "You already are, Kato. You've shown more courage and dedication than most people ever would. And I'd be honored to have you by my side."

Kato's face lit up with a shy but genuine smile. "Thank you, Mia. For everything."

She nodded, glancing back at the captured leader, who was still glaring at her with hatred in his eyes. But it didn't matter. They'd won, and more than that, they'd chosen a path that honored everything her father had stood for.

"Let's get him to the authorities," Mia said softly, her gaze shifting to the horizon. "We've got a lot more work to do."

And with that, she led the way out of the clearing, the weight of her father's legacy finally resting comfortably on her shoulders, no longer a burden but a source of strength.

The dense jungle around them was finally beginning to feel like a place of peace again. The tension that had hung heavy in the air for weeks seemed to dissipate, replaced by a sense of calm and accomplishment. Mia moved carefully through the underbrush, her eyes scanning the ground as she approached one of the last remaining traps.

With deft hands, she knelt and began dismantling the snare. A few feet away, Kato and Amina worked on a similar trap, their voices low and steady as they coordinated their efforts. Ryan was further ahead, cutting down a series of hidden tripwires that stretched between the trees.

"We're almost done here," Ryan called over his shoulder, glancing back at Mia. "Just a few more traps left on this side."

"Good," Mia replied, her tone thoughtful. "Once these are down, we'll do a final sweep of the area and call it in to the local rangers. They can take it from there."

Kato looked up, wiping the sweat from his forehead with the back of his hand. "Feels strange, doesn't it? Like... we've been fighting this battle for so long, and now it's almost over."

Mia paused, her fingers lingering on the metal loop of the snare she was disarming. "Yeah, it does." She glanced around at the team, a small smile tugging at her lips. "But this is just one step. We've made a huge impact here, but there's still so much more to do. The syndicate's been crippled, but there are other places, other threats."

"Like a hydra," Amina murmured, her voice carrying a note of both satisfaction and concern. "Cut off one head, and two more grow back."

Mia nodded slowly. "Exactly. But that doesn't mean we stop fighting. It means we get smarter, get more people involved. We take what we've learned here and apply it elsewhere. We keep pushing back."

The others fell silent, absorbing her words. After a few moments, Ryan straightened, stepping back from the trap he'd just dismantled. "You've got a good plan, Mia. We've all learned a lot from this. And you've shown us what real leadership looks like."

Mia felt a flush of warmth spread through her chest. "I couldn't have done any of this without all of you. Your courage, your skills... it's what made the difference."

Kato's eyes sparkled as he finished securing the last of the traps. "I still remember when I first joined this team. I was scared out of my mind—thought I was going to screw everything up. But you never made me feel like I was out of place. You believed in me."

"You believed in yourself, Kato," Mia corrected gently. "We all did. And look how far you've come."

He grinned, his expression a mix of pride and shyness. "Actually... I've been thinking about what happens next. You know, after this is all wrapped up."

Mia raised an eyebrow, curiosity piqued. "Oh? And what's that?"

Kato shifted his weight, glancing down at his hands before looking back up at her. "I want to keep going. Keep fighting for this cause. I want to become a conservationist, like you. I've learned so much here, and I don't want to stop. There are so many other places that need help. So many species that need protecting."

Mia felt her heart swell at his words. "Kato, that's incredible. You've already shown you have what it takes—the passion, the dedication. I have no doubt you're going to make a huge difference."

Kato's grin widened, his eyes shining with excitement. "You really think so?"

"I know so," Mia replied firmly. "And I'm not the only one. The local rangers have been asking about you. They could use someone with your skills and experience."

Kato glanced at Amina, who nodded enthusiastically. "You'd be great at it, Kato. You've got a natural gift for this work, and more importantly, you care. That's what really matters."

Kato looked around at his teammates, his smile turning soft and sincere. "I'm going to miss working with all of you, though."

"Hey, we're not disappearing," Ryan said, clapping Kato on the shoulder. "We'll stay in touch. And who knows? Maybe we'll cross paths again on another mission. Once you're a big-shot conservationist, you might even be calling us in to help out."

They all laughed, the sound light and genuine, cutting through the stillness of the jungle. For the first time in weeks, the laughter felt easy, unburdened by the weight of the mission. It was a sound of release, of closure.

Mia looked around at the team, her heart brimming with gratitude. "I just want to say... thank you. For everything. For believing in me, for believing in this mission. We've faced so much together, and we've come out stronger."

Amina smiled warmly. "You've led us through some pretty dark times, Mia. But you never gave up, even when things got tough. That's what makes you a great leader."

"Because I had all of you," Mia said softly. "And because I finally realized that this mission isn't just about carrying on my father's legacy. It's about all of us—about what we can accomplish together. My father's work is part of who I am, but it's not the only thing that defines me."

Ryan nodded slowly, his gaze steady. "You've found your own path. And you've inspired all of us to do the same."

They stood there for a moment, the weight of the journey they'd been on hanging in the air. Then Mia straightened, a determined light in her eyes.

"We're not done," she said firmly. "This was just the beginning. We'll take what we've done here and keep pushing forward. For every species, for every habitat that's under threat. We'll keep fighting."

The team nodded in agreement, their resolve clear. They might be parting ways, but they were bound by something stronger—the shared commitment to a cause bigger than any one person.

"Let's finish up here," Mia said with a smile. "Then we can get back to civilization, maybe even grab a real meal."

As they moved to dismantle the last of the traps, Mia felt a sense of fulfillment settle over her. She glanced up at the sky, the sunlight filtering through the canopy above. Her father's memory would always be with her, but now she knew—she wasn't just following in his footsteps.

She was walking her own path.

And it felt right.

With one last look around the jungle, Mia turned to join her team, the future ahead of them bright and filled with promise.

The small village at the edge of the jungle was alive with movement as the local community gathered to say their farewells. Children darted between the clusters of people, their laughter mingling with the soft murmur of conversations in a dozen different dialects. The elders, seated in a shaded area beneath a large mango tree, watched with approving eyes as Mia and her team made their way through the crowd.

Mia smiled as an elderly woman pressed a woven bracelet into her hand, muttering words of gratitude in her native tongue. Mia didn't understand all of it, but the sincerity in the woman's eyes was unmistakable. She bowed her head, placing the bracelet gently around her wrist.

"Thank you," Mia whispered, knowing it was inadequate to express how deeply she felt.

The woman patted Mia's arm, her face crinkling with a smile before she turned away, joining a group of other women who were preparing food for the farewell meal. The scent of roasted cassava and freshly cut fruit filled the air, a reminder of the generosity and resilience of this community that had welcomed them with open arms despite the dangers lurking in the forest.

"They're going to miss you," a voice said softly beside her. Mia glanced over to see Kato, his face flushed with emotion. "We all are."

Mia smiled, though it was tinged with sadness. "I'm going to miss them too. They've been through so much, yet they never stopped fighting for their home. It's inspiring."

"You're the one who inspired them," Kato said earnestly. "You came here and showed them that they weren't alone. That someone cared enough to stand with them, to protect what they cherish."

Mia nodded slowly, her gaze drifting over the village. She remembered the first days here—how uncertain she'd felt, how heavy the weight of her father's legacy had been on her shoulders. Now, the weight felt different, more like a mantle she wore with pride and purpose rather than a burden she struggled to carry.

"We all did this," she murmured. "Every single person here. It wasn't just me."

Kato nodded, his smile small but genuine. "Still, you should know what you mean to them. To all of us."

Mia felt a lump form in her throat and she swallowed hard, pushing back the surge of emotions. "Thank you, Kato. For everything."

He gave her a quick nod, his eyes bright, and then stepped back as more villagers approached, offering their thanks and well-wishes. Mia moved among them, shaking hands, accepting small tokens of appreciation, and promising to keep in touch with the community leaders. The farewell was filled with a bittersweet joy—one chapter closing, another beginning.

Ryan and Amina stood near the village's edge, conversing quietly with some of the rangers who had joined their mission. Mia saw the respect and admiration in the rangers' eyes as they shook hands with Ryan, clapped Kato on the back, and exchanged words of gratitude with Amina.

"They'll be okay," Amina murmured as Mia joined them, her gaze sweeping over the gathered people. "They've got strong leaders here. And the rangers will keep watch over the area. The syndicate won't be able to make a move without them knowing."

Mia nodded, feeling a sense of relief settle over her. "We've given them a fighting chance. That's what matters."

The sun dipped lower in the sky, casting a warm, golden glow over the village. Mia took a deep breath, savoring the scent of the jungle one last time. The rustling leaves, the distant call of birds—it was a symphony she had come to know and love, a reminder of why she had fought so hard.

"I need a moment," she said softly, glancing at Ryan and Amina. "I'll be back soon."

Ryan gave her a nod of understanding. "Take your time."

With a final smile, Mia turned and began walking toward the edge of the jungle. She moved slowly, her footsteps silent on the well-trodden path that led deeper into the forest. The trees towered above her, their branches interwoven to form a green canopy that filtered the fading light. Shafts of sunlight pierced through, illuminating patches of moss-covered ground and the vibrant petals of wildflowers.

Mia stopped at a small clearing, a place where the jungle opened up to reveal a stunning view of the valley below. The land stretched out in all directions, a lush expanse of green that seemed to go on forever. She stood there for a long moment, letting the beauty of it all wash over her.

"This is what it's all for," she whispered to the empty air. "This is why we fight. So that places like this can thrive, so that the people and animals who call it home can live without fear."

She closed her eyes, memories flooding her mind—her father's voice, the way he'd spoken about conservation with such passion, the way he'd looked at her with pride whenever she'd accompanied him on his trips. And then there was the loss, the grief that had threatened to consume her.

But now... now she felt something else. Something new.

Peace.

"I wish you could see this, Dad," she murmured softly. "I wish you could see what we've done. I finally understand now. It's not about following in your footsteps—it's about making my own. About finding my own way to protect what we both loved."

She opened her eyes, the valley below blurring for a moment as she blinked back tears. Slowly, she turned away from the view, her heart lighter than it had been in a long time. The mission was over, but her journey was just beginning. There were other places that needed help, other battles to be fought. And she would be there, leading the way.

Mia made her way back to the village, her steps sure and steady. She was ready to leave the Congo, but she knew a part of her would always remain here, woven into the fabric of the land she'd come to love.

As she rejoined her team, she smiled—a smile filled with hope, strength, and the promise of new beginnings.

"Let's go home," she said softly, her voice carrying the weight of all they'd achieved and all that was still to come.

And with that, they turned away from the jungle, leaving behind a legacy of courage and determination that would continue to grow, long after they were gone.

The familiar scent of lavender and freshly brewed coffee greeted Mia as she stepped through the front door of her Brooklyn apartment. The sunlight filtered through the tall windows, casting soft, golden light over the hardwood floors and filling the space with warmth. It felt surreal to be back after everything that had happened in the Congo—to be surrounded by the calmness of home rather than the relentless hum of the jungle.

"Mia?" Lina's voice called out from the living room, a note of uncertainty threading through it.

Mia's heart leaped, and she dropped her bag, striding forward. "Lina?"

Lina appeared in the doorway, her face breaking into a radiant smile the moment she saw Mia. "You're really back," she breathed, rushing forward to envelop Mia in a tight hug. "Oh my God, I missed you so much."

Mia hugged her sister fiercely, blinking back tears. "I missed you too. So much."

They held each other for a long moment, the embrace saying what words couldn't. When Lina finally pulled back, her gaze searched Mia's face, her eyes filled with concern and relief.

"You look... different," Lina murmured, tilting her head. "Stronger, more at peace. It suits you."

Mia gave a small, almost shy smile. "I feel different. Being out there, finishing what we started... it changed me."

Lina nodded, taking Mia's hand and guiding her to the couch. "Tell me everything. I want to know what happened—the good, the bad, all of it."

Mia settled beside her, feeling a sense of calm wash over her. "It was harder than I ever imagined. We faced things I wasn't prepared for, both out in the jungle and inside myself. But we did it, Lina. We took down the syndicate's local operation, saved entire species, and protected a community that welcomed us with open arms."

Lina's eyes glistened as she listened, nodding slowly. "I knew you could do it, Mia. I never doubted you for a second."

Mia hesitated, her gaze dropping to her hands. "There were times when I doubted myself. Times when I wondered if I was just chasing Dad's ghost, trying to prove something. But in the end, I realized... I'm not just carrying on his work. I'm building something new, something that's mine."

A smile spread across Lina's face, filled with pride. "You are. You really are. And I'm so proud of you, Mia. I know Dad would be, too."

Mia swallowed hard, a wave of emotion surging through her. "Thank you. That means more than you know."

They sat in silence for a moment, the connection between them strong and unbreakable. Then Lina leaned forward, a glimmer of curiosity lighting up her eyes. "So... what's next for you? You're not just going to settle down and become a regular New Yorker again, are you?"

Mia laughed softly, shaking her head. "Not exactly. I've been thinking a lot about what comes next. About what I want to do with everything I've learned."

"And?" Lina prompted, her eyebrows arching expectantly.

Mia took a deep breath, her heart pounding with a mixture of excitement and anticipation. "I want to start my own conservation organization. Something that builds on Dad's work but goes beyond it. I want to focus on not just protecting endangered species, but on empowering local communities to become the guardians of their own land. To create partnerships that are built on mutual respect and shared goals."

Lina's mouth dropped open, her eyes widening. "Mia, that's incredible. That's—wow, that's huge."

"I know," Mia admitted with a grin. "But I feel ready for it. For the first time, I know what I want to achieve. This isn't just about honoring Dad's legacy anymore—it's about building my own."

Lina squeezed her hand, her expression filled with admiration. "And I have no doubt you're going to make it happen. You're a force of nature, Mia. You always have been."

Mia felt a warmth spread through her chest, filling her with a sense of confidence and purpose. "Thanks, Lina. That means everything."

They spent the next few hours catching up, talking about everything from the mission to their childhood memories, laughter and tears mingling as they shared stories. It felt like coming home in the truest sense—like reconnecting with a part of herself that had been missing.

Later, as the sun dipped low in the sky and cast long shadows across the room, Mia stood in front of a large map pinned to the wall. It was filled with notes, photographs, and red pins marking places she and her father had visited together. Slowly, she reached up and added a few new pins—places she had been with her team, locations where they had made a difference.

Lina stepped up beside her, watching quietly as Mia worked. "What's next on the list?" she asked softly.

Mia paused, her fingers brushing over a blank area of the map—an expanse of untouched forest in Southeast Asia, another region at risk from illegal logging and poaching. "There," she said, her voice firm. "I want to explore that area, see what we can do to protect it. Maybe set up a new base of operations there."

Lina nodded slowly. "And after that?"

Mia turned to her sister, a smile spreading across her face—a smile filled with hope, determination, and a hint of excitement for the unknown. "There's a whole world out there that needs protecting. I want to see as much of it as I can. And I want to leave each place a little better than I found it."

Lina hugged her tightly, her voice filled with pride. "You're going to change the world, Mia. I know it."

Mia hugged her back, holding on for a long moment. When she finally pulled away, she looked back at the map, her eyes bright with purpose.

"I'm going to try," she said softly. "One step at a time."

And as she stood there, gazing at the map that symbolized not just her past but her future, Mia felt a sense of freedom she'd never known before. Her father's legacy would always be a part of her, but it no longer defined her. She was ready to face the world as Mia Evans—a conservationist, a leader, and a force for change.

With one last look at the map, Mia turned away, her heart light and her mind clear. The next chapter of her life was just beginning, and she was ready to embrace it with everything she had.

Smiling to herself, she closed the door behind her, stepping forward into a world filled with possibility.

Chapter 24
New Paths and Partnerships

The morning sun broke over the horizon, casting a warm glow on the village as the team prepared for their departure. The air was filled with a mixture of excitement and bittersweet farewells. Ryan, Mia, Amina, and Captain Morales gathered their gear, ready for the next leg of their journey.

Ryan addressed the villagers one last time, his voice calm but filled with conviction. "We've accomplished a lot together. You've shown incredible strength and resilience. Remember, the work doesn't stop here. Keep building, keep improving, and stay connected with the network."

Takashi, the village elder, stepped forward, his eyes reflecting gratitude. "You've given us the tools and knowledge to protect and support each other. We won't forget what you've done for us."

Amina hugged Takashi warmly. "You've all made remarkable progress. Keep practicing what you've learned, especially the health protocols. They're crucial for maintaining a healthy community."

Hana, standing nearby, asked, "Amina, what should we do if we encounter a medical emergency and can't reach the clinic in time?"

Amina replied, "Stabilize the patient as best you can. Use clean cloths for bandages, keep the wound clean, and make sure to keep the person hydrated. And don't forget to use the radios to call for help immediately."

Captain Morales ensured the communication system was fully operational before they left. She gathered the villagers who would be responsible for its upkeep. "Regular check-ins are vital. Twice a day at minimum. And remember, clear communication is key."

Taro, holding his radio, nodded. "We'll keep the lines open, Captain. Thank you for everything."

Mia moved through the group, capturing the final moments on camera. She paused to interview Kenji, who had been instrumental in reinforcing the village's defenses. "Kenji, how do you feel about the future now?"

Kenji's face lit up with pride. "We're ready for whatever comes. We've learned so much, and we know we can protect our village."

Ryan turned to the group, his voice steady. "Remember, you're not alone. Stay connected with the other villages and support each other. Together, we're stronger."

Takashi raised his hand in a gesture of solidarity. "We will. This is just the beginning for us."

As the team set off down the path, the villagers' well-wishes echoed behind them. They walked in silence for a while, each lost in their thoughts about the road ahead.

Mia broke the silence, her voice filled with excitement. "I can't wait to see what the next village is like. Each one has its own story, its own challenges."

Amina nodded, her expression thoughtful. "And its own unique needs. We need to be ready for anything."

Captain Morales brought up the rear, her eyes scanning the surroundings. "Stay vigilant. We don't know what we'll encounter on this leg of the journey."

The path led them through dense jungle, the sounds of nature a constant companion. They moved with purpose, their steps sure and steady. The journey was grueling, but their resolve was unwavering. They knew the importance of their mission and the lives it impacted.

Ryan paused at a clearing, checking the map. "We've got another day's trek ahead of us. Let's stay focused and keep moving."

Mia took a sip of water, her gaze thoughtful. "The more remote the village, the more crucial it is to connect them. Their stories need to be told."

Amina agreed, "Isolation often means a lack of basic necessities. We need to be prepared for anything."

Captain Morales checked their supplies, her expression serious. "And we need to ensure our radios stay functional. Communication is our lifeline."

As they continued their journey, the terrain grew more challenging. The jungle thickened, the path becoming less defined. They moved with caution, every sense alert for potential dangers.

Ryan led the way, his machete slicing through the dense foliage. "Stay close and keep an eye out for any signs of trouble."

The team pressed on, their determination unwavering. They knew that each step brought them closer to another village in need, another opportunity to make a difference. The challenges were many, but so were the rewards. They were building a future, one village at a time, united by a common goal and a shared vision for a better world.

As dusk approached, they reached a ridge overlooking their next destination. The sight of the village nestled in the valley below filled them with renewed energy. They exchanged determined smiles, ready to bring their support and expertise to this new community. The path ahead was still long, but they were ready. Together, they knew they could face whatever came their way, one village at a time.

The team descended into the valley as the sun rose higher, casting long shadows across the landscape. The village below came into clearer view, revealing a collection of huts surrounded by cultivated fields and dense foliage. The distant hum of activity grew louder as they approached, a sign of a thriving community.

Ryan led the way, his steps confident but cautious. "Stay alert. Let's see what challenges this village faces and how we can help."

As they entered the village, they were greeted by a group of curious villagers. An elderly woman, her posture straight and dignified, stepped forward. "Welcome, travelers. I am Akiko, the village elder. What brings you here?"

Ryan offered a respectful nod. "We're here to help. We've been working with other villages to build defenses, set up communication systems, and improve health and education. We want to do the same here."

Akiko scrutinized them for a moment before speaking. "We have heard of your work. Some say you bring hope, others say you bring change. What makes you different?"

Amina stepped forward, her voice warm and reassuring. "We bring knowledge and support. Everything we do is to empower you, not control you. We work with you to strengthen your community."

Akiko's eyes softened slightly. "Very well. Show us what you can do."

The team split up to begin their assessments. Ryan and Captain Morales focused on the village's defenses, inspecting the perimeter. "Your barriers are minimal," Ryan observed. "We need to fortify them to ensure safety."

A young man named Yuki, eager to help, asked, "What materials should we use?"

Ryan replied, "Use what you can find—rocks, mud, anything that can add to the stability. Adaptability is key."

Meanwhile, Amina set up a temporary clinic under a large tree, starting with a health assessment to understand the villagers' needs. She addressed a group of women about basic hygiene and first aid. "Clean water and proper wound care are essential. These small steps can prevent serious illnesses."

A woman named Miko raised her hand. "What should we do if someone is injured and we don't have the right supplies?"

Amina demonstrated how to improvise with available materials. "Use clean cloths for bandages and boiled water for cleaning wounds. It's not perfect, but it's effective."

Captain Morales gathered a group of villagers to set up the communication system. "These radios will keep you connected with us and the other villages. Regular check-ins are crucial."

A boy named Ken, holding a radio, asked, "How often should we check in?"

Morales replied, "Twice a day, minimum. And if there's any unusual activity, report immediately. Clear and concise communication can save lives."

Mia moved through the village, capturing the collaboration on camera. She paused to interview an elderly man weaving a basket. "How has life been here, isolated from the other villages?"

The man, named Haru, looked up, his eyes thoughtful. "It's been hard. We survive, but we lack many things. Medicine, education, safety. If you can help us with these, we will be grateful."

As the day progressed, the team and villagers worked tirelessly. The barriers took shape, the villagers' confidence grew, and the communication system was almost operational. By mid-afternoon, the sense of accomplishment was palpable.

Ryan gathered everyone in the central clearing for a progress update. "We've made incredible strides today. The barriers are taking shape, and the communication system is nearly operational. We're on the right track."

Amina added, "Your health practices are improving too. Keep practicing what you've learned and support each other."

Captain Morales nodded. "Tomorrow, we'll conduct a full-scale drill to ensure everyone knows what to do in an emergency. Clear communication is key."

Akiko listened intently, then spoke. "We are grateful for your help. We've struggled for so long, and now it feels like we have a real chance."

Ryan placed a reassuring hand on Akiko's shoulder. "We're in this together. Let's get to work."

As the sun began to set, casting a warm glow over the village, the team and villagers gathered around the central fire. The atmosphere was one of quiet satisfaction and growing confidence. The sense of community and shared purpose was strong, a testament to their collective efforts.

Mia captured the scene, her camera documenting the bonds being formed. "We're building something lasting here. This village is becoming a beacon of hope and resilience."

Ryan addressed the group, his voice filled with determination. "We've built more than just physical defenses. We've built trust and a sense of community. Keep working together, and we can achieve great things."

Akiko nodded, her eyes reflecting the firelight. "We will. This is our home, and we'll protect it with everything we have."

Amina smiled brightly. "Remember, we're all linked. Use the communication system to keep in touch and support each other."

As darkness enveloped the night, the team sat by the fire, discussing their next plans and reflecting on their journey. The obstacles had been numerous, but with each village they assisted, they were crafting a legacy of strength, resilience, and unity. The relationships they developed with the villagers were strong, and their shared goal for a better future was coming to life. The work was tough but meaningful, and it was making a difference. United, they knew they could face whatever challenges arose, one village at a time. The path ahead was extensive, but they were prepared. They were creating a future, one step at a time.

The next morning, the village was alive with activity as the team and villagers prepared for the final drill. The air buzzed with a mix of excitement and nerves. Ryan, Mia, Amina, and Captain Morales gathered near the central clearing to brief everyone.

Ryan addressed the group, his voice steady and encouraging. "Today, we put everything to the test. This drill will simulate an emergency situation. Remember, stay calm, follow the protocols, and communicate clearly."

Yuki raised his hand. "What's the scenario for the drill, Ryan?"

Ryan smiled. "We'll simulate a breach in the perimeter and a medical emergency. Everyone has their roles. Let's make it as real as possible."

The villagers dispersed into their assigned positions. Captain Morales took charge of the communication team. "Remember, clear and concise messages. Report any unusual activity immediately."

Ken, holding his radio, nodded. "We're ready, Captain."

Amina gathered her medical team under the large tree, reviewing emergency procedures. "If someone is injured, we assess the situation, stabilize them, and communicate their condition clearly."

Miko, practicing CPR on a dummy, looked up. "And if we're unsure, we call for help immediately, right?"

"Exactly," Amina confirmed. "Never hesitate to ask for assistance."

Mia moved through the village, capturing the preparations on camera. She paused to interview Haru, who had been organizing the villagers. "Haru, how do you feel about the drill?"

Haru's eyes twinkled with determination. "It's a lot of work, but it's worth it. We need to be ready for anything."

As the drill began, a sense of urgency filled the air. An alarm sounded, signaling a breach in the perimeter. Ryan and Captain Morales led a team to the perimeter, inspecting the barriers.

"Report in," Ryan ordered, his voice steady.

"North perimeter clear," Ken's voice crackled over the radio. "No unusual activity."

"West perimeter clear," added Yuki. "Everything is calm."

Suddenly, a shout came from the medical area. "We have a medical emergency!" Miko's voice was urgent. "We need assistance!"

Amina rushed to the scene, assessing the situation. "What happened?"

"It's a simulated injury," Miko explained, pointing to a villager lying on the ground. "He's unconscious and not breathing."

Amina knelt beside the villager, starting CPR. "Miko, keep track of the compressions. We need to maintain a steady rhythm."

Mia captured the intense scene, her camera focused on Amina's determined face. She moved to interview Ryan, who was coordinating the response. "Ryan, how's the drill going?"

Ryan, watching the teams work together, nodded approvingly. "They're doing great. Everyone is following the protocols and communicating clearly. This is exactly what we hoped for."

The drill continued, with each team responding to their assigned tasks. Captain Morales coordinated the communication efforts, ensuring all teams were in sync. "East perimeter, report in."

"All clear," came the response.

Back at the medical area, Amina continued CPR, her voice calm and steady. "Miko, how's the pulse?"

Miko checked the villager's wrist. "It's faint, but it's there."

"Good," Amina replied. "Keep monitoring. We're almost there."

As the drill concluded, the alarm was silenced, and the villagers gathered in the central clearing. The sense of accomplishment was palpable. Ryan addressed the group, his voice filled with pride.

"You all did an incredible job. The drill was a success. We've shown that we can handle any situation."

Amina smiled at her team. "Your medical response was excellent. Remember, practice makes perfect. Keep honing your skills."

Captain Morales nodded. "Communication is key. You all communicated clearly and effectively. Keep up the good work."

Mia captured the final moments on camera, turning to interview Akiko. "Akiko, how do you feel about the drill?"

Akiko's eyes shone with pride. "We've come a long way. This drill has shown us that we can protect our village and support each other."

As the sun dipped below the horizon, casting a warm light over the village, the team and villagers gathered around the central fire. The ambiance was one of quiet satisfaction and increasing confidence. Ryan spoke to the group, his voice brimming with hope and determination.

"We've built more than just protective structures. We've cultivated a community that stands by and shields one another. Keep collaborating, and great things will come."

Akiko stood beside him, her eyes reflecting the firelight. "We will. This is our home, and we'll protect it with everything we have."

Amina beamed. "Remember, we're linked together. Use the communication network to stay connected and help each other out."

Mia captured the scene, her heart swelling with pride. "We're building something lasting here. This village is becoming a beacon of hope and resilience."

As the fire crackled softly, the team sat together, planning their next steps and reflecting on their path. They had encountered many challenges, but with each village they assisted, they were creating a legacy of strength, resilience, and unity. The bonds they had formed with the villagers were strong, and their shared vision for a better future was becoming a reality. The work was demanding, but it was meaningful and impactful. United, they believed they could face any challenge, one village at a time. The journey ahead was long, but they were ready. They were building a future, one step at a time.

The next morning, the village was bathed in the soft glow of the rising sun. The team prepared for their departure, their gear packed and ready. The villagers gathered around, their faces a mixture of gratitude and determination. Ryan, Mia, Amina, and Captain Morales stood together, taking in the scene.

Ryan stepped forward, addressing the villagers with a steady voice. "We've achieved a lot together in a short time. Remember, the work doesn't stop here. Keep building on what we've started, and stay connected with the network."

Akiko, the village elder, nodded, her eyes shining with resolve. "We will, Ryan. You've given us the tools and the knowledge. We're ready to protect and grow our community."

Amina hugged Akiko warmly. "Keep practicing the health protocols, especially in emergencies. Small steps make a big difference."

Miko, standing nearby, asked, "Amina, what should we do if we encounter a medical emergency and the clinic is too far?"

Amina replied, "Stabilize the patient as best as you can. Clean the wound with boiled water, apply pressure to stop bleeding, and use clean cloths for bandages. And use the radios to call for help immediately."

Captain Morales ensured the communication system was fully operational before they left. She gathered the villagers responsible for its upkeep. "Regular check-ins are vital. Twice a day at minimum. And remember, clear communication is key."

Ken, holding his radio, nodded. "We'll keep the lines open, Captain. Thank you for everything."

Mia moved through the group, capturing the final moments on camera. She paused to interview Yuki, who had been instrumental in reinforcing the village's defenses. "Yuki, how do you feel about the future now?"

Yuki's face lit up with pride. "We're ready for whatever comes. We've learned so much, and we know we can protect our village."

Ryan turned to the group, his voice steady. "Remember, you're not alone. Stay connected with the other villages and support each other. Together, we're stronger."

Akiko raised her hand in a gesture of solidarity. "We will. This is just the beginning for us."

As the team set off down the path, the villagers' well-wishes echoed behind them. They walked in silence for a while, each lost in their thoughts about the road ahead.

Mia broke the silence, her voice filled with excitement. "I can't wait to see what the next village is like. Each one has its own story, its own challenges."

Amina nodded, her expression thoughtful. "And its own unique needs. We need to be ready for anything."

Captain Morales brought up the rear, her eyes scanning the surroundings. "Stay vigilant. We don't know what we'll encounter on this leg of the journey."

The path led them through dense jungle, the sounds of nature a constant companion. They moved with purpose, their steps sure and steady. The journey was grueling, but their resolve was unwavering. They knew the importance of their mission and the lives it impacted.

Ryan paused at a clearing, checking the map. "We've got another day's trek ahead of us. Let's stay focused and keep moving."

Mia took a sip of water, her gaze thoughtful. "The more remote the village, the more crucial it is to connect them. Their stories need to be told."

Amina agreed. "Isolation often means a lack of basic necessities. We need to be prepared for anything."

Captain Morales checked their supplies, her expression serious. "And we need to ensure our radios stay functional. Communication is our lifeline."

As they continued their journey, the terrain grew more challenging. The jungle thickened, the path becoming less defined. They moved with caution, every sense alert for potential dangers.

Ryan led the way, his machete slicing through the dense foliage. "Stay close and keep an eye out for any signs of trouble."

The team pressed on, their determination unwavering. They knew that each step brought them closer to another village in need, another opportunity to make a difference. The challenges were many, but so were the rewards. They were building a future, one village at a time, united by a common goal and a shared vision for a better world.

As dusk approached, they reached a ridge overlooking their next destination. The sight of the village nestled in the valley below filled them with renewed energy. They exchanged determined smiles, ready to bring their support and expertise to this new community. The path ahead was still long, but they were ready. Together, they knew they could face whatever came their way, one village at a time.

The evening light bathed the village in a warm glow, and the team set up camp for the night. Sitting around a small fire, they shared stories and reflected on the day's journey.

Mia looked into the flames, her voice soft but filled with conviction. "We're making a real difference, aren't we?"

Ryan nodded, his gaze steady. "We are. And it's only the beginning. Every village we help strengthens the whole network. We're building a future, one step at a time."

Amina added, "And it's not just about defense. It's about creating communities that care for each other, that are resilient and self-sufficient."

Captain Morales, ever vigilant, scanned the horizon one last time before relaxing. "We're showing them that they're not alone. That's the most important thing."

As the stars started to twinkle in the night sky, the team felt a profound sense of satisfaction and purpose. They were prepared for whatever challenges lay ahead, united by their mission and the strong bonds they had formed along the journey.

Chapter 25
A New Beginning

The team descended into the valley as the morning sun rose higher, casting long shadows across the landscape. The village below came into clearer view, revealing a collection of huts surrounded by cultivated fields and dense foliage. The distant hum of activity grew louder as they approached, signaling a thriving community.

Ryan led the way, his steps confident but cautious. "Stay alert. Let's see what challenges this village faces and how we can help."

As they entered the village, they were greeted by a group of curious villagers. An elderly man, his posture straight and dignified, stepped forward. "Welcome, travelers. I am Hiro, the village elder. What brings you here?"

Ryan offered a respectful nod. "We're here to help. We've been working with other villages to build defenses, set up communication systems, and improve health and education. We want to do the same here."

Hiro scrutinized them for a moment before speaking. "We have heard of your work. Some say you bring hope, others say you bring change. What makes you different?"

Amina stepped forward, her voice warm and reassuring. "We bring knowledge and support. Everything we do is to empower you, not control you. We work with you to strengthen your community."

Hiro's eyes softened slightly. "Very well. Show us what you can do."

The team split up to begin their assessments. Ryan and Captain Morales focused on the village's defenses, inspecting the perimeter. "Your barriers are minimal," Ryan observed. "We need to fortify them to ensure safety."

A young woman named Kiyoko, eager to help, asked, "What materials should we use?"

Ryan replied, "Use what you can find—rocks, mud, anything that can add to the stability. Adaptability is key."

Meanwhile, Amina set up a temporary clinic under a large tree, starting with a health assessment to understand the villagers' needs. She addressed a group of women about basic hygiene and first aid. "Clean water and proper wound care are essential. These small steps can prevent serious illnesses."

A woman named Nori raised her hand. "What should we do if someone is injured and we don't have the right supplies?"

Amina demonstrated how to improvise with available materials. "Use clean cloths for bandages and boiled water for cleaning wounds. It's not perfect, but it's effective."

Captain Morales gathered a group of villagers to set up the communication system. "These radios will keep you connected with us and the other villages. Regular check-ins are crucial."

A boy named Daichi, holding a radio, asked, "How often should we check in?"

Morales replied, "Twice a day, minimum. And if there's any unusual activity, report immediately. Clear and concise communication can save lives."

Mia moved through the village, capturing the collaboration on camera. She paused to interview an elderly woman weaving a basket. "How has life been here, isolated from the other villages?"

The woman, named Sato, looked up, her eyes thoughtful. "It's been hard. We survive, but we lack many things. Medicine, education, safety. If you can help us with these, we will be grateful."

As the day progressed, the team and villagers worked tirelessly. The barriers took shape, the villagers' confidence grew, and the communication system was almost operational. By mid-afternoon, the sense of accomplishment was palpable.

Ryan gathered everyone in the central clearing for a progress update. "We've made incredible strides today. The barriers are taking shape, and the communication system is nearly operational. We're on the right track."

Amina added, "Your health practices are improving too. Keep practicing what you've learned and support each other."

Captain Morales nodded. "Tomorrow, we'll conduct a full-scale drill to ensure everyone knows what to do in an emergency. Clear communication is key."

Hiro listened intently, then spoke. "We are grateful for your help. We've struggled for so long, and now it feels like we have a real chance."

Ryan placed a reassuring hand on Hiro's shoulder. "We're in this together. Let's get to work."

As the sun began to set, casting a warm glow over the village, the team and villagers gathered around the central fire. The atmosphere was one of quiet satisfaction and growing confidence. The sense of community and shared purpose was strong, a testament to their collective efforts.

Mia captured the scene, her camera documenting the bonds being formed. "We're building something lasting here. This village is becoming a beacon of hope and resilience."

Ryan addressed the group, his voice filled with determination. "We've built more than just physical defenses. We've built trust and a sense of community. Keep working together, and we can achieve great things."

Hiro nodded, his eyes reflecting the firelight. "We will. This is our home, and we'll protect it with everything we have."

Amina smiled warmly. "Don't forget, we're all connected now. Use the communication system to keep in touch and support one another."

As the night settled in, the team huddled by the fire, contemplating their next actions and reflecting on their path. They had faced numerous challenges, but with every village they supported, they were creating a legacy of strength, resilience, and unity. The connections they made with the villagers were solid, and their common vision for a better future was becoming real. The work was demanding but significant, and it was making an impact. Together, they knew they could tackle anything that came their way, one village at a time. The journey ahead was lengthy, but they were ready. They were building a future, one step at a time.

The sun rose on the village, casting a golden hue over the thatched roofs and lush fields. The team and villagers were already up and moving, the air filled with the sound of hammers, saws, and chatter. Ryan, Mia, Amina, and Captain Morales worked alongside the villagers, each focused on their respective tasks.

Ryan and Captain Morales inspected the newly fortified barriers, ensuring they were sturdy and secure. "These barriers are coming along well," Ryan said, patting a wooden stake. "Your hard work is paying off."

Kiyoko, tightening a support beam, smiled proudly. "We've followed your instructions carefully. We want to make sure we're protected."

Ryan nodded approvingly. "You're doing great, Kiyoko. Keep it up."

Meanwhile, Amina had set up a temporary clinic under the large tree. She conducted a final health training session, showing a group of villagers how to handle common injuries. "If someone is unconscious and not breathing, start CPR immediately. Remember, 30 compressions to 2 breaths."

Nori, practicing on a dummy, looked up. "Like this, Amina?"

Amina adjusted Nori's hands slightly. "Exactly. Keep your compressions steady and firm. You're doing great."

Captain Morales was overseeing the setup of the communication system, ensuring everything was operational. She gathered a group of villagers and explained the importance of regular check-ins. "These radios are your lifeline. Make sure to check in twice a day and report any unusual activity immediately."

Daichi, holding his radio, asked, "What should we do if we lose signal during an emergency?"

Morales replied, "Move to higher ground or an open area to get a better signal. And always keep spare batteries handy."

Mia moved through the village, capturing the collaborative efforts on camera. She paused to interview Sato, the elderly woman she had spoken to earlier. "Sato, how do you feel about the changes happening here?"

Sato's eyes twinkled with pride. "It's been hard work, but it's worth it. We've become a stronger, more united community."

As the day progressed, the sense of unity and purpose grew stronger. The team and villagers worked tirelessly, each task bringing them closer to their goal. By mid-afternoon, the barriers were complete, and the communication system was fully operational.

Ryan gathered everyone in the central clearing for a final briefing. "We've made incredible strides these past few days. The barriers are solid, and the communication system is operational. You're ready."

Amina added, "Your health practices have improved significantly. Keep practicing what you've learned and support each other."

Captain Morales nodded. "Tomorrow, we'll conduct a full-scale drill to ensure everyone knows what to do in an emergency. Clear communication is key."

Hiro, the village elder, stepped forward, his voice filled with gratitude. "Your help has been invaluable. We've struggled for so long, but now it feels like we have a real chance."

Ryan placed a reassuring hand on Hiro's shoulder. "We're in this together. Let's finish strong."

As the sun began to set, casting a warm glow over the village, the team and villagers gathered around the central fire. The atmosphere was one of quiet satisfaction and growing confidence. The sense of community and shared purpose was strong, a testament to their collective efforts.

Mia captured the scene, her camera documenting the bonds being formed. "We're building something lasting here. This village is becoming a beacon of hope and resilience."

Ryan addressed the group, his voice filled with determination. "We've built more than just physical defenses. We've built trust and a sense of community. Keep working together, and we can achieve great things."

Hiro nodded, his eyes reflecting the firelight. "We will. This is our home, and we'll protect it with everything we have."

Amina's smile was heartfelt. "We're all part of the same network now. Use the communication system to stay connected and help one another."

The team sat together by the fire, discussing their next steps and reflecting on their journey. The challenges had been many, but with each village they helped, they were building a legacy of strength, resilience, and unity. The bonds they had forged with the villagers were strong, and their shared vision for a better future was becoming a reality.

As the night deepened, Ryan looked around at his team and the villagers. "This is why we do what we do. Every village we help strengthens the whole network. We're building a future, one step at a time."

Captain Morales added, "And it's not just about defense. It's about creating communities that care for each other, that are resilient and self-sufficient."

Mia, her camera capturing the moment, said, "We're documenting every step, showing the world what's possible when people come together."

The fire crackled softly, a symbol of the warmth and strength of the community they had helped build. The path ahead was long, but they were ready. They were building a future, one village at a time.

The following morning dawned clear and bright, the village bathed in golden sunlight. The team and villagers gathered in the central clearing, ready for the final drill. The air buzzed with anticipation and a touch of nervous excitement. Ryan, Mia, Amina, and Captain Morales stood before the villagers, preparing to brief them.

Ryan's voice carried a reassuring confidence. "Today, we put everything to the test. This drill will simulate an emergency situation. Remember, stay calm, follow the protocols, and communicate clearly."

Kiyoko raised her hand, her expression serious. "What's the scenario for the drill, Ryan?"

Ryan smiled. "We'll simulate a breach in the perimeter and a medical emergency. Everyone has their roles. Let's make it as real as possible."

The villagers dispersed into their assigned positions. Captain Morales took charge of the communication team. "Remember, clear and concise messages. Report any unusual activity immediately."

Daichi, holding his radio, nodded. "We're ready, Captain."

Amina gathered her medical team under the large tree, reviewing emergency procedures. "If someone is injured, we assess the situation, stabilize them, and communicate their condition clearly."

Nori, practicing CPR on a dummy, looked up. "And if we're unsure, we call for help immediately, right?"

"Exactly," Amina confirmed. "Never hesitate to ask for assistance."

Mia moved through the village, capturing the preparations on camera. She paused to interview Sato, who had been organizing the villagers. "Sato, how do you feel about the drill?"

Sato's eyes twinkled with determination. "It's a lot of work, but it's worth it. We need to be ready for anything."

As the drill began, a sense of urgency filled the air. An alarm sounded, signaling a breach in the perimeter. Ryan and Captain Morales led a team to the perimeter, inspecting the barriers.

"Report in," Ryan ordered, his voice steady.

"North perimeter clear," Daichi's voice crackled over the radio. "No unusual activity."

"West perimeter clear," added Kiyoko. "Everything is calm."

Suddenly, a shout came from the medical area. "We have a medical emergency!" Nori's voice was urgent. "We need assistance!"

Amina rushed to the scene, assessing the situation. "What happened?"

"It's a simulated injury," Nori explained, pointing to a villager lying on the ground. "He's unconscious and not breathing."

Amina knelt beside the villager, starting CPR. "Nori, keep track of the compressions. We need to maintain a steady rhythm."

Mia captured the intense scene, her camera focused on Amina's determined face. She moved to interview Ryan, who was coordinating the response. "Ryan, how's the drill going?"

Ryan, watching the teams work together, nodded approvingly. "They're doing great. Everyone is following the protocols and communicating clearly. This is exactly what we hoped for."

The drill continued, with each team responding to their assigned tasks. Captain Morales coordinated the communication efforts, ensuring all teams were in sync. "East perimeter, report in."

"All clear," came the response.

Back at the medical area, Amina continued CPR, her voice calm and steady. "Nori, how's the pulse?"

Nori checked the villager's wrist. "It's faint, but it's there."

"Good," Amina replied. "Keep monitoring. We're almost there."

As the drill concluded, the alarm was silenced, and the villagers gathered in the central clearing. The sense of accomplishment was palpable. Ryan addressed the group, his voice filled with pride.

"You all did an incredible job. The drill was a success. We've shown that we can handle any situation."

Amina smiled at her team. "Your medical response was excellent. Remember, practice makes perfect. Keep honing your skills."

Captain Morales nodded. "Communication is key. You all communicated clearly and effectively. Keep up the good work."

Mia captured the final moments on camera, turning to interview Hiro. "Hiro, how do you feel about the drill?"

Hiro's eyes shone with pride. "We've come a long way. This drill has shown us that we can protect our village and support each other."

As the sun began to fade, bathing the village in a warm glow, the team and villagers came together around the central fire. The atmosphere was one of serene contentment and growing confidence. Ryan addressed the group, his voice filled with hope and determination.

"We've constructed more than just physical safeguards. We've built a community that supports and looks after each other. Stay united, and you'll achieve incredible things."

Hiro stood beside him, his eyes reflecting the firelight. "We will. This is our home, and we'll protect it with everything we have."

Amina's eyes shone as she smiled. "Don't forget, we're all connected. Use the communication system to stay in touch and support each other."

Mia captured the scene, her heart swelling with pride. "We're building something lasting here. This village is becoming a beacon of hope and resilience."

As the fire crackled softly, the team sat together, discussing their next steps and reflecting on their journey. The challenges had been many, but with each village they helped, they were building a legacy of strength, resilience, and unity. The bonds they had forged with the villagers were strong, and their shared vision for a better future was becoming a reality. The work was hard, but it was meaningful, and it was making a difference.

Together, they knew they could face whatever came their way, one village at a time. The path ahead was long, but they were ready. They were building a future, one step at a time.

The next morning, the village was alive with a new energy. The final drill had been a success, and the villagers were brimming with confidence. Ryan, Mia, Amina, and Captain Morales gathered their gear, preparing for their departure. The villagers assembled in the central clearing to bid them farewell, their faces a mixture of gratitude and determination.

Ryan addressed the villagers, his voice calm and filled with purpose. "We've accomplished a lot together. Remember, the work doesn't stop here. Keep building on what we've started, and stay connected with the network."

Hiro, the village elder, stepped forward, his eyes reflecting deep gratitude. "Your guidance has been invaluable. We feel prepared and more confident than ever before."

Amina hugged Hiro warmly. "Keep practicing the health protocols, especially in emergencies. Small steps make a big difference."

Nori, standing nearby, asked, "Amina, what should we do if we encounter a medical emergency and can't reach the clinic in time?"

Amina replied, "Stabilize the patient as best as you can. Clean the wound with boiled water, apply pressure to stop bleeding, and use clean cloths for bandages. And use the radios to call for help immediately."

Captain Morales ensured the communication system was fully operational before they left. She gathered the villagers responsible for its upkeep. "Regular check-ins are vital. Twice a day at minimum. And remember, clear communication is key."

Daichi, holding his radio, nodded. "We'll keep the lines open, Captain. Thank you for everything."

Mia moved through the group, capturing the final moments on camera. She paused to interview Kiyoko, who had been instrumental in reinforcing the village's defenses. "Kiyoko, how do you feel about the future now?"

Kiyoko's face lit up with pride. "We're ready for whatever comes. We've learned so much, and we know we can protect our village."

Ryan turned to the group, his voice steady. "Remember, you're not alone. Stay connected with the other villages and support each other. Together, we're stronger."

Hiro raised his hand in a gesture of solidarity. "We will. This is just the beginning for us."

As the team set off down the path, the villagers' well-wishes echoed behind them. They walked in silence for a while, each lost in their thoughts about the road ahead.

Mia broke the silence, her voice filled with excitement. "I can't wait to see what the next village is like. Each one has its own story, its own challenges."

Amina nodded, her expression thoughtful. "And its own unique needs. We need to be ready for anything."

Captain Morales brought up the rear, her eyes scanning the surroundings. "Stay vigilant. We don't know what we'll encounter on this leg of the journey."

The path led them through dense jungle, the sounds of nature a constant companion. They moved with purpose, their steps sure and steady. The journey was grueling, but their resolve was unwavering. They knew the importance of their mission and the lives it impacted.

Ryan paused at a clearing, checking the map. "We've got another day's trek ahead of us. Let's stay focused and keep moving."

Mia took a sip of water, her gaze thoughtful. "The more remote the village, the more crucial it is to connect them. Their stories need to be told."

Amina agreed. "Isolation often means a lack of basic necessities. We need to be prepared for anything."

Captain Morales checked their supplies, her expression serious. "And we need to ensure our radios stay functional. Communication is our lifeline."

As they continued their journey, the terrain grew more challenging. The jungle thickened, the path becoming less defined. They moved with caution, every sense alert for potential dangers.

Ryan led the way, his machete slicing through the dense foliage. "Stay close and keep an eye out for any signs of trouble."

The team pressed on, their determination unwavering. They knew that each step brought them closer to another village in need, another opportunity to make a difference. The challenges were many, but so were the rewards. They were building a future, one village at a time, united by a common goal and a shared vision for a better world.

As dusk approached, they reached a ridge overlooking their next destination. The sight of the village nestled in the valley below filled them with renewed energy. They exchanged determined smiles, ready to bring their support and expertise to this new community. The path ahead was still long, but they were ready. Together, they knew they could face whatever came their way, one village at a time.

Mia turned to Ryan, her eyes sparkling. "What's our first step when we reach the village?"

Ryan's eyes were focused on the distant village. "We'll meet with the village leaders, assess their needs, and start building from there. The process will be similar, but we'll adapt to their specific circumstances."

Amina added, "And we'll ensure they understand the health protocols from the start. Prevention is key."

Captain Morales nodded. "And we'll set up the communication system as soon as possible. Keeping everyone connected is crucial."

The team continued their trek, the sense of purpose driving them forward. As night fell, they set up camp, the firelight casting warm shadows around them. They sat together, discussing their plans and reflecting on their journey.

Ryan looked around at his team, his voice filled with conviction. "Every village we help strengthens the whole network. We're building a future, one step at a time."

Amina smiled. "And it's not just about defense. It's about creating communities that care for each other, that are resilient and self-sufficient."

Mia, her camera capturing the moment, said, "We're documenting every step, showing the world what's possible when people come together."

Captain Morales, ever vigilant, scanned the horizon one last time before relaxing. "We're showing them that they're not alone. That's the most important thing."

As the stars began to twinkle in the night sky, the team felt a deep sense of satisfaction and purpose. They were ready for whatever lay ahead, united by their mission and the bonds they had forged along the way. The path was challenging, but it was making a difference. Together, they could face any challenge and build a future of hope and resilience, one village at a time.

Epilogue
A Legacy of Hope

Mia stood at the bow of the small boat, watching as the green expanse of the Congo's dense jungle slowly drifted past. The engine hummed softly, a steady rhythm that matched the gentle lapping of water against the hull. The river wound through the thick foliage, sunlight filtering down in fragmented rays that danced across the water's surface. The air was thick with the familiar scents of wet earth, moss, and the faint tang of blooming orchids.

She traced the edge of the compass in her hand, her father's old keepsake, feeling the smooth, worn metal beneath her fingertips. This compass had guided them through countless terrains—both literal and figurative. Now, as she prepared to leave this place behind, it felt like she was finally saying goodbye to a chapter of her life that had defined her for so long.

Ryan leaned against the railing beside her, his eyes scanning the treetops. "Hard to believe we're actually leaving, huh?" he murmured, his voice a low rumble that carried easily over the sound of the boat's engine.

Mia glanced at him, a soft smile forming on her lips. "Yeah. It feels… surreal." She turned her gaze back to the jungle, the trees a blur of green and gold. "Part of me feels like I'm leaving a piece of myself behind."

"You're not leaving anything behind," Amina's voice chimed in from Mia's other side. She placed a hand on Mia's shoulder, squeezing gently. "You're taking everything you've learned, everything you've fought for, and carrying it forward. That's what matters."

Mia nodded slowly, absorbing Amina's words. "It's just… so much has happened here. We accomplished more than I ever thought possible, but I couldn't have done it without all of you. I don't know how to thank you."

"You don't have to thank us," Ryan said with a grin. "We're a team. We believed in this mission because we believed in you."

"And because we believe in what we can accomplish together," Amina added. "This was just one chapter, Mia. There's so much more ahead."

Mia's eyes misted over, but she blinked back the tears, unwilling to let emotion cloud this moment. "I know," she said quietly. "And I promise I'll carry on. Not just for my father, but for all of us. For everything we've achieved here."

The boat slowed as they neared the dock, where a small group of local guides waited to bid them farewell. Their faces, lined with age and wisdom, bore expressions of gratitude and respect. As the boat gently bumped against the wooden platform, the guides stepped forward, speaking in soft, reverent tones.

"Thank you, Mia," one of the older guides said in halting English, his voice thick with emotion. "For everything you've done. You have given us hope. You have given the forest hope."

Mia bowed her head, humbled by the sincerity in his words. "No, thank *you*," she replied, her voice steady but filled with emotion. "For welcoming us, for trusting us. This place, these people... I'll carry all of you with me, wherever I go."

Another guide, a woman with a weathered face and kind eyes, stepped forward and pressed something into Mia's hand. It was a small carved wooden figure—a representation of an okapi, one of the endangered species they had fought so hard to protect.

"This is for you," the woman said softly. "A reminder of the life you have helped save. The forest will remember your spirit."

Mia swallowed hard, her fingers closing around the delicate carving. "Thank you. I'll treasure this always."

Ryan and Amina joined in the farewells, exchanging handshakes, smiles, and promises to stay in touch. As the last guide stepped back, Ryan turned to Mia, his expression thoughtful.

"So, what's next for you?" he asked, a hint of a smile tugging at his lips.

Mia glanced down at the compass in her hand, then back at the jungle that had become both a battleground and a sanctuary. "I'm not entirely sure yet," she admitted. "But I know I want to keep fighting—for other places like this, for other people who need support. It's time to build something new. Something that's mine."

Amina's smile was radiant. "And we'll be there to support you, wherever that takes you. You've got an entire network now, people who believe in you and what you're doing."

"Speaking of which," Ryan interjected, his tone turning teasing, "don't think you're getting rid of us that easily. Wherever you go, we'll be just a phone call away. Who knows? You might even find yourself dragging us into another jungle before too long."

Mia laughed, the sound light and genuine. "I wouldn't have it any other way."

The boat nudged gently against the dock, and Mia took a deep breath, savoring the moment. She felt a sense of closure, of peace. As she stepped off the boat and onto solid ground, she felt something lift from her shoulders. The weight of her father's legacy, of the expectations she had carried for so long, was gone.

She turned back one last time, looking at the dense, vibrant jungle that had tested her in every way imaginable. She'd faced her fears here, wrestled with her past, and found her true strength. This was no longer the place where she was trying to prove herself. It was the place where she had become her own person.

"Goodbye," she whispered softly, more to herself than to anyone else. "Thank you for everything."

With one final glance at the trees swaying gently in the breeze, she turned and walked away, her steps light, her heart free.

There was a whole world out there, filled with places that needed protecting, voices that needed amplifying.

Mia was ready.

The mission was far from over, but she no longer felt bound by the past. She was stepping into her own future, a future filled with possibility and purpose.

And she couldn't wait to see where it would take her.

The steady hum of the airport terminal buzzed around Mia as she walked through the arrival gate. People rushed past her—business travelers, families, and tourists—each wrapped up in their own world. Mia took a deep breath, the crisp, air-conditioned breeze a stark contrast to the humid warmth of the Congo jungle. It felt surreal to be back. Her backpack, still caked with the red dust of the Congo trails, seemed out of place here among the shiny floors and neon signs.

She spotted Lina instantly, standing just beyond the security barrier. Her sister's face was a mix of relief and excitement, her eyes searching the crowd until they landed on Mia. A wide smile spread across Lina's face, and she waved, her hand trembling slightly as if she couldn't quite believe what she was seeing.

Mia lifted her hand in return, and before she knew it, they were running toward each other, weaving through the throng of people until they collided in a fierce embrace.

"You're really here," Lina whispered, her voice choked with emotion as she buried her face in Mia's shoulder. "I can't believe it. You're really home."

Mia hugged her sister tightly, feeling the tension and exhaustion of the past months melt away in Lina's familiar presence. "I missed you so much, Lina. You have no idea."

They pulled back just enough to look at each other, tears brimming in their eyes. Lina's gaze swept over Mia's face, lingering on the lines of fatigue and the hardened determination that hadn't been there before.

"You look different," Lina said softly, a note of awe in her voice. "Stronger. More… yourself."

Mia smiled, the weight of Lina's observation settling in her chest like a warm glow. "I feel different. It's been a long journey—one I don't think I could have finished without knowing you were here, waiting for me."

Lina shook her head, a tear slipping down her cheek. "I'm so proud of you, Mia. I know I wasn't always supportive—I doubted you, questioned if you could really do this on your own, and I'm sorry for that."

"Don't be," Mia said gently, squeezing Lina's hands. "I needed your voice of reason. You made me think, made me really consider what I was doing. And in the end, it helped me find my own path."

Lina laughed through her tears, a shaky sound that was half relief, half joy. "I guess that makes me the overprotective sister, huh?"

"Always," Mia teased, her smile widening. "But that's why I love you."

They stood there, lost in each other's presence, ignoring the bustle of the airport around them. Finally, Lina glanced down at the worn backpack slung over Mia's shoulder, her smile fading into a thoughtful expression.

"What's next for you?" she asked quietly. "I know you won't be able to sit still for long."

Mia's heart thudded as she considered her answer. This was the moment she'd been turning over in her mind since she'd left the jungle—the new chapter she was ready to start. "I'm going to start something of my own, Lina. I'm going to establish a new conservation organization, one that builds on Dad's work but goes beyond it. I want to focus on empowering local communities to protect their own environments. It'll be called the Evans Foundation for Global Conservation."

Lina's eyes widened, a mixture of surprise and admiration shining in her gaze. "Mia, that's… that's incredible. It's huge! Are you sure you're ready for something like this?"

Mia nodded, a smile spreading across her face. "I am. For the first time, I feel like I know exactly what I want to do. This isn't just about carrying on Dad's legacy anymore—it's about creating something new. Something that's mine."

Lina laughed, a sound filled with pride. "I always knew you'd find your way, Mia. You've been through so much, and you've come out stronger, more determined. I have no doubt you'll make this a success."

"Thank you, Lina," Mia murmured, emotion thickening her voice. "For believing in me, even when I didn't believe in myself."

Lina shook her head, blinking back tears. "You never needed me to believe in you. You've always had it in you, Mia. You just needed to see it for yourself."

Mia reached into her backpack and pulled out a small, worn journal—her father's notebook, the one that had guided her through some of her darkest moments in the jungle. She held it out to Lina, who took it with a puzzled expression.

"I want you to have this," Mia said softly. "It's Dad's research, but it's also a record of everything I've done, everything we've accomplished. I wouldn't be here without you, and I want you to be a part of whatever comes next."

Lina opened the journal carefully, her eyes scanning the pages filled with handwritten notes, sketches, and pressed flowers. She looked up, her voice trembling. "Are you sure?"

Mia nodded. "Yes. I'm going to keep going, and I want you beside me. You've always been my anchor, my reminder of who I am. I'm not the same person who left all those months ago, but you're a part of who I've become. I want you to be a part of this new beginning."

Tears slipped down Lina's cheeks, and she reached out, pulling Mia into another fierce hug. "I'd be honored, Mia. Whatever you need, I'm here."

They stood like that for a long time, holding each other, the bond between them stronger than ever. When they finally pulled away, both were smiling, faces flushed with excitement and hope.

"Come on," Lina said, taking Mia's hand and tugging her toward the exit. "Let's get you home. We have so much to talk about."

Mia glanced back one last time at the bustling terminal, then turned toward the exit, her heart light and her mind clear.

"Yeah," she said softly, squeezing Lina's hand. "Let's go home."

As they stepped out into the bright sunlight of the city, Mia felt a surge of determination fill her. She was ready to take on whatever came next, to build something beautiful and lasting. The Evans Foundation would be a new beginning, but it would also be a continuation of everything she and her father had stood for.

It was time to chart her own course—one that would change the world, one step at a time.

Mia sat cross-legged in the middle of her Brooklyn apartment, surrounded by a sea of papers, maps, and charts. The space, usually neat and orderly, now resembled a bustling headquarters for an emerging organization. Stacks of documents labeled with various regions and species lay beside blueprints of conservation projects. A whiteboard on the wall displayed timelines, goals, and potential partnerships, each box meticulously filled with notes.

At the center of it all, pinned above her workspace, was a freshly printed banner that read: *Evans Foundation for Global Conservation.* The words were bold and powerful, carrying the weight of both her father's legacy and her own aspirations.

Taking a deep breath, Mia glanced at the banner, feeling a thrill of excitement and a twinge of nervousness. The vision she had nurtured through late-night reflections in the Congo was now on the cusp of becoming reality. She picked up her phone, the familiar weight of it steadying her nerves, and dialed the first number on her list.

The call connected, and a warm, familiar voice came through the line.

"Dr. Richards? It's Mia Evans. I hope I'm not catching you at a bad time."

"Mia! It's wonderful to hear from you," Dr. Richards replied, his voice genuine and filled with delight. "I've been keeping up with your work in the Congo—impressive doesn't even begin to cover it. What can I do for you?"

Mia smiled, encouraged by his enthusiasm. "I'm starting something new—an organization that focuses on community-led conservation efforts and sustainable practices. It's called the Evans Foundation for Global Conservation. I'm reaching out to build a network of supporters, and I thought of you first."

There was a brief pause, then Dr. Richards' voice came back, stronger. "Mia, that sounds incredible. Your father would be so proud of what you're doing. Count me in—whatever you need, whether it's connections, resources, or advice, I'm here."

"Thank you, Dr. Richards. That means more than I can say," Mia said softly. "I'll be in touch soon with more details, but knowing I have your support gives me a huge boost."

They exchanged a few more words of encouragement before Mia ended the call. She closed her eyes for a moment, savoring the small victory. One call down, many more to go. She picked up the next number and dialed, her confidence building with each ring.

"Hello, Mr. Tanaka? This is Mia Evans. We met at the conservation summit in Kenya last year."

A pause, then recognition bloomed in the man's voice. "Mia, yes! I remember you well. You spoke passionately about community partnerships. What a surprise to hear from you. How are you?"

"I'm doing well, thank you," Mia replied, warmth spreading through her. "I wanted to tell you about a new initiative I'm launching—the Evans Foundation for Global Conservation.

It's focused on integrating local communities into the process of environmental protection, empowering them to be the stewards of their own land."

"Now that's a vision I can get behind," Mr. Tanaka said thoughtfully. "Tell me, what do you need? Funding? Connections?"

"Both, actually," Mia said with a small laugh. "But more than that, I'm looking for people who believe in this mission—who want to be a part of something that has the potential to reshape how we approach conservation globally."

There was a brief silence, and Mia held her breath, waiting.

"You know what? I think I'd like to get involved personally. I can introduce you to some key players in Southeast Asia who share your vision. And count me in for a donation to get you started."

Mia exhaled, her heart soaring. "Thank you, Mr. Tanaka. This is… it's incredible. I'll send you a detailed plan soon. I can't tell you how much this means."

They spoke for a few more minutes, Mia jotting down notes as ideas flowed. When the call ended, she felt a surge of energy, a renewed sense of purpose. Two calls, two commitments. The pieces were falling into place.

She glanced at the list of names, each one a potential ally, each one a step closer to turning her dream into reality. Without hesitation, she dialed the next number.

"Hi, Mrs. Ortega? It's Mia Evans. I wanted to reach out and share some exciting news. I'm starting a new foundation, and I think your experience could be invaluable..."

The hours passed in a blur of conversations and laughter, of shared visions and mutual excitement. With each call, Mia's network grew. Support poured in from people who had known her father, as well as those she had met through her own work. Offers of funding, connections, and strategic advice flowed freely, each one a testament to the respect and admiration she had earned.

Her voice grew hoarse, but she pressed on, determined to speak to every person on her list. Each conversation solidified her resolve, filling her with a sense of fulfillment she hadn't realized she'd been missing.

Finally, as dusk settled outside the apartment's windows, Mia made the last call.

"Hello, Mr. Johnson? This is Mia Evans. I wanted to share some news about a new project I'm launching—the Evans Foundation for Global Conservation."

"Ah, Mia," Mr. Johnson's deep voice rumbled warmly. "I've been hearing wonderful things about you. What you did in the Congo—well, it was extraordinary. What can I do to help?"

Mia felt a smile spread across her face. "Thank you. I'm building something that honors my father's legacy but also moves beyond it. I'd love to have your support as I take this next step."

"You have it, Mia," Mr. Johnson said without hesitation. "You have it one hundred percent."

The call ended on a note of promise and possibility. Mia set her phone down and leaned back in her chair, staring at the banner above her desk.

She took a deep breath, letting it out slowly. For the first time, the future didn't feel daunting or overwhelming. It felt like an open book, ready to be written.

A small smile tugged at her lips. She was ready—completely and unreservedly ready—to step into this new chapter.

This was just the beginning.

Mia stood in front of the massive world map pinned across the entire wall of her home office. The soft light of early morning filtered through the curtains, casting a gentle glow over the pins and notes scattered across the map's surface. Dozens of brightly colored flags marked the places she had already been and the ones she hoped to go, each representing a new dream, a new mission, and a new chance to make a difference.

She picked up a small green pin and carefully placed it on the Amazon rainforest, right beside the black line she had drawn to represent a region threatened by illegal logging. With a firm press, the pin stuck in place, standing out brightly against the textured surface of the map.

"Amazon rainforest," she murmured softly, her fingers lingering on the spot. "Restoration and reforestation efforts."

Beside it, a blue pin already marked the Great Barrier Reef, accompanied by a sticky note that read: *Coral restoration, local community education, marine protection initiatives.*

Mia reached into the box of pins on her desk, picking out another—this one a deep, vibrant red. She placed it on the border between Southeast Asia and Australia, marking a new potential project site she had discussed with Mr. Tanaka just a few days ago. The pin gleamed brightly under the soft light.

"You're really filling that map up," Lina's voice interrupted her thoughts, a note of playful admiration in her tone.

Mia turned, a smile spreading across her face as she saw Lina standing in the doorway, holding two steaming cups of coffee. "I'm trying," Mia said with a laugh. "So many places I want to go. So many projects I want to start."

Lina walked over, handing Mia a cup and taking a sip of her own. "You've got your work cut out for you," she teased, her eyes sweeping over the map. "But if anyone can make it happen, it's you."

Mia felt a surge of warmth at her sister's words. "Thanks, Lina. It feels different this time. It's not just about following Dad's path—it's about creating my own. I want to protect these places, but I also want to empower people to protect them long after I'm gone."

Lina nodded thoughtfully, her gaze shifting to the map. "That's the right approach. Conservation isn't just about the land or the animals—it's about the people who live there, too. If they're not part of the solution, then it's not going to last."

"Exactly," Mia agreed, feeling a sense of pride at how well Lina understood her vision. She turned back to the map, tracing her finger along the network of pins. "I want to build partnerships that aren't just about funding or logistics, but about creating a real, lasting impact. I want to bring in experts who can help local communities manage these projects themselves, to share knowledge and skills."

Lina was silent for a moment, as if weighing her next words carefully. Then she glanced at Mia, a soft smile playing on her lips. "I've been thinking... maybe I could be one of those experts."

Mia blinked, her heart skipping a beat. "What do you mean?"

"I mean, I've been considering joining the foundation," Lina said slowly, her gaze steady. "Not just as your sister or a supporter, but as an active part of it. I could help with the legal side of things—advocating for policy changes, securing permits, making sure everything's above board. I could bring in my experience to protect the work you're doing."

Mia's breath caught. "Lina... I don't know what to say."

Lina's smile widened, and she reached out to squeeze Mia's shoulder. "Say yes, and let's do this together. We've both been on our own paths for a while now, but I think it's time we teamed up again. For Dad, and for everything we want to achieve."

Mia felt a swell of gratitude and love, her eyes misting. "I'd love that. I'd love to have you with me, Lina. It would mean so much more knowing we're doing this side by side."

They embraced, the connection between them stronger than ever. When they pulled back, Lina gestured to the map with a playful grin. "So, where are we going first?"

Mia laughed, stepping back to admire the colorful array of pins. "Well, the Amazon is high on the list. And I've got contacts in Southeast Asia who are eager to start a project there. The Great Barrier Reef needs all the help it can get, too. There's so much to do, it's hard to pick just one."

"Sounds like you need to clone yourself," Lina quipped, then her smile softened. "But seriously, Mia, I'm excited for you. For us. I believe in what you're doing, and I'm honored to be a part of it."

"Thank you, Lina," Mia murmured, her voice thick with emotion. "I couldn't have done any of this without you."

They stood together in companionable silence, the map in front of them a vivid tapestry of dreams and plans. Each pin was a promise—to the world, to their father's memory, and to themselves.

"Here's to new beginnings," Mia said softly, breaking the silence. She reached up, gently placing her father's old compass beside the red pin she'd just added to the map. "And here's to making my own path."

She stepped back, taking in the map in its entirety. It was no longer just a representation of places—it was a testament to everything she hoped to achieve, a roadmap for the future she was ready to build.

With one last glance at the world of possibilities spread out before her, Mia turned to Lina, her smile bright and full of determination.

"Let's get started," she said.

Lina nodded, her expression mirroring Mia's resolve. "Yes. Let's."

And with that, Mia stepped away from the map, her silhouette framed against the glowing city skyline outside. The world was waiting, filled with challenges and opportunities. She was ready to face it all—with courage, conviction, and hope.

The Evans Foundation for Global Conservation was just the beginning.

Her journey was far from over—it was only just beginning.

And this time, she was charting her own course.

Milton Keynes UK
Ingram Content Group UK Ltd.
UKHW040258181024
449757UK00001B/122